Moon Lust

I0676499

To my parents Tim and Virginia, I love you both very much.

To one of my best friends and fellow writer Kathleen thank you for being there to offer me advice when I needed it helping me find the inspiration I needed to get this published.

To my beta readers Lisa and Richard I owe a lot of thanks. If it wasn't for the both of you helping me fix this story and make it more readable. You both know the struggle was real.

To Lauren who came to me in my hour of need and was able to help draw the cover for Moon Lust. Thank you for taking time out of your own busy schedule.

And of course to everyone who read Moon Lust when it was just a story I posted online. Thanks to your encouragement what was once a simple story has become something so much more.

Introduction

The fact I am writing this now is very surprising to me.

I always loved reading, my love first began with comics and picture books. I went through a rebellious stage for a time, refusing to read anything unless there was at least one picture to go with the story.

I never dreamed I would write my own books if I did I would have put more of an effort to pay attention during English class in school and save my beta readers a terrible burden.

I first began my exploration in writing in the form of fanfiction. I enjoyed moderate success with my works and then moved on to writing my own original work which I posted online.

Moon Lust was the second original work. I have always enjoyed the genre of sci-fi and fantasy and of course it comes to no surprise that I would write about werewolves.

Moon Lust was fun to write, what began as a simple story soon began to evolve and take a life of its own. Everything from the plot to the characters I wrote began become more and more complicated and before I knew it the simple story had turned into something far more complicated and rich than I had ever intended.

I never meant to turn it into a book. Mostly because at that point in my life I was still in the early stages of trying to figure out what kind of book I wanted to write. And partly because I knew that if I published Moon Lust, I would have to come out as bisexual which even now only a small handful of people know and the reactions have been mixed.

As my fingers press the buttons to bring my thoughts into words, I feel a sense of anxiety and excitement. That I can finally bring a dream to fruition and share this world with more people is exciting, but the ramifications it will have for my personal life cause doubt to follow me like an unwanted shadow.

But in the end the sense of freedom I will feel will be well worth it.

So thank you to my friends, my readers and those who have given their time and energy to help me turn what was once a simple story into a book for the ages.

3

To those who have read Moon Lust since the beginning I hope you enjoy this new, edited version. And to the new readers I hope you find it just as entertaining as I did when I wrote it.

Love conquers all, and so let us surrender ourselves to love

-Vergil *"Eclogues 10:69"*

1

Jeremy

We pulled into the driveway behind the U-Haul. Already they had the ramp down and went on opening the door.

"Welcome home sweetie," mom said patting my shoulder excitedly. She got out of the car happy as a bee. I, on the other hand, was one apathetic bastard.

"Yippee," I whispered.

I got out and looked at the house. It was okay, a simple two story structure, red in color. A bit smaller than our old house.

Autumn was in full effect. The tree leaves were an explosion of reds, yellow and orange. My new home looked good surrounded by all the brightly colored leaves. My camera was packed away in a box. Instead, I pulled out my cell and took a few pictures. Looking at the building I would be occupying for the foreseeable future made me think of my old home.

It had been little over two hours since we left and I was already home sick. I lived in Cambridge for over ten years. There are so many memories back home. There was comfort and a sense of belonging. But there is nothing here, a blank slate. A book with no words waiting to be filled. That is what I needed. A fresh start, a new beginning, and yet as I looked at the place I now called home I felt a yearning in my heart for the place I once lived.

Moving can suck. I had to leave all my friends behind. I didn't know anyone in this town. Though my mom knew almost everyone, she would have an easier time being here than I would. People were already coming out of their own houses to come greet us. I wasn't looking forward to shaking hands and talking to our new neighbors.

Perhaps I'm being a bit moody, but after the events of the last several months my mood was bound to be dark and broody. Mom is excited to be back in her hometown. She said we needed something fresh and new and exciting; we needed to start over. Wolf Fang Falls was where she had been born and grew up, so she thought it would be a good place to start over. You know the whole going back to your roots thing.

I had no friends, no support system save for her. And I was a junior so making any lasting strong bonds of friendship seemed kind of pointless.

Mom had told me all kinds of stories of her hometown when I was growing up. There had once been a time when I believed I might have fun if I ever came here.

Wolf Fang Falls sounded badass, but as I was quickly learning, the town was far from it.

It was dull. Very dull.

I would have been happy to move out of state or at least to a city where things would be more interesting and I could find more ways to preoccupy myself. But this was important to mom so like a good son I put on a happy face and shook hands and made conversations when all I really wanted to do was lock myself away from the world.

I had to do it for her; it's my fault we had to move after all. After what happened back in Cambridge we had to leave. Mom acted like I wasn't the reason but I know better.

Let's put it like this: I am gay. had a boyfriend whom I loved more than anything besides my mom. The bastard broke my heart which was followed by severe stress and depression and was ended with my mother's desperate attempt to make things better for me.

Which is part of the reason for my pissy attitude. I was angry about what happened, I was bitter how we had to move because of it. Bitter and guilty: and afraid.

But on the other hand I am kind of glad we moved. I needed to get away from there, from Lucas. Mom knew I was in a relationship, but she didn't know the guy was-among other things-a tad bit older. I went to school with him and we started dating when he was a senior and continued to do so after he graduated. We had to keep it a secret for obvious reasons.

I still haven't told mom. If I wanted to be a real dick I would, but I was not some bitter tween who couldn't handle rejection. I wasn't going to act like those early days didn't mean something and throw him to the dogs because of what happened.

I still miss him, I miss the time we spent together; I miss the feel of him holding me at night. But that part of my life is over. Time to start again.

God, school was going to suck bad. Everyone knows being the new kid blows. Especially when you look like I do. Plus in a small town like this everyone has known one another since they were kids. They possessed long established ties of friendship. More than likely a lot of people at school would consider one another family even.

I would be the new guy, an out of towner. In a small town like this a new family is a hot topic. I remember back home whenever we got a new student he or she would be the talk of school. It doesn't last, sooner or later the excitement and fascination will wear off, then you are just another face in the crowed.

It did not take long for people to emerge from their homes to welcome us to the neighborhood; they were quick to offer us assistance. With their help we quickly got everything out of the U-Haul and into the house. Mom introduced me to all of them because of course she knew them all.

Then I met their kids as well and by the time I had been introduced to everyone I barely remembered any of their names. Once every box was inside mom herded everyone outside and thanked them for their help. Many of the women asked if mom wanted their help to unpack. She politely declined.

Once she closed the front door she turned around and rubbed her hands together.

"I can't believe I am living here. I must have passed by this place hundreds of times on my way to school. It's amazing when you see a place all the time then find yourself living there later in life."

"Did you know the family who lived here?" I asked.

"They had a son and daughter who I went to school with but we weren't friends," she said.

She walked over to one of the box's and opened it up. She began to reach in and pull out some picture frames.

"I am going up to my room to unpack," I said.

I walked upstairs, leaving mom to go through the boxes by herself; closing the door softly behind me I looked around my new room.

The walls were blue like the sky on a sunny day; I liked the color. There were two windows, one facing the front of the house and the other to the left of the building. I peered outside and could barely see our neighbors home thanks to the cover of trees. Once the leaves withered their house would be more visible.

I would have to remember to keep my curtains closed on this window

I grabbed my computer and turned it on. We didn't have Wi-Fi yet. Mom had called to have it installed with our cable service and it would be about a week before a worked came out to instal everything.

Once the computer was on and running I pulled up my pictures and began scrolling through the folders.

I loved taking photos.

There was something about capturing a single moment and preserving it for years and years that appealed to me. To show future generations of moment in time that happened before they were born, or showing a single second of awe and wonder that could inspire a person.

I took pictures of a lot of things. People, animals, nature.

I get it from my grandfather. We have box's of photos he had taken over the course of his life. I remember sitting next to him as he showed me places he had visited and people he had met.

I wanted to be like him. To travel around the world, experiencing the world and all its wonders. To meet people who viewed the world from a different perspective and lived in different ways.

I want to be face to face with some exotic animal in its natural habitat and capture nature in all its wrathful glory. To record scenes of joy or terrible pain, to capture pure, raw emotion in a single frame and show what humanity looks like.

I feel like people today lack the drive our ancestors had. That it is pointless to travel and explore all the wonders of the world when you can just turn on your TV or go on your computer and go to Google and look up images online.

But seeing is different from experiencing. I recently turned seventeen and I have already seen some amazing things. It gave me a new appreciation for the world I live in.

As I scrolled down the numerous folders filled with the countless pictures I had taken over the years I soon found myself staring at the folder with the pictures of me and Lucas.

All our dates and intimate moments. All the photos of him that I loved. Once they were treasured memories for me to savor at my leisure.

Now they are a bitter reminder of what I had lost. I highlighted the folder and my finger hovered over the delete button.

I should just get rid of them all. I didn't want to be one of those pathetic exes who stare at pictures of their former loves, feeling nothing but self-pity and bitterness.

The whole point of moving here was so I could start over. But I wasn't ready to forget my old life just yet.

Letting go had been easy, but forgetting?

That's the real bitch.

*****

Three days after we moved to town Mom dropped me off at the school.

We still had more unpacking to do, but we got most of it done and

10

all the major nick-nacks were put away so now we could work at a slow pace.

She had to go to work at the hospital today. She had been a nurse back home and transferred over here. I took a deep breath and walked into the school with a nice smile on my face. The secretary handed me my schedule, and I made my way to my first class.

The secretary had even given me a map so I could navigate around the place. It wasn't too hard, the school wasn't that big. My first class was History, so I made my way first to period.

Students were already inside and all eyes were on me as I went in. I took a deep breath and ignored them. I took a seat, quite aware that people were looking at me as they talked amongst themselves.

I was used to the stares and the looks. Even back in Cambridge, people would watch me, even though I grew up knowing just about everyone there. Though the looks I was getting from these people were more intense and I could tell they were surprised at what they saw.

They saw a new guy, five foot eight, with black glossy hair and a shade of eyes that was between blue and violet and skin so pale it was the color of a blank sheet of paper. I had been a big target for bullies. With my eyes and delicate appearance I drew in the assholes who thought it fun to beat up the girly boy.

I hated the way I looked. My fingers were too long and thin, my lips were too small and soft. My body was sleek and smooth and my skin was so white you could see the veins on my arms and around my neck, I did have some muscle but only as much as God and Nature (who seem to both have enjoyed making me girly) would allow.

I worked out a lot, it helped give me the muscles and a six pack which helped balance my appearance. It was an advantage though, bullies would look at me and figured I was an easy target, then they got a fist in the face and found out I wasn't someone to dick with.

I dressed in jeans and a blue shirt. The shirt helped bring out the blue in my eyes and made them seem less violet.

When I am at home, I like to wear loose fitting cloths but when I go out, I wear tight t-shirts that show off my muscles. Not for the sake of vanity, just to make it easier for people to see I am not a girl.

I looked over at a group of guys, obviously jocks. I envied them for their physiques, their burliness, and their masculinity. They could protect themselves; no one would dare go after them. They were mighty beasts. I on the other hand, was a little helpless lamb with a mean right hook.

And I fucking hated it!

"Hello," a voice said.

I turned and saw a girl; she had blue eyes and red hair with freckles on her cheeks. There was something familiar about her.

"Hi," I replied back.

"I am Rachel, welcome to our school," she said. "We met yesterday. I helped you and your mom move."

I remembered her now. There had been so many people I barely remember them all. She had been one of the few who didn't introduce themselves.

"Things were so busy and I am sure you would lose my name among everyone else," she said.

She stared into my eyes and I knew she was checking out the odd color. Because of my eyes and my skin tone people assumed I was an albino.

"Your name is Jeremy right?" she asked.

"Yes," I answered.

She offered me her hand. "Welcome to Wolf Fang Falls."

"Thanks," I said and shook her hand.

Class started and the teacher, Mr. Kristof started the class by letting everyone know that I was the new student (like they didn't already know) and my name. He told them all to make sure to help me out and make me feel welcome.

Luckily he didn't make me stand up and introduce myself and talk to the class. He was one of those polite but not overly nice teachers who went out of their way to make you feel like you belonged; which I was thankful for.

"I have notes you can copy," Rachel said next to me.

"Thanks," I told her.

"If I get overbearing tell me. I have moved around a bit so I know what it is like being the new kid," she said with a warm smile.

I was quickly starting to like her. She seemed to be a genuine and honest person, but I have only known her for five minutes.

But at least she is being honest so that gave her some extra points in my book. I only had two more years of school left, wouldn't hurt to make some friends.

*****

I sat with Rachel and some of her friends at lunch when she saw me walking into the cafeteria she flagged me over to her table. We talked a little when we had a chance, she didn't overload me with questions which I appreciated. Many of my other classmates had practically interrogated me.

Swear to God if I have to tell someone I am not a freaking albino I am going to go apeshit!

Rachel sat next to her boyfriend; a scrawny guy with trimmed brown hair and a pair of wide circular glasses that seemed to make his eyes bigger than they actually were. His name was Gabe.

There was Heather, a girl with long, curly brown hair olive skin and a thin face who was a member of the cheer squad. I thought she was rather on the skinny side but kept it to myself.

After all, who was I to bitch about appearances?

Heath was Heather's boyfriend, he was on the swim team and the football team; he had wide shoulders and a muscular body with dark coffee-colored skin and short trimmed hair.

"So where do you come from?" Gabe asked.

"Cambridge," I said.

"Oh, I have family there," Heather smiled.

"Yeah, my mom and I moved, she wanted to find a better paying job and found one as a nurse at the hospital here," I said. "She has old school friends who live around here and one of them was able to find her a position at the hospital."

That was a half truth. We were doing quit well over in Cambridge but my personal issues forced us to move. But mom had been able to find work as a nurse over here thanks to some old friends who put in a good word for her.

"Must suck to have to move, especially in junior year," Heath commented.

I nodded. "Yeah, but I have two more years. Plenty of time to make new friends."

"Can I ask you something?" Heather asked.

"Sure."

"How did you get so beautiful?" she asked giving me an inquisitive look.

"Heather!" Rachel admonished.

I blushed, I tried not to, but with my skin it was impossible to hide even a little. I was used to being called beautiful before, I preferred manly or buff but no one would lie about that.

Gabe and Heath laughed at my reaction.

"What? I am sorry but you have beautiful skin and amazing eyes," Heather noted.

"Yeah, I get that a lot," I said.

"Do you use some kind of cream?" she asked.

"No, I am all natural. I got some good genes is all," I said.

"More like great genes," Heather retorted.

"Believe me, I would give anything to look different. I look like I should be an extra on some fantasy movie," I said.

14

They all laughed at that.

"You're not that bad," Heather said. "Nothing wrong with being different."

I could have made an argument about that but decided to drop it instead.

Then I noticed a group of students walking in. It was a small group and the first thing I thought when I saw them was Socs. If you have ever read *The Outsiders,* you would know what I mean.

They were all dressed wonderfully and stylishly. All looking like they were getting ready to walk down a runway. Their clothes were more expensive than anything I ever owned.

They blended in with one another well, but they stuck out like a sore thumb compared to everyone else.

They had an air of charisma and superiority about them. They walked close together and in perfect sync. Their looks all screamed high class. And other students seemed to avoid crossing paths with them or gave them a wide berth.

"Jesus, are we next door to a prep school or something?" I asked.

Everyone turned to look to see what I was talking about.

"Oh, yeah. The Commune kids," Gabe replied with a note of irritation.

"The who?" I asked.

"We call them the Commune kids, see they all live in a gated community, hence the name Commune kids. They have everything there; swimming pools, tennis courts, playgrounds, clubhouses, golf courses and of course everyone who lives there is filthy rich," Rachel explained.

"The mayor lives there. So does the sheriff, one of the doctors that work at the hospital, a lawyer and a bunch of other upper crust folk," Heather added.

"The kids from there go to our school, but they keep to themselves. Always have, always will," Gabe said.

I noticed that the Commune kids did not get trays; instead they all opened up their own lunch bags.

It was than my eyes were drawn to one of them. He had an extremely beautiful blonde girl sitting next to him, her hand on his arm. She looked at him with adoring eyes. I didn't blame her for the look, he really was a specimen.

He was about six foot six, he had tan skin. I could see no signs of a tan line so I figured it had to be his natural skin color. His hair was glossy black like mine and was long in the front and short in the back. His cheeks were thin and firm. I was willing to bet he had some Native American in him. His lips were plump and red and they looked very kissable. He wore a school jersey. It had the black and red colors of our school and had the image of the school mascot on the left breast; a wolf baring its teeth.

His arms were thick like tree trunks and his neck was just as thick. Thick was a word you would use to describe him, or husky. There wasn't a part of him that seemed small; his waist, his legs, even his feet seemed noticeably large.

He was the biggest one, he sat at the center of their table and his woman wasn't the only one giving him adoring looks.

Another word you would think of when you looked at him was strong; he seemed to reek of strength that with his large body made him seem very intimidating.

The blonde said something to him and he smiled, showing off a set of perfectly white even teeth that seemed to make him appear wolfish.

If he was a wolf, he would definitely be an alpha male. Not just because of his size, which I was sure made people think twice about pissing him off. No, there was a way the others looked at him with a look of respect and admiration; it was the look a leader gets from his followers. There was also something very charismatic about him; when he smiled I wanted to smile as well, there was an energy to him that drew you in.

I didn't even know this guy, and I already felt respect for him, like if he told me to do something I would do it because he didn't strike me as someone who you said no to. As I looked at him I found myself becoming more and more interested in him. Not just because of his good looks but because he was just glowing with a positive aura.

I was willing to bet a whole year of my allowance he was a major prick.

I could feel my fingers twitch with the familiar urge to get my phone and take a picture. The whole group looked like they could be on the cover of a brochure for our school. But the urge I felt was most directed at the guy who was at the center of it all.

"Who is he?" I asked.

"Amazing," Heather remarked.

"He said who, not what babe," Heath chuckled.

"That is Richard Farkas. His family is one of the founding families of Wolf Fang Falls. They are very prestigious and have a lot of pull." Rachel explained.

"And he is a total prick," Gabe added.

"Let me guess, he preys on the weak?" I asked.

"Like a wolf going after a wounded deer," Gabe said.

"Did he wedgie you?" I asked sympathetically.

Given the way Gabe looked I was sure he faced his own issues with bullies.

"Not since fifth grade, but he does get off on putting me down verbally," he grumbled.

Looks like I was right about him being a prick. Add money, good looks and popularity and it seems to sour a guys personality. I learned that the hard way.

"Well, with me walking around I think he will focus on me more. I have a bad history of being a bully magnet. I think it is my masculine good looks that make men feel threatened," I said with a smirk.

They all laughed at that, I was about as masculine as a Pomeranian dog. I was a little disappointed though why are all the good looking ones such dicks?

"His sister isn't so bad, Elizabeth actually is the only one he listens to and she keeps him in line," Heather commented.

"Yeah, she was the one who stopped the wedgies," Gabe said with a note of gratitude.

"Which one is she?" I asked.

"Here she comes now," Heath said with a tone of awe.

A girl walked into the cafeteria. She was similar looking to Richard. She had the same tan skin which had been powdered, adding a lightness to it, and her eyes were a honey brown color and shined with a warmth that made you feel at ease. Her hair was down past her shoulders in fabulous waves of glossy black, she was buxom with a slim waist and stood at five foot nine. Her height complemented the aura of grace and respect she had. She was a real looker alright. Her and her brother came from good stock.

If I was straight or bi, I would be drooling over her like Heath and Gabe though I still appreciated her good looks.

But she was as different from the other Commune kids as she was as different from us. The other Commune kids dressed in preppy clothes while she dressed in Gothic Victorian.

She wore a black corset, a matching frock coat and a smooth black skirt which went down to her ankles. She had on a pair of high heel shoes and had painted black nails.

I saw lots of eyes on her as she walked. Many people seemed more....welcoming of her, whereas they would have liked to avoid the others. No one had said hi to the Commune kids but people were waving at her and smiling which she returned.

"Isn't she something?" Gabe asked.

"She sure is," Heath said dreamily.

Their girlfriends elbowed them in the arm.

"Ow, damn baby," Heath complained.

"Pig," Heather said.

"Weren't you just drooling over Richard?" Heath asked.

"Not as obvious as you," she said with a blush.

I had to agree with Gabe. She was *something* alright. I felt the urge in my fingers shift, I would have loved to get her photo.

She had it all, poise and good looks and that aura of confidence that could draw a whole crowed.

Elizabeth sat with the other Commune kids. A bunch of them made a space for her and I saw the same look of respect and awe they gave to Richard focused on her.

So if Richard was the alpha male, she was the alpha female.

She stuck out among the preppy looking Commune kids, but she didn't look any less gorgeous. Despite her clothes, she seemed more serene and at ease, as if she was having such a lovely day. With the Commune kids you felt like you couldn't approach them because they were so high up the ladder, but with Elizabeth you felt like she was capable of coming down to your level.

Her sense of style was odd and a little out there. But every small town needs a bit of strange to keep things interesting.

I looked over at Richard, to see what he was up to. He was very good to look at. Too bad he didn't swing my way, I wouldn't mind being the center of his attention.

I saw he had a curious look on his face, at first I wondered if it had something to do with his sister's entrance but then I noticed he seemed to be sniffing the air. He closed his eyes and a look of pure ecstasy was on his face, he gave a slight smile and when he opened his eyes they were looking dead at me.

I gasped as his honey brown eyes landed on me. They were warm like his sister's and the same color, but there was a quiet fierceness in them. His sister's eyes were like a warm stove fire. His warmth was like the heat that powered some great machine.

But when his eyes fell on me that heat focused on me. A part of me wanted to look away and not appear to be a weirdo who stared at people. But I could not help but look at him.

He was so...perfect.

Suddenly his body became rigid and his mouth opened as if in a gasp. I couldn't look away, the heat of his gaze was too intense and his reaction to me was too puzzling.

Something passed between us, I don't know what it was but I felt like a deer caught in the headlights of some oncoming car. I saw something coming for me but I couldn't move; I was too afraid to.

But it was a ridiculous idea that I should be afraid. What was there to be afraid of? I had done nothing wrong.

He stood up suddenly and it caused everyone to look at him funny. Then he practically ran for the door, as he ran past he stared right at me and I fought the urge to squirm under his gaze, which had a hint of anger to it. As if I had done something to offend him.

Once he left, the cafeteria broke into quiet whispers about what happened and people were looking at me to see what I had done to cause Richard to leave.

"What the hell was that all about?" Rachel asked.

"Dude, what did you do to piss him off?" Heath asked.

"I...I don't know," I replied, stunned by what happened.

Elizabeth left next, her walk was calmer, as if she was in no hurry. She looked at me curiously as she walked by. she knew whatever had caused her brother to run off had something to do with me. She silently examined me as she walked by. Her gaze was neutral neither friendly nor unfriendly. She continued to make a slow exit though it was clear she was following her brother.

"Did you look at him funny?" Heather asked.

"I just happened to look at him," I said.

"Maybe he assumed you were a girl and thought you were good looking," Heath teased.

"Heath!" Heather exclaimed.

"Err, no offense," Heath smiled, he rubbed his head looking at me sheepishly.

"No, it's okay," I said with a small laugh. "Actually, it has happened before. Someone thought I was a chick and then realized I was a guy and got all pissy about it," I admitted.

There was a time when I let my hair grow out a bit, but it made me look too girly so I always kept it short now. There had been times when a boy thought I was a cute girl, and then he saw I was dressed like a boy and made the realization. And of course being homophobes, they hated me for making them think outside their comfort zone. I tried growing facial hair, but it looked too odd on me; I didn't have one of those faces that went well with a goatee or a mustache.

"Shit dude, better be careful," Gabe warned. "They all think you did something to make him mad."

He was looking over at the Commune kids table. They were all watching me. And unlike Elizabeth their expressions were hostile looks that I had to flinch at.

"Don't worry, I can help you avoid them," Gabe said.

"What do you mean?" I asked.

"Well...no one messes with the Commune kids. See, they have a rep. They stick together and if anyone crosses them they get their asses kicked," Heather explained.

I gulped.

Great, my first day and I was pissing off the most popular and dangerous group in the school...I hate my life.

2

Richard

What the absolute fuck?!

What the hell just happened? Seriously, what is happening to me?

One minute I am following this nice scent, the next I am looking at some new kid in the eye and felt....God, I can't and won't describe it.

Let me back up. First, my name is Richard Farkas, I am eighteen years old and I am a werewolf. My dad's side of the family came from Hungary back in the nineteenth century. They immigrated and moved to the states and made their way here where they found out the Shoshone tribe was also home to a pack of werewolves.

Instead of fighting and killing one another they made a peace treaty and coexisted even though they came from two different packs.

After the Battle of Rosebud my great-great-great-grandfather realized they needed a place to call home and not worry about being bothered by humans. So they helped build Wolf Fang Falls.

If you go to our community, you will see a lot of dark-skinned people. The Shoshone werewolves were not moved to some reservation; the two packs joined forces and formed their own community separate from the humans. After a few generations they eventually were assimilated into our tribe.

Though there were still a few who were keeping the old tribe's way of life alive.

From my mom's side I am descended from the Shoshone werewolves and on my dads side I come from the Hungarian werewolves. So I had werewolf blood from both Hungary and America, cool, huh?

Anyway, I am getting off topic.

Ever since I was young, I have always had one goal in life.

To become Pack King of my pack.

Pack Kings are the rulers of a wolf pack. The only way to become a Pack King is to either beat the old one in combat or if you are named his or her successor so if they die you become the new leader.

Our current Pack King is Daryl Farkas. He is a cousin of mine three times removed.

In order to earn the right to be the Pack King you had to prove you had what it took, and this naturally involved a lot of fighting and duels.

Did I want to be the leader of the pack? Hell yeah! One day I was going to challenge Daryl and I would beat him in combat....did I challenge him once? Yes. Did I get my ass beat?

Sadly...yes.

It is not uncommon for young wolves to get cocky and think they are tough shit and try to challenge the Pack King. I wasn't the only one who challenged him and I wasn't the only one who got an ass whipping.

Don't get me wrong, I love Daryl as we all do. But I want to be the Pack King. I have been groomed by my parents since I was born to take the role.

It wasn't about pedigree of course; you had to prove you had what it took. Before I challenged the alpha I had to pass some tests, the elders make us go through to make sure we have the right stuff.

There was a bunch of other things I won't bore you with the details of, but in the end only five wolves in my generation were proven to have what it takes to one day be the Pack King.

My parents were so proud. Even when I lost, (which they knew I would), they were still happy I made the cut.

I remember after it happened (or from what I can remember) Daryl kissed me on top of the head and said.

"You have the strength to lead a pack Richard. But being Pack King is more than power. It's a responsibility. Like being a parent. Do not think you can have one without the other."

I was born to lead, I was idolized by the younger wolves as the person they wanted to be when they grew up and I had a smoking hot girlfriend. She was an alpha and a pureblood and I intended to marry her one day for her to be the mother of my kids, and I also ran the whole damn school. Wolf and human alike feared and respected me.

I had everything going for me; power, authority, good looks, a bright future, all of it. The world was mine, and I was going to own it.

But everything changed when I looked into a pair of eyes so blue, they were almost violet. See....when I looked into those eyes...I fell in love...with a dude.

I know, what the fuck right?

*****

My day started off as any other would. I got up, got dressed, got ready for school and all that. I was sitting down eating breakfast with my family. Mom was telling us something about a family moving into town.

"So, I heard Diane Moonvine is moving back to town," mom said as she sat down to eat with us.

"I think Rick mentioned that last time I saw him," dad said.

"Who is she?" Liz asked.

"She used to live in Wolf Fang Falls. We went to school with her. Her mother got sick around the time she got ready to leave for college. They moved with her so she could still get her degree and help care for her mom."

"Did you know her?" Liz asked.

"Not personally. Rick used to date her though. He was really into her. It caused some tension in the pack because she is human. But they broke up when she left. He wanted to stay here, and she wanted to leave the state to go to college. I hear she has a son who will be going to your school."

"Wow, one more human attending school. Big deal," I muttered.

"No need to be such a jerk about it," Liz said.

"What? It's not like we're going to be friends with him," I said.

"Unlike you I enjoy human company. Maybe if you weren't so narcissistic you could see humans make good friends."

"Blah blah blah. Every time you open your mouth that's all I hear," I said waving my hand in the air.

She kicked my shin from under the table I was about to retaliate when mom spoke. "Alright now kids, no fighting at the table."

She gave us her stern voice, letting us know she was serious. Dad looked at us warningly from behind the newspaper he was reading, backing mom up silently.

Liz and I may be twins, but we fight like cats and dogs sometimes.

Don't get me wrong, I love her to death. I anyone messes with her I will tear them limb from limb.

But sometimes she can be so damn high and mighty about being *nice* to humans and all that shit.

She still lectures me because I used to rough up the human kids when we were younger. A few wedgies never hurt no one.

Like I said, I love her. But when we fight, it is hardcore.

Thank God we heal fast. I would look like a veteran from some war, covered in scars.

Yeah, I admit, there were times when I got my ass handed to me by my sister. You think I can be nasty when I am in a mood?

Liz is the embodiment of '*Hell have no fury*'.

After we ate Liz, and I drove over to my best friend Trevor's house to pick him up. We then drove over to my girlfriend Mary's house. Mary lived with her family not to far from my home.

Liz sat in the back with Trevor so Mary could sit up front with me. I knew she rather sit up front only because she would love to make Mary sit in the back.

Mary and Liz did not get along but for my sake opted to not speak to one another. Liz thought Mary was stuck up and a bitch, Mary thought Liz was a weirdo goth chick who was full of herself.

As Mary got in the car, she leaned over and kissed me on the cheek.

"How do I look?" she asked me.

"Perfect, as always," I said with a smile.

We drove all the way to school. Several of our classmates (of the werewolf kind) were waiting for us.

We got out and walked over to the others. Everyone was making plans to go on a run tonight outside the community.

We were allowed to run and hunt outside our sanctuary, but there were rules of course and they were easy to follow. Don't hunt humans, don't go near humans and always stick together.

And above all, never let a human see you shift.

If a human finds out we are werewolves, the law says they either die, or are turned.

Of course, there are exceptions. All the human members on the town council know what we are; they knew our community is a paradise for werewolves. Those mortals who are not members of the council are mated with a wolf.

It wasn't a big deal. I mean they were married/mated with a werewolf so it wasn't like they were going to tell right? Being married to a werewolf was the only thing that kept a human safe from the law, unless the elders decided the said human was trustworthy enough, but it was rare if that happened. Usually the human had to be useful to us in some way, capable of moving about the human world in ways we could not without attracting attention.

A few humans in the hospital and law enforcement knew. They were promised to be turned if they served us well enough.

Some in our pack chose to live with the humans in our territory.

I don't know how they did it. I mean in the Gates we could be ourselves. We didn't have to worry so much about hiding what we are.

But those who live among the humans have to be extra careful.

So, school was going good right? We arrived and of course the humans look at us in awe and respect. Which we naturally deserved.

But as we were walking through the front doors, I stopped walking. I caught this scent; it was heavenly. Like vanilla and cinnamon with a dash of something like warm bread.

"Do you guys smell that?" I asked.

"Smell what babe?" Mary asked.

"That scent in the air," I said.

My little pack of friends sniffed the air.

"All I smell is humans," Mary answered with a frown.

"You're kidding, right?" I asked, "whatever it is it's divine!"

I scented the air again, I got the smell of humans, with their deodorants and body soaps. The air tinged with the tang of their anxiety, their lust, their bitter anger along with their bitter hormones that were playing hell with their chemistry.

But whatever it was that I along seemed to smell cut through all that. It blessed this whole building with its divine aroma.

"I don't smell anything dude," Trevor sniffed the air, double checking for the scent.

Trevor had been turned. His mom married his stepfather who was a turned werewolf as well. Trevor got cancer, and he was allowed to be made into one of us to save his life. He was below me in rank but he was a good friend of mine. When we allow a human to be turned, it is usually the Pack King who does the turning. When a wolf turns a mortal, it creates a powerful bond between the two. It makes the one who was turned feel a powerful sense of loyalty to the wolf who turned them, and therefore they have a powerful desire to do as they say.

It's easier for a Pack King to run his pack if he made most of them into werewolves. That bond keeps them in line and makes them want to please him.

Not that Daryl needed the power of the blood to earn loyalty and respect. He is stern as hell, but he also fair.

"Dude, I swear, there is something in the air," I announced.

The smell was having a strange effect on me. My wolf instincts were starting to become stronger, they wanted to find the source of this amazing scent. It wasn't food, it was something better. I didn't know what but, I wanted to find it and mark it with my scent; to keep it to myself and roll around in it, mixing its scent with mine.

I was a bit surprised by my wolf's reaction, sometimes a werewolf will find something like a flower or something else it likes and rub their bodies against it to cover themselves in that scent. But I had never had a reaction like this. I beat down those instincts and continued to make my way into school.

As the day went on I became more and more frustrated. I smelled that scent everywhere. And all day my wolf wanted to find that scent, it was very annoying. It was difficult to ignore those instincts and pay attention to what was going on around me. I was like a new wolf basking in the glories of the wolf sense of smell for the first time.

Even during lunch the scent haunted me, tempting me with its lure. Enticing me to find it and claim my prize, problem was I didn't know what that prize was or why it had this effect on me.

After school I was going to hunt it down and find out where it was coming from. I needed to know what could effect me like this and not everyone else.

It smelled human, but I don't know why a human scent would effect me like this.

When it was lunch time, we all sat at our usual spot. The humans gave us a wide and respectful berth as they always do. and we talked about tonight's hunt.

Elizabeth joined us after she walked from her class. I saw her smile and wave at the humans and they acted like she was one of them, I smiled to myself, if they only knew what she really was. She may seem beautiful and gentle, but she is an alpha like me and like all alphas she had to earn her place in the pack with plenty of fights.

"So you all hear of the new kid?" Keven asked.

"Is he here?" Trevor asked.

"Yeah, saw him. He looks like a total bitch dude," Keven said.

"Really?" I asked.

"Yeah, he is super pale and has the most girly eyes I have ever seen. Probably a queer," Keven snickered.

"You know Keven, a person's sexuality is not something to make fun of. Or have you forgotten that some of us are not so primitive we think it wrong to fornicate with the same sex?" Elizabeth questioned.

There was a smile on her face, but you could hear the underlining threat in her voice. She took offense to his comment. Elizabeth was bi, but she leaned more towards girls than guys.

Keven stopped smiling and quickly apologized. "Sorry, I didn't mean to offend," he said sheepishly.

Keven had challenged Liz once. When we were younger and starting to fight for our ranks in the pack.

She had him belly up in less than a minute.

"It's okay, try to be more sensitive to others feelings okay?" she said with another smile.

I grinned. Elizabeth intimidated even alpha males. She may appear delicate, but I have seen her take a few rounds out of a few guys. My sister was not above going all out for what she believed in.

I was kind of jealous of her. Dad always doted on her while he was always more strict and critical with me. She was daddy's little girl and had dad wrapped around her little finger.

I really wanted to strangle her for it sometimes.

"As a matter of fact, I have caught a glimpse of this new student. His name is Jeremy Moonvine. He recently moved with his mother from Cambridge. He has amazingly white skin and wonderful eyes. He is very stunning. As to his sexual orientation I do not know."

"How do you know he is from Cambridge?" I asked.

"Through the grapevine," she said with a smile.

Another thing about Elizabeth was she had connections. She had a way of finding things out. If she couldn't get the info, she wanted nicely she was not above using intimidation to get what she wanted. She was both lovely and scary. She was the only one who was more open to the humans.

We avoided them because well, they were human. They were beneath us. They were inferior to us. But Elizabeth had plenty of human friends and had her fare share of human lovers. She was all about humans and werewolves getting together and living side by side.

I don't hate humans, but I just thought they should stay separate from us. I wasn't like some of those wolves out there who thought we should kill humans for fun or that we should rule them.

I was fine with humans, but we were better off on our own sides of the fence. And that was what made what happened next extremely ironic.

Once again the smell began to call to me. It was strong in the lunch room, fresh. I closed my eyes and took in that smell. My whole body seemed to relax and become warm.

The wolf began to pace back and forth in my mind, it whined, begging me to follow the scent.

It was beginning to piss me off. Why was I the only one who could smell it? Why did it affect me so?

I needed to find the scent, find out what it was and why it made my wolf restless.

And when I found it...I don't know what I was going to do, but at least I would know *what* was causing this reaction.

"Hey, isn't that the new kid looking at us?" Jason asked.

I opened my eyes and, I saw him. He was like a little china doll. His skin really was white, so white I saw the veins underneath his skin. I had never seen someone so pale in my life. His hair was black and combed to the side and had a natural glossy tint to it. His lips were small and thin, his face was round and soft. If it wasn't for the way he combed his hair and his clothes, I could have confused him for a girl, but it was his eyes that stood out. They were a shade of dark blue, I would say violet even.

The second I laid eyes on him my wolf froze. We stared at this beautiful creature with his pale skin and pretty eyes which stared at us. I found myself falling into them, lost in a sea of deep-dark-blue.

A slew of emotions began to rise in me, to many and to quick for me to properly feel them. My wolf was clawing at the surface of my mind.

It took every ounce of self-control I had to keep *him* at bay.

I knew then I found the source of the scent.

In that moment, this creature was the most beautiful being I ever saw. I looked at him and I saw pure perfection. I saw an angel; I saw something so delicate it needed to be protected.

Ours!

My wolf growled the world with such ferocity that I could taste the words on the tip of my tongue.

I stood up. I was going to go over there. I was going to introduce myself to him and take him home with me. I was going to own him, I was going to take him. He was mine; I would let no one else have him.

I stood up and was about to go over there and introduce myself when the wolf's next words stopped me.

Mate

In that instant I snapped out of it.

The word was like a song my wolf was dancing too. The thought of it made me want to dance with joy.

Mate?

What the fuck!?

The wolf howled at my resistance and tried to regain dominance, but I wouldn't let it. I could not stay here though not with this new kid, this Jeremy kid so close.

Jeremy, what a perfect name.

I quickly made my way out of the cafeteria, the wolf begged me to at least look at him and I indulged him. Jeremy looked at me with confusion, wondering why I was staring at him so hard.

The wolf howled sadly and tried to convince me to go back.

No! Must go back! Claim him! Claim him! It demanded.

I gritted my teeth and ran outside. The memory of him haunted me; it was burned into my mind. I tried to figure out what just happened as to why I was having such feelings for a human-and a human guy at that-and how to make it stop!

I made my way to the parking lot. I stopped at my car and took a deep breath. The air was clear, and the scent was gone, making it a little easier to think, but the memory of his face was still with me, more fresh and vivid than anything else in my mind.

"What the fucking fuck!" I yelled.

I heard footsteps and knew from the slow motions it was Liz. She always walked with careful steps, like a dancer.

"Richard, what is wrong?" she asked.

"Nothing," I lied.

"Really?" she asked, not buying it at all.

"I am fine, not feeling good," I lied again.

My heart was pounding in my chest. I felt like I had run a thousand miles, only it was not exhaustion I felt. It was pure exhilaration; yet I didn't know what I had to be *exhilarated* about!

She was still there, patiently waiting for me to say something else. I sighed, knowing she would not leave until I did or I said something more to put her to ease.

"Look, I just...I just felt odd all of a sudden. My wolf is acting up and I don't know why," I explained.

She put her hand to my head, feeling my temperature. "You feel a bit warm. Odd," she noted.

Werewolves don't get sick unless we drink Wolfsbane. We have a powerful immunity to diseases and poisons. We don't get sick by the flu or other kinds of infections.

"I just need a moment to get some fresh air, I think my wolf is excited for tonight is all," I lied again.

She knew I was lying, she always knew. It was like she was a fucking psychic, but I had to lie, because the truth was too horrible to confess.

"Very well. But...if there is anything wrong, you know I am here right?" she said

A part of me wanted to tell her. I wanted her help and console. If anyone could help me, it would be Liz.

But I wasn't ready to speak about it. I was still too confused, too conflicted.

"Yes. Thank you."

She kissed me on the cheek. "I am serious Richard. I will go back in and let the others know you are okay."

She turned and left me alone. Once I was sure she was out of ear shot, I took a deep breath and looked up into the sky.

"Gods, what has happened to me?"

3

Jeremy

The rest of the day went by without incident. Which I was thankful for. I didn't see Richard for the rest of school and I wondered what happened?

When I got home mom was there, getting ready for work. She was already in her scrubs when I arrived.

"Hi sweetie, how was school?" she asked.

"Alright," I said.

"Make any new friends?"

"Yes, I did," I stated.

"See, I told you. People are so friendly around here," she said with a smile.

I thought of Richard and his strange reaction today. "Yeah, friendly," I repeated.

"Sorry I have to go, I hate leaving you all alone," she said.

"It's alright mom, I need to finish unpacking anyway," I said.

"I ordered a pizza, it should be here in another fifteen minutes, and the money is on the counter. I left my number on the notepad. I have a key so make sure you lock up before you go to bed. I should be back before midnight but don't wait up for me, school tomorrow," she said.

"Alright," I said.

I hugged her, and she kissed me on the cheek. "I love you, I will see you tomorrow."

"Love you too mom," I said.

She left, leaving me alone. I walked into the living room and pulled out my homework. I found something to watch and did my homework while I waited for the pizza to show up.

When it did, I handed the man his money and took a break from work to eat.

Thinking about my day, besides the strange incident with Richard, it all went really well. I was only concerned what the Commune kids had in store for me.

After lunch I had a few classes with some of them, and every time they saw me they glared at me. As if blaming me for their friend's reaction.

I don't know what freaked him out. I just hope to God he doesn't try to start shit with me. I don't care if he is rich and badass, I won't let him treat me like I am a floor mat.

Soon it got dark outside, and I went upstairs to go through some of the things I still had boxed up. When I was going through one of the box's I found a letter from my ex, Lucas. I forgot I even had the thing.

I opened it up and smiled sadly, it was a letter he wrote to me when we were still together, telling me how much he loved me, and how I was his little snowflake. How happy we would be when I turned eighteen and we could reveal our relationship to the world.

I crushed the note and tore it to pieces. I went into the bathroom and tossed the pieces in the toilet and flushed it. I wiped my face of the tears that ran down my cheeks.

I missed Lucas. I missed him so much.

I should have known better than to be involved with him. He was older than me and his lifestyle put all kinds of complications on things.

But I was a fool in love.

I unpacked some more than decided to call it a night. I took a shower and then dressed for bed. I went downstairs and locked all the doors and went back up to my room.

As I lay down, trying to sleep, I heard the sounds of wolves howling in the distance. Wolf Fang Falls had a lot of wolves, always had; that is how it got its name

I always liked wolves. So I fell asleep, listening to their howling.

*****

Richard

I skipped school the rest of the day. I visited the nurse, and she took my temp. When she saw how hot I was she sent me home with an excuse to give to those old birds in the office.

We werewolves normally have a high temp, but I was running a fever higher than normal even for us.

When I got home mom asked why I was there, and I told her I was sick. She felt my head, not believing I was ill for the first time in my life.

Her eyes had widened when she touched my forehead. I must be warm to get a reaction like that from her.

She made me something to eat and sent me off to bed. Mom was always so sweet on me. Dad could be a hard ass but mom was more gentle and supportive of me.

I tried to sleep, but images of Jeremy haunted me, I couldn't get the damn kid out of my head.

His dark hair which was glossy like mine. I wondered if it had the same texture as mine? If I ran my fingers through it would it be soft? Would his skin feel like smooth polished marble? Then of course there was his eyes, such a dark blue!

And his scent! By the White Wolf nothing I have ever smelled has come close to his.

How could no one else be effected by it? Was something wrong with me? Was I suffering from some rare genetic disorder that caused my sense of smell to react to him in such a way?

It was rare but, it was possible for some of our kind to be born with a defect. Some of us could be born color blind or have a physical deformity; or even mental conditions!

Could that be what was wrong with me? Was I defective in some way?

I staid in my room for the rest of the night, receiving several texts from my friends checking on me.

They all wanted to know what was wrong why I had left so early. I got one irritated text from Mary because she had to catch a ride with her friends because I left without telling her.

texted them all back, letting them know I was fine and planned a time to meet up with them for tonights run.

At around eight, I met up with Keven, Trevor, their girls Cora, Vivian and Mary.

Mom checked my temperature before I left, it had gone back down so she let me leave, she made the others promise to keep an eye on me.

We took my car, Mary sat up front with me while the other sat in the back.

Once they were inside car, they began to ask if I was okay and what happened to me today. I lied and said it had something to do with my pureblood werewolf physiology. I told them all I needed was a good run and I would be better.

I was sure they could sense the bullshit I was trying to feed them, but no one pressed me.

I tried to act like I was excited for tonight as well. But the truth was my mind was focused only on one thing.

Or rather one person.

We drove out of the Gates to a private piece of land we used for runs. Lots of people came here, there were already a few cars parked from people in the pack who decided to go out for a run tonight as well.

We got out and stripped. We left our cloths in my car and began to transform. There is a difference when a pure blood shifts compared to a turned wolf. With pure bloods the change is more fluid, graceful and quicker. The turned taking a little longer, their transformations are a little jerkier and you can hear sounds of bones and muscle shifting and rearranging themselves.

When we were all changed, we went out and ran. Werewolves in their wolf form are much larger than the average wolf, being about the size of a tiger. I was at the head of the pack and the others followed me. I may not be the Pack King but I ran my group of friends, I am their alpha.

In my wolf form I had black fur, but I had white on my front chest and jaw. Like someone rubbed a white paint brush on my underbelly. Normally a good run helps me focus, but even as I ran with my pack my wolf would not let me forget about Jeremy.

He was unlike any human or werewolf I had ever seen; I wish I had gotten a chance to speak with him. Normally I would target someone like him. But the idea of harming so much as one hair on his body made my stomach twist painfully.

I was sure he was no stranger to being picked on. Guys like him were always a target.

I thought what it must be like to be him, to deal with people taunting him for his looks. And the idea of someone else harming him made my blood boil with rage.

I growled low to myself, trying to rid myself of these stupid thoughts. I needed something to distract me from them. I needed to remind myself who and what I was. Mary ran up beside me and rubbed against me, trying to comfort me; she sensed my agitation.

We found the scent of an elk and hunted it down. I was the first to take it down and being an alpha male, I got to eat first. Mary being my mate ate with me. The others waited for us to get our fill, and then when we did we let the others finish it off.

Mary licked my ears and bumped into my side. I could smell her arousal and knew what she wanted.

She continued to rub against me affectingly, licking at my ears, low whines escaping her mouth. She walked over past some trees and stopped to look at me, she jerked her head out in the woods. I could sense her lust and knew exactly what she *wanted*.

I decided that it was exactly what I *needed*, a nice romp in the woods with Mary would get rid of these fucked up thoughts.

Mary would remind me I am not gay.

We left the others to their meal, wanting a little privacy for what was to come next. Trevor grinned at me when he saw I was following Mary, but continued on with the elk. Once we were far away enough where the others would not see us we turned back into our human form. Mary walked up to me and ran her hands down my chest. Her long golden blonde hair covered her perky breasts, and my hands cupped her generous bottom. Mary was proud of her ass, many people make a big deal about women having big butts, but Mary was proud of hers, anyone who told her different would find their own ass's being handed to them.

"Baby, are you okay?" she asked looking worried.

"Yeah, I am fine," I lied.

"Are you sure? You seem like something is bothering you."

I smiled and kissed her on the lips. "I am fine. My wolf is acting up a bit," I explained.

It happens with us all, even born wolves have trouble with their animal instincts from time to time.

She smiled. "Well, why don't we try to tame the beast a little," she winked.

She wrapped her arms around my waist and kissed me, she rubbed her breasts against my chest. Normally at this point my wolf would be going wild with the scent of her lust.

But now he seemed apathetic to her in all ways as did I. She was beautiful. We had been together for four years and had sex on more than one occasion. We were supposed to be together, everyone always said we were good together, that we fit perfectly.

She was an alpha, I was an alpha. We both knew what we wanted in life and were not afraid to take it. We both knew where we stood in the world; at the top, and we both knew no one was better than us. Sure, she could be a bit bitchy and could annoy me by being needy sometimes, but women were like that.

I always enjoyed being with her, I planned on marrying her one day. On having a family with her. When the day came when I became Pack King she would be my mate and together we would rule the pack.

But now...it all felt wrong. Like all those plans had been tossed out the window, and I had a great big blank piece of paper that needed to be written on. But I did not know what to write. I knew what I wanted but now she no longer fit into the narrative.

She was still a good kisser, but her lips did not feel right. I needed lips that were smaller, thinner. Lips like.....

This is stupid! I need to snap out of it! I berated myself.

I picked her up and laid her on the ground. She had not noticed I was not hard, but I was not going to let that stop me.

She was ready to rut, but she was not fertile. One of the perks of being a wolf was we could sense when our mates were in the state to be impregnated. It saved a fortune on condoms.

I began to lick and kiss my way up her body. She moaned and became more and more aroused as I worshiped her most sensitive and intimate areas. Yet I still remained soft, I still felt nothing. The wolf was not interested in her, she was still beautiful but she just didn't do it for me, though her scent was putting me on edge.

It was like when you are starving, yet the only thing you are offered are foods you do not care for or find distasteful. You'll eat it but it won't give you the same pleasure to eat as your normal palate would.

Never before have I had such a problem! And why should I? I was a young werewolf! I had more raging hormones inside of me then any human man had his whole life!

How many times have I taken her! Ravaged her! Hissed in pleasure as her nails bite into the flesh of my back as I brought her to climax!

Now I found myself facing one of the most feared conditions a man could face: Impotence. The mere word fills the mind with images of failure and damages a mans honor.

I was not just a man! I was an alpha! I was a Farkas!

My own self-loathing fueled my desire to achieve erection. Whatever sickness had infected me I would not allow it to keep me from enjoying the most basic and primal pleasures a man can experience.

"Holy shit Richard!" she panted, gasping for breath.

She was having no problem what so ever, I knew my actions were making her feel all kinds of pleasure.

For the first time since we began to know one another I felt envy for her. Envy that she could still feel something from all this.

I growled, and she thought it was a growl of lust, but it was actually one of frustration, how was this happening to me? Me of all people? I loved having sex. Mary wasn't my first, and I never had a problem getting a hard on before.

I was a fucking teen werewolf! I got enough raging hormones in me to send a normal teen into shock!

This was all that fucking new kid's fault!

And like that the rage I felt towards him caused the memory of him to burn to life inside my head; his skin, his eyes, his sinfully delicious scent.

And just like that I began to grow hard.

Oh come on! Really? I thought to myself.

Of all the things to turn me on...another guy?

No! I wasn't a fucking fag! I was going to prove it!

I got up and positioned myself at her entrance. I then shoved straight into her "Oh my God! Richard!" she cried as I suddenly filled her up.

I began to pound into her, but as I stared at her face I was horrified to find myself growing soft. It was a man's worst nightmare, and I was living it.

I closed my eyes and tried to focus. I tried to think of how good it felt to be fucking Mary, but there was nothing to feel. The flesh was willing, but the passion was not there. I began to imagine the things I found sexy or arousing to help keep myself up. It worked a little, but I needed something to get my head back in the game.

Come on! What is it going to take to get you into this again?! I asked myself.

Mate my wolf replied.

An image appeared in my head; Jeremy, on the ground, beneath me, moaning as I pounded into him, his sweet scent filled the air, and his soft moans were like music to my ears. My dick turned as hard as steel and something flared inside me.

I began to thrust hard and deep inside of her, the wolf was aroused now, loving the image of Jeremy beneath us, soon the night was filled with the sounds of our fucking. I didn't look at her one time because I knew if I did it would ruin things.

She said my name many times, begged me to fuck her harder and deeper, she said many things that before would drive me wild. But now they had no effect on me.

My wolf was no longer satisfied with her, the desire I felt was not for her but for a guy who looked like he should have been born a girl.

And when I came, I threw my head into the air and let out a howl as I emptied into her. I felt my canines grow, my fingernails turned into claws and I could tell from how sharp and vivid my vision was that my eyes had turned into their wolf form.

The veins in my arms and neck bulged as the most powerful orgasm I had in my life hit me. I had imagined Jeremy shaking on the ground beneath me as he came too.

I pulled out of Mary and rolled over and stared up into the nighttime sky.

"Fuck," I swore under my breath.

"Tell me about it," Mary panted.

I looked over at her; she was covered in sweat, and her hair was covered in twigs and leaves. She was glowing from satisfaction.

"Sweet Christ I thought I was going to have a heart attack, I must have came three times. What got into you tonight?" she asked with a smile. "Not that I am complaining."

I shrugged. "Just...needed to vent," I commented.

After we took time to catch our breath, we returned to the others. The elk was a pile of bloody bone when we returned, but the others had their own party while we were gone. The air reeked of sex.

They were all in their human form now. All of them were sweaty and out of breath and I knew Mary and I had not been the only ones to rut in the woods

"Dude, what the fuck?!" Keven yelled at me.

"What?" I asked.

"Dude, one minute we are enjoying the elk, then your energy hits us like a ton of bricks!" Trevor stated.

I couldn't believe what he said. Had I really let my shields down and not known it? God, I should have better control than that!

"Next thing you know we are shifting back and fucking," Vivian said. Vivian was Keven's girlfriend.

"Shit, sorry guys," I said feeling bad.

"Thank God we are not fertile," Cora noted, next to Trevor.

"Yeah man, I don't think I would have cared if she was at that point! But now I am not ready to be a dad!" Trevor said, obviously just as pissed off as everyone else.

"Look, I said I was sorry, get off my back!" I snapped.

They all flinched at the harshness in my tone.

Alphas have a gift that the lower class wolves like betas and omegas don't. We can manipulate other werewolves...I don't know what you would call it-people call it. Chi, aura, energy? Whatever it is alphas can use their own energy to affect lesser wolves. The more powerful the alpha the more control he can have over another werewolf's energy. It hits the weaker wolves harder and other alphas are more resistant to it.

With this ability an alpha can sense and manipulate another wolf or even use it to cause a werewolf to change between human and wolf form. There are even alphas that have enough talent to manipulate another werewolf's energy to trap them in their human or wolf form.

There are three kinds of werewolves. Alphas, beta's and omega's. Each one has their own talents, but alphas are by the laws of nature designed to be leaders. Any one of the three can make a human into a werewolf.

But alphas are natural born leaders. A pack functioned easier to have an alpha as Pack King because our ability to not only sense but manipulate energy kept even the most unruly of werewolves in check.

I have been told that I am unusually talented for an alpha. My abilities were so precise that I could effect the moods of my fellow wolves. Even other alphas were effected by my power.

During our little tryst in the woods my power to manipulate such energy went out of control and caused my friends to get all hot and heavy with one another. My lust literally caused them to become as horny as sex crazed as I was when I was thinking about Jeremy.

Alphas are taught to control this ability. I especially have had to go through rigorous training so I don't accidentally manipulate my wolf brothers and sisters subconsciously. But I lost control, and they paid the price. Sure it was a good price to pay, but no one likes being controlled, right?

My friends were all beta level. If my shields had completely crumbled, and they got hit with it before they had a chance to prepare then they wouldn't stand a chance. All werewolves are taught to resist an alpha manipulating their energy, but like I said, if it hit them when they were not expecting it then they wouldn't be able to resist it.

One of the tests you have to pass to become a candidate for Pack King was showing the elders how good you were at manipulating and controlling such energy. I had done extremely well.

It was one of the reasons why I had such a good chance of becoming the leader of the pack one day. When even alphas can be swayed by my power, I could be a force to be reckoned with.

"Dude, what is up with you? First you flip out at school, and then you lose control of your power? That is not like you," Keven complained.

"Look, I am sorry. I have a lot on my mind. I don't want to hear another word about it!" I said firmly. They all bowed their heads in respect. "And I don't want anyone talking about this."

The last thing I needed was for one of the other wolves in the pack to think I had gotten weak and challenge me. Wolves prey on the weak after all.

You didn't have to be an alpha to be the Pack King. You either defeated the current king in a duel or if he died before he could surrender his position or name a successor then those who wanted the spot had to fight for it.

So far our Pack King Daryl had not named a successor. I was only one of several wolves who were considered eligible for the position.

If they learned I was going through whatever, this is they could use it to discredit me to the rest of the pack. And every future leader needs supporters.

We made our way back to the car as humans and silently got changed.

Everyone was quiet. There was a tension in the air. But no one dared address it out loud. I knew they were still angry over my loss of control, but they respected me enough to not bring up the subject.

We went back to the Gates, and I took everyone home. After I dropped Mary off at her house, I left the Gates again and headed into town.

I stopped by the school and found his scent. Even after all these hours his smell caught my attention above all else.

Above the smell of the sweat, perfume, cologne, body wash and other scents of the other students his was like a beacon in the dark

I followed the scent until it led me to his house, he must have walked all the way home. I parked the car a little ways down the street and walked up to his house.

I circled the place, being quiet as a mouse, making sure I was not seen or heard. I could hear him inside, he was all alone. I jumped to his roof, it was easy seeing how I was able to jump twenty feet in the air.

I went to his bedroom window and peered inside. He was asleep on his bed, looking so peaceful and serene.

I placed my hand on his window and once again my nails had turned into claws. My inner wolf wanted to go to him, to lie in his bed and cuddle with him.

I growled lowly. I should kill him! He had some kind of adverse effect on me. There was no way he was human; no human ever did this to me. He was making me weak! I would not tolerate weakness! I was Richard Farkas and one day I was going to be the Pack King of the Wolf Fang Falls pack!

I was not going to let some effeminate little human hinder me!

But yet, the idea of him hurt, the idea of him dead, bleeding, by my hands no less, it caused an ache in my heart that only made me whimper and inflamed my anger.

"I don't know who you are kid, but you fucked with the wrong wolf!" I said, too quiet for him to hear.

4

Jeremy

The next day things did not stop getting any stranger.

It was Wednesday, and I had biology for my first period class.

Gabe and Rachel were there, so that was a plus. The minus however, was Richard. He was there as well sitting with some of his group. But when he saw me I was once again I was the center of his focus. He glared at me with such intensity I wanted to turn around and walk the other way.

But I wasn't going to be intimidated by some rich pompous freak! So I took a deep breath and went inside.

I sat at a table with Gabe and Rachel. I passed Richard and his friends and I saw Richard stiffen as I walked by him.

"Dude, what did you do to piss of Farkas?" Gabe asked.

"Hell if I know," I said as I pulled out my books from my bag.

"He is acting really strange," Rachel noted. "I mean, he can be a jerk but he never just...hates someone in an instant. Did you say something to him or-"

"I haven't, I have not said a single word to him or interacted with him in any way," I said feeling frustrated.

"Well, maybe you should make sure you never wander around alone. Wouldn't be the first time he and his friends jumped someone," Gabe warned me.

"Alright class, today we are going to dominant and recessive traits," Mr. Hale said. "Now, we are going to work in groups of two. I want you to write a five-page paper, due on Friday about the subject; how are recessive genes passed and how can they become dominant in future pairings. Now, I have chosen the pairings."

I stopped listening to him when I noticed that Richard seemed to be turning his head back as if to look at me. The muscles in his neck strained as he turned his head, and I thought he had a really nice neck.

Stupid I know, to think such thoughts about someone who had some kind of beef with me. But damn if he wasn't good looking. He kind of looked like a younger, more buff version of Antonio Sabato, Jr.

"And Jeremy and Richard."

"What?"

It was a question repeated by both Richard and myself.

"You two are going to be working together on the assignment," Mr. Hale intoned.

Before we could protest, he clapped his hands and told us all to get to work. Everyone got up to move to their partner's desk to work. I did not. I looked over at Richard and he was still sitting down, looking tense about something.

He wasn't getting up, so I figured it was up to me to as they say, break the ice. I got up and grabbed my bag. "Good luck," Gabe said.

I walked over to his table and sat down next to him, his fists were clenched and he seemed to be shaking a little.

I looked back over to Rachel and Gabe. They both gave me the salute from the Hunger Games, Gabe even whistled the tone.

"So, how do you want to do this?" I asked turning back to Richard.

"Don't talk to me!" he snapped.

I sighed. "Look pal, I don't know what your deal is and I don't care. Let's just hurry up and get this shit done so we can forget this ever happened okay?"

His jaw clenched. He turned to look at me, his eyes burned fiercely. "Don't. Ever. Speak. To. Me. Like. That. Again!" he punctuated each word angrily.

"Whatever," I muttered.

In a flash his hand was around my wrist. He was rather warm and although his grip was not bone crushing, it was not gentle either. The second our skin connected I felt an odd, but pleasant tingle that went up my arm and down my spine.

"I mean it!" he all but growled.

I pulled my hand out of his grip. "Did I do something to piss you off or what?" I asked him.

He looked forward and ignored me.

"Fine, but at least pull out your book. I am not doing this alone."

He reached into his bag and pulled out his book. He slammed it on his desk so hard Mr. Hale gave him a look. He opened the book and crossed his arms, acting like a spoiled brat.

"Whatever," I said again.

I rubbed my wrist. It still felt warm from his touch. I don't know what his problem is but I am in no mood for this.

✵✵✵✵✵

Richard

God Fucking Damn It! What do I have to do to get a break around here! My wolf is positively delighted to be next to this ivory colored freak. I couldn't believe Hale put him and I together! What the fuck was he thinking?

Then the little bitch had to go and give me some lip! The wolf and I didn't like that. He was not our equal I thought, and the wolf did not like him defying us.

When I grabbed his arm my hand felt tingly. His skin was so soft. I can still feel it on my skin where I touched him. I rubbed my thumb over my palm. While he was looking in the bio book, I brought my hand to my mouth and smelled it. His scent was on my skin and I loved it.

I quickly put my hand down before anyone noticed.

Gods, what was wrong with me? Why was I feeling this way? The wolf wanted me to take him somewhere private and teach him who the dominant one was; to claim him; to mark him as ours.

Why was this happening to me? What did I do to deserve this? Obviously the kid is fucking with me, no way is he human. But why am I the only one affected? Is he targeting me?

None of this makes sense! But it's not like I can talk to someone about it. What am I going to say? That I have these confusing sexual urges directed at some human?

Bob and Henry looked at me. They must sense my agitation because they were starting to get tense as well, shit my energy must be leaking out.

I took a deep breath and calmed down. I reached into that part of me and called out to my power and pulled it back inside me. The boys relaxed but still looked at me worriedly.

Shit! I had to get this under control, I can't let the others sense something is wrong, and I especially can't let this go on. What if my power started to leak out and affect all the wolves in the school?

"Hello?"

"What?" I asked.

Jeremy sighed. "You are not even listening are you?" he asked.

"No," I simply replied.

"You know, if you're going to be dead weight then I am going to ask Mr. Hale to find me someone who is not going to make me do all the work," he informed me, standing up

"Would you sit the fuck down!" I hissed.

I grabbed his hand and pulled him down and a jolt ran up my arm when I touched him.

"Would you stop manhandling me?" he asked.

"Look, what do you want me to do?" I questioned.

"Well, what do you think is a good subject for us to write about?" he asked.

"Eye color...how they are inherited and what colors you can get even if your parents have the same colored eyes," I replied.

"Finally, we are going somewhere," he sighed.

"Eye color is about dominant and recessive alleles. But there is also a bunch of other factors that determine our eye color." I remarked.

Jeremy wrote some notes, he seemed impressed that I knew these things. Probably thought I was just some dumb jock. I felt a little bit of pride to prove him wrong, and a bit of pleasure to have impressed him.

We continued to go over the subject, about how alleles are passed from parent to child and the genetic disorders that can affect eye color as well. I enjoyed the fact we were getting along now. There was still tension of course, but now we were talking and...he did have such a nice voice. I liked hearing him talk.

The wolf was pleased as well; it liked hearing him speak, it liked how the tension between us seemed to lighten up. But it still wanted to take him away somewhere private.

When the bell rang, he put his stuff in his bag I felt a pain of disappointment. Since when do I wish class lasted longer?

"Well, we'll have to work on this some other time," he said.

"How about tonight!" I blurted.

The wolf liked the idea. Of going inside Jeremy's house, of seeing what his home was like, of entering his mate's domain.

He's not our fucking mate! I screamed at myself.

Jeremy seemed a little taken back by my outburst. "Oh, okay. Sounds like a plan. I live on-"

"I know where you live," I interrupted him.

He looked at me with a surprised expression. "How do you know?" he asked.

"It's a small town, people talk," I replied with a shrug.

I grabbed my stuff and went on my way. "I have things to do after school, I'll come over after later," I said.

I left the room before he could say any more. Bob and Henry followed me side by side, both not daring to comment on what happened in the class.

My wolf was sad to leave Jeremy, but it was also pleased we would be in his house tonight.

Claim him tonight! Take him to his den and mark him!

I ignored the wolf. I had to find out what was wrong with me. But who do I turn to? There are no gay werewolves in this pack. And I wasn't gay! This was just some stupid wolf thing.

That's all it was, a *wolf thing*. I wasn't attracted to Jeremy in any way.

****

Jeremy

The day continued to run smoothly after first period.

Fourth period was gym, I love gym.

Heath and Heather had gym with me, problem was Richard and a few of his Commune friends did as well. Richard looked amazing in his normal school clothes, but in a pair of black shorts and a black shirt he looked absolutely delicious. The guy was made of pure solid rock hard muscles.

The other Commune guys were extremely fit as well but Richard beat them all hands down.

I tried not to stare, but it was hard. Damn, why did all the super hot guys have to be bipolar or assholes or- in Richard's case-both.

The twitch in my fingers returned, the longer I looked at him the stronger the sensation got. IF I had a camera in my hands I don't think I could resist taking a pic of him.

I was nervous about him coming over to my place, mom had to work late again tonight and I wasn't sure I wanted to be alone with him. His mood swings and his extremely big physique, not to mention the aggression he has shown me made me a little uncomfortable with the idea.

I caught him looking at me a few times too, but when he saw I was looking he quickly looked away. It wasn't too odd he was doing it. I had caught many of the students and even some of the teachers staring at me. Back in Cambridge everyone was used to them, only the rare new student would stare.

Mom says when I graduate I should become a model or something. She says I would make a killing in that business.

We were all outside, the sun was shining and the air was nice with a cool breeze. It was a good day to be outside.

Our gym teacher, Coach Howard had us get in a line. "Alright class, today we are going to play field hockey."

I smiled, loving the idea of playing this game. It was one of my favorites. Lots of people complained about it because the rubber ball could hurt if it hit you or getting whacked in the shins by a stick could hurt too. But I loved it; I loved the roughness of it, I loved the adrenaline rush.

"Alright, let's split into two teams. We'll need two captains, Richard and Heath."

Richard and Heath stepped forward.

"Heath, you get first pick."

"Alex."

A guy who was tall and lanky walked forward.

"Richard, your turn," Coach Howard said.

"Trevor," Richard said.

One of the Commune kids stepped forward and joined Richard.

One by one they each chose a person. I noticed that Richard had chosen all his commune friends. He didn't start picking others until he had already gotten everyone from his little gated community on his team.

I wasn't surprised. Heath told me in the locker room that the Commune Kids never played against one another. Against the rest of the kids, yes but never against one another.

So Heath didn't bother trying to pick any of them, he knew they would not do much.

I was one of the final five kids to be chosen. I wasn't surprised; when I was younger, I would usually be picked last because I looked so weak. But then I grew up and people saw how good I was.

I guess I was going to have to show people here how *good* I was too.

Heath picked me for his team. Richard did not seem pleased, nor displeased about that. But he did scowl as I joined Heath's team.

Once everyone was picked, we got our sticks. My team was the blue team.

Heath and Richard went to the center of the field, Coach Howard stood between them, the rubber ball in his hand. Heath looked a little intimidated by Richard, but he was doing his best not to show it.

Heath was built like a boulder, similar to Richard. But there was something dangerous about Richard. The way he glared at Heath made even me feel worried for my friend. But Heath was on the football team, he knew how to face off against tough guys. I could tell he was trying to seem brave but was cautious.

He knew Richard's skills more than I did. I had to give him credit for bravery.

Richard seemed to know about Heath's feelings. He smiled, showing off his teeth, reminding me of a giant animal getting ready to pounce on a smaller, helpless creature.

Coach Howard dropped the ball and blew his whistle.

Richard rammed his shoulder into Heath. He took the ball and ran down toward our goal. No one on my side dared to get in his way, and I was pretty sure the goalie was getting ready to jump to safety when Richard was about to hit the ball.

No one on Richard's team really moved, it was like this was the norm.

I couldn't blame my teammates for not wanting to get in Richard's way. There was a wild look in his eyes; it clearly said Richard would give his all; that he would stop at nothing to win. And this was just gym! I could only imagine how competitive he was with everything else in life.

It wasn't just the his look, it was his massive frame, the way he knocked Heath down so quickly and easily showed not just strength, but skill as well.

Yep, you would have to be crazy or stupid to get in Richard's way...you see where I am going with this right?

Maybe it was the stress of the past several months, maybe it was me wanting to get a little payback at Richard for his shitty attitude. But I decided to show Richard there was one person at this school who wasn't going to let him get what he wants without earning it.

Richard was about to pass me and I acted like I was going to move out of his way, like any sane person would have. But as he was about to pass, I brought my stick out and took the ball from him.

I had played field hockey many times back in Cambridge, I was one of the fastest players.

I didn't waste time to see what his reaction was though I could imagine the look of shock or indignation. I took the ball and began to run towards the red team's goal. I saw a lot of shocked faces as I ran.

I was just some new guy, yet here I was stealing the thunder of one of the schools golden elite.

But my unbelievable act seemed to motivate my team and soon they were charging with me. I dodged a few of the red team members who tried to get the ball from me. I saw I had a clear shot of the net and was about to take a swing, next thing I know something slams into me hard, sending me onto the ground. The ball went sliding across the field and one of the red team kids got it and smacked it away.

I looked up to see one of the Commune kids smiling at me. "Better be careful or someone might hurt your lily white ass," he warned me.

I got up and was about to say something, but before I could Richard came up like a bat out of hell and grabbed the kid's shoulder in what must have been a bone crushing grip. He looked like he was about to breathe fire.

"What the fuck are you doing?!" he growled.

"Richard I-" the kid started to say, looking alarmed.

"Get the fuck out of here before I rip your throat out with my teeth!"

He pushed the kid away who made a quick exit. He then walked up to me and I was afraid I was about to get the same treatment. Instead he cupped my cheek gently and went from fire and brimstone to soft and gentle.

"Are you hurt?" he asked.

"I-I'm fine," I answered, taken aback.

He let go of my chin and regained some of his sternness. "You need to be careful. You could get hurt," he scolded.

It was not a threat, merely a warning. But still I felt a stab of annoyance.

"I'm fine, I am not a china doll you know," I said feeling irritated.

I got up and went off and joined the blue team as we tried to take back the rubber ball. As I ran Richard appeared next to me.

"You're better than I thought you would be; you have some wicked reflexes," he complimented me.

"Thanks. People like to think I'm slow, or weak because of how I look. I love proving them wrong," I said.

Speaking of good reflexes; I noticed the Commune kids seemed....really good. No, seriously, like Olympic level good. They were fast, agile, and had ridiculously good reaction times. There is good and then there is just ridiculousness.

Seriously, I think it would have been better to have the Commune kids fight everyone else in this class, but even then I don't think it would have made much difference.

I noticed the Commune kids seemed to work together and more or less ignored their other teammates. The others didn't seem to mind, the majority of them stayed on the red side while the Commune kids did all the work.

I would have liked to help my team more, but Richard kept getting in my way, not only that but every time one of the Commune kids got close he would give them a look that would send them in the other direction while he shot the ball away.

"Do you mind?" I asked him.

"What?" he asked.

"Get the hell out of my way!"

"No," he said.

"Why not?!"

"I can't risk you helping the blues. You are very quick," he said.

"For God's sake!"

I tried to get around him but he blocked me. I growled, feeling irritated. I looked for Heath and found him trying to help out our team. I waved at him and pointed at Richard and mouthed 'help me' to him. He nodded in understanding and tapped two of our teammates on the shoulder and said something to them.

They made their way over and Richard watched them closely.

"Hey Jeremy, come help us," Heath said.

"Get this mountain out of my way," I said nodding to Richard.

"Piss off," Richard snarled at my teammates. The two paled a little but Heath didn't back down.

"You can't pin down one of my players Farkas," Heath exhaled.

"I can do as I damn well please," Richard objected.

I looked at Heath and I nodded at him and he nodded back. I ran around Richard I felt him moving after me, but Heath, with his friends' help, blocked him. Judging from the sound of bodies hitting the ground Richard may have taken all three of them out.

I didn't bother to look back, instead I ran to where the ball was being fought for in the corner of the field. I rammed into the dick who had rammed into me earlier. I grabbed the ball with my stick and ran off with it. I knew I wasn't going to get very far with it so I smacked it over to the red side.

I went after the ball, taking it from a couple of reds and was about to take it to the net to try to score. Then someone slammed into me, trying to push me back down to the floor. I pushed back, not letting whoever did it, keep me away from the ball. I ran as fast as I could and saw one of the reds with the ball, but he didn't see me coming.

I came up behind him and took the ball. I was close enough to the net and my team was doing their best to give me an opening by blocking the reds so I took the shot.

There was a crack and the rubber ball went flying through the air and it went into the net, scoring us a point.

The blues cheered, and the goalie tossed the rubber ball out into the middle of the field and the game continued. I noticed one of the reds had to go and sit down on the bleachers; he had a slight limp. It was the same guy who had slammed into me, one of the Commune kids.

I knew I hadn't hit him hard enough to hurt him, hell judging from the throbbing in my shoulder he had done more damage to me.

I saw Richard was glaring at him, and then his eyes found mine and he made his way over to me and I sighed.

"Here we go again," I muttered.

*****

We were back in the locker room. I was in my briefs, changing into my school clothes. Heath and I were talking. We had lost, but we did get some points in at least.

I was going to have some nice bruises form the game. But I didn't care. It had been one hell of a game.

"Dude, that shit was sick! You got some good moves," Heath laughed.

"Thanks," I said feeling pleased I had proven myself.

"What was Farkas's deal though?" he asked. "He was like your second shadow."

He wasn't kidding. Richard had stuck close to me for the rest of the game. It kept me from being much help because with *him* following me around it was almost impossible for me to get to the ball. And after Richard took down Heath and the other two players, no one wanted to help me after that.

I sighed. "I don't know. He is starting to irritate me though."

"You got balls going up against the Commune kids though. They are wicked at sports."

He was right about that. I was surprised to learn no one from the Gates was on any of the sports teams. They didn't even seem to put any real effort into the game and they still won.

"Are they taking 'roids or something? I mean they are too good," I probed.

He shrugged. "They have been tested before but the results are always clean," he said. He looked me up and down. "Are you okay?"

"Yes, why?"

"You got some battle scars."

My right elbow and upper arm was red from where I got slammed by the ball, my shins had various red stripes from where I got whacked by some hockey sticks and you could already see the bruises forming.

It stung like a bitch but I saw it as a game well played.

"I'm fine. My skin shows the damage quicker than most," I explained.

I turned around to grab my socks. But I noticed one was missing. I looked on the floor thinking maybe it fell down but it wasn't there either.

I looked around but couldn't see it anywhere. I sighed and put the sock in my gym bag and pulled out my clean socks and put them on.

Probably someone pranking me.

5

Richard

I admit I have done a lot of things that would be called wrong. And I am certain stealing someone's sock is on the list.

Gym class had been hell. Jeremy's scent had become even more enticing when he started to sweat; it filled the air like a muggy mist that made it hard to breathe.

I had been conflicted about choosing him or not for my team. On the one hand I wanted him close, on the other I wanted him far away from me. But then Heath chose him and I cursed myself because I knew now Jeremy was going to have to go up against my team.

My only consolation was thinking he would not be good at sports. Boy was I wrong.

He was wicked fast, not as fast as us but faster than I thought he would be. The kid obviously was into sports. He was never afraid, he always had this crazy look on his face, you could tell he got a major rush from the match.

I wondered if he had been on a track team or played some other games. He had quick reflexes too.

I thought maybe soccer; from the way he moved, the way he avoided the others, it just screamed that he had lots of practice.

The wolf and I were torn; on the one we were delighted to see his skill, on the other we were worried something bad might happen to him and we were right.

First, Keven slammed him onto the floor, were it anyone else we wouldn't have cared. But our anger and indignation rose like a storm.

Protect! The wolf growled.

After that we tried to keep an eye on him, keep him out of danger. There were so many ways you could get hurt in this game; what if someone rose the stick too high, and it hit him in the face?

But then he got his friends to help him and even though I did manage to take down all three idiots, it gave Jeremy the time he needed to get back in the game.

When I saw Scott slam into him trying to knock him down to the ground, I fought the urge to transform. While everyone was distracted with Jeremy trying to get the goal I walked up to Scott and hit him on the leg with my stick, but before he could howl in pain, I covered his mouth with my hand and ordered him to sit the rest of the game out.

He nodded and limped to the coach and told him he had gotten hurt and needed to sit down and he let him.

After that I made damn sure to keep close to Jeremy, he wasn't going to fool me again.

After we won we went to change. Scott and Keven did not talk to me, but they did act timid around me. I know it wasn't their fault, they were just doing what they always do, but I could not let them hurt my...fuck I almost said it!

While we changed I spotted Jeremy in his briefs. He had more muscle than I thought; he had a six pack and had beef on his biceps. He looked amazing, so amazing I actually popped a boner.

It wasn't the first time I got wood from playing a game- when all that blood starts pumping a guy can get worked up. But the fact I was hard from looking at another guy that was really messed up. I covered erection with my bag before anyone could see. I walked down the lockers and as I passed- them, I heard Heath and Jeremy talking about me, wondering about my behavior.

I noticed his socks, the ones he wore during the game were on the bench and without really thinking about it I reached down, grabbed one and put it in my gym bag.

Freaking fucked up I know, but I knew it was going to have his scent and I wanted to keep it.

Lunch once again found me hanging with my pack of friends. The mood was different; tenser and we were not talking as much as we usually do.

I was sure Scott and Keven told everyone what happened, but no one dared ask openly about it.

I hated the way things were going. My friends should not be afraid of me; they should not be suffering because of me. I had to do something about Jeremy. But what? Who could I turn to? One of the elders of course, but how do I go to them without telling them my situation?

"So, who is all going to the party?" Stacey asked, trying to break the ice.

"What party?" I asked, trying to show everyone I was calm.

She reached into her bag and pulled out a flier. "Elizabeth is throwing a party in the woods this Saturday. She has hired a DJ and is providing food and drinks for everyone."

I recalled Liz mentioning something about it. She loved throwing parties. I am sure dad gave her the money for the DJ and food. All she had to do was ask him and he broke out the checkbook for his little girl.

Anytime I needed money he told me to go get a job.

"I wish I could go but I can't. My grandma is coming over this weekend," Stacey said.

"I don't know, she always invites humans," Henry said.

"Hey, being a human isn't a sin," Trevor said sticking up for his former people.

He was a turned wolf, so he did not have the same view on humans the rest of us did.

"I know, but we always have to be so careful around them so not to reveal what we are. I hate having to act like them, they're so....mundane," Henry grimaced.

"Wow, you used a big word; good for you," Trevor said sarcastically.

Henry flipped him the bird.

"Looks like she will be inviting humans, she's handing some fliers out at the new kids table," Vivian noticed.

My head shot up to see what she was talking about, sure enough my sister was at Jeremy's table, handing them fliers for her party.

I glared at my sister, not liking the situation at all. I was sure she knew my actions as of late had something to do with Jeremy and she was going to find out why.

I hate having a nosy sister.

✶✶✶✶✶

Jeremy

We were having lunch when Elizabeth showed up, which surprised everyone at the table.

She wore a red lace printed dress and a black shawl on top of that. She had on black eye shadow and a few pearl necklaces hung from her neck. She held in her hand a bunch of papers.

She walked up to us, a nice smile on her face.

"Hello, are you guys doing anything this weekend?" she asked.

We all looked at one another and Rachel spoke. "No, nothing important."

"Good, then maybe you would like to come to my party," she said handing each of us a paper. It was a yellow paper with giant black words telling the time and place of the party. In smaller print it detailed the professional DJ, the food and drinks as well as the dancing.

"Sounds like fun," Heather commented.

"Can you expect anything less at my parties?" she asked with a smile. "Now, we have to keep this a secret, just between us teens. Don't want the rents to ruin things."

She turned her eyes to me. "Oh, you're the new student right?"

"Yes I am," I replied.

"I believe you are called Jeremy?"

"Yes, it's nice to meet you," I said.

She smiled kindly. I was liking her a lot more than Richard. She seemed to actually be sane. Sure she dressed odd, but I of all people know not to judge someone on how they look.

"You must come, it'll be like a welcoming party for you," she smiled.

I blushed.

It's okay, I don't want to take your thunder," I responded.

"Nonsense, it's not every day we get a new student," she said. "Wolf Fang Falls can be so boring. It's nice to get some new blood around here."

"Dude, you have to go to Elizabeth's parties; they rock!" Gabe informed me with excitement.

Elizabeth smiled. "Oh, you guys, they're not that great," she laughed.

It was the kind of laugh a person makes when they are only disagreeing to be polite.

"Well, it would be nice to go to a party. I could use to blow off some steam," I chuckled.

That was true; I haven't been to a party in a long time. And after everything that has happened, my break up with Lucas and moving; I could do with a nice party.

"Great! Well, I will see you all later."

She leaned over and kissed me once on each cheek.

"I am especially looking forward to seeing you there Jeremy."

Her eyes flickered behind me and her lips turned to a smile.

"Well, I better go, see you all later."

She got up and went about handing out fliers to other people. I looked behind me to see what made her smile. Richard was glaring murderously at his sister. I wondered what she had done to piss him off.

I was wondering if going to this party was a good idea after all.

But I had a feeling if Liz wanted me to come to her party she would find a way to get me there. She was so different from Richard, yet so similar.

Where Richard was a pompous jerk who stuck with his own kind, his sister actually reached out to everyone besides the other kids from the Gates.

Whenever I hear people speak about her, it was with respect and admiration.

And while Richard dressed in a preppy fashion, his sister stuck out. Not just from the other Commune Kids but from the whole school.

From what I have seen she is the only one who dresses in Goth.

Some days she dresses elegantly, others she dressed, looking like she was ready to kick ass. But I noticed there were similarities between the two of them. She walked with the same confidant strides he did and radiated the same aura of control and intimidation her brother did.

I was thankful she did not have his personality.

One asshole in this school is bad enough.

After school I went home and got ready for Richards arrival. Mom was all ready for another late shift at the hospital.

"I am sorry sweetie, I feel horrible leaving you all alone after we just moved," she said as she put her shoes on. She had her scrubs on and her hair was pulled in a bun.

"Mom, it's okay, I'm a big boy. Besides, I won't be all alone," I told her.

"What do you mean?" she asked.

"A guy I go to school with is coming over to study," I informed her.

She raised her brow and smiled. "Oh?" I could tell from the look on her face she was already starting to make assumptions.

"He isn't gay and I am not interested. Believe me," I vowed.

She laughed. "I sense a lie, my mother senses are tingling," she smiled.

"Alright, he is good looking, but he is a total ass," I commented.

She sighed. "It's always the good looking ones."

Mom had dated a few guys. I liked some of her boyfriends, but others turned out to be total jerks.

I liked a few of them. But things never seemed to work out between her and her guy friends. She says she doesn't feel *it* with any guy. That although she enjoys their company she doesn't see herself in a long term relationship.

"Oh and can I go out on Saturday?" I asked her.

"Out?"

"Yeah, I was invited to a party by Elizabeth Farkas," I said.

"Farkas? Like the founding family?" mom asked looking surprised.

"Yeah. She seems really cool, her brother Richard is the one coming over tonight," I stated.

"Wow...the Commune kids are more sociable than I remember," she noted.

"Wait, what do you mean?" I asked.

Of course she would know about the Farkas family, and the Commune kids who lived in the gated community. Growing up in Wolf Fang Falls she was sure to know all about them.

"Well, for as long as anyone can remember, people who lived in that gated community have always stuck to themselves. They never really interact with anyone else. Most people think it's a rich people thing, you know?"

"Did you ever know any of the Commune kids?" I asked.

She paused for a moment then smiled. "Well there was this one guy. He was sweeter than most of them. We kind of...sort of dated but things changed."

That perked my interest. My mom dated one of the Commune Kids?

"What changed?"

"Well, when we graduated I wanted to leave Wolf Fang Falls and see the world. I wanted to get out of here, you know? He wanted to stay. We wanted very different things in life so we parted on good terms."

"Does he still live here?"

"Oh of course, he happens to be the sheriff," she laughed.

"You dated the sheriff?" I asked.

She giggled. "Well he wasn't the sheriff back then. His name is Rick; he has a daughter who also lives in the Gates."

"Is he married?"

"No. I heard he is divorced now."

I smiled. "Well, maybe you should see if you can rekindle an old flame?"

She slapped my shoulder. "How did we go from your love life to mine?"

I wanted to point out I didn't have a love life anymore and wasn't looking for one anytime soon. Love was not on my list of priorities right now.

"So, Saturday?" I asked, reminding her of my earlier question.

"You can go, but I want you to call me if you need a ride and if you are going to spend the night somewhere, okay?"

I couldn't tell if she meant spending the night at a friends house or if I decided to spend the night at a guys house. Mom wasn't too stern when it came to my sex life. She already had the *talk* with me a long time ago.

As long as I was safe and used protection she was okay with me being sexually active. I really lucked out; having her for a mom really was great. Most parents blow a gasket at the idea of their kids doing anything sexual.

"Yeah, I will."

She kissed me on the cheek and left to go to work. I sighed and decided to get ready for what was to come.

I wasn't sure if having Richard come over was a good idea, maybe he was bipolar. It would explain the mood swings.

Whatever the case, hopefully nothing weird would happen tonight.

We still didn't have internet yet, so I had to use my phone to go online and look up anything I could find about eye color and how it could be passed from parent to child.

The more I can learn for our paper the quicker I might be able to get Richard to leave. I still had my doubts about him being in my house.

Hopefully he takes his time doing whatever it is he has to do after school.

6

Richard

"Yeah! Just like that!"

After practice I went straight home, mom and dad were out and Elizabeth was not home yet. I forgot I had Jeremy's sock in my bag so when I opened it up his scent hit me hard. I picked it up and smelled it, the memory of his half-naked body filled my mind and I was soon hard.

Despite her best efforts, Mary had been unable to satisfy my urges. So I had a lot of pent up energy I needed to vent. And smelling that stupid sock-as pathetic as it sounds-made my urge for relief too much to bear.

I kicked off my pants and took off my shirt and jumped on my bed and went to work, I puled my shorts down my hips and gripped my shaft.

It was a fucking shame, I know; beating off to some sock that belonged to some albino freak. But fuck if this didn't feel so good.

I imagined I had Jeremy on my bed, I imagined I had him tied up; his naked body covered in sweat. I imagined him begging me to take him, to claim him, to do to him what I wanted.

"Gahhhh!"

I came, and it was one of the best orgasms I ever had. I have jerked off a lot before but this was different. It was as if his scent drove me places I didn't think I could go to. It was like some kind of aphrodisiac.

I reached over to my nightstand and grabbed a bunch of tissues and cleaned up the mess.

There was a knock on the door. "Richard? We need to talk," Elizabeth said through the door.

"Shit!" I cursed. I quickly put on a pair of shorts and tossed the sock under my bed. I ran into my bathroom and tossed the tissues into the toilet and flushed them. I washed my hands and grabbed a bottle of air freshener and a bottle of AXE body spray.

The air freshener I sprayed in the air and the AXE I sprayed on myself to hide the scent of what I did. One of the drawbacks of heightened senses was that it let you smell things best left un-smelled.

I put the bottles down and went to the door and opened it. "What the hell do you want?" I growled. I was still ticked at her for kissing Jeremy. Sure it was on the cheek and totally innocent, but still.

She walked into my room and I clenched my teeth in irritation. She sat on my bed and crossed her legs.

"Enough with the bullshit big brother. What is going on between you and Jeremy?"

"What the fuck are you going on about now?" I asked.

"Do you really think I haven't noticed? Need I remind you I have the eyes of a hawk?"

"You mean wolf?"

"I mean, I can't help but notice how you look at him, I can't help but hear how you overreacted in gym today, I also noticed your energy fluctuates when he is around. Oh, then there is this."

She reached down and grabbed the sock from under the bed.

She looked at me with disgust. "Seriously? A sock? I am all into kinky things but this is a little much don't you think?"

She threw it at me and I caught it with my hand.

71

"Though I guess I should be thankful, it is not his underwear. That would be really disgusting," she said with a teasing grin.

I let out a deep animal growl that did not sound human at all. The wolf began to push its way through my body. My canines grew, my eyes turned into those of a wolf and I started to grow hair on my arms, chest and face.

"Do you think I enjoy this? Ever since I saw that little fucker I have been all fucked up! I think he is a monster or something! Why else would I be acting like this! I am not a fucking fag! I can't even get a hard on with Mary; I have to think of him, how fucked is that?"

Her face went from amused to concerned to sympathetic. I wasn't one for getting all emotional, so when I start pouring out my heart to Liz she knows it is bad.

"Oh Richard, why didn't you come to me?" she asked.

"How could I? How could I go to anyone about this?" I replied.

She got up and walked over to me and gave me a hug. "It's okay, I am sure there is a reason."

I calmed down and began to turn back. "Please don't tell mom and dad," I begged her.

"I won't. But I want you to know this does not change the way I think about you, you are still my brother and I love you," she smiled and pecked me on the cheek.

"Thanks Liz," I said.

Sometimes I want to kill my sister, other times I want to hug her. We had been that way since we were born; fighting one minute but always being there to look out for one another.

"No one else can know, if any of the other alphas find out they would challenge me, seeing this as a weakness," I stated.

"I agree, but we can't ignore it, that isn't working now is it?" she asked looking at the sock I still held in my hand.

"But what do we do?" I asked.

She put her finger on her head. "Tell me exactly how you feel about Jeremy. Tell me what draws you to him."

I told her everything, how his smell is so intoxicating to me and me alone, how everything about him just draws me to him. How my wolf wants me to claim him.

"I think I have heard about this, there is only one person we can go to," she told me.

"Who?" I asked.

*****

"Grandma!" Liz yelled.

Grandma Susan wrapped her arms around Liz and gave her a big hug. "Oh my little grand babies have come to visit me, how nice it is to see you," she said with a smile.

Grandma Susan was our mom's mother. She was a werewolf as well. She was five foot four with long white hair. She had tan russet skin which was wrinkled around her face, but her eyes shined with an energy that could only be described as youthful.

She was a descendant of the Shoshone werewolves who merged with the Hungarian pack all those generations ago.

She told us all kinds of stories of her tribe, passed down through the ages for hundreds of years. I grew up on those stories as did Liz.

She ran a little gift shop that sold all kinds of things like paintings and homemade jewelry. Most of them she made herself.

She was also the pack shaman; she was there for important rituals. She was a heavy believer in spirits and shit like that.

"Richard, look at you, I swear you look more and more like your grandfather every time I see you," she smiled, giving me a big hug as well.

"It's nice to see you Grandma," I said.

"Come in, come in. Are you hungry?" she asked.

We entered her home, it smelled of sage and moonflowers. Pictures lined the walls. Pictures that reflected the many events from her life; from when she was a child, to when she was a teen, to when she was married and raising her kids, to more recent pictures with us.

We walked into her living room and sat down.

"Would either of you like something to eat?" she asked before she sat down.

We both declined.

"Grandma, we need to ask you an important question," Liz started.

"What is it? Is everything okay?" she asked seeing the serious expressions on our faces.

"Well...one of our friends is acting...odd," she hesitated.

"Oh?" She sat down, her face was a little more serious.

"See, there is this human who has attracted our friends attention."

"Really attracted," I added.

"Like, something about his scent calls to our friend, and when he saw him....it changed him."

We went on to explain the symptoms to her, but being careful to not hint it had anything to do with me. If anyone knew it what to do, it would be Grandma Susan. She was my only hope to figure out what was happening to me.

She was quiet for a moment, she had a faraway expression on her face. I could almost hear the knowledge in her head like the pages from an old book being turned.

"Hmmm, well, from what I have heard it sounds like this wolf may have found their soulmate," she stated.

"Say what?" I asked not liking the sound of that.

"You have heard the term before? Two people being destined to fall in love, being perfect for one and having a blissful romantic life. In our world it is a little trickier than that."

"What do you mean?" Liz asked.

"Well, as you know, when our kind mates, we form strong attachments to our lovers, it is for life. Similar to our wolf kin. Now, like humans, it takes countless hours of courting to find that special someone so like humans we can have several lovers before we chose one, but when we find our soulmate, the effects are instantaneous. When a wolf finds his or her soulmate, everything about them calls to us; their scent, their voice, their touch, and the very sight of them calls us and draws us to them."

"Why isn't it like that with Humans? Don't they have a soulmate," I questioned.

"Well, some humans are lucky enough to sense their soulmate, but it is easier for us however, because we are more in tune with our animal instincts than humans. Or wolf knows who our soulmate is. And their are accounts of humans who have been turned into a werewolf experiencing the same symptoms on their werewolf mate."

"But the human is a guy. I mean, soulmates can't be of the same sex right?" I asked.

"And why the hell not?" Liz asked looking a little miffed.

"Well, isn't that the point of love? To have sex and make babies?" I asked.

Grandma Susan rolled her eyes. "You take after your father," she said. "Reproduction is simply the biological means to continue as a species. But love, especially love like this, is about more than having babies; it is about finding fulfillment in life with another person; it's about finding that one person who makes you happier than you could ever dream. Who makes you stronger and better."

"Grandma, how often does this soulmate thing happen? I don't recall anyone going through such a thing," Liz inquired.

"Sadly, it is a rare thing. I mean, there are so many people in the world, the odds of the two finding one another is amazing when it does occur. This young man is lucky to have found his."

"No he's not!" I shouted.

"Richard," Grandma Susan said with a shocked expression when I raised my voice.

"Grandma, it's another guy, isn't that wrong?" I asked.

"True love is never wrong Richard," she said wisely, "despite what other people say. I pity people who would try and degrade such a thing. They obviously do not know what *love* is."

"But, the others would never accept him; it is one thing to be with a human, but a human of the same sex?"

She sighed sadly. "Yes, you are right. I fear many in the pack would not make things easy for the two. Our culture can mirror the humans. I know some packs are more open-minded about such things, but there are those who would actually kill any involved in such a thing. Our pack is not that severe, but there are still those who would overreact about it."

"So what should our friend do?" Liz asked.

"Well, how does your friend feel about the situation?" she questioned.

"Freaked out, until this human showed up, he never had feelings for a guy," I spoke up.

"And does the human know what he is?"

"No."

"Well, the first thing he should do is tell the human. I am sure he is feeling a pull to this wolf friend of yours as well, but because he is mortal, the process is a bit slower. Tell him to spend more time with the human, that way the bond between the two will grow so when he does reveal the truth the power of their bond will make it easier for him to accept," she instructed.

"And then?"

"Tell him the situation, that way they can decide if they want to come out or not as an item," she continued.

"You're so wise grandma, I hope I am as clever as you when I hit your age," Liz complimented.

She smiled and kissed her on the cheek.

"But Daryl has to give us permission to tell a human the truth. You know the law," I said.

"Then your friend should go tell Daryl the situation. He will understand. Soulmates play an important role in our culture. A lot of our ancient laws guarantee their safety for the loss of one's soulmate can be a hellish experience for either."

"Have you ever met a werewolf who found their sou mate?" Liz asked.

She shook her head. "No, like I said it is very rare. Your friend is the first wolf in our pack to find his soulmate since before my time."

She got up and walked over to her bookcase. She grabbed a few books and handed them to me.

"Here. Give these to your friend. They will tell him everything you need to know about soulmates."

We talked with her for a little while longer about things like school and how things were going with our lives. Liz told her about the party she was going to throw.

When I saw the time I remembered I was supposed to meet with Jeremy so we could go over our paper. A part of me was happy to see him again, but then I felt irritation at my sense of delight.

We kissed Susan goodbye, and she told us to make sure our *friend* read the books. Liz carried them as we got in the car. The second we pulled out of the driveway Liz opened one of them up and began to read from it.

"What am I going to do Liz?" I asked her as I drove.

"Take Grandmother's advice," she replied.

"You're telling me to fall in love with another boy?!"

"You already have fallen in love Richard, you just haven't accepted it yet," she threw in.

"But I am not gay!"

She continued to read from the book, slowly turning the pages as we spoke.

"Give it a shot Richard, who knows, maybe we are mistaken. Just spend time with him okay? See what happens."

I sighed.

"This sucks."

"I know what you are going through Richard. It took me a while to accept I like men and women. But I am happier now that I accept that part of myself. It is who I am."

"But not everyone accepts stuff like that," I said.

"Richard. Let me ask you something. Are you attracted to other guys?" she asked.

"No, of course not!" I said hotly.

"But you are attracted to Jeremy right?"

I mumbled a yes.

"Well, maybe you are not gay?"

"But I-"

She cut me off. "Just because you got the hots for one guy doesn't define you. Stop thinking like a human by trying to label this thing. Trust your instincts, trust your wolf. A wolf doesn't care about shit like that."

"It's not that easy Liz. Or have you forgotten Mary?" I asked.

"Deal with your crazy girlfriend later. Right now focus on Jeremy. If he really is your soulmate, then worry about her some other time. Or maybe if you're lucky this is some phase that will quickly go away."

"You don't believe that," I said dryly.

"Of course not. But what other option do you have Richard?"

"I don't know Liz, I can't believe in soulmates. That's a bunch of romantic bullshit. But I can't ignore this. It's like a disease slowly spreading through my body. But you know what the real fucked up thing is? I can't tell if I hate it...or like it. Or perhaps some combination of both."

"Grandma said those who found their soulmates are lucky. That they find fulfillment. How many people do you suppose in our generation alone will spend their days craving such a connection? We throw the word love around so often we forget its meaning. You are one of the few people who have a chance to know what the real meaning of love is."

"I love Mary, I had our whole life planned out. It would have been perfect."

She leaned her head on my shoulder. "Life is far from perfect Richard. Just because you find yourself down a path you did not foresee does not mean it is not a good one."

I dropped Liz off at home. She took the books and promised to make sure no one would see them. After that I drove back out of the Gate and headed for Jeremy's house.

Liz's words played themselves over and over in my head. And each time they did I had to ask myself the same question.

What life could I have with Jeremy? What could he offer me I could not get from Mary?

And why was this happening in the first place?

Was I being punished by Niveus for some indiscretion?

Grandma Susan made it sound like this was supposed to be some kind of blessing, but truth be told; I feel more cursed than blessed.

*****

Jeremy

I was a bit irritated.

It was going on eight and Richard hadn't shown. I know I wanted him to take his time, but this is a bit ridiculous. I swear if he thinks he can put all the work on me than-

The doorbell rang, breaking my train of thought. I got up and answered the door and saw it was Richard.

"S'up?" he asked all nonchalant.

He walked in without waiting for an invitation. Not even five seconds and already I wanted to kick his ass out.

"Oh yes, please come in," I said sarcastically.

He looked around the house, not looking impressed with what he saw.

"You're late," I commented.

"Actually I never specified what time I would be here," he said with a grin.

"You're not the only one with shit to do you know!"

"Oh? And what do you have to do that is so important?" he asked with a sneer.

Smarmy prick!

He took his shoes off and put them on the welcome mat. Glad to see he has some manners. "Well, let's do this," he said with a scowl.

We headed into the living room and he sat down. "So, are you hungry?" I asked.

"No," he said.

"Okay. So, I did some research about eye colors." I opened the notebook I had used to take down notes.

"What was my sister talking to you about?" he asked suddenly.

"Huh? Oh she invited me to her party this Saturday," I answered.

He got a thoughtful look on his face. "Are you going?"

"I am thinking about it, it's been awhile since I went out," I replied.

"I am going," he told me.

"Okay," I said.

He looked at me oddly, but then he shook his head and grabbed his book and opened it up. He propped his feet up on the table and leaned back into the couch.

"Excuse me," I bristled.

"What?" he asked flipping through some pages.

"Do you mind?"

"What?" he asked confused.

I waved at his feet. "Could you get your feet off the table?"

"What? I am wearing socks," he frowned, with a shrug.

"So, it's rude."

He ignored me and continued to read from the book. I used both of my hands to grab his legs and push them off the table.

The confusion and anger that has been slowly building inside me since I first met him finally snapped.

"Look, I don't know how everyone else treats you, but I am not going to pamper you or let you get away with shit! There are rules to follow when in someone's home; and propping your feet on their table, is a no-no!"

He slammed the book shut, and I jumped at the sound. He leaned forward and his eyes glinted with a dark look.

"I do as I damn well please. Don't tell me what to do," he spoke lowly.

I stared him in the eyes, not backing down.

"Not in my house. You either follow the rules or you can leave. I won't let you treat me like shit in my own home!"

Damn him! Why did he have to be such an obnoxious ass! Seriously, who doesn't teach their kids proper manners? All I ask is he not disrespect my table, and he goes and gets all pissy!

Before I knew it he was on top of me, our books fell to the ground but I didn't care, all I cared was the massive mountain now on top of me. I had my hand on his chest, trying to push him off but he was too strong.

He leaned down as I struggled to get away from him. He buried his face in my neck and I froze. I felt him inhale, taking a deep breath.

Then something wet and warm was snaking out and lapping at the side of my neck.

Holy fuck he is licking me!

I tried to move but a growl in my ear kept me where I was. "Don't move," he snarled.

He continued to lick my neck as his hand snaked to the back of my neck, and he gripped it tight. He pulled back and made me look at him.

"I don't care if this is your house. I do as I damn well please. Now, let's hurry up and get this done, and if you give me lip one more time, then I am going to do a lot more than lick you. Understand?" he hissed.

I nodded, too stunned by what was happening to even dare dish out any sass.

"Good."

He got off me and took his seat, but didn't put his feet on the table.

"Hurry up, I don't have all night," he griped.

I shakily got up, I grabbed my book off the ground and we began to go over our assignment. A few hours later and thankfully, there really wasn't an incident. He continued to be an ass though, but he didn't attack me, so that was a bonus.

By the time he got ready to leave we were pretty much done with the project. I escorted him out, eager to get him the hell out of my house.

"Good job tonight," he commented.

"Thanks," I muttered.

"So, I will see you at school?"

"Yep."

God this was awkward.

One minute he is assaulting me now he is acting like nothing happened. I wish he would leave!

"And the party?" he asked.

I looked at him in disbelief. Was he really asking me if I was going to the party after what just happened?

Really!?

"Maybe not," I replied, trying to stay calm.

"Why not?" he asked with a scowl.

I shrugged. "I just remembered I have stuff to do."

That is a total lie. I just did not want to be around this guy, not after what he pulled. Obviously there was something seriously wrong with him.

"You're lying," he spat.

"No I'm-"

He grabbed me and pushed me up against the wall.

When he spoke, his voice was harsh. "Another thing, don't lie to me, I always know when someone is lying," he glowered.

He brought his head down close to my face; he was so close our lips almost touched.

I felt like my heart was about to jump out of my mouth. He was so close,

I could count the number of eyelashes he had.

And dam if he didn't smell good!

I pushed those thoughts aside and took a deep breath and moved my leg so if I had to I could knee him in the groin. I wasn't going to let him abuse me in my own home!

"You're going to that party and if I don't see you there, then I will hunt you down. Don't think I won't or can't."

He spun me around so I was face first against the wall. I felt him pull the neck of my shirt back then he grabbed the top of my pants and pulled them out. I had no idea what the hell he was doing, but it was freaking me out.

I felt him lean forward and whisper in my ear. "See you at the party Jeremy."

I shuddered at the tone in his voice. Then he let me go and walked out the door. I quickly shut it and locked it. I heard his car start roaring to life and then taking off down the street.

I fell to my knees, my whole body was shuddering. I had no idea what the fuck just happened. I rubbed the spot on my neck where he had licked me.

My whole body was shaking, from fear, anxiety and.....excitement?

I realized I was a little turned on; the way he handled me, the danger of the situation; a part of me was attracted to it.

"What the fuck!" I yelled.

I made sure all the windows and doors were locked, I turned out the lights and went to bed. As I lay under my sheets, I remembered to put my aluminum baseball bat under my bed just in case.

I thought moving to Wolf Fang Falls would be boring and dull. God, I wish I had been right.

I tried to sleep, but I kept on replaying the events of the night in my head.

I had a feeling Richard would be a jerk, but licking me. Pushing my against a wall. Something is seriously wrong with that guy.

And something is seriously wrong with me for feeling a rush of excitement when he manhandled me.

Now I like to get a little rough for foreplay. But Richard was a stranger and a total dick.

Yet every time I touched my neck I shuddered at the memory of him dragging his tongue over my skin, and his scent, like trees and fresh cut grass.

I gripped the bat like a small child might hold their favorite stuffed toy.

How could it be I was both afraid and excited at the same time?

I know one thing for sure, I was not going to that party.

No way in hell.

*****

Richard

Well, that didn't go as well as I had planned.

I didn't mean to do that to him. Everything was going okay, but then he had to get an attitude with me; he even stared into my eyes! It's a stupid thing to do to a werewolf. Staring us in the eye during a confrontation is just like staring into a wolf's eye, we take it as a challenge.

My wolf didn't like he was challenging us; he was our mate and shouldn't be chastising us. So acting on instinct, I pushed him onto the couch, but when I touched him, it was just like earlier when I touched him during class.

My skin felt tingly and sensitive. I noticed how warm and soft he was, like he was made out of clouds or something. That, plus his scent, made the wolf stronger, gave it some control.

The smell of his fear both aroused us and made us pause. He struggled of course but that just made it more exciting and then he bared his throat to me; in wolf culture, a sign of submission.

But seeing that long pale throat and the long blue vein in it; made the wolf go in for the kill.

Not literally of course, but he and I couldn't resist. We wanted to show him we were not going to hurt him that we were not cross.

So I licked his neck.

And God if he didn't taste so fucking sweet! Even better than a sugar cane dipped in lamb's blood......what? I'm a werewolf so sue me!

After I got in a few good licks, I firmly told him who was the alpha and he didn't say anything, thank God for that. After a few hours of tension and studying I went to leave.

I was still a little high from being around him and what happened. I had hoped being around him for a while might desensitize me to him, but it didn't. The entire time I was fighting with my wolf.

He wanted me to move closer to him, to hold him, to lick him some more. It wanted to hold him tight and make him feel more comfortable, to make up for our little tiff.

I licked my lips for the hundredth time at the memory of his skin on my tongue.

When he lied to me about the party, it made the wolf angry that our mate would lie to us, and once again I was pushing him against the wall. Then I smelled not only fear but arousal. He enjoyed the treatment I was giving him.

God, he had no idea what he did to me. I wanted to rip his clothes off and fuck him right then and there! I am still fucking hard from his arousal! My wolf wanted to go back and finish the job but I was stronger than that.

I pretty much scared him into going to Elizabeth's stupid party. I had checked the tags on his clothes to find out what size he wore so I could get him something to wear.

I wasn't satisfied with his home; it was not worthy of him.

My wolf agreed; it wanted to take him home with us, to move him into our den where we would care for him and provide. I mean, it wasn't a dump; it was a nice clean home; well-kept and all that.

But Jeremy deserved something larger and more grandeur as befitting the alpha's-

"He isn't my mate!" I growled. "Gods can my life get any worse?"

*****

Unknown

I drove on my way to Wolf Fang Falls.

I killed a wolf recently; I tortured the beast before I finished him. It took a while but after force feeding him enough water laced with silver he talked. They always talk in the end.

He told me about his pack in Wolf Fang Falls. I couldn't believe a pack would live in such an obvious place. Werewolves were more common in towns than cities. They preferred to live as close to the wild as they could and it was easier for them to hide in small communities.

He told me his pack was extremely large; there was over two hundred of the monsters running around this town and the surrounding counties. It was an unusually large pack.

I was on my way there now to bag a few of the fuckers. I was going to get me an alpha. The werewolf I killed gave me a list of names. I couldn't get him to give me the name of the Pack King; no amount of torture could break his loyalty to his king. But still I can pick off the others one by one.

Wait until the guys see all the alphas I am going to get, I will be a legend!

7

Jeremy

Today was Saturday.

I should be more excited about tonight, but I am scared.

Since Wednesday night Richard has kept his distance. But there were still times when I caught him looking at me with that same burning look.

I am happy to report that we finished our paper and got a B. Richard didn't seem to care, I was just happy I didn't have to study with him no more.

He continued to act like what happened between us never happened, luckily he kept his hands (and tongue) to himself. What was bothersome was he kept on insisting we study after school, but I always managed to keep our interactions in the school where there we plenty of people.

I did not want to go really, but yesterday Richard reminded me he expected to see me there. And from his tone I had a feeling not showing up would be a bad thing.

I was so nervous about tonight I decided to go for a jog. I took my iPod and listened to some tunes as I ran. I tried to figure out what I had gotten myself into.

Why was Richard so....whatever he was? Why did he have a thing for me? He has a girlfriend, Mary; a gorgeous blonde-haired green-eyed girl with a generous figure. She reeked of stuck up bitch. She was a mean girl all the way. The kind who likes to make snarky hurtful comments directed to people she viewed as her social, physical or mental inferior.

So, pretty much everyone.

Whatever Richard saw in her it wasn't her charming personality.

Maybe he was bi? Or maybe he was in the closet? Could I be living the dream? Having the hottest, most popular guy at the school fall for me but no one knows he is gay and our relationship has to be a secret?

God I hope not, the last relationship I had that was like that didn't go so well.

Maybe he really was attracted to me?

I had boyfriends before Lucas. Of course they were all rather hush-hush and didn't last long because it's hard to have a relation with someone when most of your energy is invested into keeping everything you do a secret.

But none of them acted like this, they had been shy and nervous in that way young love can cause you to act.

None of them were aggressive and moody.

Was that what Richard saw in me? What set him off? My eyes and skin? Was there something about my personality that rubbed him the wrong way?

God, why does everything have to be complicated?

I stopped running and took a deep breath. This situation with Richard was giving me a headache. Normally I wouldn't mind a looker like him being into if he wasn't so....creepy about it.

I mean, he licked me; no one has licked me since Lucas. He was a very...oral person.

What's worse was a part of me was thrilled by how rough he was with me. Yeah, I liked it like that when it comes to sex and stuff, but I didn't even know Richard. I wasn't one of those people who bend over for a good looking guy.

The last couple days I have been thinking a lot about him. It was stupid I know, but I couldn't help it. I kept wondering little things about him. What was his house like? What was it like living in a gated community? What were his parents like? What did he do for fun? What was he like when no one was around?

And the one million dollar question: What the fuck was his problem?!

A police car pulled up next to me. A man stepped out. He had short, trimmed brown hair and a small beard growing around his face that was well groomed. It helped make his jaw look square giving it a stronger look. He had hazel colored eyes with crinkles around the corners that matched the friendly smile he had on his face.

"Hello son, need a ride?" he asked.

"No, I am okay, just jogging," I said.

He looked at me for a few seconds. "You're Diane's kid, right?" he asked.

"Yes, I'm Jeremy," I said.

"Jeremy, you are aware one of our fellow citizens has gone missing?"

"Yeah, I heard something about it," I replied.

It had been on the news. Some guy had vanished without a trace. Reports say he vanished somewhere over in Ethete. Apparently he had been there visiting a friend and left but never made it home.

"Then you should know it might not be safe to be jogging all alone," he said. "Let me give you a lift home."

I decided there was no point in arguing with the law so I took him up on his offer. I got in and made sure to put on my seat belt. We drove to my place and talked a little.

"So how do you like Wolf Fang Falls?" he asked.

"It's nice and quiet, I like it," I said.

Except for one tall, handsome pain in the ass

"Yeah, not too much happens around here. Most folks wish it was more exciting, but I am glad it is like this," he commented.

"Yeah, I am not one for excitement myself. I like things quiet," I agreed.

We pulled up to my house, we both got out, and he followed me to the door. It opened before we got to it, mom must have seen the car. She looked a little worried at first but then her eyes widened in surprise.

"Rick?"

I looked from mom to the officer. *Rick?*

He tipped his hat to mom. "Hello Diane," he said.

Wait...this guy was my mom's ex and the sheriff?

I suddenly had a sneaking suspicion his reason for taking me home was less to do with my safety and more an excuse.

"Is everything okay?" she asked looking from him to me.

"Oh yeah, I saw Jeremy jogging and thought it best if I give him a ride, what with Wayne going missing and all," he explained.

"Oh, thanks for that. Jeremy, thank Rick for giving you a lift," mom said.

I shook Rick's hand. "Thank you sir," I said with a grin.

"Please, call me Rick," he said with a friendly smile. He turned to look at mom. "So, how is it to be back home?"

"Nice, it's good getting back to my roots," she said with a smile. "Sorry I haven't called or stopped by to say hello. Been busy with the move and work."

He shook his head. "No problem. It's good to have you back."

I was sensing some vibes going on between them. I so can't wait to tease her about this later.

"Hear you got a job at the hospital," he noted.

"Yeah, long hours but the pay is good," she said with a smile.

"Well, I won't keep you any longer. I will see you all around," he said. He turned and walked to his car and drove off, giving us a small wave as he drove by.

"God, he is still fine, his ass still looks tight," mom said with a smirk.

"Mom!"

"What?"

"He is an officer of the law," I exclaimed.

"I know, damn he looks good in that uniform," she gushed placing her hands to her mouth and hopped around.

"Oh my God," I huffed.

I walked into the house and went to head to my room. "Oh sweetie, you got a package in the mail, I put it in your room," she said.

"Huh?" I asked.

"Yeah, it was on the porch, there was a note on it. I left it on your bed. Did you order something?" she asked.

"No...I wonder who sent it?"

I walked up to my room. There was a box on top of my bed with a white envelope on it. I opened the box first to see what was inside. It was clothes.

"The hell?" I asked frowning.

It was a V-neck shirt, a pair of jeans and.....a blue pair of red briefs that seemed a little small for me. I knew if I put them on they would show every curve and leave little to the imagination. The jeans were dark blue denim, and the shirt was blue with a black swirly pattern on it. I checked the tags and found they were my size.

I grabbed the note and opened it, pulled out the letter and began to read.

Make sure you wear these tonight, including the briefs-R

I remembered that night he was here and recalled how he had me pressed against the wall. I remembered how he had pulled my pants and shirt back, I didn't know what he had been doing but I realized then.

"He was checking what size clothes I wear. That psycho!" I snarled.

If he thought I was going to play his little game he had another thing coming. No way was I going to wear his clothes!

No matter how good they would look on me.

This is getting ridiculous!

If he thinks I am going to play his games, he has another thing coming!

Fuck him! Fuck his bi-polar attitude and fuck his cloths.

I am going to have words with him tonight!

If he doesn't leave me alone, then I will go to Rick! I'm sure that will get him to back the fuck off!

Maybe mom crushing on him will turn out to be a good thing.

*****

Richard

"Oh Richard! Oh God!" Mary panted as I thrust into her.

We were in the woods and I had made plans to take her out on a little picnic. We drove out deep where we knew no one would see us or find us.

It started out easy enough with us eating the food, drinking some Moon Lust I stole from my parent's supply and talking. Or rather she did the talking, I just listened.

Eventually it started to go where it usually went; in the old days I would love to do this but now I have to force myself to do this, to get into it.

Mary was still beautiful with long, smooth blonde hair and bewitching green eyes. She had a plump bottom, a generous chest, and long legs that I used to love having wrapped around my waist.

I had her on all fours and took her from behind. I had to think about Jeremy again to get hard. I still had some hope that maybe this was just a mistake and I wasn't destined to be with another man. I had even tried reading as many dirty magazines and watching as much porn as I could, but although I got wood from it and found the girls hot, none of them appealed to me like *he* did.

Right now I was thinking about Jeremy.

I left the package with his cloths on his porch today. I was hoping he wore what I got him.

I needed to speak with him. I needed to work something out with him because not being around him was quickly becoming torture.

But when I was close to him I felt more at ease, more relaxed. My instincts weren't scratching at my mind. I felt more calm and relaxed.

But I am well aware my actions have scared him, so I got him the cloths to apologize and hopefully entice him to want to hang out with me.

I wasn't sure if the cloths I got were his style but they would look real nice on him.

As usual, I came, and I pulled out of her and fell to the side. Mary lay down next to me but I could tell from her silence something was bothering her.

Usually by now she would be cuddling with me and we would make some pillow talk but she kept her distance from me.

"What's wrong babe?" I asked her.

She looked at me, her eyes were glossy. "Richard, do you still love me?" she asked.

"What? Of course," I lied.

"Then why do I feel like this?" she asked.

"Like what? Wasn't it good?" I asked.

"It was but...I feel like we are moving apart. Richard, did I do something to make you angry?" she asked her lips pouting.

"Don't be stupid, we're fine," I lied.

She wiped her face. "But it feels like you've lost interest."

I put on a fake smile. I tried not to show any sense of fear or anxiety.

"Babe, if I had lost interest would I be out here giving you another earth-shattering orgasm?" I asked with a grin.

She laughed softly. "So...we're good?"

"Of course," I lied again. I pulled her close and kissed her cheek. "I just got a lot on my mind lately. Dad wants me to work for him after I graduate, but I want to go away to college for a while. You know how he is, my thoughts don't matter," I said bitterly.

"Your dad is an ass, what does your mom think?" she asked.

"She is all for me going to college. But dad thinks going to college is a waste of time and money. Says the way the world is now, college is pointless."

"But let me guess, he is all for Elizabeth going to college?"

"Oh, you know he is. Thinks it will help her in life," I said.

She rubbed her hand along my belly. "Don't listen to him. He has always been such a hard-ass on you."

"It's been his dream for me to become Pack King. He never made the cut and his dad never let him forget it, now he puts the pressure on me to succeed."

She kissed my cheek. "Don't worry, when you do become Pack King then you can tell him to go fuck off," she said with a grin.

I smiled. "I dream of that."

"So, are you still going to Elizabeth's party?" she asked.

"Yeah, too bad you can't come," I said.

I lied; I was kind of glad she wasn't going to be there. She would only complicate things.

"Me and some of the other girls are going to hang out with Stacy before her grandmother shows up. I think her parents are just keeping her in the Gates because Wayne went missing."

"Maybe we should all stay at home. It's not a good sign if one of us goes missing," I commented.

"Wayne was alone. No one in their right minds would attack a group of us."

She climbed on top of me. Running her hands gently up my chest, tracing the lines of my stomach.

"It doesn't matter to me if you go to college or not Richard. I know we will be together no matter what. One day you'll be Pack King and I will be your mate and we'll rule the pack just as we have always wanted."

I didn't answer her. I was done lying for the day.

She bent down and kissed me and we resumed our love making.

And yet, using the term love for what we had seemed like a terrible lie.

*****

Unknown

I watched the two werewolves from afar.

I made sure to stay downwind and smeared plenty of dirt and moss on my body to help hide my scent.

I watched them with a pair of goggles I paid a pretty heavy price for. It allowed me to see all kinds of shit from pretty damn far away.

I knew all these freaks were hanging out in a gated community so I have been watching the place from afar, with my trusty new high tech goggles and noticing who goes in and out.

Every once in a while I would follow a wolf or two that left the Gates, I kept journals on them; their routine and what they did outside their little fortress. The place was locked up tight; there were tons of security cameras, and the walls were lined with razors to keep someone from trying to jump them and plenty of security guards patrolled the perimeter.

But even I was not dumb enough to try sneaking in there. The place was full with wolves and it would not be long before I was sniffed out and killed. I knew the Pack King and all the other alphas I targeted lived there but it would be suicide going in there.

So I waited and watched.

I saw these two leaving and decided to follow them. I knew the male was Richard Farkas, a member of one of the founding families. The female was Mary Volkov. Both went to the same school and from what I saw were going out.

I did research on both families. The Farkas clan came here from Hungry more than a century ago and helped build the town. The Volkov family had lived in the are for several decades.

From what I saw it appeared they were mates.

And boy did I see a lot. Figures werewolves would be fucking in the woods with no dignity. But damn if the blonde didn't have nice tits.

While they talked I used a special device that let me hear their conversation; another piece of equipment that cost me a pretty penny. I knew all about this party now and I decided tonight would be the perfect night for me to strike.

While those little wolf shits were getting wasted, I would pick them off one by one, starting with Farkas, that wolf I tortured gave me a list of the alphas in his pack.

I was surprised by how many alphas. Normally too many alphas in a pack caused strife because all alphas had a need to rule.

But seeing how this pack was unusually large it would explain why it had so many *top dogs*.

Either way, I was not leaving the state until I nailed at least one person on my list.

And who better than a member of one of the founding families.

*****

Jeremy

I was nervous about tonight. Should I go? Should I stay? What if Richard comes after me? He doesn't seem very stable.

I told myself I should go and put him in his place, but at the same time I was afraid he might snap again.

Who could I tell? I was the new kid and Richard was the rich guy everyone adored.

I was sure mom would believe me but we just moved here and I didn't want to cause problems for her. We were still settling in and she liked her job.

So I decided to go. I would talk to Richard tonight and warn him to stay away.

I was waiting Rachel to come pick me up; I wasn't going to wear the clothes Richard got me; I would not give him the satisfaction of seeing me wearing the clothes he bought me. I was more than some lap dog he could dress up.

"Sweetie, your friends are here," mom called from downstairs.

"Okay, you can do this. Don't let Richard intimidate you," I said to myself.

I walked downstairs and saw mom at the front door talking to Rachel.

"Jeremy, I know Rachel's mom, we graduated together," mom informed me.

"When I told my mom I was taking you out she told me she knew your mom, cool huh?" Rachel asked.

Rachel had her hair done in curls and she had done her mascara to draw attention to her eyes. She wore a green shirt with some glittering images of flowers on it and a pair of cotton pants.

"Yeah, she also happens to have had a thing for Sheriff Rick when they were young too," I said with a teasing smile.

Mom blushed but Rachel smiled. "Way to go Miss Moonvine," Rachel smiled. "I think he is cute, he looks so good in his uniform."

"I know right?" mom nodded in agreement.

I hugged mom and kissed her on the cheek. "I will text you when I get there," I said.

"Call me if something happens or you need a ride," she stated.

"I will. I won't be out to late."

"Bye Miss. Moonvine," Rachel said.

"Call me Diane and be safe; don't drink and drive," mom warned.

We walked out of the house and headed for the car. I could see Heath, Heather and Gabe inside waiting for us.

"You look cool Jeremy," Rachel noted.

"Thanks," I said. "You look great yourself."

I wore a pair of faded black jeans with a navy blue shirt and black sneakers. I liked to dress in blue, it brought out the color in my eyes.

Made them look less violet.

We got into the car and I sat in the back with Heather and Heath. We pulled out of my driveway and headed for the party.

"So where is this party at?" I asked.

"It's out in Hunter's Meadow," Gabe replied.

"It's this really awesome place near the woods. People have been partying there for generations. It is covered in all these beautiful flowers and there are these boulders where the DJ sets up his equipment, and it is so open and we can be as loud as we want!" Heather explained.

"Sounds like fun," I smiled.

"Oh it is; everyone will be there. Tonight is going to be a blast!" Gabe gushed.

I smiled, but inside I was still worried about what was going to happen when Richard saw I wasn't wearing the clothes he wanted.

"Plus, I am sure there will be plenty of chicks who want to dance with you man," Heath said, "I heard some girls talking about how they have their eye on you."

I laughed nervously. Time to fess up.

"Well, I won't mind dancing with the girls but I won't be going out with them," I started.

"Why? You got a girl back in Cambridge?" Rachel asked.

"No....I'm gay."

"....."

"....."

"......"

"......"

Awkward.

"Pay up!" Heather laughed, holding out her hand to Gabe.

He mumbled and handed her a twenty dollar bill.

"What?" I asked.

"I bet him twenty dollars you were gay," she answered with a smile.

"Was it my looks?" I asked with a sigh.

"No, it's the way you eye hump Richard. No straight boy looks at another boy like that," Heather explained as she placed her money in her purse.

"I don't eye hump him!" I said indignantly.

At least I hope to God I don't. Maybe I have let my eyes linger on him a few times but I am not the only one!

Well, maybe I'm the only guy who does.

"Yeah....and the sky isn't blue," she teased.

"So....are you guys cool with it?" I asked looking at them all.

"Yep," Rachel said honestly.

"It would be cool to have a gay friend!" Heather smiled.

"Fine by me," Gabe shrugged.

"Doesn't bother me," Heath agreed.

"Huh....I didn't think it would be that easy," I commented.

"Hate to break it to you buddy but you are the only gay kid in school," Heath noted.

I remembered Richard's kiss and although I was tempted to correct Heath, I wisely kept my mouth shut. I doubt Richard would like me outing him. Or that they would believe me if I told them.

"It's fine. I had a bad break up with my last boyfriend and am not looking for romance right now. Believe me."

It struck me then that tonight I would be a fifth wheel. Gabe and Rachel were together and so were Heath and Heather. It had been me and Lucas for so long.

While they were all having a good time with one another, I would be dealing with some bipolar ass with personal space issues.

Why the hell did I decide to go out tonight?

*****

We parked in the woods. We had driven off a road on the highway that took us down a dirt path. Cars lined the side and the distant sound of music could be heard.

We got out and walked the rest of the way there. I could see lights and the music got louder. When we broke past the trees, I finally got a glimpse of Hunter's Meadow.

It was a vast and open, big enough to build a football stadium. There was more than enough room for people to park their cars here. But this was private property and although parties were allowed here if you had permission from the town council, the rule was to keep the place nice and tidy.

And if people parked their cars in the meadow, then it would tear the flowers that grew here.

There were a series of rock formations, like small hills at the center of it; that was where the party was. The formation reminded me of Stonehenge.

The DJ was on top of the largest boulder and his loud speakers were spread out around a little boulder. He had a computer system set up and was playing music, strobe lights and fog machines were spread about, and people were wearing and carrying glow sticks, making their dance movements hypnotic.

I immediately took a liking to the place. Not because of the music or the party goers that filled it, but the rock formations which were in a crescent moon formation with the stones on the outside being smaller and the ones in the middle being larger.

There was something about it that had a sense of antiquity. Like something old and important. A piece of some ancient history that survived through the ages.

I took out my phone and started taking pictures. The urge was too strong to resist, and I wasn't going to bother resisting. No way was I *not* going to add this to my folder.

Some people danced, some walked around talking with their friends. A few sat on top of the other rocks, having walked up the back and sat down on the edge, watching the dancers below.

I spotted Richard. He, along with the Commune Kids, sat on top of one of the larger boulders next to the DJ. They were dressed less preppy and more...seductive? Their clothes were still expensive looking, but were now more revealing, and the colors were darker.

Vests that showed abbs and biceps, shirts that bared midriffs and showed cleavage. Not the kind of things you wore at school, but at a party where you wanted to flaunt your assets than yes.

I noticed many of the girls wore flowers in their hair and a few of the guys had a flower tucked behind their ear. I saw one of the girls smell the flower behind the ear of one of the boys and then kiss his neck. It was odd but the Commune Kids seemed to enjoy smelling the flowers.

They were the same ones littered about the meadow: Moonflowers.

Richard sat in the center of his friends, they watched the people dancing below them, some were swaying to the music while others were busy making out with their partners.

Before I knew it I was aiming my camera at him and taking a pic. The strobe lights hit him perfectly, illuminating his features.

He sat with the posture of a ruler. With the way he was dressed with his shirt which was tight enough to show every line of his muscles, his jeans which were torn at the knee and his fierce expression he looked like the leader of some band of badass delinquents.

Or a king observing his kingdom.

I had to admit I was glad I did come. The smell of the moonflowers which hung heavy in the air, the thumping beat of the music and all the dancing put me in a good mood. There was energy in the air, a flow of life and a rush of glorious madness that comes from a party that has great music and people willing to let it all out.

Soon I was aiming my camera at everyone! The Commune Kids, the DJ, the people dancing, by the end of the night my phone was going to be bursting with pictures.

"Who's ready to fuck this place up?!" Heather shouted throwing her arms up in the air.

"We are!" we all yelled, laughing.

We headed for the inner part of the formation to party, they had tables set up with food and drinks like punch, but I saw people carrying beer bottles and figured some of the ice coolers had beer in them.

We stopped by one of the tables to get something to drink. I got punch, and the guys got beer while the girls, like me, decided to start out with punch.

I knew if I started drinking now than I would soon be too tipsy to be able to get more pictures.

Once I start throwing back the drinks I have a hard time stopping.

Elizabeth appeared, weaving her way around people in a way I could only describe as half-walking and half-dancing. She wore a black and red dress that left her arms and upper chest bare. She wore a choker with a ruby on it. She had red eyeliner on and her hair was tied in a knot with a silver comb in it.

Her cloths were on point with her friends for once.

"Hello," she greeted us. "Did you all just arrive?"

"Yes, party is great as always Elizabeth," Rachel praised.

"Thank you, I am glad you all made it, if you need anything let me know," she said. She bent down and plucked a flower from the ground and put it behind my ear. "Moonflower, meet Moonvine," she chuckled.

"Thanks, are these the ones that get you high?" I asked.

They looked similar to morning glories. My grandmother had been a gardener, I spent a lot of time helping her plant flowers. She had many books on flora that I enjoyed reading for the pictures.

Lucas and his friends had loved moonflowers. Though not for their LSD properties. You could say it was...part of their culture.

She laughed.

"No. This species though edible don't send you on a trip to the moon. These bloom at night," she said warmly as she inhaled from a flower. "Kind of like your namesake. The moon vine is a night bloomer, I wonder if tonight you will open up to us all Jeremy."

She pushed the flower further behind my ear and gave me a wink.

I had to give her props, she had a flair for the dramatic.

"I have nothing to open up about, I simply intend to have a good time tonight," I threw in.

"Good, I won't have anything less," she said. "If you need anything, please let me know."

She left us alone, going back to the party, dancing her way through thee crowd.

"I bet she has the hots for you dude," Heath said leaning close to speak to me.

"No, she likes girls," Rachel said.

"No, she swings both ways," Heather said.

"You should tell her your gay dude. She is the last girl in the world you want to lead on," Gabe warned.

"Why? She crazy?" I asked.

"No, her brother will fucking kill you," Gabe said with a wince.

I took a drink of my punch and glanced up and saw Richard looking down at me, his gaze once more heated, and judging from the look he was giving me...he was not happy that I was not wearing his clothes.

"He might do it anyway," I muttered to low for anyone to hear me.

I raised the camera and took one more picture.

*****

Richard

I watched Jeremy dance.

I watched him the entire time. Never once did my eyes leave him.

He wasn't wearing the clothes I got him. I had told him to wear them in my note, and he defied me.

But he still looked amazing. I should have gotten him red cloths; he would look good in red. It was dark out, yet he seemed to glow in the darkness, even with the roar of the crowd and the blaring music, I could still sense him.

Even with so many sweating humans, humans with their colognes and perfumes, I could still smell him, and if I closed my eyes and focused I could even hear his heartbeat through the din of the music.

We stood on our rock, watching the humans. The night was young, and we were getting high on moonflowers.

Moonflowers are like catnip for a werewolf. For normal humans it can cause hallucinations, but for a werewolf it causes a pleasant high and is also an aphrodisiac of sorts for us, like chocolate is for humans.

This meadow was a sacred spot for our pack. Hell it was sacred to the humans and werewolves. They believed this place was a gateway to the spirit world.

Now we came here every full moon to run or for our pack meetings.

We also liked to have our parties here. It was far enough we didn't have to worry about disturbing anyone and the whole place was so serene. Perfect to sing and dance.

The elders didn't mind if we used it as a place to party. As long as we cleaned up the mess and didn't fuck the place up, we were cool.

And we made sure it was well taken care of. If any human tried parking their cars in the meadow we made sure they moved it out into the woods.

This was our sacred place. My ancestors have come here to pray and worship for centuries. I would gladly tear anyone apart who dared desecrate it.

When I was young a group of seniors, thought it would be cute to graffiti the stones. We *politely* told them not to do it.

They told us to fuck off, so we had to add a little of their blood to the paint.

Liz still has a picture of me slamming one of the seniors face into the stone.

It was the one time I started a fight and didn't get in trouble. Rick being the sheriff made sure they cleaned up their mess and Daryl patted me on the head and told me I did a good job for protecting our sacred place.

Even dad was proud of me. Because no one in the pack had sympathy for a bunch of little pricks who were warned not to fuck up the meadow.

I had taken a few flowers and eaten them, hoping they could calm me down. Help take the edge off what was slowly building inside me.

But they didn't.

Jeremy was having a good time with his friends; they all danced and swayed to the music. He was obviously no stranger to the party scene.

I watched mesmerized as his body moved with both style and grace, he was in perfect sync with the music; he went with it, never missing a beat.

I wanted to jump down and join him, to ride the flow with him, to press my body against his and dance.

But I had to keep myself in check.

Then it happened.

A girl, some random bitch, walked up to him and whispered in his ear, he nodded and began to dance with her.

I could tell he was not interested in her, it was just a friendly dance. But I could see the look in her eyes that she was interested in him.

That is when I snapped.

The wolf wanted to tear her apart! How dare she dance with our mate! She was not worthy! And Jeremy was dancing with her! He knew I was there and yet here he was with some slut, dancing!

I couldn't help it, maybe it was the Moon Flowers effecting me, or maybe it was the need of the wolf to be released. But I decided it was time to teach Jeremy his place.

My chest burned with jealousy and anger like a deadly acid.

I looked up, almost expecting to see the Moon in all her glory above us. But tonight was not the night of the full moon and her song was only a faint echo in the sky.

Yet the wolf began to take over and soon the instincts and subconscious desires were taking action while the rational of my mind was pushed back until I felt like I was in a dream.

The wolf was in charge now and all I could do was whisper in the back of my mind.

I could not punish him here, not in front of the humans. And Liz?

She was dancing with a human female, I could read her energy; she was distracted.

I had to use this moment before Liz decided to check on me. I poured my power out, slowly and subtlety so Liz wouldn't catch it. It washed over my pack, at first they didn't sense it, but soon they felt its effects on their minds.

I called to their wolves, I called to my pack. I was the alpha, and I needed my pack's help.

I stood up, and they followed me, having sensed my silent call, waiting for their orders.

"Vivian, Cora, Tracey, keep Liz distracted. Do what you have to but don't let her leave to look for me," I commanded.

The girls left to go dance and keep an eye on Liz.

"What are we going to do Richard?" Trevor asked a slight empty tone in his voice.

"We're hunting," I replied.

"Hunting what?" Keven asked.

I smiled.

8

Rick

I got out of my car and walked to where the others were gathered.

There was no one else save us on the property. The barn was abandoned. It looked like it was about to fall to pieces.

I had gotten a call from our contacts in the Etan police department. They had found Wayne. I could smell the decomp before I went inside. Pain and anger filled me at the smell.

One of my pack was dead.

I braced myself and walked inside. Evidence was already being gathered. I froze at the entrance of the barn.

Wayne was hanging by a pair of silver chains that continued to burn his skin even after he died. He was naked, stripped not only of his life but of his dignity.

I could see burn marks on the rest of his body though there was no silver touching him save for what held him up, I could smell the dried blood. I could smell the wolfsbane in his system. It has such a sweet smell, yet it is so lethal.

I steeled myself. I would mourn him after I avenged him, but before I could do that I needed to find the bastard that did this.

I walked inside. The deputies and crime scene investigators nodded.

Those who were in my pack gave me the same look I was sure I gave them.

They lost a pack brother to.

The closer I walked to Wayne's body the more enraged I became.

He had been tortured.

The scent of his pain lingered. I don't believe in ghosts, but the evil that had been committed here was soaked into the air. I had to breathe through my mouth because the smell sent shivers down my spine.

I stood next to Jesse Harden. He was a police officer and another pack mate.

"How did you find him?" I asked.

"Decided to check any abandoned buildings that could have been used to hold him. Caught his scent as soon as I got out of my car. Knew right away he was dead. The bastard left him here to rot!" he growled.

"We sure it's just one?" I asked.

"Yes, there was only one other scent besides Wayne's, it took a while to catch because of the chemo-smells."

I took a deep breath. The scent of death and torment was still there. But if I concentrated I could detect another scent.

My wolf was thirsty for retribution. I had hunted with Wayne, both as a man and as a wolf, gone fishing with him and invited him over to my place to have dinner with my family.

He had been a good man, he didn't deserve this.

But I had to push the rage down. I was the Sheriff of Wolf Fang Falls and the Enforcer of my pack. I had a job to do. So I focused on the evidence.

"See the burn marks on his body?" I asked.

"Yes. It's like silver burns. But it's like he is still being burned,"

Jesse commented. "I know silver burns us and injuries heal more slowly."

"They injected him with liquid silver. I've seen the effects it can have when it gets in the bloodstream," I answered.

He took a deep breath. "Wayne was a good man. He didn't deserve this."

"No, but who ever did it does. And I think we both know who did this."

"Had the knowledge and skill to capture and contain a werewolf," he said.

"Tortured him using silver, and wolfsbane," I said.

We both looked at one another.

"Hunter," we both said.

Hunters. Hell, any human can pick up a silver knife and call themselves a Hunter. But this guy was the real deal. He had the training to capture a werewolf and hold him.

But what's worse he was obviously a rogue.

A Hunter who hunts werewolves whether they are peaceful or not. They do not follow the Hunters code.

And if he tortured Wayne he was trying to get info out of him.

I knew Wayne was no snitch. But I also know even a werewolf can be made to break. As much as I wanted to believe Wayne didn't tell the Hunter anything I could not take that risk.

I reached into my pocket and grabbed my phone. I needed to call Daryl. I was not going to lose another pack mate to this guy.

*****

Jeremy

"Say cheese!" I said and took another photo of Heath and Heather.

Heath stood behind her, wrapping his arms around her and hugging her close to his chest. The flash of my phone went off, and I examined the picture with satisfaction.

They both walked over to see and were pleased with the shot.

"You're really good at this Jeremy," Heather said.

"Thanks, I want to be a professional photographer when I graduate," I said.

I had taken dozens of photos already. I couldn't wait to save them on my computer back home.

Heath and Heather left me to go back to dancing, and I went to get something to drink.

I was sweating quite a bit; I have been doing nothing but dancing since I got here. I was having a good time. I danced with a lot of girls, but I had to make it clear to them, (especially the ones who were a little too frisky), that I was not on the market.

As I was getting another drink, a hand fell on my shoulder. I looked and saw it was one of the Commune Kids. He was not alone; about five others were with him.

I didn't like the look in their eyes. It was like they were not all there; like they were in some kind of trance. Probably high on pills or something.

"Come with us," the guy said.

"Bit busy now," I said, brushing him off.

His grip on my shoulder tightened.

"Now!"

Before I could say anything he grabbed me, he shoved a piece of cloth into my mouth and covered my face. His friends brought up the rear, their massive frames blocking the view of them abducting me.

We headed for the woods, away from the party. I already had a feeling as to why they were doing this. I tried to break free, but this guy was strong like an ox.

I tried to call out for help but the cloth kept me from yelling, and the noise from the music made it impossible for anyone to hear me.

We headed into the woods where the music became more and more distant. I continued to struggle, but it was all in vain. Finally we stopped and he let me go. I pulled the cloth out of my mouth and glared at him.

"The fuck is wrong with you?!" I yelled.

"We brought him, Richard," the guy said, his eyes never left me with their vacant gaze.

"Good work Trevor."

I turned around and saw Richard.

"What is going on?" I asked.

"Hold him," he ordered.

Two of his friends grabbed my arms and held me. Richard walked up to me and my heart beat hard in my chest. He put his hand around my throat and lightly squeezed it, keeping me from running.

"Leave us," Richard demanded.

The guys all left without a word. I dared not struggle against Richard with the grip he had on my neck.

He stared into my eyes, never once blinking. He looked positively feral.

Not quite angry. His gaze had the same expression as the others only more aware, more emotion.

"You dare defy me?" he whispered.

"Look if this is about th-"

"Stop talking!" he growled. "First you disobey me, and then you dance with a bunch of human whores!"

Human?

"Look, leave me alone, please. I just want to go back to my friends," I pleaded.

He closed his eyes and took a deep breath. "God, your scent. Do you have any idea how bad you fuck with me?!"

"Fuck with you? I don't bother you at all!" I shouted.

"Oh, but you do!"

He backed me up into a tree, pinning me against it with his massive frame.

"My life was perfect until you showed up! I had everything going for me. But now...it doesn't matter. You are mine, and it is time you accepted that. That I accept it! I can't keep doing this no more! It's killing me!"

"What the absolute fuck are you talking about?" I demanded.

He kissed me.

I felt like all the breath had been knocked right out of me, fire burned right to my core and I felt like I was at the center of something wonderful and terrifying. I kept my mouth shut though his tongue tried to get past my lips. He growled and pulled back, he looked positively insane now. He let my throat go and ripped his shirt off and threw what remained to the ground.

Even though the situation was fucked up, I couldn't help but look at his chest. Damn he was ripped. There was no hair on his chest. Though there was a thin trail of hair under his navel that disappeared into the waistband of his boxers. There wasn't an ounce of fat on this guy; his body was tight with muscles, but he wasn't bulging with them, he was smooth and perfect.

"Can't you feel it?" he asked, "I know you have to feel something."

He grabbed my hand and placed it over his heart, his skin was hot to the touch and I could feel his heart beating fast in his chest.

A terrible need grew inside me as if touching Richard had created a connection between us and everything he felt came pouring into me.

I suddenly focused on him more intensely then anyone I ever have. I went limp and pliant, I grabbed his wrist and gently squeezed it.

I felt a raging chaos inside of my being, feelings I recognized only on a much more intense and terrifying level.

I wanted him. I needed him so bad it hurt. I wanted to see him smile and hear him laugh and wrap him around me like a blanket.

But where was this coming from? These could not be my feelings could they?

He grabbed my waist and brought me close, pleased by my submission to him. "Mine," he growled with an expression of fierce delight.

He bent down to kiss me again and this time I welcomed his advance.

God if his lips weren't so fucking perfect!

His mouth moved do my chin to my throat. I tilted my head to the side to give him more of my tender flesh to kiss and nibble. I felt numb; it was as if he was sending jolts of electricity through my body.

Such joy I felt, such happiness.

All the sorrow and pain I have felt, the depression and bitterness was all washed away. For the first time in too long I was free, thanks to Richard.

In that moment I was his, in that moment he owned me and I was more than happy to let him have me.

But then his teeth suddenly bit down a little too hard on my neck and the small jolt of pain I felt woke me up from whatever spell I was under.

Anger blossomed in my chest and I knew I had to get away from him.

So I slid my leg between his knees. He was so focused on my neck he didn't notice.

Then with all my strength I brought my knee up between his legs, striking the most vulnerable part where a man can be hit.

A howl escaped his mouth and he let me go as he cradled his groin and whimpered in pain. I ran past him as fast as I could, trying to head back to the party.

I heard a loud snarl that didn't sound human, but it sounded disturbingly familiar.

I could hear him chasing after me and I tried to run faster, thankfully I jogged a lot, so I was good at running.

Sadly, he was a lot faster.

Before I knew it I was back on the ground with him on top of me. I was stunned for a moment by being thrown to the ground by such a massive body. Then he spun me around, his teeth bared, his eyes were still honey brown but they looked different; almost wolfish. He was making these growling noises that no human should make. Sounds that I was sure I had heard before.

"That was a big, fucking mistake!" he glowered.

I tried to shake him off, but he was too heavy. He smiled as I struggled as if he took pleasure from it. He ground his crotch into mine and I froze. He was hard, and even through the fabric of his jeans I could feel he was big.

He bent down and began to lick my neck while he rubbed himself against me. I closed my eyes, wishing this was some kind of nightmare.

"Richard, stop!" I cried.

He stopped.

He pulled back and looked at me, maybe it was the tone in my voice or maybe it was the tears running down my face, but he seemed to snap out of it.

The feral madness left his eyes, and he became calmer. He looked shocked, like he couldn't believe what just happened.

"Oh God! Jeremy I am so-"

Before he could finish, there was a sound of something flying through the air. Richard roared, got up and turned around. I saw there was a dart in his back.

He growled and went to charge but his body jerked and he fell to his knees.

"Richard!" I yelled.

I got up and went to him, three more darts were in his chest and something strange was happening. Where the darts had hit him, dark purple lines were spreading, as if a terrible poison was moving through his veins.

A man walked towards us, he had dark skin and a bald head. He wore combat boots, camo pants and a black shirt. He carried a rifle and there was a combat knife attached to his utility belt.

He held up a tranquilizer gun which he had used to shoot Richard.

"Not so tough now, huh big guy?" he asked with a sneer.

"What...who are you?" I asked.

"Name's Joseph. Don't worry kid, he won't be getting back up," he informed me.

The lines were spreading further along Richard's body and sweat began to run down his body, like it was trying to fight off an infection. He began to pull the darts out of his chest, but it did not matter, whatever was in those darts was in his system now.

CLICK.

I looked and saw Joseph had his cell out and he took a picture of Richard. "There, now I can prove to the others I got him."

I kneeled down next to Richard and helped him pull out the dart in his back.

"Richard? Richard?" I whispered urgently to him.

He looked at me, he looked so sick. "Run," he croaked.

He fell down, and I caught him, I gently laid him down on the ground. He almost took me down with him, he was a heavy guy. Good thing I lifted weights.

"What did you do to him?" I asked Joseph.

He was still looking at his phone, his thumb was moving over the screen, I was sure he was sending a text.

"I put him down; the wolfsbane is doing its job."

"Wolfsbane?"

And then I had an epiphany.

From the first moment I came to Wolf Fang Falls. To seeing Richard and the Commune Kids. The way they moved together and how they lived in a gated community shut off from the rest of the world. The way they seemed to get high just from sniffing the moonflowers and Richard's strange behavior.

In that moment everything made sense, and I cursed myself a fool for not seeing it sooner. How could I have not connected the dot sooner?

"You're a Hunter," I stated.

He looked surprised. "You know about Hunters?"

"Yes."

"So you know that thing is-"

"I didn't until now," I said.

"Good, last thing I need is to explain to a frightened kid about the monsters of the night. I mean, Christ kid, he scared you so bad you're as white as a piece of paper," he commented.

I scowled at him. "This is my normal skin color."

"Oh....you an albino or something?" he questioned.

"What are you going to do to him?" I asked, ignoring his question.

"Well, after he dies, I am going to drag his carcass to my fellow Hunters. I am sure to get some serious cash for bringing in an alpha," he said. He began to tap his phone with his thumb again. "Matter of fact, I need to make a call."

He turned his back and talked on the phone. I did not bother to listen; instead I grabbed the moonflower Elizabeth put behind my ear and brought it to Richard's mouth. I opened it and put the flower in.

"Come on, chew the damn thing!" I whispered to him.

His mouth began to move as he chewed the flower. I looked up and saw that Joseph was still talking on his phone. I quickly felt around Richard's pants, hoping he had his cell.

I found it and reached into his pocket and pulled it out. I quickly went through his contact list and found Liz's number and hit dial.

I prayed she could hear it over the music.

"Richard? Where the hell are you? Are you with Jeremy?" she asked sounding annoyed.

"Elizabeth it's me," I tried to whisper.

"Jeremy? Wh-"

"Listen, I am in the woods, Richard has been attacked by a hunter named Joseph; he shot him with darts filled with wolfsbane!"

"What!? Where in the woods?"

"I don't know; Richard's friends dragged me into the woods when I was by the punch bowl, tell them the situation and be sure to bring moonflowers," I stumbled out.

"Wait...how?"

"Later!" I hissed.

"Hey!"

I looked up and saw Joseph had finished his call and was now glaring at me.

"Hurry!" I snapped.

9

Elizabeth

I cursed and put the phone back in my pocket.

I immediately gathered as many Moon Flowers as I could and went to find Jeremy. If what he said was true, they were the only thing that would be able to save Richard.

They are a cure for wolfsbane poisoning.

We werewolves loved moonflowers for more than just their sweet scent.

They were our protection from aconite. One flower that killed us, one flower that saved us. Two flowers, one deadly and one sweet.

Ironic how simple flora can have such sway over creatures like us.

Which begged the question how Jeremy knew about them in the first place. A question I was going to make sure was answered.

Once I gathered enough, I quickly began to try to track Richard's scent, but there was so many humans and the noise was so loud.

As I made my way to the punch table hoping to catch Jeremy's scent some of the girls got in my way. They had these dreamy expressions on their faces.

I figured they had been eating the moonflowers and were a little high.

"Move it!" I growled at them. "Richard is in trouble!"

"What's the rush Liz?" Vivian asked.

"Yeah, come dance with us," Cora said.

Are they for fucking real!

I unleashed my power on them, now was not the time for simple shit. They whimpered and then seemed to wake up from a dream. They looked around confused.

"Where are we?"

"What happened?"

"Where are the guys?"

"Come on! Richard needs us!" I yelled.

They followed me as I hunted down Jeremy and Richard and I filled them in on the situation. I caught Richard's scent and followed it.

We happened on the guys who were walking from the forest.

"Keven, where is Richard?" I asked.

"Back there with Jeremy," he said.

"Why is Richard along with the new guy?" Cora asked.

I had a rather good idea of why Richard and Jeremy were alone together. I dreaded to think of what may have transpired between the two of them, but one crisis at a time.

"We need to get to them right now!" I reminded them.

I went to move past Keven, but he grabbed my arm. "No! You can't interfere with this!"

"Keven baby what's wrong with you?" Vivian asked.

Something was wrong, the guys had the same expression the girls had.

Could Richard have used his gift to make the others help with whatever crazy scheme he came up with?

I was really good at reading a wolf's energy to accurately judge their emotions and feelings. But Richard had a way of messing with our minds. Even I could be effected by it, which was why I was always on my guard around him.

There were times when he was younger when his power caused a dew incidents with the pack.

If it was Richard using his unusual gifts, I knew how to break his hold.

I unleashed my power. I let it slam against the guys. I let it hit them all full force.

I knew from experience a powerful werewolf unleashing her power on another would could feel like the air was being knocked out of them. But it would help knock some sense into them.

Luckily the guys snapped out of it. Just like the girls they were confused, not knowing how they got there. I told them the situation, and we all ran into the woods to find Richard and Jeremy.

Once we were in far enough where humans couldn't see us, I threw my head back and let out a howl and the others followed.

It was a howl to let our brothers and sisters know there was trouble and help was needed, it was a howl to let our pack brother know help was on the way; it was a howl to let our enemies know we were coming.

Close by, a single wolf howled, we recognized it as Richard and ran to help him.

I swear I can't leave him alone for a minute without him getting into trouble.

*****

Jeremy

I dropped the phone to the ground and stood up.

"What the fuck are you doing?" he demanded.

"I just called for help, so you better leave," I retorted.

"You did what?"

"You heard me!"

"Why the hell would you do something stupid like that?" he demanded.

"Because I don't want you to kill him," I explained.

It was true, sure what happened between us was some serious shit, but now that I know what is really going on I know I can't let Richard die.

At least not without giving me one good fucking explanation about what just happened between us.

I stood up and faced the Hunter. I blocked him from Richard.

I gave him a single moonflower, but I knew he was going to need more to clean the wolfsbane from his system.

"Idiot, he was going to kill you!" Joseph ranted.

Obviously he didn't know how wrong he was. But I didn't tell him that.

"Just leave, go before his pack shows up," I suggested.

"I don't think so." He dropped the tranq-gun and took his knife from his belt. "I am not leaving without my kill."

I stared at the knife he held. It was obvious from the way he held it he knew how to use it.

I was more than sure he could beat me in a fight. But if I played it smart, I could buy Elizabeth and hopefully the others time to get here and help.

I was wishing Richard's friends were here right now.

"You'll have to kill me to get to him," I said bravely.

He leered at me. "Oh, a sympathizer. You think I won't cut you because you are human? Wrong. Your type are nothing but traitors, you deserve to die as much as they do."

I knew he meant every word he said. I could see it from the look in his eyes. He would kill me and take satisfaction from it.

He had gone from hero to psycho in less than a second. All friendliness gone and only deadly intent remained.

He walked up to me, his knife in hand.

"But I will look the other way, just turn and run and I will let you go, no reason to get yourself killed over a stinking-"

WHACK!

Once he was close enough, I brought my leg up and kicked the knife out of his hand. It flew through the air to the side. Joseph looked shocked but before he could recover I swung my leg into his gut, then I did a spin kick right into his face.

Thank you mom for letting me take martial arts classes when I was young.

It helped me with bully's growing up now it *might* save my life.

Might being the key word here. Because I am sure I just made myself a target.

He fell to the ground, but then he got back up. I took a deep breath and got ready for round two. I had surprised him the first time, but now he would be ready, more cautious.

He was trained to take down werewolves, so I was sure he was more than capable of defending himself against me. My skills would surely pale in comparison to his.

He glared at me and wiped the blood from the side of his mouth. "How the hell did you do that?"

"Dude, you think I could look the way I do and not need to learn how to defend myself from bullies?" I asked.

He stood up. "Well, you got lucky that time but now I-"

He froze. He looked behind me. I turned and saw Richard was standing up. He didn't look that much better, but at least he could stand.

"Get away from him!" he roared.

He staggered forward, trying to resist the effects of the wolfsbane. Good thing I gave him that moonflower though I fear it was going to take more to cure him.

Joseph pulled the rifle hanging from his shoulder and aimed it at Richard. I wave of fear hit me, I was willing to bet the bullets were made from silver.

Then before Joseph could fire the air was filled with the sound of howling wolves, Richard threw his head back and howled in response.

"See, those are his friends coming, you better run," I warned Joseph.

I prayed he would run. I hoped to God he wouldn't pull the trigger first before he fled.

Luck was finally on my side.

"Fuck this! I'll be back, this ain't over runt; I won't forget this!"

He lowered the rifle and grabbed his knife and dart gun and took off running. Richard tried to run after him but stumbled and fell to his knees. "Easy," I soothed, grabbing his shoulders to keep him from falling forward.

He looked at me with a look of what I could describe as pride.

"You fought him? How?"

"Like I said, when you look like me you have to know how to fight. Mom let me take karate classes when I was young," I explained.

"Jeremy...I...I am sorry....I can explain," he started to apologize.

"You don't have to Richard.....I know what you are," I said.

"What? What do you mean?" he asked, trying to act like I hadn't figured everything out.

"I admit that I should have figured it out sooner. But now, it all makes sense," I replied.

"What are you going on about?"

"Richard....you're a werewolf," I stated.

The look on his face was priceless; there was shock, disbelief, confusion. Then it turned to worry and fear.

"Don't tell anyone else! Not just the humans, but the others....if they know you know about us...."

He trailed off, not daring to finish the sentence. He didn't need to. I was all to mindful of what would happen if his pack found out I knew about werewolves.

"I know."

"Richard!"

Elizabeth came running with Richard's friends. I saw she carried moonflowers, and I knew they would be enough to save him.

I hadn't even been here a week and already I had werewolves and a crazy Hunter to deal with.

What the fuck.

*****

Richard

Even though Liz brought the Moon Flowers, I still had to go to the hospital.

We called for an ambulance and they drove me there. Mom and dad had been called as had Rick. We had to bring Jeremy so he could tell everyone what happened.

It was....tricky to say the least. First, we had to make sure no one knew he knew the truth; that would be very bad. Second, we had to come up with an excuse as to why I was alone with Jeremy in the woods and why the others had no memory of going there with us.

I felt bad for doing that to them, I seriously had to work on my control. I didn't even realize what I had done. I was too lost in my instincts to realize just how bad I had messed with their minds.

Dr. Samuel was going over some last minute tests with me, making sure I was alright. Even with all the moonflower nectar in me I still felt weary.

"Well, I advise you to take it easy, your tests all clear but no need to over exert yourself," he said.

Samuel was a human, his mother had been a werewolf and his father a human. He was offered the right of transformation when he came of age but he rejected the offer and opted to remain human.

It was easier for him to be a doctor as a human than it would be as a werewolf. He didn't have to schedule his work around the lunar cycles.

Rick was in the room as well, so was mom, dad, Liz and Jeremy. Mom had almost hugged him to death, thanking him over and over for saving my life.

The story was that Liz made me hang out with Jeremy and be nice to him to make up for how mean I was to him in the past. Everyone believed it; they knew whatever Liz wanted, Liz got, no matter what.

She knew Jeremy would be in danger if it was revealed he knew the truth. So she helped validate the story.

I knew she was sticking her neck out for me by lying and I was so going to pay her back for this.

As for the others, we blamed the moonflowers. The ones in Hunter's Meadow didn't have the hallucinogenic properties that others types did but they were still capable of effecting werewolves.

"Thanks doc," I said.

"Are there any more questions you need to ask my son, Rick?" dad asked.

Rick shook his head. "No, we are looking for the guy now. It won't be long before we find him," Rick said. He turned to Jeremy. "I called your mom, she is on her way to pick you up," he added.

Jeremy groaned. "She is going to be freaked."

"I told her you were safe," he insisted.

"She will still be frantic, trust me," he complained.

"I know the feeling," mom said as she petted my hair soothingly, her face filled with distress.

Dad stood silently by her, but I could tell he was upset as well. When he looked at me, his expression lacked the hardness it usually did.

We got ready to leave and Dr. Samuel left us to take care of another patient. Rick also left, and we started to leave. I left my family and walked up to Jeremy. He was sitting in the lobby, waiting for his mom.

"We need to talk," I told him.

"Okay," he said his face neutral.

We stared at one another.

The air between us was heavy. I didn't know what to say.

Of course I had a slew of questions I wanted to ask him. But I was also freaked out about the attack.

That Hunter could have hurt him, killed him! If Liz and the others hadn't come when they did. Thank the gods they got there in time.

"We both have some explaining to do," I finally said.

"I agree," he nodded.

Before I could speak Liz appeared. "Do you mind?" I asked irritated.

She stuck her tongue out at me, and then turned to Jeremy. "I can not thank you enough for what you did. You saved my brother."

He shrugged his shoulders. "It was nothing."

"You were brave Jeremy. Braver than anyone I ever saw," I said.

"Thanks. But what are we going to do about your pack? Won't they be pissed I know?" he asked with a whisper.

Liz and I placed a comforting hand on his shoulders. "Just keep to the story I came up with." Liz looked at me. "You to. As long as we don't screw up no one has to know."

"How do you know about us?" I asked him.

He sighed. "That is a long story. One I'd rather not talk about right now."

He got this sad look on his face. I wanted to wrap my arms around him and hold him. To give him comfort.

Liz touched my arm. "He's right. It's been a long night for all of us. Come now Richard. Let's get you home."

She took my arm and dragged me away. I didn't want to leave him.

"Thanks again Jeremy," she called out.

"No problem, see you later," he said tiredly.

Once we were out of earshot she rounded on me, her eyes furious.

"You are an idiot, you know that?!" she hissed at me.

"Get off my ass! I almost died tonight!" I growled at her.

"Goddess, why couldn't I have had a twin sister instead of a brother!" she complained.

"Fuck off," I retorted.

"You're lucky I was able to break your hold on the others. Seriously, what the hell?"

"The wolf was in control okay?!" I grumbled.

"And Jeremy knows?" she asked with a worried tone. "How the hell does he know?"

"That wasn't me, but trust me; I am going to find out how he found out," I continued.

"Jeremy has more surprises than I thought," she said.

"I know," I agreed.

I don't know how he knows, but I will find out. I intend to know every single detail about Jeremy. After my little near death experience, I had decided that I needed to reevaluate my life. And I intended to make sure he was in it.

*****

Rick

I stood next to Wayne's sister Gina as the coroner pulled the sheet back.

She looked at his body like the wind had been knocked out of her.

"Oh Wayne," she whispered, covering her mouth with her hand.

She turned her head unable to look anymore. I nodded. and the sheet was pulled back up. I placed my hand on her back and gently led her out.

"I'm sorry for your loss Gina. Wayne was a good man," I said.

"How could someone do this? He never hurt a fly Rick! He hated violence! He was studying to be a nurse!"

Her whole body shook as the grief began to take over.

I wrapped my arms around her and held her. Lending my strength to my pack sister in her time of need.

"We think the Hunter wanted to know more about our pack."

"So he tortured him?" she asked horrified, "I smelled the wolfsbane."

"We'll find who did this. I swear," I said.

"Rick."

Gina and I turned to see Daryl walking to us.

Two of my deputies and three of our pack brothers followed him.

They were here to protect Daryl. With a rogue hunter running around we had to make sure our Pack King was safe.

"Daryl, Wayne is dead," Gina cried.

Daryl opened his arms and hugged her as she began to sob.

"He was supposed to come to Joey's birthday next week! What am I supposed to tell him now?"

Joey was her son. Wayne dotted on his little nephew much to Gina's irritation. He always bought him toys and would let him stay up past his bedtime so they could play video games. Poor kid was going to be crushed when he found out.

"Be strong Gina, it's what Wayne would want. I need to speak with Rick, we will find who did this I promise," Daryl said soothingly kissing the top of her head.

"Barry, take her to get some coffee upstairs," I said.

Barry nodded and took her from Daryl and let her lean her head on his shoulder as he took her away.

"Have we had any luck finding the Hunter?" Daryl asked.

I shook my head. "No. He knows how to cover his tracks. But he can't hide for ever. We have his scent and we have already had Richard and Jeremy give a description. If he's smart, he'll have left the state."

"If a Hunter goes through all this trouble. I doubt he'll give up that easily. How bad was the damage to Wayne?" he asked.

"Bad enough. This hunter has done this before. Niveus knows how long he spent torturing him for information."

Daryl turned to look to the others. "Let's keep that bit quit. Wayne was a good man and I don't want his name besmirched. Last thing his family needs is people accusing him of being a traitor. I doubt many could withstand the torture he went through and not break," he firmly stated.

The all nodded.

Daryl turned back to me.

"I am concerned about the boy, Jeremy. How much does he know?"

"Richard says he thinks the guy was just some raving lunatic but..."

"But what?" Daryl pressed.

As an enforcer of both the human and werewolf law I know I should not let my emotions get the best of me.

I did not want to place Jeremy under any scrutiny. Any other kid I wouldn't mind but he was Diane's boy. But I took an oath and I could not let my personal feelings get in the way of my duty.

"I questioned him myself. I think it might have just been shock, but he was acting really...calm."

"Calm?"

"Yes. Most people would be freaking out after something like this happened to them. I could tell he was a little upset but, he just seemed to...together. Like it wasn't something he had never seen before."

"Has he ever faced a similar situation like this before?" Daryl asked.

I shook my head. "Not to my knowledge."

Daryl was quiet for a moment. "We'll have to keep an eye on him and his mother. We need to make sure he doesn't suspect anything. And in case the Hunter comes after him again."

"Why would he?" I asked.

"He might think Jeremy saved Richard because he is a friend. He might see him as useful to gather more information."

I shuddered at the idea of Jeremy being interrogated like poor Wayne.

"Rick. I know you have feelings for his mother. But you can't put your own feelings ahead of the safety of the pack. If the boy becomes a danger to us, he will have to be taken care of. You know the law."

"I do Daryl. And I have never let my personal feelings interfere with my duties," I said sternly.

He placed his hand on my shoulder. "I was not implying anything. I just don't want you getting confused."

"If Jeremy turns out to be a threat to the pack, I will take care of it

Daryl. I promise you that."

10

Jeremy

I woke up that morning at first believing I had dreamt the events of last night.

But the I quickly realized that was wishful thinking when I saw the mark on my neck from where Richard had bitten me last night.

I shuddered at the memory. I don't know what was scarier, the Hunter or Richard.

I know Richard freaked out on me and I should have been grateful for being saved by Joseph, but I didn't want Richard dead.

Before he showed up and attacked him Richard snapped out of it. He seemed shocked at what he was doing. Like some new werewolf with no control of his instincts.

If Richard and his sister were werewolves I am more than sure the other Commune Kids are werewolves as well.

Now that I think about it, I should have noticed the signs sooner.

I wonder how many of them there are? How many have I met and not even known it?

But I knew better than to think I was not in danger. Liz and Richard were willing to keep me safe but that doesn't mean the rest of them would be less than gracious in that aspect.

The once boring town I thought I knew was now suddenly something more sinister and dangerous.

Now I would have to fear discovery and the repercussions my knowledge would bring.

As I walked out of the bathroom, I heard mom walking up the stairs.

"Oh good, you're awake," she said when she reached the top of the stairs. She placed her hand on my forehead. "How are you feeling?"

"Fine," I said gently removing her hand.

"God, I can't believe we are not even here a week and some psycho is running around. I'm so glad I let you take all those karate classes."

"You and me both," I said with a grin. "I was a total bad ass!"

Just then the doorbell began to ring, letting us know we had company.

"Whole town is probably outside wanting to know what happened," mom said with a sigh.

We walked down the steps. I went into the kitchen to get something to eat while mom answered the door.

"Jeremy, it's your friends!" she called.

I grabbed my bowel of cereal and walked to the front door.

Rachel, Heather, Heath and Gabe came walking in.

"Oh my God are you okay?" Rachel asked giving me a hug.

"Yeah, Richard was the one who got attacked," I said.

"Dude everyone is talking about it," Gabe said.

"Told you," mom said as she headed into the kitchen.

We all moved to the living room. "So what did happen? Why were you with Richard in the woods man?" Heath asked.

"Liz heard he has been kind of shitty to me so she made him apologize to me. But since he is such a prideful prick he didn't want to do it in public," I said remembering the story Liz came up with.

"Who was the guy that attacked you?" Heather asked.

"Was it the same guy who kidnapped that nurse?" Rachel asked.

"Rick thinks so. It would be too much of a coincidence if he wasn't."

"I can't believe we have a killer running around. I'm scared to be alone," Rachel said.

"Don't worry, Rick will find him. He's the best sheriff we've ever had. He always finds his perps," Gabe said putting a comforting arm around her shoulders.

A werewolf who always finds his perps?

Imagine that.

*****

They staid a little while longer to talk.

They told me what happened after I vanished (actually kidnapped).

How they looked for me and when they couldn't find me they knew something was wrong. I was a little glad when they left. I had repeated the story of what happened so many times I was beginning to feel like a robot.

I always made sure I repeated the story word for word. I took my time, I didn't want to make even the slightest mistake.

I was not sure they were all human. Though I had a feeling, they were not werewolves I could not take that risk.

And even if they were human who is to say they did not serve the werewolves. I know some packs keep humans as servants or even have human lovers or family members.

I needed to try to learn more about what and who I was dealing with.

So after they left I went on my computer and began to do some research into Wolf Fang Falls.

It was built during the eighteenth century around the time of the Battle of Rosebud. Through the combined efforts of a group of Shoshone Indians and several other families.

One of them named Farkas.

I found an old photo taken of the founding families along with the Shoshone. The photo showed the founders up front with their families behind them.

One of them was Sami Farkas. A man with a stocky build, thick eyebrows and a mustache.

I did some more research and found out the Gates were built in the fifties where the states rich would gather to live. I was almost certain it was actually built to house the werewolves.

Maybe the whole pack lived there.

How big was this pack? How big was their territory? What tribe were they affiliated with?

I did research into the Farkas family and the other founding families of the town. I looked up old news clippings and police reports.

Anything and everything I could find about the town and its residents.

Surprisingly there wasn't a lot to find. You'd think a town with its own wolf pack would have all kinds of odd incidents or wolf sittings.

But werewolves were very big on secrecy. How else had they remained in the mists of myths and legends?

The phone began to ring, and I heard mom answer it.

The question is what should I do now? Obviously Liz and Richard were going to keep me safe. But how much could I trust them?

I still don't know what is up with Richard or why he is acting the way he is acting. I also don't know why they are so trusting of me or so willing to keep me safe.

I am sure they feel grateful to me for helping Richard out. But something tells me there is something more going on here.

I had to talk to Richard...or more preferably Liz. I was sure they wanted to know how I knew about werewolves.

Maybe in telling them the truth I can get the truth.

Mom walked into my room. "That was Richard's mother. She has invited us over to their house for dinner tonight to thank you for saving her sons life," she said.

A feeling that was a mix of dread and trepidation settled into the pit of my stomach.

"That sounds great," I said with a smile.

"I know, I've never been there before. Should be interesting."

She smiled and left me alone.

I groaned and covered my face.

Great, just great.

My phone began to beep as someone tried to call me using Facetime. I smiled when I saw it was my buddy Jeff from back home.

I hit accept and a second later his face was on my screen.

"Hey man!" he greeted.

"Hey what's up?" I asked.

"Dude I heard a rumor from Joey Fitzsimmons who has a cousin in Wolf Fang Falls that someone was attacked last night at a rave."

"Dude...you won't believe what happened," I told him.

I spent the next twenty minutes telling him an abridged version of everything that happened since I came to Wolf Fang Falls and of the events of last night.

Jeff was human and did not know anything about werewolves. He was one of the few people who knew I had been dating Lucas. He knew I left home because I had *issues* with Lucas, but he didn't know the true reasons.

He knew it had something to do with Lucas, but I never went into full details.

"Dude, you have the worst fucking luck," Jeff said.

"Tell me about it," I said.

"Have they caught the guy yet?" he asked.

I shook my head. "No, he is still out there somewhere."

"Jesus. You sure you don't want to move back?"

I almost told him I was more safe here then there.

"Tempting, but I am sure this lunatic will be caught soon. I mean if I could take him down he can't be that smart."

Jeff laughed. "He probably thought you were some helpless little girl."

"Dick."

We both laughed.

"I got to go, I just wanted to call and see how you were doing," Jeff said.

"Yeah, nice talking to you man."

The call ended, and I put my phone back in my pocket.

I really did miss my friends. I missed my home. I missed...Lucas.

I had left Cambridge to escape werewolves and found myself living in the territory of another pack. And if they found out, I knew my life would be in danger.

I touched my neck. I thought of Richard and the look in his eyes when he told me to run.

He had been afraid, but I think he was more afraid something would happen to me.

What was it about me that would make a werewolf risk the wrath of his pack to keep me safe? What happened between the two of us last night?

Too many questions, not enough answers. Something I am going to rectify tonight.

11

Mom and I drove to the Gates.

I was kind of nervous about going to the Farkas' house. Now that I knew the gated community was a haven for werewolves it made me kind of nervous to think I was going into their den.

And after what happened with Richard last night, before the Hunter showed up, I was starting to get nervous again.

I knew Richard wanted answers, but so did I, and the only way I was going to get them was if I talked to him at his home. The only thing that made me feel at ease was the fact that mom and his family would be there, so he wouldn't be able to pull another stunt like last night.

I hope.

I feel stupid for not realizing he was a werewolf sooner, I have spent time with them; I should have recognized the signs. But even his being a werewolf didn't explain his bizarre behavior.

Mom was excited because she had never been inside the Gates, even when she was dating Rick. She had asked him to take her but he always changed the subject.

If only she knew why.

It was below a hill you had to drive up. When we arrived at the top, we got a good look at it and I gasped.

From what I could see it was huge! I saw dozens and dozens of houses, and it went on and on, how big of a gated community was it?

"Amazing, huh?" mom asked.

"How big is it?" I asked.

"Big enough that we used to joke it was its own little town," she said. "See the razor wire?" she asked.

I saw at the top of the wall rows of razor wire sat menacingly.

"When I was your age, the big thing to do was to try too sneak into the Gates and get back out without being caught. Eventually they put razor wire up. They take their privacy very seriously," mom said.

Of course, last thing they want is for a bunch of humans running around watching them turn furry. If everyone knew what was really inside the Gates, they would never dare go near it.

We drove down past the wall until we came to the main entrance. There was a guard stationed at the main entrance in a booth. We pulled up to the gate up to his booth.

"Can I help you?" he asked looking at us suspiciously.

"The Farkas family is expecting us for dinner," mom explained.

"Name."

"Moonvine. Diane and Jeremy Moonvine," mom stated.

The guard checked his computer. Once he confirmed who we were he opened the Gates for us.

"Have a good night," he said politely.

"Thanks," mom smiled.

We drove past the Gates and they closed behind us. Mom followed the directions Mrs. Farkas had given her. As we drove, I took in the sights.

My friends were going to freak when I tell them I got in.

Inside the gated community was filled with houses bigger then our own. Many of them had rows of beautiful flowers and neatly trimmed bushes and green grass.

Some people were walking on the sidewalk, others were outside talking to their neighbors, there were even children playing with one another; riding their backs or playing hopscotch.

It was like a giant housing district, cheerful, beautiful and serene. I could feel my fingers develop a familiar twitch.

But as we drove, one thing stuck out. Every person, man, woman and child stopped and looked at us. Some leaned in to whisper as they watched us, others just stared.

We passed a house where a group of guys I recognized from school were playing basket ball. Like everyone else they stopped to watch us drive by.

"Okay, not creepy at all," mom muttered.

"I know," I said.

I admit my nerves were starting to act up. Knowing what we were surrounded by now made me uneasy.

But I had to stay calm.

If any of the werewolves found out, I knew my life would be in danger. Not just my life but my mothers.

I may have saved Richard, but that did not mean it would save us from their wrath.

We continued to drive. We passed a golf course which I couldn't wait to tell the others about. I thought they were exaggerating about this place but they weren't. It really was like its own little town.

We drove to an area that had much bigger homes, like mansions; they were large, some had fountains in their yards and unlike the more close-nit houses we passed these had larger yards, both front and back.

I realized there was a class division in the community; the rich and the filthy rich. I wondered how they managed to stay afloat given today's economy.

We finally arrived at Richard's, no surprise that his family lived in one of the larger houses.

It was a lavish, sienna colored mansion, it had a Victorian style to it, I could see Elizabeth living in a place like this; it was just her kind of style. It looked like something you would see in a movie about the twenties or thirties. The yard was neatly trimmed and dark green, I knew they had to have a sprinkler system.

We pulled up into the driveway and got out.

"Man, this place is awesome!" mom exclaimed.

"I can't wait to tell everyone at school we got in," I said.

"I know all my coworkers will be grilling me for details," she added.

We walked up to the door. There was an old fashioned knocker, but instead we settled for using the doorbell. After it rang it didn't take long for us to hear footsteps and then the door opened.

Mrs. Farkas was standing in front of us. I had met her last night at the hospital. She looked a lot like Elizabeth only her skin was a shade darker and her hair was smoother. Richard and Elizabeth got their eyes from her; they were like Elizabeth's; a friendly warm honey brown.

"Jeremy, Diane, thank you for coming," she said giving us each a hug.

"Do you remember me from school?" mom asked.

"Of course, you went out with Rick," she answered.

"Guilty as charged," mom smiled.

"Thank God it wasn't a crime to date him, all the girls envied you so much," she said with a smile and mom laughed. She let us in and we took our shoes off.

"It is nice to have you back. When you left, everyone was talking about how you went out to see the world," she commented.

"Well after being in Wolf Fang Falls my whole life I wanted to see what was out there after I graduated college," mom explained. "Didn't see as much as I wanted but it's nice to be back after all this time."

I knew I was the reason she didn't get to explore the world as much as she wanted. She had gotten pregnant with me while she was in college and between that and her mother falling ill she dropped out.

"We really don't travel much besides going to visit some relatives out of state. We've never wanted to travel too far from home I guess."

You mean you didn't want to travel far from your pack I thought to myself.

Elizabeth came walking in; she wore a blue gown with a matching corset. She had on blue eyeliner and looked so delicate with her tiny figure but I knew she had more strength in her left pinky then I did in my whole body.

"Jeremy," she said. She leaned in and kissed me on the cheek. "That was for saving my brother." She turned to my mom and offered her hand. "Nice to see you again under better circumstances," she said.

"You to Elizabeth, you look very lovely," mom said.

"Thank you," Elizabeth said giving her a bow.

"Richard, Frank, our guests are here!" Mrs. Farkas called.

Mrs. Farkas turned to me and gave me a hug and a kiss on the forehead. "That was for saving my son," she said.

"It was nothing Mrs. Farkas," I said.

"Please, call me Janice. Thank you again for coming, we wanted to properly thank you for what you did."

"Yes, thank you," a voice said.

Richard and his dad walked in from what I assumed to be the living room. Mr. Farkas was big like Richard, his eyes were hazel and he did not have the same kind of cheekbones Richard had. His skin was lighter than his wife and children's. He had a gruff and husky build and didn't look very trim. You might say he was a tad fat.

But I had a feeling if he took off his shirt you would see he was more built then he looked. Some guys are just made like that, they have a body that makes you think they are packing the pounds, then they show off their stocky muscles and they go from flab to rock solid.

Richard took after his father, Mr. Farkas had the same aura Richard did and the same fire in his eyes Richard did. I could feel him looking through me, studying me, analyzing me. I had a feeling he was not too impressed by what he saw.

He seemed a lot sterner than his wife, he made you feel like you had to be on your toes around him.

He reached out his hand and shook our hands. He had a very firm grip and his palms were rough with calluses. I wondered if maybe he was into construction. Definitely something with his hands; maybe carrying heavy things.

Thank you sir for having us into your home," I said politely.

He didn't correct me when I called him sir, I had a feeling he was stricter about titles then his wife. "It is the least we can do, had it not been for you my son would be dead."

"Have they caught the maniac who attacked the boys?" mom asked.

"Sadly no, Rick is still looking, but it is only a matter of time. No one harms our children.....ever."

I cringed at the tone in his voice. I hoped for his sake Joseph was far, far away from Wolf Fang Falls. I knew that werewolves like humans can carry a grudge and can be very.....creative in their punishments.

I looked over at Richard and saw he was looking at me, his face was neutral.

"Hi Richard, how are you doing?" I asked.

"Fine," he said simply.

"Well then, let us go eat," Janice said.

*****

Dinner was nice. We ate at a long mahogany table.

Frank sat at the head, of course. Mom and I sat together. Mom sat across from Janice who was sitting on the right of Frank, Elizabeth sat next to her mom and Richard sat next to Elizabeth.

They had a fine meal prepared for us; steak, cauliflower, carrots, mashed potatoes, gravy, bread and butter, and drink of our choice.

Mom and Janice were getting along fine. They talked the most out of all of us, talking about their high school days and talking about people they went to school with. About who had gotten fat and who had made it big, about the once popular people who were now down on their luck.

Richard and I kept on glancing at one another, I had a feeling he was as eager to talk to me as I was to him. I noticed Elizabeth watching us from the corner of her eye.

"So, Jeremy. How do you like Wolf Fang Falls?" Frank asked me.

"Well sir, it is a lot like Cambridge, I like it. Much more exciting I think," I answered.

I wonder if they know about the werewolves over in Cambridge. I know there are hundreds of wolf packs all over America alone. Should have been obvious there was one here.

Wolf Fang Falls? Duh.

"I am sorry you had to face such an unpleasant event. We like to pride ourselves in the safety of our town," he commented.

When the residents have fangs and claws and go bump in the night, it is no wonder why crime rate is so low that it is almost none existent.

"It's okay, if I hadn't been there then Richard or some other poor soul wouldn't be here with us," I said quietly.

"Well, when they do catch him I hope they give him the chair, honestly, what kind of monster ruins a good party?" Elizabeth asked, obviously pissed that Joseph had ruined her night.

Hell hath no fury like a woman whose party has been wrecked.

I saw Richard shoot her an annoyed look because she was more pissed that Joseph ruined her party then attempting to kill Richard.

Frank gazed at his daughter and his eyes softened quite a bit. I am thinking Frank is wrapped around Elizabeth's finger.

"Don't worry baby, the bastard will get his comings soon enough," Frank said.

"So Jeremy, please tell us how you fought him off again?" Janice asked.

I told them how I kicked the knife out of Joseph's hands, then I kicked him in the stomach and my whirl kick sent him on the ground. I finished by telling them how I had called Elizabeth using Richard's phone and told them where we were.

"Jeremy took lessons when he was young," mom said proudly.

"I still practice now and then," I added.

"That is amazing, forgive me for saying but you don't look the type to be violent at all," Janice noted.

I smiled. "Well, people who look the way I do have a tendency to attract trouble."

"Jeremy has faced bullying because of his appearance," mom explained, "it was one of the reasons he took lessons; to learn how to better defend himself."

"Oh, that is terrible. To think some people would harass a fine looking young man like yourself," Janice chided.

I wondered if she was aware of her son's reputation for being a jerk at school.

From what I heard from people like Gabe he was exactly like the bullies who used to pick on me.

Except none of them were werewolves and tried to make out with me.

"I think you look beautiful Jeremy," Janice continued.

"Thank you. I do wish I was a bit manlier though. I hate to say it but there have been times when I was confused for a girl."

Janice giggled and Elizabeth smiled.

"So, tell me Diane, what of the boy's father?" Frank asked.

Mom didn't flinch or show signs of distress at the question. She had been asked it many times before.

"His father left when Jeremy was born. He sends us money every once in a while but we never see or speak with him."

I stared at my plate. My father was a sore subject at the best of times. I have never met my old man. Sure he sends us money; his way of making up for being absent I guess. Mom still has a thing for him, every time she gets his checks in the mail she gets really sad.

It's one more reason for me to hate his ass.

"Oh, I am sorry to hear that, forgive me for bringing it up," Frank said sounding sincerely apologetic.

"It is okay. I know it seems bad but I can't complain, after all, I got Jeremy out of it," mom said giving me a warm smile.

After I finished my plate Richard stood up. "Mom, dad, can Jeremy and I go up to my room? I want to show him my new game."

"If it is okay with Jeremy sure," Janice said.

I looked at mom and she nodded. I got up and thanked Janice for the dinner. I followed Richard to his room, leaving mom to talk with the Farkas family alone.

Richard's room was on the first floor, and it had a window that showed the backyard. I saw they had a magnificent garden with different kinds of flowers growing.

A part of me wanted to go out there and inspect it more closely. If my grandmother was here, she would fall in love with it instantly.

Richard's room was big and fit for a king. A seventy-inch plasma screen TV with surround sound and a game console was set up against the wall across from his king-size bed. He had his own bathroom and there was a bookcase filled with books. I never pegged him as a reader.

He had a large stereo system with an assorted collection of CD's. The room had posters of famous football players and it was a bit messy.

I spotted a wooden guitar propped up next to his dresser.

I had this image in my head of Richard playing a tune and maybe singing a song. It made me smile a little to think about it.

He closed the door behind me and turned to face me.

"Alright, time to talk," he said.

12

Richard

My wolf was giddy because our mate was in our den now!

But I kept the bastard under lock and key, I was not going to let him screw things up like last night.

Jeremy stood there, looking so serene and angelic. But I could smell he was nervous, his heartbeat was a little faster than it had been when we were eating dinner.

I did not like he was scared to be alone with me, but after last night I don't blame him.

"So...is it okay to talk? I mean your-"

"Our rooms are insulated. We can't hear what is going on in the bedrooms unless we are right outside the door," I explained.

Super hearing can be useful but it sucks to have when you hear things you don't want to hear.

"Oh...so...how are you?" he asked.

"Good. The moonflower helped cure me. But you knew that."

"Still, I haven't seen one of your people hit with wolfsbane before. It was scary."

"Yeah, it's some nasty shit....listen...about last night. I am sorry, I fucked up bad...I didn't mean to do that to you...it's just....fuck," I spluttered.

"So, any luck finding Joseph?" he asked quickly changing the subject

"Like they said, no. He is a professional Hunter, knows how to stay hidden," I griped.

I walked up to him until we were about a foot apart. "But what I want to know is how you know about us?"

Jeremy sighed. "Can we sit?"

"Sure."

We sat on my bed, my knee was touching his but he didn't move his leg, my wolf took that as a good sign.

Touching him made me feel more relaxed.

"Did you know there is a wolf pack in Cambridge?" he asked.

"Yes. We have had a few dealings with them," I nodded.

"Well...God I can't believe I am talking about this. Just....don't judge me okay?"

My wolf and I didn't like the sound of that. Why would we judge him? What could he possibly have done to deserve to be judged?

"Jeremy, you saved my life. I won't be judging you for shit," I smiled.

"Good. Not that you have the right seeing how you were about to rape me," he scolded, giving me an angry frown.

"I was not trying to rape you!" I growled, "I was asserting my dominance over you to put you in your place."

He gave me a blank look.

"Just tell me how you know! Fuck!" I exclaimed, not liking being reminded of last night.

"Sorry...anyway....before I moved here with my mom, there was this guy-"

Reaaallllly not liking where this conversation was going now.

"-but I broke up with him."

Reaaaaallllly liking it now.

"It is why I moved. See, he was a member of the wolf pack from over there. We went to school together, and we had to keep our relationship a secret."

Cambridge. I knew of several wolf packs in the state, but unlike us, they were of the red tribe, though we were friendly with them.

"Because you were both gay?" I asked figuring it out.

"No....because I was fifteen, and he was eighteen."

"What?" I asked.

"I know, I know. But it was only a three-year difference, and I really liked him. His name is Lucas. I always had a thing for him, he was tall with dirty blonde hair and blue eyes and was a member of the lacrosse team and he was popular. I never thought he was interested in me; turns out he had a thing for me. He said I was one of the most beautiful people he ever saw."

I took a deep breath and fought the urge to growl. Though I did have to compliment Lucas on his taste. But when Jeremy talked about him he got this dreamy look on his face that I didn't like.

"One night some of my friends and I snuck into a party he and his friends were having. We were caught, but he hid me away while my friends were tossed out. I was so scared, and I didn't know what was going to happen. I was afraid he was going to get his friends and they would kick the shit out of me or something. Instead, he told me he liked me and wanted to go out with me. But it had to be in secret and I said yes. We would go out on dates, mom never knew, if she did she wouldn't approve. After he graduated I was afraid he would break up with me because I was still in high school, but he didn't."

My hands clenched into fists, I felt such a powerful feeling of jealousy over this asshole.

"It was on our first anniversary that he told me what he was. He transformed right in front of me and of course I was freaked...but I loved him and I learned to accept it. He introduced me to his friends, and they accepted me as a human member of their pack. We still kept our relationship a secret from the older wolves though his dad Kent knew. He wasn't too thrilled about his son dating a human male but he was nice enough and advised us to keep it a secret.

"But eventually the whole pack found out. It seemed like every other day he was being challenged by some asshole who thought he was weak for loving not only a human but a guy. But Lucas always put them in their place. Yeah everything was going great, absolutely perfect."

"So what happened?" I asked.

He took a deep breath. "He...was chosen to marry a woman from another pack."

"Oh."

"I guess his pack and another pack decided to merge. According to their traditions, the children of the Pack Kings had to mate and produce children from their union, an arranged marriage to ensure peace and happiness between the two groups."

I was not an expert of the red tribe's rituals and rules. Each of the tribes had their own traditions, and I knew some of them would arrange a union between certain wolves to ensure a proper pact between their two packs.

"When I found out I freaked, I tried to get Lucas to find a loophole, this wasn't going to be a once in a lifetime hook up. It was going to be permanent; they were going to be married as according to their werewolf traditions."

"What did he say?" I asked.

Jeremy took a deep breath. I could hear the change in his heartbeat. I could smell his scent change. My wolf whined, it did not like that he was hurting, it wanted to hold him, to wrap him up in our scent and keep him safe and happy

"He was ambitious, wanted to be the Pack King one day, mating with her would help him achieve his goal. Plus he wanted kids and since nature made that impossible with me he had to do it the old natural way with someone else. Plus he was under a lot of pressure; he was Kent's only son, so it fell on him. If he didn't do it, it could be seen as an act of war."

He wiped a tear that fell down his face and continued his story.

"I tried to understand, I tried to accept it, but I couldn't. I really did. Lots of Kent's pack warned me dating a werewolf comes with all kinds of complications and I thought I could handle anything. I had been patient and as understanding as I could be with the other stuff but I couldn't do this. So I broke up with him."

"Oh Jeremy that sucks," I said sympathetically, though a part of me was grateful for the separation.

"It gets better," he said darkly. "Even though I ended things with him, he wouldn't let me go. Said we could still be together and shit."

"But he mated with a female and bred her," I argued.

"I know it's normal for you werewolves to mate for life. But in his pack it is acceptable for werewolves high in the hierarchy to have a lover even if they are married. Since he was an alpha he had the right. He tried to convince me we could do that. We could never marry but we could still go on dates and have sex and could still have our own little family together. In his pack being someone's lover is not seen as a bad thing, especially if they are an alpha."

"How did his mate feel about this?" I asked.

"She was pissed, bad enough he fucked around with a guy, but a human? She is a real prejudiced bitch," he said getting a dark look on his face.

"Did she ever attack you?" I asked.

"No, but she did like to publicly humiliate me and degrade me. She always called me the family pet."

"You deserve to be more than someone's other lover," I noted.

"I know. But Lucas wouldn't let me go...he was calling me and texting me. I tried to avoid him but he wouldn't let me be. His friends took his side of course so they were no help. They encouraged me to take him up on his offer. Both of them."

"Both?"

"Yeah, he started to get real pushy about me becoming a werewolf. See the pack tolerated the fact I knew about werewolves because Lucas and I were together. But when we broke up, they got worried I might do something stupid to get back at him so they wanted me to be changed to guarantee I would not reveal them to the world."

"And he wanted it as well?"

"Of course, he even wanted to do the....what do you call it? Siring? Turning? He wanted to do this himself. I knew he would have a hold on me, he had told me how a werewolf's bond to their creator is powerful. I knew if that happened then I wouldn't be able to deny him anything. Even being the other one you know? I got real depressed and mom noticed. She knew it had something to do with a guy, but I wouldn't tell her. So she decided to move us away."

I felt a new level of respect for Diane. She was willing to uproot her whole life for the sake of her son. Even though she wasn't fully aware of the details, she knew Jeremy needed some place better.

She really did love her son.

"Didn't he know you planned to move?"

"Well we kept it secret. By the time he did find out it was too late. I didn't tell him where we were going. I wrote him a note telling him I still loved him but I couldn't be with him anymore. I wished him and his wife well and haven't seen him since we moved."

"You were too nice to him!" I growled.

My wolf was enraged as was I. How dare this fucker hurt our Jeremy! He should have fought for him! After all the shit Lucas did to him Jeremy still obviously had feelings for him and even hoped he had a happy life!

I wanted to hunt this bastard down and rip his throat out! I wanted to bathe in his blood and bring his skin as a prize to Jeremy!

"Richard...what's wrong?" he asked looking worried.

"You deserved better!" I growled.

"It's over now. It doesn't matter," he said softly.

I took his hand in mine and stared into those pain filled beautiful eyes.

"I mean it! He had no right to ask you to share him! A real wolf would never hurt someone he loved. In our pack there is no other lover. Sure, we fuck around and date and shit but when we marry or find that special someone, we never let anyone else into our heart or our life!"

Jeremy smiled. "I wish they were more like that in Cambridge....but now...I think it is your turn to explain. Why are you so....bizarre around me? Why did you attack me in the woods?"

I took a deep breath. I was going to tell him everything.

Lucas made the mistake of lying to him and hiding the truth. I would make no such mistake.

*****

Jeremy

"I need you to listen to me and not interrupt okay?"

"Alright," I said.

"What do you know about soulmates?" he asked.

"You mean like true love?"

He nodded.

"Well I know of the concept."

"When a werewolf finds his or her mate, it's like...being hit by lightning. Everything about your soulmate calls to you. Their scent, their voice, everything. I found my soulmate recently."

"Okay but what does that have to-"

It hit me then. The odd behavior, the kissing, the sniffing, the touching.

I knew werewolves could be very tactile. Most people would mistake their actions for something intimate. The werewolves from Lucas's pack were not as bad as Richard but they could still be touchy feely with me.

"I'm...your soulmate?" I asked.

He nodded. "That day I saw you I didn't know what was wrong. I caught your scent, and it was driving me crazy but I couldn't figure out why I was so drawn to it. Then I saw you during lunch and...well...like lightning."

When Richard finished his story, I was stunned.

"So...we're soulmates?" I asked.

"I believe so," he said grimly.

"And last night.....was what? A dominance thing?"

"Something like that. Wolves and dominance go paw in paw. When you defied me about the clothes and I saw you dancing with those sluts I just...flipped. I wanted to show you who you belonged to, I wanted to mark you, claim you. But I snapped out of it when you were crying. Then the Hunter showed up before I could explain myself," he explained.

He ran his hands through his hair.

"I need you to know what I did...there is no excuse. But I wouldn't have hurt you Jeremy. I wasn't trying to force myself on you-he made a gagging sounds when he said that-I would never do something like that. But you make me lose control. I have been trying to fight it but it's only made things worse. I've been treating my friends like shit, even Mary knows something is up."

I stood up off and so did he.

"But...what about Mary?" I asked. "What about your feelings for her?

It was obvious she adored him. The way she looked at him screamed love.

"I....care for her....but not like you. I have tried to make it work with her, but now the spark that was between us is gone...I can't even get hard without thinking about you," he replied.

"Too much info," I grimaced.

"It's true! I really have tried, I have done everything with her I normally do," he complained.

"Even sex?"

"Yes."

I flinched and felt a bit upset at that bit of knowledge. "Does she know?"

"Are you insane? She would go bat shit crazy if she did," he uttered.

"Does anyone else know?" I asked.

"Liz, she is too damn perceptive. But that's all, and that is the way we have to keep it. Our pack is a lot stricter about humans knowing the truth than the Cambridge pack."

I nearly told him how *strict* Lucas's pack could be. But I doubt telling him the only reason I am alive is because Lucas (whose dad was the Pack King) protected me would go over well.

Lets just say more than one of his pack mates protested not only our relationship but the fact Lucas told me about their existence.

"Dare I ask what happens?" I asked.

"The human must be silenced, turned or may stay human if they are mated with a werewolf or have werewolf family members. Sometimes we may let humans know if they can be useful to us."

"Could I be useful?"

"Are you rich or have connections that would benefit the pack?"

"I run fast." I shrugged. "And I take pictures."

"....That would be no then," he said giving me a dry look.

"So...what do we do?" I asked.

"Fuck if I know, you're the first and only guy I ever wanted," he grumbled.

"But why me? What is so special about me?" I wanted to know.

"Well....you are just beautiful," he answered.

"Really?" I asked grumpily, "why is it always beautiful? Why can't it be...I don't know, good looking?"

"You are." He walked up to me, and rubbed my soft cheek with his rough knuckles, enjoying the feel of my smooth face. "Your skin is white, smooth, and flawless. Your eyes are warm and burn with an inner strength and they are unlike any shade of blue I have ever seen; like violets." He brought his other hand up and began to run it through my hair. "And your hair is like black silk, smooth and strong."

His hand went from my face to my stomach, feeling that nice six pack I had. "You may look soft but you are tough; tough enough to fight anyone who disrespects you, tough enough to fight someone bigger and deadlier than you. You are far from weak."

He began to lean down, his sights set for the side of my neck where he had bit into last night.

"Richard?"

"Shhh, let me try something," he said gently.

He leaned down and put his face into the crook of my neck, his breathing became shallow and he took a deep breath.

"Gods your scent! If you were a blanket, I would wrap you around me wherever I went, if you were a cologne I would wear you every day, if you were a flower I would scatter your seeds so I could smell you wherever I went....I...I try to fight it...I really do.....but fuck, my will is slowly breaking Jeremy. I can't keep fighting this hold you have on me."

He kissed my neck softly, then his tongue snaked out and began to lick the spot on my neck that was still tender.

I pulled back suddenly, leaving him whining for more.

"Richard, stop!" I yelled rubbing my neck.

I didn't need any more hickies after last night.

He took a step forward. "More," he whined.

"Richard, please...our parents are here," I said gently.

He took a deep breath and seemed to control himself.

He raised his hands up in surrender. "Sorry...see, you make me lose control. Just like last night, my wolf took over, and I used my power to control my friends into helping me. Thank Gods they don't remember," he said.

"What I felt last night, was that because of our connection?" I asked him.

"What do you mean?"

"I remember feeling this...need. A terrible longing that was eating me up from the inside. I was like putty in your hands Richard."

"Tell that to my balls," he said with a grimace.

I rolled my eyes. "Well I snapped out of it, thank God."

"I don't know, maybe it was because of our connection. My grandmother gave me books to read. Maybe they can tell us something."

"Richard...this can't happen," I told him.

The color drained from his face. "What?"

"Richard....I am still recovering from a bad break up where my heart was broken into a thousand pieces," I explained.

"Then let me help you fix it," he started.

"I can't, Richard. You are with Mary, this isn't fair to her," I reminded him.

"So? What is she to you? God knows she has a low opinion of you."

"Mary had a low opinion of everyone. I know she is an A-Class bitch, but she deserves more than this. I know what it is like to be someone's other lover," I retorted.

"Then I will dump her."

I stared at him in shock. He said it so nonchalantly as if breaking her heart was not a big deal.

"You don't have to be so casual about it, she loves you, even I can see that," I persisted.

"But I don't....I care for her, we have history but...I can't keep pretending like everything is the same. I lost the feelings I had for her," he confessed.

"God this is so fucked up!" I hissed.

This was worse than I could have imagined.

I left Cambridge because my last relationship with a werewolf went terribly bad, now I was involved in another romantic triangle.

"Tell me about it," Richard mumbled.

"Are you sure I am your soulmate?"

"I am sure, I asked my grandmother. She is a shaman and an elder. She doesn't know I was asking because I found you, we told her it was because of another wolf friend," he replied. "My symptoms are just like a wolf who has found his soulmate."

"But what about your pack? When Lucas's pack found out a few actually challenged him, said he was weak for loving another guy."

"I don't care. It is inevitable for me to get into fights. Werewolves fight each other all the time to prove they're more dominant or stronger. I am an alpha after all."

"We still can't Richard."

He took my hand in his. "Tell me you don't feel something; tell me there isn't a part of you that feels a pull."

"There isn't," I insisted.

"You can't lie to me Jeremy, werewolves are good at sensing lies," he said.

"Alright fine! I think you are simply magnificent, I think you are breathtaking, mouth-watering and very pleasing to the eye. But I don't just go and date guys because I find them attractive. I am not ready for a relationship," I stated.

A whine escaped his lips, and he bit his tongue. Richard didn't whine.

"Look, I am sorry, I didn't mean to screw with your life, all I wanted was a fresh start from how fucked up my life became. I can't just date a guy after I just broke up with someone I loved with all my heart. I don't think I can trust anyone now."

"But you can trust me; I would gladly do anything for you."

His voice was raw and honest, like a child desperate for someone to believe him.

I shook my head. "You want to be Pack King? Well you can't make promises like that. You can't be loyal to the pack and be willing to do whatever I want to make me happy."

He took my hand in his and squeezed it gently.

"But if we are together, then the pack couldn't hurt you. Lots of humans who do know are family or lover to my kind. Lots of Pack Kings have had human mates."

I pulled my hand out of his. "Listen to yourself!" I snapped. "You're talking about dumping your girlfriend for some guy you just met!"

He was about to say something when there was a knock on the door.

"What!" he snapped.

The door opened and Liz came in. "Got bored, I want to play with Jeremy," she said.

She walked over to me and grabbed my arm and pulled me to the door.

"We're having a private conversation Liz!" Richard growled.

"You can't hog him all night, it's my turn now." she continued to drag me out the room, shutting the door as we left.

*****

I was still in shock.

One minute I am being told I am someone's soulmate, now I am in Elizabeth's room being used as a doll.

She took me to her room which was more lavish and decorated then Richard's. Her bed was a four poster bed with scarlet drapes and silk sheets.

She had me standing up and was taking my measurements, a note pad in one hand and a tape measure in the other.

"Sorry about Richard, he doesn't know when to quit sometimes," she said.

"So...you're cool with the whole thing?" I asked.

"Jeremy, I have had my fair share of lovers, both men and women, so I am not going to judge either of you. Besides, I think it is kind of romantic. Finding one's soulmate and having to fight for that love."

"But what if your parents find out?" I asked.

"Well, I think my mom would understand; she is more open minded and understanding like our grandma. Dad on the other hand, would flip his lid. I sometimes wonder how such opposites could fall in love, but hell, if they could, why can't you and Richard?"

"I don't love Richard," I said.

"But you feel something. I can tell," she said with a grin.

"Alright so I think your brother is hot, but he is a jerk to," I grunted.

She smiled. "Duh, you think I don't know that," she agreed. "He can be loud, cocky, arrogant and full of himself, but he can also be protective, loyal, hard working and honorable. We all have our good parts and our bad parts."

She finished writing down my measurements.

"There, now I can work on your new clothes," she explained.

"You don't need to buy me clothes," I said.

"Buy, make whatever. I love fashion; I am always buying clothes and then tweaking them to the way I like. I want to be a clothes designer one day, make my own line and everything," she said with a dreamy smile.

"Elizabeth...what am I going to do? About Richard?" I asked.

"Nothing much you can do, you guys are soulmates. True love and all that, it can't be broken or stopped. It's like a tiny snowball rolling down a mountain, gaining more momentum and more snow, getting bigger and bigger until you have a snowball the size of a boulder that smashes everything in its way."

"But...I am not ready for love."

"Because of Lucas?" she asked.

I looked at her, shocked. "How-"

"I was listening outside the door."

"But Richard said-"

"He said we can't hear anything unless we are right outside the door and I was curious," she stated simply.

"So...you know?"

"Everything? Yes. But don't worry, I can keep a secret. Maybe this will be good for both of you. You will be able to keep Richard in line and whip him into shape and Richard can give you the strength and support you need. You complete one another; you both fill a space in the other's life that you both need."

I sighed. "This is all complicated."

"Hey, cheer up. It's not like it is the end of the world. Besides, you have me to help you out. You didn't think I was going to let you do this all by yourself, right? I mean, we don't want a repeat of last night do we?"

"He told you?"

"Of course. He was distraught; he hated himself for hurting you, for forcing himself on you. He begged me to help him get better control, and my brother never begs," she shared.

She wrote some notes down on her paper.

"He never cries. But he did that as well to. Poor thing. I didn't even have the heart to chastise him."

I admit it did pain me to hear all that. I knew Richard did feel guilt for what happened. Even experienced werewolves could lose control of their instincts from time to time. I had seen it in Lucas's pack.

"So what do I do?" I asked.

"Well, try to be understanding of him. Also, don't look him in the eye. You know we consider that a challenge right?"

"Yes, I did learn a few tricks from Lucas," I said.

"Lucas wasn't your soulmate. Werewolves are very possessive; it's a mix of our wolf and human parts. The more we care for something the more we are protective of it and since you are Richard's soulmate, he is going to be super protective and possessive of you."

"God, Lucas was bad enough, I can't imagine what Richard will be like," I sulked.

If Lucas smelled the scent of a guy who I just bumped into he got territorial.

"He'll be intense. So, if you do decide to pick a fight with him and we know you will, you must not look him in the eye. Also, if you do piss him off, and we both know you will, show him your throat."

"A submissive gesture," I said.

"Bingo. It will help sooth him, also...you will have to spend a little time with him."

"What?" I gasped.

"Just enough to keep him complacent. That is why he was so worked up last night, all this time he wasn't around you, talking to you, touching you; it got him all wound up. You need to pacify the wolf, keep it nice and docile so it doesn't take over him and a repeat of last night happens."

"But what...what if I decide to date someone? I mean, no way he will like that right?"

"Well, there are no other gay boys in town, trust me, so that solves that problem."

"But I can't just go along with this." I croaked.

"Look, this isn't just about you. If the other wolves find out, they will be all over Richard, challenging him. And need I remind you we have rules about humans knowing about us," she said. "I am not trying to get you to go out with him, I am saying help him keep his shit together."

I sighed, wishing we had moved to another town.

"Hey, cheer up. Being my brother's soulmate has its perks. He is good looking, rich and will one day rule the Wolf Fang Falls pack. Face it tiger, you've hit the jackpot," she said with a cheery smile.

I gave her a funny look. "Isn't that from Spider-Man?"

She shrugged. "I know a thing or two about comics."

"Alright, then let me bring up the most obvious problem. Mary."

She bit her lower lip. "Yes she will definitely be a problem. We'll have to keep an eye on her. But don't worry about her. At least yet. Just focus on Richard."

"What about the Hunter?" I asked, "isn't he still running around."

"Let *us* worry about him. Sooner or later he'll show himself and when he does." she lifted her left hand, and I watched as her nails turned into three inch long claws. "We'll nail the son of a bitch."

How could such a pretty smile be so sweet, yet so scary?

13

I sat in my room.

It was little past ten now, mom and Janice kicked it off real well. They were now planning on getting a mani-pedi in a few days.

I lay on my bed, thinking about my situation.

I was supposedly the soulmate for an alpha male werewolf who dreamed of ruling his pack one day. This had to be kept a secret because the other wolves could use it as an excuse to challenge Richard, seeing it as a weakness. And then there were also the personal complications it could cause him as well.

And if the werewolves found out I knew the truth, they would either kill me or turn me, but if I was with Richard as his lover then I could stay human but I would have to be his mate.

But....I didn't love Richard.

Sure, maybe I did feel something for him. But I wasn't ready to be in a relationship, let alone one with another werewolf, not after how the last one ended.

To top it off, there was a psycho werewolf hunter running around and I might be on his shit list for ruining his plan to kill Richard.

Great, just fucking great.

I know this would be perfect for other people. But I am not ready for love and I don't like the idea of being forced into something.

If I am going to be with a guy it has to be because I want to. Not because I have to.

There was a tapping sound on my window.

I looked up and my jaw dropped when I saw it was Richard. He was outside my window. I got up and opened it and he climbed in.

"What the hell!" I growled at him.

"I wanted to see you," he explained.

"Okay, this is a little creepy, you sneaking into my house in the middle of the night."

"Hey, you let me in," he said.

He had me there.

"Well I didn't want the neighbors to see you," I muttered.

We stood there for a few seconds. He looked around the room, taking everything in. His eyes fell on the clothes he got me that were neatly stacked on my dresser and his lips curled into a smile.

"So, what can I do for you?" I asked.

"I wanted to say...sorry."

"For?" I asked.

"For last night....for tonight. I didn't mean to be pushy. This is all new for me too," he said.

"And you couldn't wait until tomorrow to say this?" I questioned.

He got a frustrated look on his face, then he opened his mouth like he was going to say something, but then he bit his lip.

"I just...wanted to make sure you were okay is all," he mumbled. "That Hunter is still running around and I needed to know you were safe."

"This is one of those weird werewolf things isn't it?" I wondered.

"Yeah, pretty much," he replied.

"Figured."

"So, I see you still got the clothes I got you," he noticed. He walked over to my dresser and grabbed the red briefs in his hand. "Don't suppose I can get you to put these on now?"

"Don't suppose you want me to toss your ass through the window," I replied.

"Right. Maybe one day then." he put the briefs down. "So...your dad's a dick huh?"

"Wow...way to bring up a touchy subject Mr. Sensitive," I said dryly.

"Sorry, I just want to know more about you is all," he remarked.

"To answer your question, yes. Though I have never met him, I can say he is a dick. Mom still loves him though; she gets sad when I bring him up so I don't talk about him to her anymore. She says I look a lot like him, except his eyes are a lighter shade of blue."

"Sorry. My dad can be a dick too but at least he is around," Richard said.

Actually I can see why Richard is the way he is after meeting his dad. He was more polite than Richard but he was so rigged and stony.

"So what about you? Care to share any secrets with me?" I asked.

"Well, I am part Native American. My grandma is the pack shaman and Liz is my twin sister. I plan on being the Pack King one day. My favorite colors are red and violet. I like to watch sports   shows, and work out and hang out," he announced.

"What about college? What do you want to do besides being Pack King? I know they can have a normal, human job," I remarked.

"Well I want to go to college, but my dad wants me to stay here. Says college is pointless and being a Farkas, my financial future is secure. He says I need to start making more friends in the pack, getting support and shit you know?"

"I want to become a photographer. I love taking pictures. I get it from my grandfather."

"Where do your grandparents live?" he asked, "back in Cambridge?"

"No, they both passed when I was younger."

"Sorry."

"It's okay. I still have his old camera. And a box of pictures he took over the years."

"And is that all you want to do with your life?" he asked.

"Well, I plan to settle down one day and spend my life with someone."

He walked up to me and took my hand. "Spend it with me," he said gently.

"Richard," I said tiredly.

"I will take care of you Jeremy; you would live with me in my home with a whole pack to help protect you."

"I have heard this speech before Richard, and last time it didn't end so well," I reminded him.

"Lucas was weak, I am not. No one tells me whom I can breed. Our pack is too big and strong to be challenged," he told me.

"Let's...give me some time okay?" I begged.

"Okay...but I have something for you."

He reached into his pocket and handed me a leather cuff bracelet. It had a crest with the image of a white wolf holding a green and red sword in its mouth.

"I meant to give it to you last night but then everything went to shit."

He gently grabbed my right hand, his thumb gently rubbed my wrist.

A warm feeling spread up my arm and to my chest.

He smiled, sensing no doubt the effect he was having on me.

He took the cuff and placed it on my wrist and gently snapped it on.

"Thanks." I smiled as I admired it.

"Wear it. When a wolf takes a human under their wing, they give them a token like this to show the other wolves that human is under a wolf's protection. It's my family crest, so if one of my pack sees you wearing this they will know you are under my protection."

"Won't they think that is a little odd?" I asked.

"No, sometimes one of our kind becomes attached to a human, forms a friendship. So to keep them safe from others of our kind, we give them items like jewelry or cloths so no one else from the pack will dare bother them. This way I will know you are safe from my pack," Richard explained.

"Is your pack dangerous?" I asked.

"No...well, not all of them. It will keep my friends at school from messing with you," he stated. "After you saved my life no one will be surprised if I offer you my protection. I owe you a life debit now."

"Well, this is a bonus," I joked, remembering how rough his friends had been with me in gym.

I admired it. It looked good on me.

Richard seemed pleased I liked it.

"It looks good on you," he smiled.

You read my mind.

"Thanks," I responded softly.

He turned to head out the window.

"Richard," I called to him.

He turned to face me. "I...I am sorry...for messing up your life. Believe me, I didn't mean to do this," I said.

He smiled. "I know. But I am glad it did happen."

I watched him jump out the window. I went to close it and saw him walking off. He turned back to look, and me and waved.

I closed the curtains and sighed. I looked at the leather wrist band.

"Why can't I meet a nice human guy for once?" I asked myself.

Seems like only yesterday Richard was glaring at me and being a moody bastard. Now he us saying were soulmates and planning our future.

I still wasn't sold on this soulmate thing. And I doubt moving again would solve my problems. I had a feeling no matter where I went Richard would follow me.

I decided to call it a night.

As I got into my bed and turned the light next to my bed off I realized I was still wearing Richard's cuff.

I didn't even bother taking it off.

*****

Joseph

I sat my suitcase down on the bed and opened it up.

Thanks to that little bastard I now had the whole county on my ass!

I saved him from that monster and this was how he thanks me? Probably one of those brainwashed idiots who think werewolves are they're friends.

I pulled out my gun case from the suitcase and opened it up.

I had already closed the window curtains so no one could look inside and see what I was doing.

I was far from done though. I was going to wait awhile until things cool down. I needed to visit some friends and see if I could get some help.

I would have preferred to do this solo, but now that my cover is blown I am going to need a new plan.

Those other Hunter dumb fucks are to blame for all this. They should have exterminated the werewolves not made this stupid treaty with them.

What does it matter what tribe they come from?

They're all monstrosities and perversions of nature.

I used to believe in the code, in the rules of our order until it got my sister killed.

She was sent on a job to investigate killings going on in a town of supposedly peaceful werewolves and was murdered.

The killer was never caught. The pack claimed it was a rogue wolf that did it and he left but he left before they could catch him.

But was there an investigation?

Did our fellow Hunters send in more to try to find him?

No.

They closed the case and when I went down there to find out the truth and refused the order to return I was forced with a choice.

Stay and be kicked out for disobeying orders or let it go and trust the investigation had run its course.

Obviously I chose to stay and find out what the hell happened.

I captured the Pack King and tried to get the truth from him. But his pack found us before I could learn anything more.

I had been too sloppy, I had left a trail in my eagerness to learn what happened. A rookie mistake, I had allowed my emotions to cloud my judgment.

He gave me the same bullshit story of a member of his pack going rogue. I demanded the location of her killer but he said he had already left outside their territory and they could not track him.

I had to run before I could put a bullet in his head and have been looking for the monster that killed her.

I found him eventually after killing a lot of wolves but I found him.

He had formed his own pack. A bunch of misfits and runaways easily seduced by the lure of a demon dog.

I called some friends I had made in my time tracking him down and we killed him and every werewolf he made.

But I didn't stop there.

I have been hunting and killing monster ever since. Because monsters don't care about rules or human lives. A monster is an evil thing that needs to be killed.

And I've killed my fair share of monsters.

Hell, I'll probably spend the rest of my days hunting them until one of the bastards finishes me off.

Many would call me a fool or a murder. They would ask me why keep doing it even after I avenged my sister.

Because even when we sacrificed our lives for the good of the people they just forgot all about her.

They were just wiling to believe those wolf fucks when they said she was killed they were willing to let them hunt her killer down.

They pissed on her memory and all the hard work she put into her job.

How can I go back now? How can I forget such a sin?

I was born and raised to hunt werewolves; we were expected to do what our forefathers did because we were supposed to be humanities defense against the werewolves.

And what did all those generations of sacrifice amount to in the end?

Not a fucking thing.

So I will keep killing as many as these demons as I can. Because killing is all I have left now.

Because there was once a time I wanted to be something more than a Hunter of werewolves. But my father told me and her we had a duty, a lineage to uphold.

He told us Hunters were a family; we train together, we fight together we die together. Well my family turned their backs on her and on me.

So fuck them all.

They're not Hunters. They're just a bunch of fat bureaucrats who forgot why we are here.

I know my place in the word and it's not with them.

It's out there, finding werewolves and ending them.

14

Jeremy

By the time I got to school on Monday everyone had heard what happened. I was the center of attention, everywhere I turned people were asking me for details.

Come lunchtime I was tired of having to repeat myself.

I sat with my friends. We were talking about the party; they were once again telling me what happened with them while everything went down.

"We tried to find you but then the police showed up and we thought they were busting the party, but then they said we had to return home and then the paramedics showed up," Heath explained.

"You must have been so scared, God I can't imagine what I would have done," Heather shuddered.

"The worst part is there is a curfew now. Until they catch this psycho, we can't go out anymore," Rachel complained.

"Bad enough there wasn't anything to do around here anyway," Gabe said with a frown.

"I'd rather be safe in my home instead of running around when there is a mad man running loose," Heather said.

"Don't worry babe, I'll protect you," Heath said kissing her cheek.

"Uh...Jeremy....Richard Farkas is looking at you," Rachel noted.

I turned to look at the table where the Commune kids sat. They were all looking at me, but there was one face I did not spot in their group.

Richard was not there.

Liz was sitting among them, she waved and pointed her finger to the side.

I turned and saw he sat at the furthest table on the other side of the cafeteria, all by himself. He was looking at me to. He raised his hand and cocked his finger at me.

"O...M....G....he is beckoning you!" Heather cried in delight.

"Beckoning?" Rachel asked with a laugh.

"Calling, summoning, whatever, he wants to talk to you!" Heather said, bouncing in her seat.

"Maybe he wants to thank you," Gabe said.

I looked at Richard and saw he was starting to get impatient. He was frowning now and was pointing at me and then to his table and waving his hand more urgently now.

"What should I do?" I asked them.

"Go!" they all shouted.

I wasn't sure if I should. It wasn't just my friends and the other Commune kids who noticed Richard's strange behavior. The whole cafeteria noticed as well.

The fact he was not sitting with his friends was odd to all the students, I doubt any of them had seen Richard apart from anyone in his group.

I decided I better go see what he wanted. I remembered Elizabeth's advice on how to deal with Richard. Me not going to sit with him might make him see that as an act of disobedience.

He probably wouldn't start something during lunch, but it's probably better not to risk it.

So I grabbed my food and walked over to his table, painfully aware of the stares and whispers that followed as I made my way over to him.

I sat down next to him. "Hello," I said.

"I see you're wearing the strap," he said to my wrist.

"Yeah, it looks cool," I smiled.

His eyes brightened and the corners of his lips tugged upward at the corners of a smile. I liked him better when he smiled.

"So, how is your day going?" he asked.

"Good. Yours?" I asked.

"Alright. I am dreading the future though," he said.

"Why?" I asked.

"Let's just say I am making some changes in my life. So, what are you doing tonight?" he asked.

"Nothing," I shrugged.

"I was thinking we should...do something," he said.

"Do something?" I repeated.

"Yeah."

I looked over to the other side of the room where the Commune Kids sat. None of them were watching us. But I knew how good a werewolf's hearing was.

But there were so many people between us and them I was sure even the other wolves could not her us amongst the sea of noise that filled the room.

"Like a date?" I asked.

I leaned in and whispered the question to him, not wanting to risk being overheard.

"No."

I didn't need to be a werewolf to know he was lying.

"Richard, we both know it would be close to a date," I remarked.

"I want to be around you more," he said.

"Richard, we went over this," I said frowning.

"I know, but I can't help it Jeremy. I am not asking you to go out with me, just....be around me for a while," he insisted. "Please, I hate to beg. But Not being around you puts me on edge."

I sighed. "Fine. You can come over and hang out. But there are going to be some ground rules," I scowled.

"Okay," he said happily.

"No touching. Unless it is something tame like shaking hands. That means no kissing, no caressing or groping. And for God's sake that means no pushing me against a wall either," I explained sternly.

"Alright," he agreed.

"Also, no licking or smelling me," I continued. "I know that is a polite form of greeting for your people but it creeps me out."

"Alright," he frowned, looking disappointed.

"Hey, don't get all sad and mopey. You're not the one getting sniffed or slammed against a wall," I chuckled.

"Alright, jeez."

I looked over to the table where the Commune kids sat and saw Mary watching us. For a moment I feared she might have heard us but one of her friends got her attention and she turned her head to talk.

"So...you and Mary?" I asked.

"Still together," he said.

"Good."

"So...how about tonight?" he asked again.

I had to hand it to him he was tenacious.

"What about Joseph?"

"Don't worry, I have a plan for that," he stated.

"Oh...okay," I said.

"I will come by your place at six, okay?" he asked.

"Sounds like a plan," I confirmed.

He smiled, and I smiled back. We ate the rest of lunch together and left to head for class when the bell rang. I had some reservations about hanging out with him. I kept telling myself it was nothing, but I knew I was just lying to myself.

I wasn't ready for love, but that doesn't mean Richard and I can't be friends.

And with the risk of his pack finding out I know the truth it's not like I can forsake any beneficial friendships right now.

*****

Daryl

I sat at my desk, going over some documents. I had just gotten off the phone with Rick; they had not found that damned Hunter yet. I did not like the fact that we had not caught him yet.

Knowing there was a lunatic out there praying on my pack angered me. It was bad enough he got poor Wayne and tried to get Richard.

I will not tolerate an attack on my pack. I will find this bastard and rip his throat out with my teeth!

I had already issued a statement to the local news paper about Wayne and we have the whole county trying to find this guy.

I contacted Charles Higgs, the regent for our tribe and told him about the Hunter. He was contacting the Regia Lupus so they could get hold of the Hunters Council.

I doubt they would help, but I was also certain they would not try to avenge him. Once you break the Hunter's rules you are no longer protected by them.

The only reason I even called Charles was because it was protocol. If things got to bad, I could petition for help to be sent. The Regia were always happy to lend a hand when dealing with rogue Hunters.

My phone rang, and I answered it.

"Hello?"

"Sir, it's the Cambridge Pack King on line four," Tracey my secretary said.

"Thank you, hold all calls," I instructed her.

I clicked the button and was transferred to line four.

"Greetings Kent, Pack King of the Cambridge wolves, may the white wolf smile on you," I greeted.

"Greetings Daryl, Pack King of the Wolf Fang Falls pack and may the red wolf give you strength," Kent announced back.

Something must be up for him to call me. Although we were on friendly terms with the Cambridge werewolves, we did not have much contact with them.

"To what do I owe the honor of this call?" I asked.

"I heard of your trouble with a Hunter and I hope your pack is well," he said.

So word of the Hunter has spread already?

I was hoping to have caught the Hunter before the other packs caught wind of what happened. Last thing I wanted was for other Pack Kings questioning my rule or my packs strength.

"Sadly no, one of our brothers was lost and another of our younger wolves was attacked but managed to escape," I replied.

"I am sorry to hear that, may you find the bastard and feast on his bones," Kent voiced.

This Hunter is lucky it is us and not the Cambridge pack after him. The Cambridge wolves were of the red wolf tribe. The red wolf tribe was known for their tempers and their vengeance. Among the five tribes, they were known for their blood thirsty nature.

They were known to...play with those who wronged them before they finished them.

"I thank you Kent, I hope your pack is not facing the same problem," I said.

"No mortal in their right mind would dare attack any wolf from the red tribe. I am calling you to warn you of a potential danger in your area."

I stood up a little straighter.

What kind of threat could Kent know about but I don't? I knew there was a reason for this call.

"Oh?" I asked trying to not sound too interested.

"There is a human in your town who knows of the werewolf people," Kent explained.

"A human?" I asked sitting a little straighter in my chair.

The last thing I wanted was a leak running around, especially when my pack is under threat.

"Yes. He just moved there with his mother; his name is Jeremy Moonvine," Kent continued.

I knew about Jeremy. Being the mayor I was always aware of every soul that came and went in my town. I also know he saved Richard from the Hunter.

And of course Rick had mentioned he got an odd vibe from the boy and I always trusted his instincts.

It would seem once more he was right.

But that causes more questions to be asked now.

Is it coincidence not to long after the boy arrives so does a rogue Hunter?

"Yes, I know of Jeremy. He saved my pack brother from the

Hunter," I remarked.

"Did he?" Kent asked sounding surprised.

"I am aware he came from Cambridge. May I ask how he learned of our kind?" I asked.

Kent sighed. "My son and he were.....acquainted," he said.

I could sense there was more to it than that.

"Please go on," I urged.

"They were intimate for a while and my son told him about our kind. We allowed him to be because he loved Lucas and proved he was trustworthy. But when my son mated with a she-wolf from our sister pack we feared the boy in his fury would turn on us. I pressured Lucas to turn him, but before we could do anything more about it, the boy and his mother left. They told no one they were leaving, but we looked and when we learned where to we realized we could not collect him so I decided to inform you of the situation. I am sorry you had to inherit one of our problems," he finished sadly.

I rubbed the bridge between my eyes and nose. Great, one Hunter and one human with a broken heart.

Just what I need.

"I thank you for this call Kent. Is there anything else I should know about this boy?" I asked.

"He is a good kid; he doesn't cause any problems for anyone. But I thought it better for you to have knowledge of his awareness. It is my understanding that he doesn't know about your people. But given his experience with our kind he might soon become suspicious"

"I thank you Kent, with everything else going on I don't need a human causing some problems."

"You want my advice? Turn him, that boy has a strong will. I dare say he is alpha material. No point in letting his potential go to waste, right?"

I had to hand it to Kent. For him to advise turning Jeremy into one of us instead of killing him showed Jeremy had his respect.

The red tribe value strength. I know Kent well enough he would not just recommend a transformation regardless of Jeremy's history with his son.

"I will take that under advisement. Thank you Kent."

"I hope your Hunter problem is solved soon. If you ever need help, give us a call. We love hunting Hunters."

I could hear the smile in his voice.

"No thank you, we got this," I said with a friendly tone.

"Very well. Take care Daryl."

I hung up the phone and leaned back in my chair. So the Moonvine boy knew, huh? That was going to be a tricky situation. He did save Richard but I couldn't let a human who knew about us go running around.

The Cambridge pack feared he might reveal us to the world out of pettiness, yet so far he had not tried to expose us.

Although, it was rather convenient that this Hunter arrives around the time Jeremy does.

I was going to have to have to have a little talk with him and soon.

15

Richard

I admit I was very excited for tonight. A nice night with Jeremy...and company.

I knocked on the door.

After a few moments Jeremy answered, his eyes rounded in surprise when he saw who was with me.

"Richard...you're here...with friends," he said.

Mary, Trevor, Keven, Vivian and Cora stood behind me. I had planned to spend time with Jeremy alone, but since that psycho hunter was still on the loose Daryl had issued an order that no one was to travel alone; it had to be in groups.

When I told them I was going to hang with Jeremy, they gave me blank looks. I never hung out with humans; that was Liz's thing. But I told them Jeremy was okay for a human, and he did save my life and being the new guy hanging with the cool kids would of course help his street-cred.

And of course they saw the bracelet I got him and they wanted to see what was so special about him that I would offer him my personal protection. It was not very common for a werewolf to give a human one, only the humans who were the most useful and trustworthy were given a wolf's protection.

Or if the human is loved by the werewolf but trying to avoid telling them that for now.

Doctors, lawyers or law enforcement personnel were given them; not some new kid in town. They had all pestered me about why I did it, even though I told them I did it to repay him for saving my life. I don't think they bought it. But they didn't question me, they knew better than to press me.

"Hey, I invited my friends, I hope you don't mind," I answered him.

He shook his head. "No, of course not. Come on in," he smiled.

He moved to the side, and we all walked in. We all took our shoes off and they all headed for the living room. But Jeremy grabbed my arm.

"The hell?" he asked jerking his head in their direction.

"I had to, no one is allowed out without having a pack mate with them," I explained.

My arm was feeling all tingly; I was hoping he would keep hold of it for a little while longer. It was the same feeling I got whenever he touched me.

I always wondered if he felt it to. I remember grandma saying how even the humans could feel the connection, just not as strongly as we could because they were not in touch with their animal instincts like a werewolf was.

He let me go, and I almost whined at the loss of contact.

"Great, now I have a pack of wolves running around my house, thanks Richard."

He turned and left to head for the living room. I sighed and followed him. I didn't want the others to be here, least of all Mary. I wanted to have Jeremy all to myself.

But rules are rules.

I just know tonight is going to suck.

It is hard trying to get him to open up when we are alone together but with everyone else here it will be impossible.

When I did ask them to come with me, I had to listen to them all bitch and moan about going over to Jeremy's to hang out before the curfew.

But I managed to convince them and here we were now.

Getting him to open up to me when we were alone was difficult enough.

Getting him to open up when we are surrounded by my friends was going to be impossible.

*****

I wish I could say we were having a good time.

But it was awkward.

We all sat in the living room, and we were all quiet.

The guys sat with their girls and Jeremy sat by himself. He had ordered some pizzas, and we were waiting for them to be delivered.

"So, Jeremy. Where is your mom?" I asked. I was glad the others were being polite at least though Mary had her arms crossed and a very displeased expression on her face.

She had been the most vocal about not coming over here.

"Working, I told her you would be stopping by. Ever since the incident with that psycho in the woods she has been worried about me being all alone by myself," he explained. "I text her every hour to make her feel better."

"That was really cool how you saved Richard," Trevor remarked.

"Yeah, it wasn't that big of a deal," Jeremy blushed.

"What are you crazy? You kicked ass," I praised him.

The memory of him fighting off Joseph sent thrills of pride running through me. I was pleased Jeremy wasn't the fragile china doll people assumed he was.

I had been so afraid he was going to be hurt. But like the Hunter I underestimated him.

Strength is a quality all wolves look for in a mate after all. Knowing he could defend himself relieved me.

He gave me a look that told me to shut up. I knew he was still angry because I had brought the others with me to his house. I had a feeling he was especially uncomfortable with Mary being here, do to our unique situation.

I couldn't invite the others without inviting Mary; she was my girlfriend after all. We did everything together after all.

"Yeah, it was impressive that you were able to defend yourself from a psycho in the woods. I would have figured you'd be helpless as a lamb," Mary remarked innocently.

But you could easily hear the snarky attitude under it.

I frowned at her, not liking how she was talking to him. She had complained about having to come over to Jeremy's house. I told her she didn't have to come with us, but she insisted on it.

"Jeez Mary, way to be a bitch," Keven said giving her a hard look.

"What? Just because he saves Richard one time we have to act like we like him?" she spat.

Jeremy looked down at the ground and I bit my lip so hard I thought I was going to make it bleed. The others started to look uncomfortable, not liking the scene Mary was trying to cause, and I knew it wasn't going to end.

I knew Mary; she had a bad habit of making other people suffer with her if she was in a bad mood or upset.

Now that I think about it there was a lot of things about Mary that bothered me. But until now it didn't seem to matter to me.

I had always turned a blind eye to her behavior in the past.

But why?

Had I really been so in love with her I was willing to overlook her faults for the sake of our relationship?

Had meeting Jeremy truly changed me that I could finally see what I had been purposely blind to this entire time?

"If you don't want to be here than you can leave. He saved my life so if you can't be civil than go!" I said firmly to her.

They all looked at me with surprise. Especially Mary.

We had our little fights now and then but I never took such a tone with her before.

She gave me a sharp look but kept quiet.

Jeremy was looking very uncomfortable now.

I heard the sound of a car pulling up and knew the pizza was here. I reached into my pocket and pulled out my wallet and handed him the money he would need for the pizza.

"For the food," I told him.

"I can pay for it," he said.

I shook my head. "It's fine. You shouldn't have to pay for us all to eat."

"Well it should be here soon," he said taking the money.

Just then the doorbell rang.

"Maybe that's the pizza, I'll be right back."

He got up and left the room.

No one spoke.

Mary was obviously upset. She had her arms crossed and had a petulant look to her face.

"This is a nice house," Cora said looking around the living room. She withered under the glare Mary gave her.

Jeremy walked back in carrying three pizza box's. He sat them on the table.

"I'm going to go get the plates and the soda."

He went into the kitchen and I could hear him moving around. When he came back, he had some cups and paper plates.

We all began to grab a piece of pizza and pour ourselves some soda and began to eat quietly.

Mary did not eat or drink anything, she just continued to sit and sulk but at least she wasn't causing a scene.

"So. What do you like to do?" Keven asked Jeremy.

"I like to run. I like to go camping and walk through the woods and take photos. I did that a lot back in Cambridge," he said.

He nodded. "Yeah, I talk to go camping every once in a while."

"What's your favorite color?" I asked him suddenly.

The question flew out of my mouth, I was hungry to know more about him.

Jeremy gave me a warning look.

"It's blue. I like to wear it because it makes my eyes seem less violet."

"No offense but are you an albino?" Trevor asked. "I read they can have red eyes or violet."

"Mom actually did have me checked to see if I was an albino when I was younger," Jeremy said.

"They're really pretty," Cora said.

"Thanks. I sometimes wish they were not like this. I think it only makes me look more girly," he said.

"They're perfect. Just like the rest of you. You should be happy you have such a unique and rare eye color. It makes you different from everyone else," I said.

"Yeah well different can be very lonely sometimes," he said.

He got this far away look on his face like he was remembering something.

I remember Keven mocking Jeremy for his appearance on his first day at school.

If I hadn't become enthralled by him, I would mock him as well. He was slender and lean with soft and smooth features and a soft mouth on an oval shaped face. And of course those amazing eye of his.

He looked like a Botticelli painting come to life.

Were it not for my feelings for him I would probably enjoy tormenting him for his appearance.

"Maybe you should try working out a little more. If you had some more muscle, you might actually pass for a man," Mary said.

The tension in the room became thick again.

I glared at Mary and everyone else looked between him and her.

Jeremy smiled at her, he lifted up his shirt exposing his stomach to everyone. My eyes focused on Jeremy and his abs.

Vivian let out a whistle.

"Daaaaamn," Cora said leaning forward to check out Jeremy's six pack.

I knew from gym Jeremy looked delicate but underneath his cloths he had nice muscles. I had a strong desire to run my tongue down his abs and learn each and every detail of his stomach.

"I think I am doing pretty good," he said to Mary who was looking at his six pack with surprise.

I grinned at him. How deceptive he was. He looked beautiful and soft. But there was a hard edge to him, he knew how to handle himself both physically and socially.

I learned it myself from all those times he gave me lip and attitude.

"Dude what do you do to get that ripped?" Keven asked.

"I do a lot of sit-ups and pull-ups," Jeremy responded putting his shirt down.

"You lift weights?" Trevor asked.

"I can lift about a hundred pounds," he said.

Trevor looked at him with a new found respect.

Things became a little more bearable now that the others were involving themselves more into conversing with Jeremy.

Cora complimented him on his mothers decorating skills and Vivian asked him about his skills with a camera.

He went and brought down his computer to show us some of the photos he had taken. Everyone-minus Mary- was impressed with his work.

I could tell Jeremy felt more comfortable talking about his love for photography. That was his natural element and he went into great detail about different techniques and styles.

Mary thankfully kept her mouth shut the rest of the time we were there. I was glad Jeremy was getting along so well with my friends.

It made me feel better that they liked him.

Because the day was going to come when they learn what he really means to me.

In fact that day might be coming sooner than I had thought it would.

*****

We got back to the Gates before the curfew. I dropped everyone off at their homes and was on my way to Mary's house.

The tension between us was unbearable. I could sense she was angry right now. It annoyed me she was angry at all after all she was the only one who had made a big deal about being at Jeremy's.   She was the one who had insulted him several times. And yet she was the one acting like the victim.

The others managed to warm up to him. All except her. The longer I was around her the angrier at her I became.

Why did I love her?

I have known her for a long time, she was beautiful and she was popular. She lavished me with affection and I liked how she always got what she wanted.

And yet I was beginning to realize that her faults outweighed her virtues.

She cared too much about popularity and status. When she didn't get her way, she could be so dramatic and childish.

We pulled up to her home, and I waited for her to say something.

"You know it is one thing to take him under your protection but it's another thing to expect us to try to make friends with him," she said coldly.

"What's the big deal Mary?" I asked. "All you had to do was be nice to the guy!"

"Why? He's just a human," she said throwing her hands in the air.

"So, he was nothing but nice to us and you acted like a total bitch!"

Her eyes got wide. "Oh I am sorry I would rather spend my time with my own kind than a human who looks like he doesn't have a dick!"

"What the fuck is your problem?" I asked, "I don't get why you are so upset! You didn't have to come you know."

"So sorry I want to spend more time with my boyfriend after he almost gets killed by some lunatic in the woods!"

"We have been spending time together Mary!"

"Not really!"

"What's that supposed to mean?" I asked.

"It means you're not really there when I am around you Richard! It's been like this before the Hunter showed up! I don't know what is wrong but something has changed between us!" she yelled.

"Maybe I am tired of this!" I yelled back.

"Tired of what?" she asked.

"Of this! Of us! Of you!"

She looked at me, her eyes filled with hurt.

I continued to rant, the anger and frustration that had been slowly building inside of me was starting to spill out.

"Every time you don't get what you want you make everything so fucking dramatic! It's always about you! I don't know why I put up with you for so long! I do so much for you and you can't even play nice for at least a few hours!"

"Richard I-"

I was being hard on her I know, but I was a changed man now. I wasn't saying this just because of Jeremy. Ever since the Hunter I have been reevaluating my life.

Never before had I come so close to death and as I had laid there with the wolfsbane burning through my veins, I looked back at my past.

I thought of how people would remember me; I thought of how I acted and how my actions would dictate how people would remember the kind of person I was.

And I realized that outside of my family and close friends I would be remembered as Richard Farkas, the guy who was from a wealthy family, was popular, good at sports and was a complete and total asshole.

Not the legacy I wanted to leave behind.

"No Mary, it's over between us. We're done," I said.

The second I said the words I felt a sense of freedom. One less obstacle to over come.

"Done! What do you mean?" she asked, her voice becoming hysterical.

"I mean I don't want to be with you no more Mary," I said firmly but not unkindly.

"Richard I'm sorry! Please, lets talk about this!"

I shook my head. "There is nothing to talk about Mary. I hate to do this to you-"

"Then don't!" she wailed.

Tears were running down her face. I could smell the distress she was feeling, her heart was beating hard now.

"I almost died Mary and when I thought about my life I realized...I have a lot of growing up to do. The direction I was going wasn't good for me as a person. You're not good for me."

"I have been nothing but great for you!" she screeched.

"You loved me, you looked good with me. But you never made me a better person. You always encouraged me to be Pack King. But you never tried to get me to be a better person."

"I don't get what you're saying Richard!" she cried.

"Maybe one day you will. I hope when that day comes you understand because you learn there is more to life as well."

"Richard your not making sense. Let's just talk I am sure we can work this out!"

Once we could have worked something out. But that was before the Hunter that was before Jeremy.

"There is nothing to talk about Mary. Get out," I said.

"No! I am not leaving until you tell me what this is all about!" she demanded.

My hands clenched the steering wheel. I was tired of talking. I just wanted to go home now!

"Get out!" I growled.

She looked at me with a pained expression. Then as if she was being physically forced to she got out of my car and slammed the door shut. She just stood there, crying.

I pulled out of her driveway and went home, I looked in the rear view mirror and saw she was watching me as I drove off.

The door to her house opened, and I saw her mom walking out looking concerned.

I drove to my house and sighed as I parked my car, I got out and walked inside.

"So how did it go?" Liz asked as she ate a small bowel of banana flavored ice-cream.

"I just broke up with Mary," I said as I shut the door behind me.

She stared at me with shock, the spoon still in her mouth.

She pulled it out and began to chew. "Well shit, that happened sooner than I anticipated. I thought I smelled soul crushing despair on you. Guess I know where it came from."

"This isn't funny Elizabeth!" I snapped.

"Am I laughing?" she asked.

"I just can't do it anymore. I am tired of pretending everything is okay," I said with a tired sigh.

"Better you do it now instead of later. At least now you can focus more on Jeremy."

I suddenly began to feel a lot better. Now that Mary and I were no longer a thing it would be easier to bond with him.

"But you do realize she isn't going to just give up on you right? Mary does not take rejection well," she said.

I winced.

"She'll find another guy. A girl like her doesn't stay single forever."

Suddenly a howl broke through the night. It was a pain filled call filled with heart break.

"Hell hath no fury like a woman scorned. Remember that," Liz said as she walked off leaving me alone to listen to Mary's howling.

*****

Jeremy

An hour after the Commune Kids left I was getting ready for bed.

I admit it had been awkward having Richard's friends here. Especially Mary. Iit was obvious she did not want to be here.

But it got better talking to them as time passed.

I figured they would have huge egos and be self-absorbed. (if Richard was anything to go by)

But they were not so bad.

As I got ready to go to bed, I sent mom a text letting her know I was going to sleep. Just as I hit send the house phone began to ring.

I frowned when I saw the caller ID said Farkas on it.

I decided to answer and see what Richard wanted. Though I was sure he wanted to talk about tonight.

"Hello?" I answered.

"Hey," he said.

I don't know how, but I knew right away something was wrong with him. There was something about his voice.

"What's wrong?" I asked.

"What makes you think there is something wrong?" he asked after a pause.

"I can tell from your tone. Is everything okay?"

He was quiet for a moment. "Yeah. I...I just broke up with Mary."

I heard the words but I couldn't believe them. "Why?" I asked him.

"Remember earlier I told you I was planning to make changes in my life?" he asked.

I remembered him saying that earlier today. Of course I had not anticipated him to do something so stupid.

"Why in the hell would you break up with her though?" I asked.

"Why do you care? She hates you," he stated.

"Well, I may not like her but that doesn't mean I want her to be hurt," I replied.

"It was going to have to happen sooner or later Jer, better now than later right?"

I felt a stab of irritation when he called me Jer. Lots of people called me that but none of them were Richard.

"Don't you think people are going to think it is funny that you broke up with her all of a sudden?" I asked.

"Hey, it's no one's business Jer an-"

Just then the doorbell rang. I was confused as to who it could be, this late.

"I'll call you back, someone's at the door."

I put the phone on the receiver. Feeling a little nervous I reached under my bed and grabbed my aluminum baseball bat and went downstairs to see who was here.

With Joseph running around I wanted to be ready just in case. Though I doubt my bat would do much if he had a gun.

Then again if it was Joseph, I doubt he would be ringing the doorbell to tell me he was here.

I quietly walked downstairs and peeked out the curtain in the living room. I saw Rick with two other deputies and a guy I didn't recognize but he did look familiar.

I turned on the lights on the living room and went to the front door and opened it.

"Rick? Is everything okay?" I asked looking from him to the others.

"Jeremy, we need to talk son, it's important," Rick stated looking serious.

"What is it?" I asked.

"Jeremy my name is Daryl Farkas; I am the mayor of Wolf Fang Falls," the man I thought looked familiar said.

I realized I had seen pictures of him on the internet when I was doing research on the town.

"Oh...umm...what's up?" I asked.

"May we come in?" he asked.

"Sure."

I moved to the side and let them all in. I noticed the deputies were scenting the air. I knew they were werewolves as well.

"Why are you holding that bat?" Rick asked me.

"Oh, I figured better safe than sorry. What with that psycho still on the loose and it being so late," I said.

He nodded approvingly.

"I'll take that," he said extending his hand.

"Why?" I asked holding the bat closely to my chest.

"You don't need it."

"Neither do you," I fired back.

"Why are you jumpy?

Survival instincts.

"Why is the mayor and sheriff in my house this late at night?"

Rick gave me a sharp look. "Hand it over Jeremy. Now."

The other two deputies were giving me hard looks, I knew one word from Rick and they would spring into action. Daryl was watching with a blank look, merely observing us.

My stomach was tight with anxiety. But I had to try to stay calm. Something wasn't right. But for now I would play nice.

Besides, it didn't matter if I had the bat or not. Any one of them would be able to take me down before I could use it.

I've seen what a werewolf's reflexes are like. If Rick wanted, he could have me flat on my ass with the bat in his hand before I even realized what happened.

I handed him the bat.

He placed his hand over mine firmly.

He gave me a look that was stern, but it was also the kind of look a parent gives their kid that says *behave.*

"May we take this into the living room?" Daryl asked.

"Yes, right this way."

I led them to the living room. Rick and Daryl sat next to one another while the other policemen stood behind me.

I could not see them, but I felt their presence behind me. I knew if they attacked I would not see it coming.

"Jeremy, I wish this was a more pleasant visit, but I am afraid this is rather serious," Daryl started.

"Did...did I do something wrong?" I asked.

Please don't know I know, please don't know I know! Please don't know I know!

I repeated the words over and over again in my head.

"We know you know our secret," Rick said bluntly.

Fuuuuuuuck.

"Secret? What secret?" I asked, trying to play dumb.

Maybe I could fake ignorance.

"Give it up Jeremy, Kent called me and told me your situation,"

Daryl told me.

Kent? Oh yeah, Lucas's dad. Kent had always been nice to me, he didn't exactly approve of my relationship with Lucas, but he was always polite.

I remember the last time he and I talked. He told me despite what was going on with Lucas and his new mate I was still a friend of the pack. Said there was nothing wrong with being his sons lover even if he was married. Alpha privilege and all that.

He even tried to convince me to become a werewolf, said I had a lot of potential.

But becoming a werewolf was nowhere on my list of things I wanted to do with my life. Besides, joining the pack meant I would have to watch Lucas and his mate and their bundle of joy. He offered to make me a werewolf himself that way I wouldn't be manipulated by Lucas into being his....what do you call someone's other lover?

If a woman is a mistress then what would a guy be?

I appreciated his offer, but I refused of course. Not that it matters now.

"Oh, well I guess I am up shit's creek without a paddle," I responded.

"Yes, quite. Normally if a human learns our secret we take care of them immediately," Daryl said simply.

I didn't need to read between the lines to know what he meant by that. When Lucas and I first started going out, he told me the dangers of dating a werewolf.

"But seeing how Kent did say you could be trusted and the fact you did save my cousin's life and the fact Rick here is willing to take responsibility for you, Though I believe it is only because of your mother. I have decided to leave you be...for now."

I remembered then he was Richard's cousin. He had paler skin then Richard but, he was built like Richard. His eyes were sterner looking; more disciplined, and he was more like Frank in his mannerisms.

"However, I can't help but feel uneasy Jeremy. I don't like wild cards in my pack or in my town," Daryl continued.

"I am not a wild card sir, believe me, I don't like drama in my life. It's one of the reasons why I left Cambridge," I said.

"Then tell me Jeremy, who else knows you know our secret?" Daryl asked.

"We can smell other wolves have been here Jeremy, don't lie to us," Rick pointed out.

"Richard and some of his friends were here earlier," I explained.

"I know Richard. He might have felt an obligation to visit you as a favor for saving his life. But he would not have brought his friends."

"Don't lie to us Jeremy. We have rules and if someone broke them, they must face the consequences for it," Rick said

I knew it was pointless to lie to them. The only way one could lie to a werewolf was to have top notch training. I may have been around Werewolves for several years but I was not good enough to lie to a werewolf.

But I knew it was possible to bend the truth. So long as I didn't go into full details. Sometimes the best way to lie was to answer, but leave out a few details.

"I...figured it out on my own, seriously I did," I said. That was true; after Richard was attacked and Joseph was going on about wolfsbane, all the clues seemed to click into my head."

"Well, you are telling the truth. But who knew you knew?" Daryl asked. "I want names."

I sighed, I had hoped I could work around telling the truth by only answering the exact question but obviously that wasn't going to work on Daryl. "Richard and Elizabeth," I answered.

Daryl and Rick shared a look.

"Anyone else?" Daryl asked.

"No," I shook my head.

They stared at me for a few moments.

The tension that had been in this room earlier when Richard and the others were here was nothing compared to the atmosphere now.

My life could very well hang in the balance right now.

One word from Daryl and the deputies behind me would kill me before I knew what happened.

"Very well. I will talk to the elders about this and we will talk more. But for now you may go about your business. But keep in mind we will be keeping a very close watch on you Jeremy. So don't think about leaving," Daryl informed me.

"I won't," I said.

Relief flooded through me. I wasn't going to die.

"Oh and one last thing."

He suddenly had his hand wrapped around my throat. I could feel the tips of his claws pressing against my throat.

It had been so quick, I hadn't even seen him move!

His face was still calm and collected. Though his eyes were now wolfish.

"Are you working with the Hunter Joseph?"

"N-no!" I quickly said.

"Have you in any way helped him?"

"No!" I answered, more forcefully.

"Do you intend harm to my pack?"

"For fucks sake no! I just want to be left alone!" I yelled.

He let go of my neck. I grabbed my throat. I looked over to Rick to see he looked relieved.

"Just had to make sure, you have to admit the Hunter showing up when you did was rather a coincidence right?" Daryl asked.

"And had I lied about any of your questions?" I asked.

"Why ask a question when you know the answer."

They got up to leave, and I saw them to the door. Keeping a good amount of distance between them and myself.

"Daryl...Richard and Elizabeth, they won't be punished will they?" I asked.

I didn't want the twins to suffer because of me. Elizabeth was my friend; strange to refer to her as that because I don't know her very well, but she has been nothing but nice and supportive and was willing to risk the wrath of her pack to keep me safe.

And Richard.....God I just didn't want him to get in trouble at all.

As much as I try to deny it, I do care for Richard. Yes he is cocky, yes he can be egotistical and he can be a jerk, but there is a part of me that can't help but feel right when he holds me, and it does feel right being around him.

"Richard and Elizabeth will be reprimanded, but it won't be too severe. Take care, Jeremy."

Daryl and the two deputies left but Rick remained.

"Does your mom know?" he asked me.

"No, she doesn't know nothing about your kind. And I won't tell her."

"Good," he nodded.

"Rick, Daryl said you were willing to take responsibility for me. It's because of my mom isn't it?" I asked.

"Of course it is. I know Diane wouldn't raise an idiot for a son. So do yourself and her a favor and don't do anything foolish. You're not out of the woods yet."

Before he could walk out of the door I spoke. Maybe I was pushing my luck, but I was feeling pissed and angry about what had just happened.

"Isn't it a conflict of interest?" I asked. "To be the sheriff and enter a mans home and threaten him?"

His back went rigid with anger. He turned to face me, his eyes hard. "I am the enforcer of my pack. Their safety and protection will always come first."

With that he left, tossing me my bat on his way out.

I locked the door and took a deep breath. I walked back up to my room and dialed Richard's number and he answered on the third ring.

"Hey Jer, so-"

"Richard...we need to talk," I interrupted him.

16

Days passed.

It has now been three weeks since I arrived in Wolf Fang Falls and luckily not much has happened.

Richard and Mary are still broken up, which sent waves through the whole school.

Liz told me their father was beside himself. He had high hopes Richard and Mary would marry one day. Mary was part of a well respected family in both the human and werewolf community. He couldn't understand why his son would just break up with a girl he planned to marry.

Of course Richard didn't tell him the truth.

He did get into a fight with her brothers. Mary was the middle child and the only girl and was doted on by her parents and brothers. When they learned Richard broke her heart they immediately challenged him for her honor. Richard won, but barely.

Mary was still in grief. Their split also seemed to cause a division with the Commune Kids. On one side, (the majority of whom were women), were on Mary's side and thought Richard a right bastard for hurting her.

The other side, (made up mostly of men), were on Richard's side. Though they didn't get why he would dump a hottie like Mary, they stood by him. I guess even werewolves have a concept of bro's before ho's.

I spent a lot of time dividing my attention between my human friends, and my new friends I made thanks to Richard.

I made it clear to him I wasn't going to hang out with him all the time and just dump Rachel and the others to be with him and his group. He didn't raise a fuss because he understood which I was thankful for.

When I started dating Lucas, he demanded a lot of my attention and didn't hand out with my friends as much as I used too. Something I regret now and did not want to repeat.

Rachel and the others were happy I wasn't going to dump them for the Commune Kids. They feared I was going to stop talking to them altogether now that I was in Richard's *inner circle* as they liked to call it.

Rachel and Heather loved to pump me for info; asking me what I talked with the Commune Kids about and what it was like being around them.

They weren't the only ones; lots of people were talking to me, asking me about what it was like to hang with Richard and his group.

No one outside the commune was friends with them. Even less could say they had been inside the gated community.

Truth was, Richard and the other kids from the Gates were just like any other group of teens. Sports, cars, women; they all talked about the usual. I got along well with his friends but preferred to listen instead of talk.

Mary still had a thing for Richard. Every time she saw him she would stare at him so hard I was surprised he didn't get a bruise. The look was part anger, part want.

There were times when she would catch my eye and her eyes would turn purely hateful as if she knew I was to blame for Richard breaking up with her.

I hoped to God she never found out. Hell hath no fury like a woman scorned, so imagine what a she-wolf is like.

Richard and I had talked about his decision to end things with her.

He said I wasn't the only reason. Almost dying changed him. Made him rethink things. Made him want to be less of a dick.

The Hunter had not attacked again. Richard said they were thinking he was either long gone or waiting. So far no one else had disappeared so things had lightened up.

It was Thursday, and I was talking to Richard. He leaned against my locker, looking just as devastatingly gorgeous as always. We were still not going out; I still wasn't ready for love though there were times when he came over to my house.

We would talk a little and watch TV. Sometimes he would bring Liz or his other friends.

I was slowly starting to warm up to him.

And he was getting better. Now that he had finally accepted things he wasn't so angry and frustrated and easier to be around.

But Richard was...frustrating. In public he was so cocky, arrogant, charismatic, and full of zeal. But despite our unique relationship he could still be rather prejudiced against humans.

I told him if he wanted us to work he needed to play nice with the other humans. He was trying, but there were times when he would slip and make a comment about how feeble humans were.

He tried to blame it on his wolf nature. "Wolves prey on the weak."

To which I would remind him it was a *human* who almost killed him and it was a *human* who saved him and of course it was a *human* who was his soulmate.

That shut him up.

Yeah, he could be a bit pigheaded in public. But when we were alone, in those rare moments when no one else was around and we were alone, and he would look at me...really look at me, no longer having to hide his feelings...God, I felt like I could faint.

We would watch TV and he would slowly make his way closer to me until our hips were touching and his arm was around my shoulders. When I spoke he listened to every word as if it were some kind of revelation. Yes, there were times when we made out. I wasn't too proud of myself when I gave in to that damn smile, or those plump lips. But we have not had any kind of sex.

Just really hot, steamy make out sessions that made me want to say fuck it and just get my world rocked.

Richard could be a dick, but there was another side to him. There was the side that showed how much he cared for his friends and family, a side that showed him to be brave and caring even.

A part of me wanted to throw caution to the wind and give in to the need, but the other part warned me, reminded me of what happened the last time I did such a thing.

Richard didn't pressure me, cocky bastard was confident I would give in to him sooner or later.

And I do think he is right.

"So, I have a gift for you," he announced.

"Oh?"

Another thing he did for me was buy me stuff. Clothes, electronics, I had to draw a line when he bought me a bunch of scarlet red and navy blue man thongs. He said red looked delectable when compared to the whiteness of my skin and the blue brought out the color in my eyes.

I was tempted to accept his offer to let me use his Mercedes.

He reached into his pocket and handed me a plastic card. It had my picture on it. Next to it was my name, my address and some other details.

"What is this?" I asked.

"Your pass into the Gates. I went to Daryl to get approval and he okay'd it. Now you can visit me whenever you want," he explained.

I quickly pocketed the card. I realized how precious a gift I had. Only those married to a werewolf or who had a special connection to the werewolves were given one of these.

If any of the students found out I had this many of them would try to get me to take them inside the Gates. I wouldn't be surprised if someone tried to steal it.

So I resolved not to tell anyone about it.

"Thanks, I really appreciate it," I smiled.

He took a deep breath and his face become more serious. "So...as you know the fall formal is coming up," he started.

"Yeah, Rachel was talking about it last night," I said.

"Well, I was thinking...we should...go together," he blurted out.

"Okay, I wasn't going to go, but it sounds like it could be fun," I agreed.

He took another deep breath. "I meant as a couple."

I stared at him in shock. I looked around to make sure no one had been listening in.

"Richard...do you mean...like....a couple, couple?" I asked.

He rolled his eyes. "Is there any other kind of couple?"

"But Richard, no one knows about us," I said solemnly.

Well Daryl knew, Richard told him why he and Elizabeth kept me a secret. It was their duty to inform him when a human knew the truth. Daryl knew for them to be willing to put the packs safety in jeperody they had to have a damn good reason. Needless to say Daryl was shocked, but he agreed it best to keep it a secret.

He knew it was a delicate situation and the revelation Richard's soulmate was a human male would cause a huge uproar in their pack.

Richard and Liz's punishment had been a stern talking to by Daryl and they had to do some hard labor for not telling that I knew about werewolves, even f I was Richards soulmate and already knew; Rules were rules.

Mostly they had to help clean up the Gates. Mowing the lawn, trimming hedges, helping the older members who needed a ride or someone to help them buy groceries. Community service stuff.

I had been relieved they hadn't been beaten or something harsh. Lucas's pack were not afraid to draw blood for even minor infractions.

I told Richard about my meeting with Daryl, but I left out the bit where he threatened me. Werewolves were very protective and if I told Richard he might snap and attack Daryl.

Though I had a feeling Richard figured it out himself.

True to Daryl's word I was now under watch. Rick was showing up around my neighborhood more often now. And sometimes when I would leave home I would notice I was being followed.

When I would go for one of my walks, I would notice a cop car following me from a distance. Or parked somewhere close to my house.

No one in the neighborhood, no one thought it odd. They figured it was simply a precaution after the attack and felt better knowing the law was still on alert for trouble.

I may be Richard's soulmate, but I was still a stranger and needed to earn Daryl's trust. So for the time being I was under watch.

"So. It's time they did. I want to be able to kiss you and touch you in public," he spoke up.

"Richard...we're not together," I said gently.

His gaze became heavier. "Aren't we?"

I had to think about it.

"Yes...no....I don't know Richard. I like being around you. You make me feel things I haven't felt since Lucas. But I still am afraid some werewolf bullshit will ruin things for us."

It was true. As much as I wanted to give him a shot I was too worried about going through the same thing I did with Lucas. Sure the rules were different because apparently we were soulmates, but I couldn't bear going through another fiasco like I did with Lucas.

"We're soulmates Jeremy. I have been reading up on our laws. It says that a werewolf's soulmate is by the law of the white wolf herself, a member of the pack and is to be treated as such. No other law, oath, or pact may come between that," he persisted.

"But Richard, what would your dad say? He was so angry when you dumped Mary and I highly doubt he wants his only son to marry a human, let alone a man," I lamented.

"My father is not my boss. I will be with whom I chose, he will have to accept it," he stated defensively.

"But, what about the other wolves? They might challenge you," I remarked.

"So let them, I will be running this pack one day. Everyone knows that."

He smiled that cocky confident smile that both drove me crazy and made me feel at peace.

"Richard...I just....can I think about it?" I asked.

"Sure. Just think about it," he said softly.

He brought his hand up and dragged his thumb across my cheek. "I know this seems so sudden, I am still trying to wrap my mind around it. And I know I wasn't nice to you when you first got here, but I am glad you gave me another chance."

He leaned in close and whispered into my ear, I shivered as his warm breath blew into my ear.

"Take all the time you need Jeremy. I already know what your answer will be."

Smug bastard.

*****

I was walking home, I could have taken the bus, but I needed time to think and walking always helped me clear my head.

What was I going to do about Richard? This soulmate stuff is serious. I try to resist but the more time I am around him the more I find myself falling for him.

Yet I still pine for Lucas; I still miss him even though he broke my heart.

I still think about him sometimes; I wonder how he is doing; if he is happy.

Why can't I have a normal gay relationship?

Lucas was my first love; the boy I lost my virginity to. He was like Richard, popular and loved by all. He has a million dollar smile and a body that was pure perfection. There was also a charm to him, he had charisma and style. You just couldn't help but be drawn to him whether it was his good looks or that aura of excitement and adventure he had.

I mean he told me he was a werewolf. You have to trust someone to share a secret like that; obviously he loved me.

Plus there was also the taboo of our relationship; he was older than me. Our love was wild, spontaneous, intense, forbidden. The kind of love people crave.

But don't all great loves end in heartbreak?

Maybe that was why I was so hesitant with Richard. He and Lucas were a lot alike; they were popular, amazingly handsome werewolves. Maybe I was just projecting my fears onto Richard.

But I can't just let go and give in, I need to be smarter. I can't let my emotions get the best of me. If this thing with Richard went as bad or worse as it did with Lucas, I don't think I could handle it.

Richard says we are soulmates. He says since I am human the attraction is not as strong as it is for him. It takes time to build up.

At first I thought he was just exaggerating. But every second I spend with him I find all my fears and doubts slowly melting away.

Now I am starting to wonder if Richard was telling the truth.

Were we really soulmates?

Were we really destined to live happily ever after?

I thought soulmates was just something romantics made up to give themselves something to fantasize about.

A love so strong it can overcome anything and is eternal. The kind of shit you see on a Disney movie where the princess marries some guy she just met and knows nothing about him yet they make everything work out.

Richard and I did not start off on the right foot. There are a ton of complications and I just don't know if I am ready to deal with them.

I wanted to explore the world and become a photographer, how could I do that if I was with Richard? To my knowledge Pack Kings rarely left their territory.

And I wasn't going to ask him to give up on his lifelong dream.

I was so lost in my thoughts I did not notice the van pull up beside me until the door flew open and I was pulled inside.

I struggled of course, but I felt something hard hit me on the back of my head and I lost consciousness.

17

Richard

"I can't believe you asked him to the dance!" Liz shouted gleefully.

We drove home in my Mercedes. The wind blew through our hair. "Well, I had to do something to show him I am serious about this," I explained.

I had finally come to terms with what has happened. Jeremy was my soulmate. And I wanted to be with him. I was ready to reveal us to the pack.

I was tired of having to hide what we were, I was tired of acting like he was just a friend.

I wanted to be able to hold him and kiss him in public, I wanted us to be able to walk down the halls of our school with my hand around his shoulders while people watched us go by.

I know many people at school were impressed by his good looks.

Many of the girls bemoaned the fact he was gay. And I heard more than a few people make rather nasty comments about it.

I wasn't expecting a warm welcome by the whole town when I announce our relationship. But I swear to the Moon if anyone gets in my face or tries to give Jeremy shit about our relationship I'll make them bleed!

But the biggest problem I had to worry about was my own family. I was sure mom would be okay with it. But dad...Daryl and I both agreed it was best to wait to tell him.

All I wanted was for people to know this beautiful creature made perfect by the gods was all mine. And that I loved him.

"I can't wait; this is going to be the biggest thing to happen to the pack and the town! Richard Farkas, taking another guy to a dance," she gushed. "Oh, I can't wait to buy Jeremy a suit!"

She smiled, I can only imagine the plans she is making right now for Jeremy; the kind of suit she was going to get him. I knew it was pointless to stop her once she sets her sights on someone there is no stopping her.

"But...what do you think Mary is going to do when she finds out?" she asked me.

That darkened my mood. I have been dreading thinking about what Mary would do. When she discovers I dumped her for a boy and a human; it would be a huge blow to her ego.

"Besides flip her fucking lid?" I asked.

"That is putting it mildly big brother. Rumor has it she has been planning on seducing you and winning you back," she threw in.

I wouldn't put it past her. Before when Mary and I fought, and I didn't talk to her she had some really inventive ways to get me back in her good graces.

"Mary will have to deal with it, if she tries to hurt him I will punish her," I said firmly.

"Do you really think Mary would dare hurt Jeremy? To harm another werewolf's soulmate is a serious offense among all the wolf tribes. Even the black tribe has harsh punishments for wolves that harm another's soulmate and the black tribe doesn't follow many rules," she proclaimed.

That was true. Soulmates were such rare and precious things that all werewolves treasured them.

If even the black tribe the; the worst of all werewolves

acknowledged their importance it goes to show how special they are.

"People do foolish things when rage controls them," I said.

Gods know Mary has a serious temper. Lots of people have found out first hand how vindictive she could be.

Just then my cell phone alerted me of an incoming text. I went to look at it but Liz slapped my hand away. "Now, now. Haven't you heard about not texting and driving?"

She opened the text and her face quickly fell. I knew something was seriously wrong; her face was filled with horror and silent fury.

"Richard! Pull over!" she yelled.

I instantly did as she said. I quickly pulled over to the side of the road.

"Liz what is it?" I asked.

She took a deep breath and showed me the picture. My blood turned to ice in my veins. The text was a picture of Jeremy. He was on a concrete floor, his hands tied behind his back and his mouth covered with a gag.

His hair had been cut horribly, like someone took a pair of scissors and just began to hack away clumps of his hair.

Just then another text came in and I quickly grabbed the cell from her hands. I read the new message.

If you want him to live, come to us. We will leave you a trail of his scent between the school and his house for you to follow, come alone.

I shifted the car into reverse and turned around kicking up dust.

I knew Jeremy had a route he took when he was walking from school to his house; it took over thirty minutes to walk between the two. Jeremy liked walking. I learned that in the time we spent together. It helped him clear his head.

Liz took my phone and read the text. "Richard no!" she yelled.

"I have to Liz! That Hunter has Jeremy!" I growled.

My wolf was enraged; growling, snarling inside me, wanting to be released, to track down our mate and make sure he was safe, then hunt down that bastard and hang him with his own intestines.

My nails turned to claws, and I felt my teeth begin to sharpen.

I hit the brakes when I caught Jeremy's scent; he had only been fifteen minutes from his house when he had been captured.

I jumped out of the Mercedes and began to sniff around. I smelled Jeremy and the faintest whiff of other humans. But I noticed a scent leading into the woods; it was not Jeremy's, but I could smell him very faintly.

"I smell Jeremy here," Liz said next to me.

"His scent leads into the woods," I said.

"Are you sure? I smell someone but it's not Jeremy," she frowned.

"Trust me, Jeremy's scent is mixed with the other," I said.

We followed the scent into the woods. Eventually we found a tree with some of Jeremy's hair taped to it. That explained why Jeremy was missing so much hair, the bastards cut it off so they could leave me a trail to follow.

"How did you smell his hair?" she asked.

"He is my soulmate, my senses are tuned into him remember?"

I went to follow the next trail but Liz stopped me.

"Richard, think about this, there is obviously more than one Hunter now. We don't know how many there are," Liz warned me.

"They have Jeremy!" I growled.

"I know, but think. Who's to say they won't kill him after they kill you?"

"They're Hunters; they protect humans," I said.

"You call this protecting? These aren't just Hunters; these are rogues," she said.

"Rogue what?" I asked.

She sighed. "My God, don't you ever pay attention to what dad says?"

"Not when he is bitching at me."

"Rogue Hunters do not follow the code normal Hunters do. They care little to nothing about human life and seeing how Jeremy saved your life I doubt they are going to give two shits about him. So what will stop them from killing him when they are done with you?"

She was right.

I was not dumb enough to just turn myself over to these fuckers. But I could not just let them hurt him. I had to try to save him.

"I can't wait Liz, I just can't! Call Rick, I am not waiting!"

I ran off into the woods with Liz calling my name. I turned into my wolf form, shredding my cloths in the process and ran. My senses picked up Jeremy's scent much better.

I wasn't going to just rush in; I had to be smart, crafty. I had to plan an attack because when I find these bastards I will kill them all.

They dared kidnap my mate!

There will be blood!

18

Jeremy

I woke up with a headache.

The back of my head hurt, I could feel it throbbing.

There was a foul smell in the air. Where ever I was it smelled old and moldy and there was a bitter scent like piss that burned my nose.

I slowly began to remember what happened; I was abducted.

I had a gag in my mouth and my legs and feet were tied up. I tried to wiggle out of them but they were too tight. Whoever did this knew what they were doing.

I looked around and saw that I was in what appeared to be a basement. There was a window on the wall but it was so small I didn't even entertain the idea of climbing out of it.

I sat up and tried finding something I could use to cut my ropes but didn't find anything. Like they were dumb enough to leave something sharp down here.

The door above the stairs opened and Joseph began to walk down the steps.

"Well, if it isn't sleeping beauty," he commented.

"Fup hu," I said despite the fact I had a gag on.

He just smiled and leaned down and took the gag off. "There, now we can have us a nice talk," he said.

"You are dead, so freaking dead!" I snarled.

"Oh? Your wolf boyfriend is going to kill me?"

"No, I am you asshole!" I growled.

He just laughed. "You got spunk for such a girlie looking kid."

I seethed at the girlie part. What I wouldn't do to have these damn ropes off so I could kick his ass, again!

"What do you want with me?" I asked.

"Isn't it obvious? The alpha you owe me; the Farkas boy," he replied.

"Look pal, just because I saved him doesn't mean he-"

He reached into his pocket and pulled out the wrist brace Richard got me, the one that had the crest of his family on it.

"I know what this means: It's the Farkas family crest. Means you are under the protection of a werewolf. Werewolves only protect a human if they mean something to them such as a good friend, a powerful ally, a dear lover. Which one are you?"

"A good friend," I lied. Well half a lie, we are not lovers although Richard has implied many times he wished it was otherwise.

He smiled. "Don't lie, we have been watching you," he informed me.

"We?"

"Yes, after I had to run, I called some friends of mine, they have been monitoring you and the other wolves. They have seen the way he interacts with you."

I tried to think of when we could have been spied on. Richard and I had been very careful being around one another; we didn't want the other wolves to know of our situation. Daryl had promised he would not tell because he understood the delicate situation we were in. I was grateful for that.

"I don't know what you are talking about," I lied.

Joseph just smiled. "Please, no need to lie. We bugged your house."

"What?!"

"Remember when the handyman arrived to install your cable network? He was working for us, so while you weren't looking he put a few bugs in your house. Imagine our surprise when we heard things like soulmate."

I remembered that day. We had been waiting for someone to be sent to instal our Wi-Fi and cable network. The guy who installed everything had been a stern looking and rather rude.

My body shook with rage, how dare this man come into my house and intrude in such a way! God only knows the things they have heard.

"You bastard!"

He just laughed. "I am sure lover boy is on his way. I know how powerful the bond is between a wolf and their soulmate. He won't be able to think straight; he will come running in here and we will shoot him dead."

"You're crazy, his pack won't let you leave this town alive if you kill him," I pointed out.

"We'll be long gone before they find us. We'll have us a nice big alpha as a trophy."

"Why are you doing this? Richard has done nothing to you!" I shouted.

Joseph's eyes turned hard and cold. "He is a monster. I was raised to hunt freaks like him."

"That is stupid! Look, I am not saying all werewolves are saints, believe me, I have been burned by a few. But Richard is just a kid, like me. All he wants to do is to graduate and become Pack King one day. He doesn't want to hurt anyone...well besides you, but you have that coming."

Joseph just shook his head. "People like you make me sick; people who defend those mutations, acting like there is something human about them. I'd kill you now for being a traitor to your race but I want that werewolf to watch you die. I have seen what happens when a wolf loses his true mate. Look up the word soul-crushing-defeat and you will see the picture of a werewolf who lost their true love."

He turned and walked back up the stairs and I sighed in frustration.

I sat there alone in the cold basement, hoping to God Richard doesn't do something dumb.

*****

Richard

I stayed hidden in the bushes.

I followed the trail all the way to a small house in the woods. Clumps of hair had been left for me to follow.

The thought of those bastards hurting him, touching him and cutting off his hair made my blood boil.

It didn't take me long to figure out where I was going. I have run around this area many times before. I was betting they would be staying at this old abandoned house no one had lived in for years.

The only ones who go there are kids who want a place to get high or homeless people who need a place to crash.

The house was old and in poor condition; the paint was faded and green moss had begun to grown on it as well. The wood on the porch was rotted and the whole thing looked kind of crooked.

I kept to the shadows of the trees, keeping low to the ground. Canines may be color blind but werewolves are not, even when we shift we are still able to see color.

And thanks to our sharp vision we can see from a further distance. Allowing me to inspect the house.

I saw two Hunters on the porch, holding guns in their hands. Several more patrolled around the building.

I was sure the bullets were laced with wolfsbane. I always wondered why werewolves never tried to wipe out that damnable flower and save ourselves the trouble of a slow and painful death.

As I observed the Hunters, I thought it stupid for them to be outside where anyone could see them. But I could only imagine what it must be like inside the house. Even from this distance I can smell it.

Jeremy was in there. In that rotten shit hole where druggies and homeless go to stay. When I rescue him I nee to remember to make sure he got a tetanus shot just to be on the safe side.

I listened, focusing my hearing. Werewolves have better senses then either our human or wolf kin. If I concentrated I could sharpen my already phenomenal sense of hearing and listen in to what was going on in the house.

I closed my eyes and focused.

The wind blew causing the leaves to shake and the grass to tremble, I could hear the birds in the trees and the bugs that crawled on the ground.

But it was not just my hearing that increased it was my sense of smell as well.

The scent of the racoons, squirrels, deer, bobcat, bear, elk and all the other creatures of the land that had passed through and left their mark.

I could smell the building in all it's rotting glory, I couldn't smell the Hunters. I had to give them credit. They were smart in choosing it to hide, I couldn't catch their scent.

But I could smell Jeremy. The smell of him was a blessed relief to the foul stench wafting from the house.

His was the first heartbeat I heard, I instinctively knew it was his, and I felt a surge of relief to know he was still alive.

I could hear someone talking inside and struggled to listen.

"-era's spotted a wolf heading our way," a voice said.

"He should be here soon then. Might be here already."

I growled in recognition of the second voice.

It was Joseph.

"If he was, we would know. If that kid is his soulmate no way could he resist rushing over here," the first voice said.

"True. But we also must consider he went to his pack for help."

"What should we do?" the first voice asked.

"Have the men get ready. And keep an eye on the cameras. His pack might show up soon."

"Maybe we should just kill the kid now."

"No. Once we kill the wolf we'll kill the kid," Joseph said. "Until then he is our leverage. As long as we have him Farkas will be ours."

So they have camera's hidden in the woods.

I had been so preoccupied with getting to Jeremy I had not considered the possibility they had prepared for this. That they would have counter measures. Traps even.

I needed to get my shit together!

I was no use to Jeremy running around like a newborn pup! But at least they intended to keep him alive for the moment. I needed to look around for an opening. A way to get inside.

I had to study my prey, I had to be patient.

The wolf does not just attack until he finds his opening.

First. I had to patrol around the area so I could find out how many more Hunters there were. These assholes have been hunting my kind for God knows how long; this was going to be tricky.

I circled the house several times and every once in a while I would spot a Hunter walking by a window or peering out. I saw an open window in the back that was not guarded.

I almost ran to it but my instincts told me it was a trick. Old man Lewis, the fighting instructor of the pack seemed to speak in my mind, reminding me that if something looked too good to be true, it probably was.

If I survived this, I was sure he was going to kick my ass for running off to deal with the Hunter's all alone without help.

I focused again until I could hear more heart beats coming from the house. But I could not pin point their exact location in the building. I could not get any closer without risking being seen.

I considered the open windows but thought better than that. Even if I was able to get close to one without being seen the fuckers were probably waiting for me to pop my head in the window to blow me away.

No way they were dumb enough to leave an open window unguarded.

By the time I finished patrolling the house I decided if I couldn't go to them, I would make them come to me.

I shifted into my human form and walked around to the front of the house and out of the bushes where those fucktards in the front could see me.

"Hey assholes!" I called.

The stood to attention when they saw me they aimed their guns. I looked around in confusion. "Hey, where's the human woman at? I'm looking for an easy lay and everyone knows human women put out even for an omega."

They cocked their guns and began to walk towards me.

I decided to really piss them off for good measure. "After all, why would they want some limp dick human guy, when they can get fucked by a real beast of a man!"

I flipped them off and rubbed my dick at the same time. They aimed their guns at me and I quickly ran back into the trees. Gunfire sounded in the air.

I ran faster than a deer in the woods. I hid behind a tree and took a deep breath. I opened my mind up to my wolf, tapped into the power that made me an alpha and I sent out a howl for help.

Not a real howl, a mental one. Using the power of an alpha I sent out a wave of my power in all directions; a distress call. A trick a werewolf could do to summon help.

Birds flew away, squirrels hid in their trees, deer ran in fear. The animals sensed something, not knowing exactly what it was that frightened them; just knowing that a call had gone out and something deadly was coming in response.

Any werewolf within several miles would feel it and know on instinct a werewolf was in dire need of help.

It was a trick I learned during my training to learn to control my alpha powers. A technique werewolves could do when stealth was needed. Normally we just howl to one another, but there may come a time when staying hidden is vital to our survival.

A way for us to silently communicate with one another. It's not telepathy. There is no exchanging of silent words or thoughts.

We like to call it the dog whistle trick.

I felt a few responses. One of them I recognized as Rick and some other pack brothers. They were close and were coming for us.

I just had to stall for enough time so they could get here and help.

I heard the two Hunters coming from behind me. I smiled and focused my power into my hands. My nails turned darker and longer, transforming into deadly claws. The muscles got a little tighter and firmer, which would help add strength to the coming blows.

I crouched down low and heard them stop just behind the tree. I heard them moving around, making such a loud noise. I took a deep breath; I could smell sweat, adrenaline, and a very small tinge of fear.

I could hear their hearts beating, hear the blood racing through their veins. I could hear the air entering and leaving their lungs.

I licked my lips in anticipation. My wolf was hungry for the kill. These bastards harmed Jeremy, my sweet, feisty little Jeremy; so strong, yet so vulnerable.

He was tough, yeah. All that outer soft beauty hid a tough interior. Yet he carried his own scars.

The wolf goddess of my tribe Niveus preached peace and understanding between all creatures. But she also told us to defend those we love with our lives. To strike down those who would mean us and our pack harm. To smite evil when it dared show its face.

I have never been much of a believer but there were parts of the teachings I did enjoy.

Like eviscerating your enemies.

I jumped out from behind the tree and rushed at the one Hunter. His back was turned to me so he didn't even see it when I opened the back of his head like a can of chicken noodle soup.

The other hunter turned his gun on me and fired, using speed and reflexes no human possessed I dodged the bullet and tore out his throat.

His body fell to the ground, and I licked my lips from the blood that stained my face.

They were my first kill.

I had killed my fair share of animals for food, but I have never taken a human life before.

I was no stranger to blood and gore, having gutted and torn many mighty beasts apart myself.

But these men were not killed for sustenance. They were killed for vengeance.

Was it wrong for me to feel victorious? To feel a vengeful satisfaction as their blood ran down my claws?

I couldn't care less.

I could hear more Hunters coming so I shifted into my wolf form and ran back to the house, circling around to avoid them.

I decided to make my way to the back of the house where I saw that open window. I didn't see any Hunters, so I ran up to the window, shifting back into my human form.

I listened for a heartbeat and didn't hear any save a few by the front of the house. I jumped through the window, quiet as a mouse and deadly as death.

I creeped through the halls, a door to my right opened and I quickly moved to the wall so as not to be seen. A Hunter came out, but I snapped his neck before he could realize I was there.

I could smell Jeremy on him, my wolf growled in rage at the idea of this filth touching our Jeremy.

Just then the sounds of gunshot could be heard as could the howl of wolves and I knew the pack was here. I heard the remaining hunters shouting and yelling; preparing for my brothers and sisters arrival.

While they ran around preparing for the oncoming onslaught, I quickly followed Jeremy's scent. It led me to a door and I could finally hear his heart beating. It seemed louder than all the other noise but I knew it was only because he was my soulmate and his scent was the first and foremost of what my senses detected.

I quickly ran down the stairs. Jeremy was tied up, and he had a gag in his mouth. His hair was a wreck; entire clumps of it were missing. Those bastards hacked chunks of his hair, obviously not caring about the damage they caused to those beautiful locks.

Jeremy stared at me, looking horrified. I figured it was the blood coating my chest. I walked to him, eager to free him. But then his eyes looked behind me and it was then I realized there was another heartbeat.

It had been beating so lowly. So full of calm it had been faint. Easy to hide amongst the symphony of gunshots and hungry howls.

Before I could spin around something hit my back and then my whole body erupted in pain. I howled and fell to the ground, twitching as the electricity coursed through me.

"Gotcha."

I looked up and saw Joseph holding a stun gun in his hands.

"Knew as soon as I heard the guns going off you would be the first to try to rescue the kid. You werewolves can't resist the urge to save your soulmate."

"Give it up asshole! My pack is almost here and they will tear you to shreds!" I snarled.

He gave me another shock, and I screamed in pain.

"Foolish boy, I never intended to live. This is how I was meant to die. Doing what my family has been doing for generations. What my sister died doing. What Hunters are meant to do. Killing your kind."

Just then there was the sound of guns firing and men screaming. The sound of growling could be heard as was flesh being torn and blood being spilled.

Joshua looked up and smiled.

Something rushed past me, it was Jeremy. He had somehow got his legs free and had gotten up and now rushed at Joseph. He slammed into him, causing them both to fall to the ground.

Joseph dropped the stun gun, but I was still suffering from the after effects. Electricity wrecked hell with our ability to transform.

Jeremy was still on the ground; he hadn't been able to untie his hands and Joseph was already up.

"You fucking twink!" he yelled.

He kicked Jeremy in the face and he fell down. The scent of his blood filled my nose and my rage broke.

My power exploded outward. I stood up and turned into my hybrid form, ignoring the pain as my sore muscles were forced into transformation.

My wolf and I were one, a perfect synchronization: kill, protect, avenge.

Joseph reached for the gun he kept at his waist but I lunged at him, grabbing him by the shoulders, enjoying his squeal of pain as my nails dug into his flesh.

Much to my disappointment it was not fear nor rage that he looked at me with.

It was acceptance and for extra insult a smile.

I closed my jaw on his neck and with one shake, severed his head from his body.

I let his body drop and quickly made my way over to Jeremy. I cut the ropes from his hands and helped him up. The right side of his face was starting to swell and there was a nasty cut on his head.

I could hear the fight waging on above us.

My pack was quickly dispatching the Hunters if they could be called that. They had not planned on such a massive attack. Had Joshua not told them how large we were?

Why else would there be so few? Why else would they be so ill equipped and sloppy with their work?

Joshua did not strike me as a fool, so why did he make such a half-assed attempt at murder?

It didn't matter, he would never hurt anyone ever again.

Acting on instinct I began to lick his wound. Werewolf saliva is a wonderful antibacterial agent. It would keep him from getting an infection and would prevent the wound from scarring.

The second my tongue met his blood my sense of taste exploded. It was truly heaven; better than anything I have ever tasted. It was sweet, spicy, and quenching.

I moaned in pleasure at the taste and continued to messily lick him; soon the whole right side of his face was covered in slobber.

The blood was affecting me in another way as well; my junk started to swell and harden.

I was so horny for Jeremy right at that moment and if he wasn't hurt, I would have had my way with him. The idea pleased me, taking my mate, covered in the blood of my enemies, as my pack feasted on their victims; it would have been perfect.

Some sane part of me told me Jeremy would not be up for sex even if he wasn't hurt. Sex and violence could easily mix for a werewolf but most humans are not into that mix. That is what happens when you open yourself up to your wolf; soon the two instincts of man and wolf mix and you find yourself feeling all kinds of strange things.

I have tasted many kinds of blood before. The animal blood of my prey, the werewolf blood of a challenger, the human blood of the Hunters

I had just killed who had the honor of being my first mortal kill.

But none of them could compare to Jeremy's blood which was like liquid fire!

How could he have such strong blood?

Was the power of our bond so strong his blood could effect me so.

I felt like I was high on his blood. I felt so light and warm as if I drank a gallon of none-distilled Moon Lust all by myself.

It was silent now, the battle was over. I could hear and feel my pack above us.

I picked Jeremy up and walked up the steps. The house was a bloodbath. Dead bodies littered the floor. My wolf brothers feasted on the remains of the Hunters. The beta's did so in their wolf forms, and the omega's in their man-beast forms.

Omegas could not transform into a wolf unless it was the night of the full moon. Otherwise they retain a humanoid form with extra amounts of hair, fangs, claws, pointed ears and wolf eyes.

If you saw an omega, you would think they were humans with very good prosthetics. I saw three of them over the body of a Hunter whose neck I snapped. They were feasting on his intestines. Their hands and mouths were covered in blood and gore.

I was glad Jeremy was unconscious. I did not want him to see this horror.

I walked out of the house to see more of my pack gathered, some eating the Hunters, others merely observed hungrily. Many of them crowded around me, trying to get to Jeremy, thinking he was another snack. They were drawn by the scent of his blood. I snarled at them, letting them know he was not for eating. They whimpered and backed down.

Rick and Liz walked over to me, both naked after having transformed back into their human forms.

I did the same and gently sat Jeremy on the ground. The others circled around us, watching with hungry eyes. Rick kept them back while we inspected Jeremy

Liz kneeled next to me, peering at Jeremy. "Is he okay?" she asked.

"He will be fine. But we need to get him to a hospital," I said.

She ran her hand gently down his face. Some of his blood smeared on her fingers. She brought her hand to her nose and sniffed it.

Her eyes widened in disbelief. "He smells wonderful!"

Jeremy opened his eyes. He looked around in confusion, his eyes settled on me. "Richard?"

"Yeah, it's me Jer," I answered softly.

He looked me up and down and a goofy smile crossed his face. "Wow, I am really loving heaven right now," he said.

Liz and I laughed. He looked over to her, realizing she was there.

"Liz?"

"Yes, I am here too."

"I'm gay, but I have to say, you have really nice boobs," he commented.

Liz laughed harder, and I felt a pang of jealousy. Stupid I know, but wolves were territorial by nature.

I lifted him close to my face and smiled. "You're not dead Jer."

"I'm not?"

"Nope."

"So you're really naked?"

"Yep."

"And-"

"About to kiss you? Yes."

I leaned down and captured his lips in a kiss. It was not the first time we did it but this time it was sweeter; maybe it was because the taste of his blood was still on my tongue or maybe it was because I came so close to losing him.

I heard a collective gasp from the others. I didn't care though; I didn't care if they were shocked or offended. I didn't care if they would gossip to the rest of the pack.

I pulled back and looked down at Jeremy. His face was flushed and his heart was beating a little faster.

"So, seeing how I just saved your life I think you owe me a date," I smiled.

"You saved my life, I owe you more than a date," he said with a smile.

19

Jeremy

"Those sons of bitches!" I yelled.

Liz and Richard sat in my room. It was the day after the incident with the Hunters.

They brought me to the hospital where I was diagnosed with a concussion. Mom arrived not an hour after I did, crying hysterically. When she found out Richard had saved me she gave him a major hug, thanking him over and over for saving me.

She stayed with me the rest of the day, doting on me the entire time. I convinced her I was going to be okay, I was safe now.

Richard stayed with me the whole night. It was useless to try to get him to leave, he was still too nervous about leaving me alone. He pulled a few strings so he could stay the night. I was actually glad he did. I felt safe knowing he was there in the same room with me.

I was going to be released today and wanted to see what the cut on my head looked like. Liz handed me her pocket mirror, and I saw not only the cut but what they did to my hair.

Turns out while I was unconscious they had cut chunks of my hair off to leave for a trail for Richard to follow. I looked horrible!

"We can fix it, we'll just have to do a trim," Liz said soothingly.

"Are you kidding me? I might as well shave my head bald!" I cried out.

I handed the mirror back to her and sulked.

"Don't be dramatic, it will be a bit short but we can fix it. I think a nice buzz cut will make you look manlier," she chuckled.

"Really?" I asked happily.

"Of course," she stated, smiling at me.

"I think you look perfect no matter what," Richard complimented.

"Of course you would say that, we're soulmates," I grumbled.

"You still look perfect to me," he repeated with a shrug.

I was quiet for a moment.

"So....I take it the whole pack knows?" I asked.

They knew what I was talking about. After seeing Richard and I kiss I was sure the werewolves who had been present had talked about what they saw.

"Oh, they all know by now I am sure," Liz teased.

"Do your parents?" I asked them.

"Judging from the very angry voice message I got from my dad I think they do," Richard said with a sigh.

"So…what happens now?" I asked.

"Now you two can stop hiding and come out in the open about your relationship," Liz said happily clapping her hands together.

"It's not going to be that easy Liz," I commented.

"I know, I just like being an optimist," she agreed.

"We'll have to have a pack meeting to discuss this. You will have to come so I can announce you as my soulmate to the whole pack," Richard said.

"Then what?"

"Then what happens, happens. You will be initiated as a full-fledged member of the pack," he explained.

"Just like that?" I asked.

"You are my soulmate. It's the law," he stated.

"But what if the other werewolves object?" I questioned.

"All the tribes have the same beliefs when it comes to soulmates. 'Thou shall not harm the true mate of another wolf, thou shall welcome your brother's true mate into your pack and hunt with the true mate as if they were your kin'," Liz recited.

"What's that from?" I asked.

"The Book of Niveus. Basically our version of the Bible."

"Werewolves have a bible?" I asked.

"Technically five; one for each tribe. Each one is filled with the teachings and traditions of each tribe. But some of the commandments are different," Richard said.

I remembered Lucas mentioning a few times that his pack was of the red tribe. I never really inquired to what the difference between a pack and a tribe was.

Since I was about to join them I think I should know.

"So what does it mean to be a member of a tribe? How is that different from a pack?"

"There are thousands of packs all over the world. But each pack belongs to a tribe. There are many tribes, but there are five major tribes who are the largest of all; the white tribe, the black, the yellow, the blue and the red. Each tribe has their own rules and laws and the pack of that tribe follows those laws. We are the white wolf tribe. We worship the white wolf goddess Niveus. We are firm believers in law and order and believe in co-habitation with humans," Liz explained.

"Do the other tribes have their own deities?" I asked.

"Yes they do. Good thinking Jer," Richard said looking proud that I figured it out.

"There is one wolf God for each tribe. The Cambridge pack is the red tribe. The red tribe are the warriors of the tribes; following a strict warrior's code of ethics and honor. Very traditional and old fashioned if you ask me. Life in their tribe can be tough; they believe in the philosophy of survival of the fittest and tend to look down on humans," she told me.

"I know what you mean," I muttered. I had seen how brutal and warrior-like Lucas's pack could be. He once took me to a get together his pack was having. Basically it was a werewolf fight club. No one died though it had been a pretty close call.

I remember the savage energy that was in the air that night; the look of immense blood lust that filled their eyes. Luckily Lucas was with me, I got a lot of looks that said many of them thought I would make a good snack.

"The next tribe is the blue tribe. Of all the tribes they are the most human; they are more in touch with their humanity than anyone else. They tend to be philosophers and scientists. Many of them live in large towns or cities. They help make inventions to help our people." Richard continued where Liz left off.

"I like the sound of them," I said.

"You'll like the yellow tribe even more. The yellow tribe is like the hippies of the werewolf people. Unlike the blue tribe the yellow tribe is more in touch with their wolf side. They prefer to live out in the wild, away from technology, living in harmony with nature. They are friendly with humans but prefer to live away from them. Of all the tribes they are the most spiritual and peaceful," Liz threw in.

"And finally the black tribe," Richard growled. Liz bared her teeth when he said their name and I was sensing some tension in the air.

"Let me guess, they're the evil werewolves?" I asked.

"Got that right. They believe werewolves are the apex beings. That we should enslave humanity. Killing humans is allowed. No, it is encouraged in their tribe. They only turn a human into a werewolf if the human has done something to earn their favor or if the human is useful, which is a very rare thing. But even then, turned wolves are treated as second class. I heard it is punishable by death to procreate with a human in that tribe," Richard said.

"So not a tribe you'd want to run into in a dark alley?"

"They are the reason humans fear us. Legends tell of the black tribe wiping out entire villages hundreds of years ago just for fun. They still do shit like that now but on a smaller scale," Liz lamented.

"Wow, glad I will never ever have to meet them," I noted.

Liz gave Richard a sharp look. "You dumb ass, you didn't tell him!" she scolded.

"I was waiting for the right moment," Richard mumbled suddenly looking uncomfortable.

"Tell me what?" I asked.

"Once every year as dictated by our laws, all the tribes within certain areas gather together to celebrate the Nox de Lupus," she said.

"That's Latin isn't it?" I asked. "Night of the Wolf."

"You speak Latin?" Liz asked looking surprised.

"I went through a phase when I was younger. I tried to learn it but never finished," I explained.

"The Nox de Lupus it is our most sacred holiday. It is a time when all the tribes gather and forget what divides them, and for one night become one pack," Richard explained.

"And the black tribe is coming here for it?" I asked.

"It is our turn to host it this year. Last year it was the yellow tribe; the only pack I hate visiting more than the black tribe," Liz said.

"Why? I thought you said they are peaceful," I reminded her.

"They are, but they're nudists as well. They only dress when they have to, otherwise they go commando," Richard chimed in.

I thought it funny they were making a big deal about werewolf nudists seeing how they didn't seem to have been bothered by me seeing them naked last night.

Even Lucas and his pack were not-

Just then I had a horrible realization. I prayed I was wrong, I hoped *they* were not coming. "Guys, when you said all the tribes....you meant the red tribe too?"

Richard and Liz looked very awkward then.

"Yeah, the Cambridge pack is coming as well. And their new Pack King." Liz said gently.

"New Pack King?" I questioned.

Lucas's father Kent had been the Pack King last time I had been in Cambridge. Someone must have challenged him and won.

"Yeah, a couple of days ago we received word that the former Pack King Kent lost a duel of leadership with his son. Lucas."

"Lucas...is coming to Wolf Fang Falls?" I gasped.

"Next month," Richard said sounding angry. "And he is bringing his pack with him."

"Well fuck," I muttered.

I had left Cambridge to get away from Lucas and the drama his life brought. But now it seems he would unknowingly follow me to Wolf Fang Falls.

I wonder what his reaction to me and Richard was going to be. Knowing a werewolf's temperament I think the answer was very obvious.

There was a knock on the door and I expected one of the nurses to come in.

Instead it was Daryl and Rick.

Liz and Richard stood up. Richard placed a hand on my shoulder, he gave both Daryl and Rick a sharp look. As if he was daring them to try hurt me.

"Calm down Richard, we're just here to check on Jeremy," Rick said sternly.

"Samuel tells me you should be fine. I am happy to hear this," Daryl spoke to me.

"Going to take a lot more than some Hunter to take me out," I said.

"He was a shit Hunter. Seriously, the whole set up was garbage," Richard said.

"Yes, those friends of Joseph's were Hunters in name only. We have been in contact with the Council about this," Daryl said.

"Hunters have a council?" Jeremy asked.

"True Hunters do. Joseph was rogue, and the rest were a bunch of drop outs and failures who did not pass training," Rick said.

"Why would Joseph get help from a bunch of loser Hunters?" I asked.

"He said he never intended to live. That he was supposed to die killing werewolves. And he was never afraid, even when I was about to kill him. He seemed kind of happy."

Daryl and Rick shared a look.

"The Hunter Council told us Joseph went rogue after his sister died. Before that he was one of their best and never broke the rules," Daryl explained. "My belief; and I may be giving him more credit than he deserves. Is that Joseph wanted to die."

No one said anything. I saw Richard frown and Liz look puzzled.

"I don't think he started off as a bad man. But losing his sister caused something in him to break. And he crossed a line that tipped him over the edge of the abyss. People are such complex creatures so I can only make assumptions of course. But when a good man goes against his nature, it can ware him down. A part of him was driven by rage and wanted to keep killing, but the better part got tired of it all and wanted it to all end."

"So he was trying to go out in a blaze of glory?" I asked.

"What better way for a Hunter to die than to do it trying to kill werewolves," Rick said.

"I guess it makes sense, in some twisted way," I said.

"Like I said, people are complex," Daryl said.

"I hope the Hunter Council is not going to cause us trouble for all this," Liz said.

"No, in fact they apologized for the whole thing and have helped us cover this whole incident up."

"I didn't think Hunters and werewolves got along so well," I said.

Whenever Lucas talked about Hunters, he made it seem like they were the scum of the Earth.

"A proper Hunter is trained to hunt only those werewolves who hurt humans. For those like us who live in harmony with humanity we have little to fear of them. Save for the few like Joseph and his accomplices who decide to hunt us regardless of our moral standing."

"But for other tribes like the black tribe they are a problem," I said.

Daryl nodded. A look of distaste on his face as if he ate something sour. "Yes, the black tribe are made up of the worst of our kind. They have warred with the Hunters for centuries. Were it not for their vast size and resources they would have been wiped out a long time ago."

"Not that anyone would complain really," Rick said.

Daryl took a step toward me and Richard tensed. Daryl gave him a sharp look.

They just stared at one another for a tense moment. I saw Rick was keeping equal distance between his king and Liz. I doubted Richard and Daryl would come to blows in a hospital.

But when it comes to a fight between werewolves, it was never wise to make assumptions. And if there was a fight I was sure who Liz would side with. So was Rick, which was why he was keeping his distance from her so if she attacked he could pull out his taser gun.

"I mean him no harm Richard," Daryl said.

I never told Richard about Daryl's threat to me. But Richard was smart enough to read between the lines. He also knew Daryl would need to put pressure on me to guarantee I wouldn't do something to hurt the pack.

Richard let out a low snarl; but he relaxed. He nodded and sat down next to me, grabbing my hand and giving Daryl a hard stare, as if daring him to try something.

Daryl stood by me, he looked down at me and I fought the urge to squirm under his gaze. The memory of his claws around my throat was still fresh and after the events of yesterday I was still feeling jumpy.

"Jeremy, I know our first meeting was less than ideal. I won't apologize for what I did. As you have learned our lives can be very dangerous. I had to be sure you were not a threat. And thank the goddess things didn't go differently."

"I understand. I still think you're a bit of a dick. But I understand."

The look on everyone's face was one of shock. It was kind of funny.

Liz had her hand to her mouth to cover a silent gasp, Rick made a choking sound and Richard seemed to be fighting a smile.

Then again calling the leader of a werewolf pack a dick was kind of dumb; I blame the concussion.

Daryl let out a bark of laughter. "Oh you got balls kid. Richard is going to have his hands full with you."

*****

Later that day I found myself at home.

Rachel, Gabe, Heath and Heather were visiting me.

The story was the psycho who attacked Richard and I at the party came after me again. Luckily, I was able to call for help and Rick came to the rescue.

Don't know how they were going to explain the bit about him lacking a head.

"Man, you are so lucky," Gabe said.

"I know, mom says I have to take the bus from now on. No more walking by myself," I told him.

After she got down crying she was quick to scold me when she found out I had walked home when there was a psycho running around. Rick promised her he would make sure I got home okay.

As much as I appreciated his gesture I also felt a little irritated by it as well.

I had no doubt in my mind he would personally make sure I kept safe, even if it meant he had to take me home himself.

But at the same time I knew he would make extra sure as to my safety for mom.

I was glad she had someone who obviously cared about her so much. But ever since I figured out he was a werewolf I have felt a lot more worried about them dating.

Maybe it was my own experience with dating a werewolf or maybe I didn't like such a dangerous being around my mother.

Hypocritical I know but I didn't want her to have to go through the bullshit I went through.

"What happened to the good old days when we didn't have psychos running around?" Heather wondered.

Rachel was examining my hair. Her mom worked at a beauty salon and Rachel had a thing for cutting hair as well.

"It would be a buzz cut, that's the only thing we could do with it. I can't believe someone would be so evil as to cut such lovely hair. You must have been so scared," she said.

"I was," I nodded.

"I can do it, or if you want, I can get my mom to do it. She said she would cut it for free," she offered.

"You can do it; all you have to do is just trim it all off, right?" I asked.

"Yep. Don't worry though, I think it will be a nice look for you, very manly," she smiled.

I smiled back. That was a plus about this; looking manlier. I preferred to have longer hair, but the longer it is the more people would think I was a girl. So I would keep it cut short to draw more attention to my masculine features.

I once considered cutting it shorter, but I didn't want my hair that short. But now I don't have a choice.

I smiled, remembering Richard's words on how he thought I would look good no matter what. The look in his eyes said he spoke the truth.

I was going to need Richard next month; when they have the Noxd de Lupus meeting. When Lucas and his pack come for the celebrations. I like to think nothing will go wrong, and that he won't find out I am here.

But I have a feeling he already knows. Kent was the one who called Daryl and told him I was here and that I knew about werewolves. If Kent knows, then I am sure Lucas knows.

But I won't worry about that yet. The full moon will be in three days. The pack is planning to initiate me in as a member that night. Liz and Richard said I will only have to swear a few oaths and meet the other pack members, human and werewolf. It would be a small kind of party with drinks and food. The werewolves would then run off and frolic in the woods for a while.

Richard would also officially declare me as his soulmate to the pack. I didn't know if I could say for sure that we were going out...sure, I did promise to go out with him for the dance and on a date. But I was kind of concussed at the time, and I still have reservations about dating again, let alone dating a werewolf.

Not only that but I am sure Mary is going to be my new personal enemy. She didn't strike me as someone who handled rejection well and when she finds out I am the reason Richard dumped her I have a feeling my name is going to be at the top of her shit list.

I was wondering how Richard was doing right now? I had a feeling his ass was feeling a bit sore from the chewing he was getting from his dad.

20

Richard

Liz sat next to me on the couch. Mom stood up her arms crossed, looking both calm and peaceful.

Dad however, was pacing back and forth, pissed and furious.

They both heard what happened; about the kiss. As soon as Liz and I got home dad demanded I sit down and tell him why he heard I kissed another guy.

So with Liz's help I told my parents that there once super-straight son now had a soulmate in the new kid in town.

Mom was shocked, dad was furious and had yet to speak. It had been over five minutes since I explained to them what happened.

Finally he stopped pacing and glared at me. I braced myself for what was to come. Knowing a lot of angry words were about to be said.

"Do you have any idea what you have done?!" he yelled.

I kept quiet, knowing better than to interrupt him when he was on a rant.

"I got a call last night from Mary's father that he heard you were seen by over a dozen of our brothers and sister kissing that Moonvine boy! I told him that it was a lie, my son is definitely not gay, and Mary could prove that! The phone has been ringing off the hook with the gossiping bitches in the pack wanting your mother to confirm it! Now I find out it is all true! You dumped Mary for a low level human boy!"

My wolf did not like him talking about Jeremy like that and neither did I.

"Jeremy isn't low level, just because he isn't from a rich family doesn't mean you have to speak about him like he is dirt," I said.

"Don't you dare speak to me like that!" he growled.

"I don't know why you are getting all worked up over this," I stated.

"Because my son is not a queer!"

"Frank!" mom yelled. She walked up to him and put her hand on his shoulder. "Please, we need to talk about this I agree, but not like this."

Mom looked at me, and as usual she was the calm and collected one. "Richard, are you sure?" she asked.

"Yes mom, we went to Grandma Susan, and she told us what happens when a wolf finds his soulmate."

"But you can't mate with him! He's a man!" dad shouted.

"Well technically." Liz stopped when dad gave her a look.

Liz may be dad's favorite, but there were rare times when even she didn't dare push her limits with him.

"Mates only happen for reproduction, as it was meant to be. Last time I checked men don't have children!" dad thundered.

"Grandma Susan says soulmates aren't about reproduction; they're about true love," I reminded him.

"You haven't known this boy long enough to say you love him!" dad yelled.

"Do you think I don't know that?!" I yelled back at him, standing up. "Do you think I wanted this to happen? I was happy with my life, I tried to resist; I tried so fucking hard to ignore him! But my wolf pines for him, even right now! I can't help it dad but I love him!"

248

"Then what we need to do is keep you away from him! You said it yourself; you tried to resist. Maybe we can break this thing; maybe it is a pheromone thing. If we can just keep you separated log enough-"

"No!" I backed away from him. I could feel my body starting to change. "You can't keep me from him! He is MINE!" I roared.

Liz appeared in front of me, putting her hands on my shoulders. I sensed her aura trying to keep me calm. Mom did the same with dad.

"Richard, calm down. Come on, breathe, we won't take you from him, I swear," she said soothingly.

I took a deep breath and calmed down. Liz turned to face mom and dad. "Dad, separating Richard from Jeremy won't solve this. They are meant to be. I see the way Richard looks at him, with pure love and adoration. He never looked at Mary like that. Why can't you be happy for them?"

"Happy? My son has suddenly turned gay! Do you realize how this is going to affect all of us? Bad enough Mary's family has grief with us because he broke up with her, but now when they find out it was over a human boy, this will severely damage our relationship with them! Hell, many in the pack will see this as weakness and challenge our position and authority." He took a deep breath and rubbed his head and began to pace again. "And what about children? There can be no heirs from this union!"

"I think we need to take a break. Liz, take your brother to his room. Your father and I need to talk," mom ordered gently.

"Of course mom," Liz nodded.

She took my hand and led me out of the room. We walked about seven feet past the door and stopped. She put her finger to her lips, and we stood there and listened to mom and dad talk.

"I can't believe this is happening to us! This is punishment! The goddess is punishing us for my idiot brother joining the yellow tribe!" dad yelled.

"Frank this has nothing to do with Eldred and you know that," mom said.

"Janice, our son is gay! This changes everything! I knew something funny was going on! Ever since we had the Moonvines over for dinner, I knew something was off about Richard's scent!"

"Frank, I am as shocked as you. But we must remain calm. We need to talk to my mother about this, I am sure she can help," mom said softly.

"This is my fault, I knew I should have spent more time with him!," dad grumbled.

"Oh for God's sake Frank," mom said with a sigh. "We raised Richard perfectly. This is unexpected and shocking I agree."

"Our whole world has just turned upside down Janice. Once everyone learns the truth, alphas will be challenging Richard left and right. This will be seen as a sign of weakness, you know that," dad whined.

"I know, but I know Richard is strong. He will fight for us, his mate and his honor. Just like you taught him to."

I heard dad sigh and sit down. A second later mom joined him.

"Our son is gay Janice," he said.

"Just because he has feelings for one boy doesn't make him gay," mom said soothingly.

"All those dreams and plans we had for him just flew right out the window," dad complained.

"Not necessarily. He can still be Pack King one day," mom noted.

"A gay Pack King," dad said bitterly.

"Yes, and we need to learn to accept that. Richard is going through a difficult time as well and needs our support to help him through this."

"The Nox de Lupus is coming, what will the other tribes do when they learn of this?"

"What can they do? They will be in our territory and as such will have to act cordial," mom replied.

Liz and I quietly snuck back to my room. I sat down on my bed and put my hands over my head. Liz sat next to me putting her hand on my shoulder.

"Are you okay?" she asked.

"No. Did you hear them?"

"I was right there to," she said.

"They're disappointed. I let them down," I moped.

"No you didn't. Yes, they are disappointed, but not because of you. Well, not exactly."

I gave her a hard look.

"I mean ever since we were babies, mom and dad dreamed you would be the perfect alpha son. Rich, popular, attractive, smart, powerful. Well, they got four out of five right."

"What do you mean?" I asked.

"Well you are rich, popular, attractive, and powerful," she said teasingly with a grin.

"Bitch," I muttered playfully.

"I think you mean alpha bitch. But my point is: all these years they thought you would hook up with a super good looking alpha woman and have lots of pups and be Pack King. It is just hard to imagine you with another guy, and also the no grandkids part."

"I feel bad," I said.

"Don't. At least mom is more understanding," she said.

"Man. Can this day get-"

She quickly put her hand on my mouth.

"Don't jinx us," she laughed. She let go of my mouth. "Can I ask you a question though?"

"Shoot," I said.

"Are you really gay?" she asked.

"Obviously I am," I said.

"Do you like guys besides Jeremy?" she asked impatiently.

"I...no...I don't," I said.

I tried to think if in my life I ever had a homosexual thought in my life. Until Jeremy entered my life I never considered ever being with another guy in any kind of way.

"Well maybe you're not gay then."

"Then what am I?" I asked.

"You're my brother. That's all that matters to me. I don't care if you like guys or girls or both. Not everything in life has to have a label."

"Thanks for being there for me Liz," I said. "I know I can be a jerk and treat you bad. But I am glad to have you as my sister."

"You may be a pain in my ass sometimes but you're still my brother," she said kissing my cheek softly.

21

Mary

I stared at Tiffany in shock.

"What?!" I screeched.

I was in my room with Tiffany, Zoe, and Victoria. They had called and said they were on their way to tell me something important.

Ever since Richard broke up with me I have been horribly depressed.

I locked myself away in my room, only coming out to go to school. But only because my parents refused to let me skip it.

Seeing Richard was like a dagger in my heart.

Mom says if I give him enough time he will get over it and come back to me. She says sometimes men need time to themselves and she was sure he would get over what ever it was that had been bothering him.

I got a call from my friends telling me they had to speak with me. At first I told them I was not in the mood but when they told me it had something to do with Richard, I demanded they tell me what it was.

But they said it was not something that could be told over the phone. So as soon as they got here I demanded they tell me what it was.

I thought they might have clue as to what might be causing him to hate me so much. So imagine my shock when they told me that the little pasty human got kidnapped and Richard helped save him and kissed him in front of many of the pack.

"Richard kissed that human kid Jeremy," Tiffany repeated timidly.

"What do you mean he kissed him?" I asked. My brain seemed to be incapable of comprehending what I was being told.

"I mean, he stuck his tongue right into his mouth and gave him the full treatment," Tiffany explained.

Zoe and Victoria looked at me, waiting to see what my reaction was. But they too had the same looks of shock and outrage that I was sure was on my face.

"How do you know this?" I asked her.

"My friend's, cousin's boyfriend was there when it happened. He wasn't the only one; the whole pack is talking about it. Lots of people saw Richard save him from some Hunters and then kiss him right in front of everyone!" Tiffany exclaimed.

I stood up and began to pace, they watched me wearily. "But Richard isn't gay. God knows I fucked him enough times to know that," I said agitated.

"But people are talking, why would someone lie about this?" Victoria asked.

"Yeah, Richard would hunt them down and beat their ass," Zoe.

"But Richard is not gay!" I repeated forcefully.

"Maybe he is bi and never told anyone," Tiffany said.

"I can't believe this! Of all the people he leaves me for, it's because of a piece of human trash! I've known him since we were kids and he dumps me for some little twink he just met! We were going to be married! We were going to have a family! Now I find out he left me for a human guy!"

"You'll be able to find out on the night of the full moon.. I heard my dad say we're supposed to be initiating him into the pack," Zoe said.

"To hell with that, I am not waiting!" I exclaimed.

I grabbed my purse and headed out the door. They followed me, scrambling to keep up.

"Mary, where are you going?" Zoe asked.

"To Richard's. I am going to get some damn answers! He owes me the truth!" I growled.

As I walked down the stairs with the trio following behind me my younger brother Neal was walking up the steps when he saw me coming down.

He frowned when he saw me, no doubt sensing my emotions.

"Sis? What's wrong?" he asked.

"Out of my way!" I snapped brushing past him.

"You told her didn't you?" I heard him ask the girls.

"You knew!" I screeched turning around to face him.

He winced. "Almost the whole pack knows," he said with a sigh.

"Why didn't anyone tell me sooner?" I demanded.

"Mom and dad were going to tell you themselves-he shot an irritated look to the girls- no one knows what the hell is going on or why Daryl is just allowing this human guy into the pack so suddenly."

"Well I am going to get answers!" I growled.

I turned and continued on my way to Richard's. I could have taken my car, but I was too pissed to drive. I might run someone over just for the hell of it.

"Mary stop!" Neal yelled chasing after me, the girls followed quietly behind.

"Fuck off Neal!"

"Mary come on, just wait for mom and dad to come home, don't go over there and cause a scene!"

"Oh I am going to cause a scene! This is serious bullshit!" I all but screamed.

Neal looked around nervously. People were peeking out their windows to see what the commotion was. I glared at them all. If the whole pack knew then they knew what was causing my rage.

"Mary look Richard is an ass, if he wants some stupid human to be his mate then-"

I spun around and grabbed him by the throat and lifted him off the ground.

"I am his mate!" I yelled.

I threw him to the side into a car. He coughed and struggled to get up. I made my way to Richard's, the girls still followed, at a safe distance.

They were smart. If anyone dared stop me now, I would tear them to shreds!

Richard owes me a goddamn explanation, and I was going to get the truth out of him.

*****

Richard

I was in the kitchen making a sandwich when I felt her.

Her energy was leaking out, and I could sense it was in an aggravated state. She must be so angry that she was losing control of her aura. Not a good sign.

I quickly made my way to the door. I was sure mom, dad, and Liz could sense her as well. Mary didn't live too far from us. I had walked her to her home many times when we were going out.

I opened the door to see her stomping up the sidewalk. Zoe, Tiffany and Victoria followed her looking uneasy and a little afraid.

Mary was a different story. Her eyes were filled with anger. The second she saw me she began to speak.

"Richard Allen Farkas, what the fuck is going on?!"

"Will you keep your voice down?!" I hissed.

"No! I have heard some real disturbing shit and I want answers now!" she shouted.

I saw movement in the houses across the street. I saw people peeking out their windows to see what was going on. Some were actually coming out to stand on their front porch to watch.

"What is it Mary, what have you heard?" I asked already knowing what it was.

The anger and hurt in her eyes told me.

"I heard you kissed that fucking Jeremy Moonvine, is that true?" she asked.

I sighed. I wished it was just her. The girls stood back, looking on eagerly, obviously enjoying the drama that was about to happen.

"Yes I kissed him," I answered.

"But why?!" she asked her voice shrill.

"Because, I love him," I said.

The girls all gasped at the same time and looked at one another shocked.

They were not the only ones. Those watching from the safety of their homes looked just as surprised.

"Love? LOVE?! How can you love him?! He's a man Richard! I know he doesn't look it, but he has a cock and balls! Not your thing last time I checked!" she yelled.

"Look, it's complicated, okay. But Jeremy and I.....well....I want to be with him Mary. I am planning on announcing our relationship to the whole pack," I stated.

Her eye bulged in disbelief. "Relationship? How long have you two been together? Is that why you left me? Because of him?" she shrieked.

I could hear her heart beating, her face was starting to get red and her eyes were starting to get watery.

"We're not technically going out, but-"

"Since when have you been gay? All those times we had sex-"

"I'm not gay!" I hissed angrily.

"Then how the fuck can you say you love another man and not be gay!?"

"It's fucking complicated okay!"

"Then help me understand Richard because one minute everything is right with the world then the next it's all fucked to hell! Was it me? Did I do something wrong?"

"No damn it's not you!" I yelled.

"Then why? Why are you doing this? What will people think when they find out Richard? What will they think of me when they find out you left me for a man? What will they think of your family?"

"I will explain more on Sunday. I am sorry Mary, but everything will make sense then, okay. Just go home and relax, alright?"

"This isn't over Richard, I don't know what the hell is going on but this is far from over!"

She turned and walked down the sidewalk. Her friends followed her, looking back to throw me dirty looks. I sighed and closed the door.

I turned and found mom standing there, obviously having heard the whole conversation. I was sure dad did to, but I am glad he didn't come down with mom.

I wasn't ready to see him after the talk we all had.

"Mom," I started.

She walked up to me and gave me a hug. "Are you okay, sweetie?"

"No...everything sucks now. I feel like I have ruined everything," I scowled.

"Richard, this isn't your fault. You can't help what happened."

"But maybe if I fought harder. Maybe if I tried to resist, then none of this would have happened," I mumbled.

"Richard, love, especially true love, should never be denied," she said kindly.

"Mom, do you believe in soulmates?" I asked.

"I remember when I was a child and your grandmother would tell me stories about werewolves who found their true mates. I used to dream about finding my soulmate one day. Then I met your father, and I realized just because two people are not soulmates, it does not mean they can't be in love. I admit there have been times when loving your father has been difficult; he can be so damned stubborn and close-minded. But I wouldn't have him any other way because I also fell in love with him because of his stubbornness."

"So, yes or no?" I persisted.

She chuckled. "Yes, I do. And if you say Jeremy is your soulmate, then I believe you. But tell me, how does he feel about all this?" she asked.

"He...he was in love with another werewolf before he came here. His ex is the new Pack King of the Cambridge pack," I explained.

Her eyes got round with surprise. "Well, I have to give Jeremy credit. He doesn't settle for anything less than the best of men."

"Yeah, but said alpha ex broke his heart in a million pieces so he is a bit hesitant about being with me. But he feels something for me, he even admitted it."

"And does it frustrate you that he has yet to give in to your advances?" she asked.

"Hell yes! I used all my best moves and he still won't just give in. I mean, by the time I finish with him he smells like he is in heat but he never-"

Mom gave me a look that said I was going a little too far.

"I mean. I try really hard and nothing works," I finished.

She chuckled. "You're your father's son alright. When he first tried courting me he tried being slick and smooth. But then he quickly learned I wasn't going to fall down at his feet like all his other conquests. Eventually he came to understand he was going to have to change his tactics. He had to reign in his ego a bit and become more mature but in the end it worked, obviously."

"So. I need to do what dad did?" I asked.

"Well, I can't say yes. Though I am sure it would help. Hearts can be as beautiful as a diamond, but as delicate as glass," she said.

"But true love can cure all, right?" I asked.

"It can also destroy just as easily. If you and Jeremy really are soulmates, then you have to be very careful. Despite popular belief, love is not just a pure force of good; it is more like a force of nature. It can be beautiful, but highly destructive as well. You be good to him Richard Allen Farkas. And I pray he is good to you as well," she said.

"Thanks mom..so....how is dad?" I asked.

She rolled her eyes. "He is being a big baby. Give him time, he will come around. He didn't kick up this much fuss when Liz told us she like men and women."

"I wish I hadn't disappointed him," I muttered.

"Your father will learn to accept it. Just give him time," mom said.

I gave her another hug and kissed her on the cheek.

"So, does Jeremy know his ex is going to be here within the month?" she asked.

"Yeah, he knows," I said.

"Well, I have a feeling this years Nox de Lupus will be very interesting," she said thoughtfully.

22

Jeremy

I stared at myself in the mirror.

Rachel had done a good job. My hair was buzzed short and luckily it did bring out my manly good looks.

The side of my face was bruising from where Joseph kicked me. It made me look more rugged.

Mom was downstairs cleaning the dishes. Our kindly neighbors had made us get well food. Our fridge was now stuffed with an assortment of sweets.

There were cakes, pies, salads, puddings, and other nice snacks and meals that I would enjoy eating in the next couple of days.

If I had known I could get such good food, I would have kicked my own ass.

There was a knock on my door. "Come in," I said.

The door opened and closed. I turned expecting to see mom but instead found Richard.

"Hey, your mom let me in," he said.

"Oh. How are you doing?" I asked.

"Fine." He walked up to me and ran his hand over my head. "You look great. The hair really brings out the muscles in your jaw," he complimented.

He looked at my face, the part where I had been kicked and a flash of anger and sorrow appeared in his eyes.

"I am so sorry this happened to you," he said softly.

Something in me broke then. Something I had been carrying since those psychos kidnapped me. I wrapped my arms around him and hugged him as a small sob escaped my lips.

"Hey, it's okay. You're safe now," he rubbed my back soothingly.

"It's not that...I thought they were going to kill you. When he tasered you I was so afraid he was going to kill you," I mumbled.

I remembered the way his body twitched on the ground as Joseph sent jolts of electricity surging through him. The look in his eyes as he watched the pain he inflicted on Richard was so menacing.

I let him go and wiped my eyes. "Sorry. So much for my new manly look, huh?"

He leaned down and kissed my head tenderly. "Men can cry too, you know."

I pulled away from him and walked over to my bed.

"So....how was it today?" I asked.

"Dad freaked, mom was cool. Oh, and Mary knows," he nonchalantly threw in.

"What?" I exclaimed wide-eyed.

"She showed up demanding answers, so I told her. Well, she doesn't know we are soulmates, I didn't think she could handle *that* so I just told her we were...sort of together."

"Sort of?" I asked.

"Well....are we?" he asked.

He sat down next to me. I had a feeling we were about to have a heart to heart.

"I...don't know yet Richard....I...I feel for you but.....God....I'm not ready," I mumbled out.

He just smiled and put his hand on mine. "It's okay. I can wait."

"You shouldn't have to. You should go back to Mary and live the dream you had with her. How would we work Richard, I can't even give you kids."

"We can work around that. We can find a donor or something. The way things are nowadays two guys having a kid is much easier," he said.

I smiled sadly. "I'm sorry you have to deal with my baggage," I said.

He had a good life, then he met me now everything has been downhill for him.

"Jeremy, you have to understand. I will never hurt you like he did. I will never leave you. You are simply wonderful. You have a strong sense of right and wrong, you don't let anyone push you around. You're better for me then Mary was. I admit it, I am a dick but she encouraged me to be one. She didn't make a better person like you could," he said.

I sighed. "Why couldn't I have met you first?" I asked.

"Let's not dwell on what if," Richard stressed.

"So, how will my initiation work? Will I have to eat raw meat? Take down a deer?" I asked.

"No. Daryl will say some words, you will make some oaths, then that will be it," he explained.

"There will be food too of course?" I asked.

"Oh yeah, when someone is allowed into the pack it is a big deal. You will be getting your own party," he smiled.

"Sweet."

"But there is going to be one other ceremony," he let me know.

"Oh?"

"The ritual of the soul oath," he said.

"Come again?" I asked.

"It's the ritual a wolf performs when he declares another as his soulmate."

"Oh....go on," I said.

"I will officially declare you my soulmate. I will declare my undying love and devotion to you and that I will feed you, protect you and shelter you. Now, this is where things get tricky."

"Uh oh," I frowned.

"I have to prove to the pack we are soulmates," he said.

"How do we do that?" I asked.

"We share our auras," he explained.

"But I am not a werewolf, you can't use any werewolf mojo on me," I said.

"Well, I talked to my grandmother. She said even if the soulmates are of different species, their souls will still resonate with one another. Our energies will intermingle and the pack will sense them temporarily merging."

"Merging?"

"Apparently it is an experience beyond words; beyond human or even werewolf consciousness. It's supposed to be intense," he stated.

"Wow....so....ummm....we don't have to have sex in front of the pack right?"

He gave me a funny look. "What?"

"Sorry, I read too much smut," I laughed.

He rolled his eyes. "Humans, you always have your minds in the gutter."

He stood up and headed for the door. "Well, I will get going an-"

"Richard, sleep with me!"

He spun around, his mouth hanging open in shock. I mentally kicked myself for my choice of words.

"I mean-shit! I mean, tonight...in my bed-I mean....damn it! I mean just-spend the night with me....that is..if you want," I stuttered out.

I couldn't help but notice the flash of disappointment in his eyes.

"Sure. I need to call my parents and let them know," he said.

"And I need to let my mom know," I said.

I quickly left the room, cursing myself for being an idiot.

I found mom in the living room watching the news.

"Hey mom?"

She looked up at me and smiled. "Yes?"

"Can Richard spend the night?" I asked.

"Oh, sure. If it is okay with his parents, then it's fine with me," she answered with a smile.

"Cool, thanks mom." I turned to leave, but she stopped me.

"You know we are going to have to talk about this," she informed me.

"What?" I asked.

"Please, I know he spent the night at the hospital. My co-workers told me," she said giving me that mom look.

"It's...not...we're just friends," I stuttered.

She smiled slyly. "Oh, I can't wait to have this talk."

"Whatever," I said feeling my neck and ears get warm.

I was not looking forward to that *talk* with mom. I am *very* lucky to have a mother who is accepting and understanding like she is. But that didn't stop her from having a bit of good natured fun about my love life.

"Oh and Jeremy," she called.

"Yes," I turned to look at her.

"Keep your bedroom door open."

"Mom!"

I left with the sound of her laughter in my ears.

I made my way upstairs and Richard was waiting for me. I immediately took notice of the grin on his face.

"You heard what she said didn't you?" I asked him.

"Oh yeah," he laughed.

I sat down next to him.

"So, about this festival coming up; is there anything I should know? Like will I have to attend?" I asked.

"Not if you don't want. I have to because we always go. Dad says being one of the most respected families we have to make an appearance. Besides, Lucas will be there and I don't want you going through that bullshit all night," he responded.

I took a deep breath. "I want to go Richard. And I will. This is a part of your life and if I am your soulmate, then I have to learn more about your culture. Your heritage," I said.

"Didn't Lucas ever fill you in?" he asked.

"Not really. I was never allowed to attend any special ceremonies or rituals. Come to think of it, I don't think there were any other humans who knew the truth," I said thoughtfully.

"Not surprising. The red tribe is very strict and disciplined. They rarely let a human know about them without turning them or killing them," he explained.

"Isn't it the same with your tribe?" I asked.

"It depends on the circumstances. All the tribes agree keeping our species a secret from the humans is important, but each tribe has a different method for dealing with exposure. I think the only reason they didn't kill you or turn you was because of Lucas. Him being an alpha and his dad being the Pack King gave him certain privileges," Richard answered.

"And how do you guys deal with a leak?" I asked.

"Under extreme circumstances we kill the human. Otherwise we determine if the human can be persuaded to keep quiet or is useful to us, we invite them to join the pack. Lots of humans agree to the latter in the hopes they will earn the right to be sired. We may not be immortal but there are many other perks," Richard stated.

"Us being together won't cause a problem with the Cambridge pack will it?" I asked.

"No, even if he is the Pack King of his pack he will be on out turf and will have to conduct himself properly," his eyes darkened and his jaw tensed. "But it is the black tribe I worry about. As long as anyone can remember the two tribes have always been rivals and have many times in the past gone to war. They are sure to make their stay miserable for us just to be dicks."

"Lucas told me things about werewolves. But never as much as you have," I said.

"What did he tell you?" Richard asked.

"He told me there are five tribes. His was the red tribe. That each tribe worshiped a different god. He told me about alpha's. beta's and omega's and how a person can be changed into one, how moon flowers were sacred to your people and could cure wolfsbane poisoning. That's all he ever told me."

"I'm surprised he never told you more," Richard said.

I shrugged. "I always wanted to know more. But he was always hesitant to tell me. I never pushed him into telling me more. I was content to wait."

"So...you really do like blue, huh?" Richard asked.

He was looking around my room. My walls were a sky blue and my bedsheets were a deep navy color which matched my sheets.

"Yeah. Not just because of my eyes but because I think it is a very calming color. What's yours?" I asked.

"Red. But I also like violet," he said with a smile as he stared into my eyes.

"Really? Since when?" I asked.

"Since I saw them staring at me when we first met."

I blushed. "I wasn't staring, I was admiring you and your good looking friends," I stated.

"You were so checking me out," he replied smugly.

"Was not!" I spat.

He tapped his nose. "You're lying."

"Jerk," I mumbled.

"What kind of music do you like?" he asked.

"Are we doing the fifty questions thing?" I asked in amusement.

"Give me a break Jer, we have been hanging out these last few weeks and I know so little about you. If were going to be in each other's lives, we should know one another better. It might make things easier," he said.

He had a point.

In the last few weeks we have spent together we didn't talk much about ourselves or each other save for a few simple basic questions.

Truth be told, I had not been comfortable telling him too much about me. Or maybe I was not ready to open up to him.

But now after everything that has happened after he saved me from the hunters and revealed his secret to the pack how could I resist telling him more about me?

"Okay. You're right. Let's see, my favorite music would be One

Republic, Florence and the Machine, Green Day, Lorde and Lindsey Stirling."

"Whose Lindsey Stirling?" he asked.

"Oh, she was on America's Got Talent. She is a violinist, and she is amazing!" I said. "She makes such beautiful music. I follow her on YouTube and love listening her music. It's so serene and soothing."

"You like violin music?" he asked.

"It's my favorite instrument. The way it can convey emotion is inspiring."

"I prefer the guitar myself," he said. "I always thought violins were too sad to listen to."

"What about you? Who do you like to listen too?" I asked.

"Jay Z, Wiz Khalifa, Drake, Maroon Five," he said.

"Do you play guitar?" I asked remembering he had one back in his room.

He nodded. "Yeah. It's more a hobby. I don't do it professionally."

"What about family?" I asked. "Do you have any other relatives besides Daryl?" I asked

"My dads younger brother Eldred. He's like the total opposite of my dad. He's more carefree and fun loving. You'll meet him and his family at the Nox de Lupus."

"Doesn't he live in the Gates?" I asked.

He shook his head. "When I was young, he met and fell in love with a woman from the Woodbeam pack. They live in Montana. He married her and converted to her packs religion."

"Isn't the Woodbeam pack from the white tribe?" I asked.

He shook his head. "No, there of the yellow tribe."

A huge smile broke out on his face. "Man, it caused quite the stir. Dad refused to talk about him for months, he's still pissed about it. We still see Eldred and his family from time to time. Liz and I call him Uncle Free-baller because he runs naked like the rest of them do."

I chuckled. "He sounds nice; I can't wait to meet him."

"He is cool, but I have to warn you. He likes to give big hugs....even when he is naked," Richard smiled.

"Yeesh," I said.

"And my cousins....Gods they are little hellions. Liz and I always get stuck babysitting them. Which I find unfair because how are we supposed to look after six wolf pups?"

"Six? My God I feel bad for your uncle's wife," I grinned.

Richard smiled. "Wives, plural. He has three."

I stared at him in disbelief. "Three?"

"Yeah. The yellow tribe is big into polygamous marriages. A man or woman can have more than one spouse. The yellow tribe has more purebloods than even the black tribe."

"They like humans right? They're the hippies as I recall."

"Oh, they like everyone. Though they aren't too fond of humans when they cut down forests. Many times they have snuck into construction sites and wrecked the machines to save nature. They are very spiritual and really close to the earth is all. If a human wants to join them they can, but they have to be willing to give up modern technology. The yellow tribe prefers to live in cabins or out in the open. They're kind of the antithesis of the blue tribe who are all about science and logic."

"Man, I never thought werewolves were so cultured," I commented.

"Hey!" Richard said indignantly.

"I mean you guys are more complex than how you are portrayed in modern media!" I quickly said. "In the movies you guys are usually just running around howling at the full moon and eating people. But the truth is your much more complex than that. You have your own religious beliefs and government. It's kind of cool."

"Yeah, it is. People always focus on the wolf part of my kind. They assume we are more beast than man. They tend to forget we are also human. Most of the time at least."

*****

It was around eleven when we decided to go to bed.

We had been talking all night. We talked about our childhoods. He told me about growing up and learning he was an alpha and how he had to train to control his abilities.

I told him about growing up with mom. My story was more dull compared to his, but he listened eagerly to anything I could give him.

As we got ready for bed, I went downstairs to get some extra blankets and a pillow for Richard.

Mom had gone to bed a few hours ago, she had to work the morning shift at the hospital.

When I returned to my room, I found Richard in only his briefs. I stared, mesmerized. I looked down and saw a large bulge in the front. I remembered what he looked like naked and I couldn't help but shiver.

Richard smiled, and I was sure he could smell the effect he had on me.

"Like what you see?" he asked in a smug tone

"I didn't know you sleep in your underwear," I commented.

"I usually sleep nude, but I don't think you want that. Yet," he smiled.

"Whatever," I said trying not to blush.

I grabbed a pair of shorts from my dresser and left to go change in the bathroom. I wasn't going to change in front of Richard; the look he was giving me said he would have enjoyed to see me strip down to my cloths

Truth was I was nervous as hell. The idea of sleeping in the same room with Richard both excited me and terrified me. I hadn't felt like this since Lucas, and it made me angry.

How long was I going to feel this pain? I still care about Lucas but I hate him for what he did. I like Richard and want to be with him but I'm afraid by how quick and intense this is.

"Just do it in baby steps," I muttered to myself.

I walked back into my room, determined to not let this end badly. I asked Richard to stay and wasn't going to hurt him by asking him to leave.

Richard was eying me up and down as I re-entered the room. I shivered at the intensity of his gaze.

"We don't have an air mattress. Unless you would prefer the couch," I said.

He dug his heel into the ground. "I was wondering if I could sleep in your bed."

Werewolves are very tactile creatures. They took comfort in physical contact. I remember the dog piles I found myself in when I dated Lucas.

It took me a while to get used to, but I was quick to learn what might seem like an intimate touch from a werewolf was actually their way of showing trust and friendship.

But Richard was not any werewolf. He was my soulmate. That made things different.

"I promise I won't do anything you don't want to do. I just...I don't think I would be able to sleep. Knowing you're so close and being unable to touch you," he stated.

I thought about it for a moment. I had asked him to stay. I should have been prepared for something like this. Werewolves were all about platonic cuddling. For a human it might seem weird or even intimate but werewolves were just more tactile.

But I barely knew him and this soulmate business made things complicated. But he did make a promise and I would hold him to that.

"Sure," I said.

His face lit up with excitement.

I got in the bed first and Richard turned off the light, quickly sliding in after me.

I faced the wall, very much aware of him behind me. I could feel his breath on the back of my neck. I felt the weight of his gaze on the back of my head. I tried not to move my bottom; we were so close if I moved too much I would brush up against him.

Once again I remembered seeing him naked and covered in blood, and I remembered seeing he was erect. I figured it was the blood lust.

I remember the fights Lucas took me to see a friendly contest in his pack; the werewolves that fought had been naked. It frightened me how savage and brutal the fights could be. But the werewolves took it all in stride, even the losers.

No matter how badly they were beaten they never held grudges. They just laughed it all off and shook hands with the victors demanding a rematch one day.

Lucas was more excited than I had been to watch the fight. He cheered and stomped his feet with everyone else as we watched the men fight.

Eventually he got so worked up he fought himself. I had begged him not too, but he kissed me on the head and told me it would be fine.

He stripped off his cloths, and I had to watch him fight.

I got a peek into how violence and sex could mix that night. The more fights a werewolf won, the more honor was bestowed on him and he had more females he attracted.

I remembered one of the winners from that night; a man called Rodrick had several women licking his wounds and other....intimate areas.

What I hadn't told Richard was that the little fight club turned into a sex club. All the adrenaline seemed to tip the werewolves into a mating frenzy and soon an orgy had begun.

Lucas and I quickly left for his place and he calmed me down. It had disturbed me to see such violence, and then such debauchery. One minute they're beating the fuck out of each other, and the next they're having sex in full view of everyone.

I had asked Lucas why they did it. How could they act like this?

"Because it is who we are. We are warriors, we are a pack. We fight, we fuck and we live; it is simple as that."

After that I found out he was in need of some relief. All the sex and blood had aroused him as well. And let me tell you, it was really good sex too.

I wondered if the white tribe did that as well; had their little fight clubs and public orgies. I couldn't imagine it though because the white tribe seemed to be classier and too high maintenance for such things.

Richard snuggled close to me wrapping his arm around my waist.

He didn't do anything else. I let him have this one luxury because I enjoyed feeling him holding me.

I shut my eyes and let sleep take me.

*****

I dreamed I was in a dark forest. The trees towered over me, gnarled and leafless, baring down sinisterly at me. Their branches were sharp and reminded me of the edge of a knife.

It was cold, a sense of dread hung in the atmosphere like mist and it was deathly silent, as if the very air was holding its breath.

As if it was hiding from something.

I was barefoot, my feet burned every time they touched the ground. It felt like hot ash on my skin. My arms and face were covered in cuts from running through bushes and past branches.

It was like they purposely followed my movements, trying to cut me and draw blood.

I was running from something. Something deadly, something that wanted to hurt me.

I dared not stop, I dare not look. But I could feel it getting closer and closer. I could feel its blood lust. I knew if it caught me I was dead. I had to keep running. Because what ever was chasing would not stop.

It would never stop.

It was right behind me, I could hear the sounds of its massive paws hitting the ground, hear its vicious snarls as it chased me.

I tripped and fell on the ground. I turned and stared death in the eye.

It was massive and black, blacker than ink and the darkness between the stars. I saw eyes white as milk; like the eyes of a corpse, filled with rage and teeth as long as daggers gleaming in the moonlight.

"I found you!" it spat.

It jumped at me, it was so large I was sure it could crush me with the amount of weight it had.

"Jeremy, wake up!"

*****

I woke up covered in sweat. Richard was shaking me.

"Are you okay? You were having a nightmare," he told me.

"I...I am fine," I panted.

I was not alright though. God that dream had felt so real. My skin still felt the cold air from the forest and even my feet still felt hot. I even checked my arms, looking for cuts and scrapes.

I could still smell the breath of the wolf, like death and decay.

Richard pet my head soothingly, careful to not touch the wound where Joseph had kicked me. I lay my head on his chest taking comfort in his embrace.

The dream was so real. I could still feel the black wolf's presence.

"What did you dream of?" he asked gently.

"It was just a bad dream. I can't really remember what it was about," I lied.

Last thing I wanted to do was tell him I dreamed of a wolf attacking me, he might take that the wrong way and I was afraid it would hurt his feelings if I told him..

I was sure he knew In was lying. But thankfully he didn't press me to know more.

"You're safe now, it's all okay," he said soothingly.

He kissed the top of my head and I snuggled close to him. I breather in his scent, let it wash away the dreaded memory of the nightmare, let his warmth sink into me and warm me up.

Sleep soon claimed me again the last thing I remember was wrapping my arm around him and clung to him for dear life.

*****

Richard

I watched Jeremy sleep; he didn't whimper this time or cry out. I couldn't imagine what he had been dreaming about; whatever it was scared the shit out of him.

I gently placed my leg over both of his, careful not to wake him and covering him more with my body.

He was holding onto my so tight, even as he slept, like I was the only thing keeping him floating in a large body of water filled with monsters..

I was glad mom was taking this whole mess in stride. I wish dad could be more understanding. But I shouldn't be surprised. Growing up he was always hard on me, he wanted me to succeed and make something of myself so he gave me lots of tough love.

He dreamed I would find a nice alpha woman, have a bunch of kids, and one day be Pack King.

Well, I could still be Pack King at least.

It wasn't easy trying to please my dad as much as I love him I also resent him a bit. Things at home were going to be so fucking awkward now because dad will be in a constant state of aggravation and I was sure we're going to have a few more fights.

It didn't matter. Jeremy and I are soulmates. I don't know why it happened, but it did. I won't go back to trying to ignore it and I won't do what Lucas did to him either.

Jeremy deserves someone who will love him, and that will be me.

If dad doesn't like it, then too bad.

Daryl had been shocked, but he was accepting. And I am sure Eldred or his wives wouldn't care about Jeremy was a guy. Their tribe didn't sweat things like gender.

Everyone was accepting. When I finally told grandma she hugged me and told me she loved me no matter what. We had a long talk about why this was happening to me why even though I was decidedly straight my soulmate was a guy.

Not exactly a conversation I thought I would ever have with my her. But she is my grandmother and the pack shaman. She wanted to help me not just because she loved me, but because helping people when they were going through emotional or spiritual upheavals.

Dad is the only one kicking up a fuss. I could understand this was all sudden and unexpected. But I wish he was a little more supportive.

I took a deep breath of Jeremy's scent and let it lull me to sleep.

Soon Jeremy would be a member of the pack and everyone would know. Then we could finally work towards building a relationship.

If Jeremy wants to take things slow, then that is what we will do. I know no matter how long it takes he will be mine.

After all, I am already his.

23

Jeremy

I sat with Liz and Richard in his car.

Liz sat in the back while I rode up front with Richard. Tonight was the big night. I told mom I was spending the night at Richard's, it was the only way she would let me out of the house after Joshua kidnapped me. She always made sure I was with someone; she got nervous when I was alone and now she always made sure Richard or Rick brought me home from school.

The pack had falsified reports of what happened with Joshua and the other Hunters.

The story was that Joshua had kidnapped me but he had been seen committing the act. Rick and the other deputies found him and there was a stand off and he was shot and killed.

The whole town was relieved the threat of a mad man was over. The pack was happy the rogue Hunters were dead. But all I could feel right now was nervous about the whole ceremony tonight.

We were driving to Hunter's Meadow.

Apparently it is a sacred place to the werewolves. It is where they have all their pack meetings. It's also where the teens like to throw wild parties. As long as they clean up and don't leave any trash, the elders let them do it.

Liz told me it had been sacred to many Native American tribes. Human and werewolf. According to her grandmother it's a convergence point for ley lines and had a strong connection to werewolves.

That's why it was built by the werewolves many centuries ago. They believed Hunter's Meadow brought them closer to the Moon.

I tried to imagine the old werewolf tribes digging huge holes and moving these giant boulders to make the formation. Even with their inhuman strength it would have taken a lot of them to do.

The Meadow was highly desired by many packs and tribes. Richard told me that in its early days the pack of Wolf Fang Falls had to fight the Black tribe for ownership of the Meadow. And to this day it is still desired by many other packs.

I admit, it is a visually stunning place and I can see the appeal. But I can't imagine fighting a war for a bunch of rocks.

Then again wars are always fought over petty things.

We were all quiet. Liz and Richard were both calm, I was the only one who was tense. I was joining a wolf pack and doing some weird ritual to prove I was Richard's soulmate.

"Don't be scared Jeremy, we are backing you up," Richard said.

"I can't help it. What if something goes wrong?" I asked.

I was pretty nervous. Richard had explained to me like a dozen times how this would play out.

But as always I was a pessimist and expected the worst to happen.

"Relax. No one is going to start shit here, Hunter's Meadow is a no violence zone," Liz stated.

We drove down the same road I did when I came here last. There were cars parked here and there just like the night of the party.

We had less than two hours before the change would happen. I could tell Richard and Liz were feeling the effects. They moved more wolfish and showed more teeth when they got aggravated.

We found a spot to park, got out and walked to the stones in the clearing.

I could see dozens of people; much more than there had been at the party. There was well over a hundred wolves in this pack, bigger than

Lucas's pack had been.

I took a deep breath and followed Richard and Liz. Richard walked between Liz and me. Every once in a while his shoulder would bump mine. I couldn't tell if it was just an accident or if it was on purpose.

Werewolves communicate with touch so maybe he was trying to calm me down, or maybe I was looking to much into it.

They had started a fire at the center of the formations. I could smell cooking meat and remembered there would be an assortment of foods tonight.

I could hear lots of people talking. But then one by one they stopped and stared at us as we approached. I was very aware of dozens...no hundreds of eyes staring at us.

I was suddenly hoping I would not end up on the menu tonight.

Truth be told, I wasn't nervous about what the wolves would think or do. Though, I was hoping there would be no fighting tonight, the thing that scared me the most is the Soul Oath Ritual.

It was so...intimate. More so than sex. I mean, we would be exposing our souls to one another in front of other people just to prove we were bonded..

And the sharing of my soul, or aura, or energy, or whatever with Richard.....it just....yeesh. I mean, what if something goes wrong? What if we find out we are not soulmates? What if it is just a thing Richard is going through? Then what?

I was being stupid, I know. The way that Richard looks at me isn't the way a bi-curious guy looks at you. It's true love.

Isn't it funny how people spend their whole lives looking for true love and here I am bitching about it?

There was a tension in the air, and I became aware of people talking, whispering. Richard's parents stepped out of the crowd. His mom looked kindly at me and smiled. His dad was giving me a glare that said he would love to chew me up and spit me out....literally.

And after remembering what the pack did to those rogue Hunters, I really wanted to try to avoid pissing off Frank more than I have already.

Richard and Liz nodded to their parents, and I did the same as a courtesy.

I looked up at the rock formations and saw some people sitting on top of them like before at the party, looking down at us with the same intensity and curiosity everyone else was. I noticed Mary and her kin sitting on top of one formation and if Frank's looks were scary, then Mary.....Jesus, I have never had someone look at me with such....hatred.

The rest of her clan were watching me with mixed looks of anger and disgust. I had a feeling if anyone was going to cause an issue it would be them.

I noticed Daryl and several others standing on the highest rock formation. I knew the woman next to him was his wife Erica. The young guy next to them was their son. There were a few others with them; the elders of the pack. These werewolves were some of the oldest, the strongest and the most highly respected of the pack. They would offer wisdom and council to the Pack King.

I spotted Richard's grandmother, Susan. She was looking graceful and elegant. She smiled warmly at me, her eyes filled with the same kind of warmth I saw in Elizabeth and Janice's eyes.

I noticed many people weren't wearing much clothing. Some men had their shirts off as did some women though they did wear bras. Many were even in their underwear.

I knew it was because of the full moon; werewolves get antsy and find clothes to be too constricting so they preferred to wear as little as possible.

My fingers began to twitch, despite how nervous I was I had an urge to take pictures. But there was a strict no pictures policy during pack meetings and full moons.

We would do the initiation, then the Soul Oath Ritual, eat some grub, and then the wolves would change and run off to frolic in the woods before returning where we would have a great big sleepover. But I had a feeling it was going to be a bit more complicated than that. I don't know why, it was just a feeling I had.

We had gone over it a dozen times in the last couple days but that damn voice in the back of my head was saying something was going to go wrong. I decided to ignore that voice and instead worry about what was going on rather than what might happen.

Daryl was shirtless, only wearing a simple pair of black shorts. I could see the family resemblance between Frank and him. Daryl was Richard's three times removed cousin. But he had the same intimidating height, the same build and black hair as well as that authority of power and command.

He raised his hands and everyone quieted down.

"Tonight we welcome a new member into our pack. Tonight we also perform another ritual; one that is very rare, one we should all feel blessed to take part in," Daryl announced.

"I object this!" a voice said.

Well, that didn't take too fucking long.

I looked up and saw Mary's father was the one who objected. "What has this human done to earn membership into our pack?" he asked.

There were sounds of people murmuring in agreement. They had a right, too. I wasn't someone who could be useful after all. I was just a stranger who supposedly is the soul mate of another werewolf.

Werewolves are very picky about who they let into their pack. Wolf or human, the wrong person could mess up the balance of power in the pack.

"As you are all aware, Jeremy saved Richard from a Hunter not too long ago. We do owe him a debt," Daryl informed everyone.

"A debt we paid when we saved him from the Hunters," another voice called out.

"And we object to his joining; this boy has caused great distress for my family and I," Mary's dad said.

"He stole Richard from me!" Mary cried out.

"He didn't steal me from you Mary. I dumped you of my own free will," Richard reminded her.

"Richard, you are like a son to me. How could you hurt Mary like this? You promised her marriage one day. Your parents and I looked forward to the day when our two families would be united by the blood of the children you would one day have. You told Mary you planned to mate with her for life," her dad said.

"Jason, believe me, I know what you are going through," Frank said. Richard's face had fell a little when his dad spoke. "I myself am very disappointed and disturbed by these turn of events, but Richard made no true oaths. He did not swear on the Moon or the goddess. There is nothing binding in his promises."

If you ever make a deal with a werewolf; a deal you want to know for sure they will follow through with, make them swear on the Moon or one of their deities. It is considered the highest level of dishonor and disgrace for a werewolf to make an oath like that and then break it. Even if you were tricked into, it you were still expected to follow through.

Liz said even the black tribe took that shit seriously and they are the evil lunatics of the werewolves.

Richard stepped forward and spoke to the tribe. "My reasons for my actions are for me to explain. As you have all heard I kissed Jeremy when we saved him. The truth is, I love him, Jeremy is my soulmate."

The crowd broke out into angry growls and jeers. Some called him a liar, and some thought he was just blowing his feelings for me out of proportion.

"It is true, I am not speaking figuratively. Jeremy Moonvine is my soulmate. And tonight I will perform the Soul Oath Ritual with him to prove it!!" Richard announced.

"That's impossible! You're a man, as is he!" someone in the pack exclaimed.

Susan spoke up. Her voice was loud and clear. "It is true, for a pair of the same sex to be soulmates is exceptionally rare. But there are cases. I have gone over this myself and going by what Richard has told me; he and Jeremy are soulmates," she said.

People were talking now, they weren't bothering to whisper. I caught snippets of conversation myself.

"Ridiculous!"

"Absurd!"

"Outrageous!"

"It would explain his behavior."

"Didn't see this coming."

"But he's a man."

"I can't believe his parents are allowing this to go on."

"Poor Mary, how must she feel?"

"Susan wouldn't lie about something like this even for Richard."

"I demand proof!" Mary roared. "I refuse to believe that Richard, a man I have slept with many times, is gay!"

"And you will have proof, once we begin the ceremony," Daryl said. "According to the most sacred laws of all the tribes, a wolf's soulmate is allowed the right to join the pack. The soulmate is not to be harmed by anyone in the pack." Daryl gave Mary and her family a hard look. "The punishment of killing another's soul mate can be met with the most severe punishment. Death."

He jumped down from the formation as did Susan. It was amazing to see Daryl land perfectly on his feet from such a height. But Susan looked positively mind blowing. You would think a woman her age would break her legs jumping from such a height like that. But she landed just as perfectly as he did.

"Jeremy Moonvine, step forward," Daryl instructed, his voice was firm and full of authority.

I took a deep breath and walked up to him. "Remove your shirt," Daryl began.

I did as he said; I took my shirt off and gently laid it on the ground. One of the people who were gathered around, stepped forward, and put a fur cloak over my shoulders. I recognized it as wolf skin. Wasn't sure if it was real wolf or werewolf.....wasn't sure I wanted to know.

Another put a laurel crown made from moonflowers on top of my head. Susan stepped forward. She held a small wooden bowl in her hand.

She put her finger in the bowl and began to paint my face.

First her finger traveled down my nose, then across each eye, and then she made a vertical line on my chin.

"Who here speaks for this young man?" Susan asked.

"I do," a voice I recognized as Richard.

"As do I," another voice said. I was surprised to hear Rick.

"Step forward," Susan commanded.

Richard appeared to my right, having discarded his shirt. Rick to my left, he was only in his briefs. It was weird seeing the sheriff in his undies. It was even more awkward because mom had a thing for him.

And I had to agree with her...he did have a nice ass.

"Richard, for what reason do you speak for this human?" Daryl asked.

"He is my soulmate. I love him with all my being and know he will keep the pack a secret and never betray us. I know he is going to be a wonderful addition to our pack. As one who intends to court him, I offer to protect him and care for him as a mate should."

I heard a growl in the air. Daryl looked up sharply at who made the sound and the growling stopped, (I had a good idea who it was though), no one else made a sound, respecting the ritual.

"Rick, for what reason do you speak for this human?" Daryl repeated the same question to Rick.

"I have a history with his mother. He comes from a good bloodline that can be trusted. I also offer him my protection as one who intends to court his mother, and wish to keep him safe on behalf of his mother, who does not know our secret."

I looked sharply at Rick. He intended to court my mom?

As much as I was grateful to him for this, we were seriously going to have to talk about this whole courting thing.

"And do you both accept responsibility for this young man? To guide him in the ways of our people and if necessary, discipline him should he break our laws?" Daryl asked.

"I do," Rick nodded.

"I do," Richard agreed.

Richard told me when a werewolf takes responsibility for a human that means if the human breaks the rules not only will the wolf be punished but he or she must punish the human they are protecting.

I doubt Richard would ever punish me even if I did break a few major rules. Rick, I did not doubt would tan my hide if I did something dumb.

One of Susan's attendants handed her a larger wooden bowl. She walked up to Richard and Rick and they placed the palms of their hands in the bowl which was filled with a white paint.

They then placed their hands on me. Richard's over my heart and Rick's on my right ab.

The marks were their signature; showing how many werewolves I had vouching for me that I was trustworthy. The fact that Rick himself was willing to stand up for me changed things.

As I looked around at the other werewolves, I noticed some of the tension seemed to have slipped away. The fact that I, an unknown guy, was suddenly being made into a friend of the pack troubled many.

But the fact that the sheriff; the keeper of the law and a very well-respected alpha, was willing to vouch for me seemed to win me some brownie points.

"Jeremy Moonvine. Do you swear by the Moon and by the White Wolf to always keep our secret? To help protect each of us, just as each of us will protect you? To honor us as we will honor you?" Daryl asked.

I took a deep breath. "I swear by the Moon and by the white wolf to keep your secret, to protect each of you and to honor you," I repeated.

"Then by the authority invested in me as Pack King, and by the power of the goddess herself, I Daryl Farkas, do welcome you into my pack!"

Daryl threw his head back and a loud howl escaped his lips. One by one, dozens of voices filed the night air as the pack howled in respect of my initiation.

"And now, it is time for the Soul Oath Ritual!" Daryl exclaimed once the howls died down.

A new feeling swept over the crowd. Anticipation. The only time this ritual was performed was between soulmates. And it wasn't every day you saw that happen, so naturally lots of people were curious to see what was about to transpire.

Hell, it might not even happen in any of our lifetimes; that is how rare finding your soulmates is.

But this was also the moment when we would all find out if Richard and I were truly are meant to be.

"Richard Farkas, step forward," Susan commanded.

Richard did. Like me, he was given a wolf skin coat and a laurel of moonflowers. It was funny to see Mr. Macho-Man wearing a crown of flowers. Too bad I didn't have a camera. I would make this image the wallpaper for my phone.

"Richard Farkas. Do you acknowledge Jeremy Moonvine as your soul mate? Do you accept the responsibility this commitment carries? Do you swear to love and protect him, he who caries your heart?" Susan asked.

"I do," Richard replied.

Susan turned to me. "Jeremy Moonvine. Do you acknowledge Richard Farkas as your soul mate? Do you accept the responsibility this commitment carries? Do you swear to love and protect him, he who carries your heart?"

The whole thing was a little too wedding-like for my taste. But if this was a wedding, someone would have told me.

No way Richard wouldn't tell me if this was something like that.

But yet, it felt like a binding. I mean, I was acknowledging Richard was my soulmate; that I was in love with him. I couldn't pull out now, that might make him look bad in front of the pack, and I knew things were about to become more difficult for him and I didn't want to add any more pressure.

And to be honest, I don't think I could have said no.

Because I wanted to know beyond of a shadow of a doubt if we were soulmates. Because I no longer felt like I could trust my own feelings. So if this could finally erase any doubt I had then so be it.

"I do," I said.

"Then, let your souls touch one another. Show us all that you are indeed destined!" Susan instructed.

Richard and I had gone over this. We would face each other. We would place our hands on the others chest where our hearts were and on the center of the others head. Apparently it had something to do with the heart and head chakras.

We had practiced this, so I knew what to do. I put my right hand on his chest where his heart was. It was beating pretty fast; he must be nervous as well. My left hand I put on his forehead.

He did the same to me and looked me dead in the eyes. Eye contact was crucial he had told me. Windows of the soul and all that.

"You ready" he asked.

"I am," I said.

He took a deep breath, and I waited. I didn't know what to expect. I have never felt a werewolf's energy before.

I remembered how the werewolves from Lucas's pack would shudder or flinch when Lucas got angry or confrontational. As if they were being struck by an invisible force.

I just continued to breathe and stay relaxed. Hopefully this wouldn't hurt.

I continued to stare into his honey brown eyes. The light from the fire danced in them, making them appear more mesmerizing than they already were.

I gasped as I felt something hot spread over my body. Like the scorching wind of the desert. It started where his hands touched me as if he was pouring warm water over me.

It was unlike anything I have felt before. I felt like I was hooked up to an IV pumping me full of an energy drink with lots of sugar, caffeine, adrenaline and steroids.

Goosebumps grew on my skin as the feeling washed over me. For the first time in a long time my heart skipped a beat. It was like the air around us was becoming warmer. But it didn't make me thirsty or feel like I was drying up. I felt like a plant, soaking in the sun's rays.

I could not stop staring into Richard's eyes. They still remained the same, but now it was as if I could see into him now.

Then it happened. It was just the two of us; me and him.

I could hear nothing, see nothing, feel nothing and smell nothing but him. I saw around him and into him. I saw him for what he really was.

I saw everything that made him Richard. I saw his pride, I saw his arrogance, I saw the gentleness he showed so very few. I saw the predator in him; the one that enjoyed flaunting his power and authority over others. I saw the love and care he had for his family and pack. I saw the courage and determination and I saw his vanity.

Everything, the good and bad was laid bare.

When I looked into his eyes, I saw his soul. I can't tell you what a soul looks like..it is....indescribable. Like opening up a book, only instead of finding words you find thoughts and feelings.

I knew he was seeing the same of me as I stared into him he was looking into me and I had a terrible sense of openness. I wondered what he saw. What strengths and weakness made me, me?

In that moment I knew I was in love with Richard. I could no longer deny it. I was in love with him, and after this I could never just treat him as a very good friend.

Because at the core of this man, beyond the ego and the flesh and the man and the beast was something I needed. A piece of myself that was not a part of me yet fit me perfectly.

Sadly, I felt the warmth fade away; his power retreated back into his body and I suddenly felt cold.

"And so the ritual has been completed, let it be known that Richard Farkas and Jeremy Moonvine are indeed soulmates," Susan said, her voice a little shaky.

I broke my gaze with Richard to look around. Many in the pack were looking shocked and surprised. I noticed a lot of men and women were holding hands and looking into each other's eyes lovingly.

Some even had tears shining in their eyes as if they just witnessed something beautiful.

Richard took my hand in his and bent down and kissed me. I kissed him back, I didn't hesitate, I didn't pull away. How could I not kiss him after what just happened?

We pulled away and people began to clap and cheer, many even howled in approval. It was a change from what things had been like but a few moments ago.

"Allow me to introduce to you, Richard Farkas and his husband, Jeremy Moonvine!" Daryl shouted.

Yes, the ritual was complete, and now we were-

Wait what?

Richard and I looked at Daryl sharply.

"Wait....husband?" Richard asked.

Daryl looked at Richard with a funny look, like he didn't understand why Richard would say that. "Yes Richard. You and Jeremy just performed the Soul Oath Ritual."

"Yeah, to prove we are soulmates," Richard pointed out.

The air was silent. I looked around, and once again lots of people were looking shocked. Hell, even the Farkas family were looking flabbergasted; Frank looked like he was about to pop an aneurism.

"Well, you had to prove you were soulmates before you got married, I mean we can't just let everyone get married this way. It is the most ancient and binding of all marriage ceremonies in all the five tribes,"

Daryl explained.

"What?" I asked.

"Richard, didn't you read this in the books I gave you?" Susan asked looking confused.

"I...I...kind of skimmed it," Richard said shakily rubbing the back of his head.

"What?" I asked a little more loudly.

Frank suddenly appeared next to us, his face red as a tomato. Liz and Janice came up on our other side. They were both glaring at Richard with the same intensity Frank was.

"Are you telling us we all just witnessed my son marry this human!?" he yelled.

Daryl and Susan looked at one another. They shared a look that clearly said "Uh oh."

"Yes Frank, according to the most sacred rules of the tribes, Jeremy and Richard are husband and husband till death do them part," Daryl said.

"WHAT?!" I yelled.

24

Richard

"You skimmed it?!" dad yelled.

"I...yeah...I did," I said weakly.

"You skimmed a book detailing important ceremonies and rituals? Really, Richard?" mom asked looking exasperatedly at me.

"It was really long and boring; I figured I could just skip certain parts you know?"

Every other paragraph in the damn book was about eternal and undying love. It got old after a few chapters so I just skipped certain parts to save time.

"Richard, you just married Jeremy Moonvine in front of the whole pack!" dad shouted.

"Yeah, this sucks, I was supposed to plan your wedding, now my chance is gone," Liz said with a pout.

Dad and mom fixed her with a glare.

"Sorry, just trying to lighten the mood," she said holding up her hands.

Dad turned to grandma. "Susan, please tell me there is some kind of loophole, or a ritual to annul this."

She shook her head. "I am sorry, this is a binding ritual; once entered, only death can end it."

"Well, this is just fucking great!" Frank hollered.

"Richard, how could you be so irresponsible?!" mom screamed.

"Why didn't you tell me it was a wedding ceremony, grandma?" I asked.

"Well, I did ask you if you read the book thoroughly and that the ritual was forever binding and you said yes and you wanted to do the ritual," she said giving me a piercing look. "I assumed you read the part about it being a marriage ceremony. I should have known better!"

I looked over to Jeremy. He was talking to Daryl and Rick. I couldn't believe we were now married. I was shocked, amazed and to be honest...kind of pleased, but I don't think I should tell anyone that.

My wolf was thrilled; Jeremy and I were bound for life by ancient laws that could not be broken. It was a big step to fully claiming him.

"You are grounded mister," mom stated, drawing my attention.

"What?" I asked. Seriously? She is going to ground me now?

"You heard me. This is all your fault, young man. How do you think Jeremy feels right now? That poor boy is still recovering from a broken heart and this happens? You are not doing a good job so far as a soulmate!" she said firmly.

I felt bad, worse than when dad chastises me. I mean, he does that a lot, but when mom does it I know I fucked up. Not that I needed anyone to tell me that.

"Well, let's go talk to him, see what Daryl has to say about this," dad said.

We walked back over to them. Daryl was giving me a look that screamed *you idiot!* Rick glared at me with a look that said *I should beat the snot out of you!* And Jeremy wouldn't even look at me, which I thought was the worst.

"Way to go Richard, you really fucked up on this," Daryl said.

"What now? What happens between us now?" I asked.

"Whatever you want, you two are married now. We will have to go over the smaller little tidbits later. Now that Jeremy is your husband, he has rights to your inheritance and property."

"I don't need money," Jeremy said, still not even looking at me.

"It will be between you and Richard to work out personal details such as that. But for now, let us try to get tonight over with as quickly as possible."

Once again, he turned to address the pack.

"My people. Despite a certain overlook, (everyone save Jeremy gave me a glare), the marriage between them is still binding. Despite this surprising turn of events, let us enjoy this night. Both to welcome a new brother and to celebrate what will hopefully be a happy union."

With that he ordered for the feast to begin.

The pack was buzzing like bees. No one could believe what happened. Richard Farkas just accidentally married a human who was his soulmate.

My street-cred was not looking good right now. I just seriously humiliated myself and my family for my oversight. I just made myself look like a complete and total fucking idiot and a bad mate to Jeremy.

A feeling of shame washed over me. I was a disgrace to my family and my pack.

The worst part was people kept walking up to my family and I, welcoming Jeremy into the pack and congratulating my parents.

Scott, Keven, Bob, Trevor and Henry walked up to me. "Can we borrow Richard for a moment?" Trevor asked.

"Go on," dad said looking like he would be glad to be as far from me as possible.

My friends took me as far from the pack as they could so we could talk.

"Dude, what the fuck?" Henry asked.

"I fucked up guys, I know, okay!" I said.

"Dude, you are seriously in deep shit!" Bob exclaimed.

"Yeah, I have already heard a few alphas talking about how they plan on challenging you," Keven mentioned.

I had already expected this. My union with Jeremy and my very obvious foolishness was going to cause many of the alphas to see me as weak, and challenge me. I was going to have to start fighting for my position as one of the strongest alphas in the pack.

"What are we going to do?" Henry asked.

"We? You mean you still want to be friends with me?" I asked.

They all rolled their eyes at me.

"Richard, we won't lie, this soul mating thing with a dude freaks us the fuck out, okay. But you are still our best friend. I mean, how could I abandon you after you took me under your wing when I was turned?" Trevor said.

"How could I forget that time you fought that prick Matt when he and his group jumped me?" Bob asked.

"How could I forget when you helped me and Chelsea get together?" Henry asked.

"We ain't ditching you, man," Keven promised.

"But how many of the others will remain the same?" I asked.

They refused to meet my eye.

"Damn it," I muttered.

I was sure I had lost a bunch of my supporters. Before becoming Pack King, it is always wise to make friends and allies. That way when you take over, your reign won't be filled with people questioning your every move or other alphas challenging you.

Before, I had enough friends and allies to almost guarantee that when I did one day take over it would be a smooth transition. But now?

"Alright, before we run, I want you all to mingle with the pack. Keep your ears open and find out exactly who are still on my side and who have lost faith in me. I need to know how bad my image is now," I instructed.

"Dude, you just accidentally married your human soulmate. It will be pretty bad," Keven said.

We all went our separate ways while the guys did as I instructed I went looking for Jeremy.. He was talking to some of the other human members of the pack.

"Excuse us, we need to talk," I said.

I took his hand and gently moved him to some place private. It was pointless because all eyes were on us.

I took off the wreath still on my head and turned to look at him.

"Jer, I am so sorry, I fucked up bad, I know. Please forgive me," I begged him.

He looked at me, his face perfectly neutral. His heartbeat was steady though I did smell some stress in his scent.

"It was just supposed to be you declaring me your soulmate," he said.

"I know I-"

"Just a simple thing to help make my initiation into the pack go more smoothly and to help keep me safe."

"I know-"

"But because you skimmed a fucking book, we are now man and....man!" he growled. I was suddenly very glad he was not a werewolf. I had a feeling if he had a pair of claws he would be using them....on me. "I'm not married for even five minutes and I already want to kill my husband!"

"So...you want to stay with me?" I asked feeling hopeful.

"Not like we have much choice, idiot! I talked to Daryl, and he told me there is no way out of this unless one of us dies. Way to go, Richard."

"Jeremy, please tell me what I can do to fix this. Please don't be mad at me!" I begged him.

Since we did the ritual my feelings for him were more intense, more raw. The thought he might want to leave me now was too painful to bare, I could not imagine not having him in my life.

Not after we shared our souls to one another.

When I looked into him and saw his spirit I saw how truly precious he was. The bond between us was stronger now; I only hoped he was feeling it too.

He sighed and rolled his eyes at me. "Richard, I just shared my soul with you. Right now....I feel all kinds of fucked up. I am angry with you, but there is a part that is also happy about this and...I don't know how to feel about that. I need time to process all this, okay?"

I put my hand on his cheek. "I am sorry. I promised I wouldn't hurt you. Yet I keep on doing it," I said.

"On the plus side, the pack seems to like me now. Our show must have been really impressive," he said with a small grin.

"The werewolves felt the energy of our union, they felt our love. They can't give us shit for being together now. But after my little fuck up, I fear I am going to have to work on my image," I said.

"So....now what?" he asked.

I sighed. "I don't know."

Liz appeared then, wrapping her arm around Jeremy's. "So, how is it going my brother-in-law?" she asked teasingly.

"Shocked, can't say I am surprised. I had a feeling something would happen...just not this. I figured Mary would cause something," Jeremy said.

I looked around and realized I couldn't see Mary. Most of her family was gone save for her dad and eldest brother, Derek. They were talking to a few others in the pack.

Derek caught my eye, and we had a serious battle of the wills.

Derek and I never got along much. He wanted to be Pack King, and I wanted to be Pack King. He had his group of friends and I had mine. But we respected one another for our strength and for Mary's sake.

After I broke up with her both he and his younger brother Neal challenged me and although Neal wasn't much of a problem Derek came dangerously close to beating me.

This was the perfect time for him to make his move. My rep was shit now, and it would be a good time to take my old friends and allies as his own. Plus, I just shamed his sister and his family so now he had anger to fuel his campaign.

That reminds me.

"Where is Mary?" I asked.

"After your little show she took off like a bat out of hell. Between sensing your energy and finding out you two are married, I don't think she could handle it," Liz said.

Shit, I hadn't stopped to think about that; about how she would react. Between the shock of it all and dealing with the fallout, I hadn't had time to think about it.

One more thing to add to my list of things that will bite me on the ass, I am sure.

*****

The night carried on, people were still buzzing about what happened, of course. My friends and I had gathered again to talk.

"Dude, you are in some serious shit," Keven said.

"What have you guys learned?" I asked.

"We have been talking and a bunch of the others have jumped ship to Derek's side," Trevor said.

"Damn! I knew that fucker would be using this as a chance to bag some followers!" I growled.

"A few are ambivalent. They have not joined him but have made it clear your actions have not won you their favor. I think if you play your cards right you can get some of them back," Bob said.

"Others won't be so easy to convince. They think you being in love and married to a guy makes you a sissy and won't follow a fag," Scott threw in.

I sensed someone approach us. No not someone, someones.

I turned, and the others stood next to me, showing a united front. Derek walked up to me, his friends, and many of my now former friends with him. I saw Jack, Charlie, Dylan and Dante, among others.

Derek had a cocky smile, as if he enjoyed flaunting the fact he had my friends on his side, but knowing him he probably did.

"Well, Richard, congratulations. Your husband sure is pretty. You are a lucky man," he said.

Some of the others snickered.

"Jeremy is a good guy. This marriage may have been an oversight, but I do not regret it," I said truthfully.

"Choosing a weak human over a beautiful alpha werewolf? I thought you had more pride than that, Richard," he said.

"Oh, I have pride Derek, but even I am not so full of myself as to deny when I have made mistakes. I fucked up and I am willing to accept the consequences for it," I said.

"Oh, you haven't even begun to pay Richard, not yet," he said, his voice hardening.

"That a threat?" I asked.

The guys stood next to me. Showing they were on my side. A show of solidarity.

"A promise. For the pain you brought my sister and the shame you brought on my family, I will get satisfaction."

"I am sorry Mary got hurt. I wish I had done things differently, but I promise if I can make it up to her I will," I said.

"And I promise this, Richard. When I become Pack King my first order will be to banish you and your whole family from this pack," he hissed.

I growled and the tension between the two groups became stronger.

"If you have a beef with me, that's fine but don't touch my family!" I warned him.

"When I am Pack King, I will do what I please!" he growled.

"Well, I got news for you; I am going to be Pack King!"

"Well, neither of you are yet. I however, still am."

We all turned and saw Daryl standing in front of the two groups. We all shivered as his power slowly crept over us like a hot wind; gentle yet scorching, reminding us who was in charge.

"Now then, I suggest we keep the rest of tonight civil, no one will be banished unless they deserve it. And, unless I approve it. Unless one of you wishes to challenge me, that is," Daryl said sternly.

We all bowed our heads in submission. No one in their right mind wanted to challenge Daryl. He was still too strong.

"That's what I thought. Now, why don't you all get ready, we have less than an hour to get ready before we shift," Daryl said.

Both groups walked away. Derek and I shared one last look and left. But it wasn't over. A war had been declared; I knew it, Derek knew it, Daryl knew it, and by morning the whole pack would know it.

Becoming Pack King was no longer just the instinct for a young alpha male; it was about survival. I knew if Derek did become Pack King he would fulfill his promise. I had to become Pack King for my family now; I had to keep them safe.

Them, and my new husband.

Going to be awhile before I get used to that.

25

Jeremy

Well, I hope somebody answers the phone; because I fucking *called it*!

I knew something was going to happen! But, I was expecting a fight or something, anything but this!

I am....married, and I didn't even know it was going to happen.

I mean, seriously?

God, I really need to get drunk right now.

Everyone was congratulating me and welcoming me into the pack.

I was getting a drink. Sadly, non-alcoholic; it was some very nice lemonade someone brought to the meeting tonight. I had eaten a lot tonight and my stomach was so full. When I get nervous or anxious I get hungry, and after tonight I felt like I could eat a bus.

I turned around and accidentally bumped into someone.

"Sorry, my bad," I apologized.

I recognized the man. I remembered seeing him standing with Mary's family.

He was as tall as Richard, a little leaner and slim, but still just as ripped. He wore a pair of tight briefs that showed that despite being slimmer than Richard, he was still packing some serious muscles. He actually had an eight-pack. You don't see many of those.

He had dark blonde hair and pale, piercing blue eyes. He had no hair on his chest, which was funny seeing how you would think werewolves would be hairy even in their human form.

He didn't say anything, just stared at me. "So....ummm. Excuse me," I said.

I went to move around him but he stood in my way.

"Please, I need to-"

"You are in deep shit, Jeremy," he said.

"I am sorry, you know my name but I don't know yours," I stated.

"Derek," he said.

"Well Derek, I don't like being threatened, so please piss off and leave me be," I spat.

"You must think you are so special, now that you are married into the Farkas family. Well, I wouldn't get to happy if I were you. The Farkas clan is done; Richard has ruined them. They won't be around much longer," he said.

I gave him a hard look. "Just because Richard made a very....very....very dumb mistake doesn't mean they are done," I said.

"You obviously don't know anything about werewolves," he spoke with insulting tone, as if I was an idiot.

"Actually I do, my last boyfriend was a werewolf. An alpha in fact and guess what? He is a Pack King now of the Cambridge pack; and those guys are hardcore. So, if you think you can come over here and puff out your hairless, chiseled chest and intimidate me, then think again," I snarled.

"You have bite. Maybe you're not as big of a little bitch as you look," he smirked.

Rick appeared, glaring at Derek. "Can I help you, Derek?"

"No, just welcoming Jeremy into the pack. My sister would welcome you as well, but seeing how she just had her heart crushed, I think you can understand," Derek said icily.

"I am sorry for hurting your sister Derek, believe me I did not ask for any of this," I said.

"Funny how you and Richard keep apologizing for hurting her and yet you both still do it."

He turned and walked away, Rick followed him with his eyes.

"That boy is going to cause a lot of trouble, mark my words," he said.

"Wouldn't be the first time a werewolf has been a pain in my ass. I have a feeling it won't be the last," I intoned.

"How are you doing?" Rick asked.

"Don't even ask," I replied.

"I am sorry, had I known, I would have stopped it," Rick sighed, rubbing the bridge of his nose.

"How come Daryl and Susan knew, but no one else?" I asked.

"Susan is the shaman of the pack. She has studied all the old ways and rituals as part of her job. Daryl studied all the laws of the five tribes extensively, to show his dedication to being a Pack King. You have to remember, for two soul mates to find one another, let alone perform a Soul Oath Ritual, is so rare. That's why none of us fully knew what it meant, because it has not happened in this pack for a *very* long time."

"So...you wish to court my mom, huh?" I asked with a smile.

He smiled and blushed a little. "Yes, well. Your mom and I have been talking a bit lately and I feel like there is something between us. But, she is your mother and you are the center of her world, so I wanted to talk it over with you before I did anything," he admitted.

"You have a kid, right?" I asked.

"A daughter, she is eleven, her name is Katherine. She lives with her mother."

"Both werewolves?"

"Yes. Her mother and I divorced when she was five. We tried to make it work, but we decided it was better to just end it."

"Well, I appreciate you talking to me about this, Rick. And I also appreciate you vouching for me with the pack. I promise I will do my best to stay out of trouble. Though I fear that may prove to be more difficult," I said. I gave him a serious look. "But let me warn you, if you break my mother's heart or hurt her in any way, I will hurt you. Don't think Richard won't help me kick your ass."

He looked at me surprised then let out a bark of laughter. "Kid, I swear you have some wolf in you. I bet anything you would be an alpha if you were turned."

"Is it possible for a human to be an alpha when they are transformed?" I asked.

He gave me a deep look. "Why? Thinking about becoming a full-fledged werewolf?" he asked.

"No, just curious," I smiled.

"Well, it is possible. Some say being an alpha is about your blood. Which is bull; I have known alpha werewolves who produced an omega or two for children. Others think it is just something you are born with; while others think you have to have the mental strength. Others think it is a combination of all three. Truth is, no one is truly sure why some werewolves are alphas, some are betas, others omega, or why some are somewhere in between. I have met plenty of werewolves who were mean bastards but didn't have the powers of an alpha. And I have met wolves meek as a lamb with alpha-level abilities. Who's to say how or why it happens.

"But there is a theory it has to do with the size of a pack. As you know our pack is unusually large and we have several alpha werewolves. But wolf packs that are smaller have less. Because alphas help keep the lesser wolves in check. You can't have to many alpha wolves in a pack. It upsets the power balance. If you look at smaller packs the number of alphas tend to decrease."

I tried to imagine what it must be like to be an alpha. To be able to sense the aura of other werewolves, not only that, but control them with your own power.

I know alphas had to go through a lot of mental training to prevent their power from affecting lesser werewolves. Lucas told me in his pack, omegas were used to help train alpha werewolves to use their abilities. I thought it cruel to use them in such a way but he said it was how his pack worked.

Werewolves came in three types; alpha, beta and omega. Betas were the most numerous. They could sense energy and use it to manipulate other lower-classed werewolves to a certain degree, but their abilities were not as strong in comparison to an alpha, who could use his power to mentally dominate other werewolves.

Omegas were the lowest class; they were able to sense another werewolf's power. But they were unable to manipulate that primal energy if it belonged to a beta or alpha.

"How do you train your alpha werewolves to control their abilities?" I asked.

"Well, the shaman helps of course. As do the other alphas. We have them practice on one another," Rick said.

"But do you use omegas?" I asked.

"Only if one offers. Which is almost never. Or if an omega did something that warrants punishment," he explained.

"What is it like? Having an alpha use his power to manipulate you?" I asked.

Rick got a thoughtful expression on his face. "It depends on the alpha's skill. Some can be real subtle with it so you don't even realize what you are doing. Kind of like hypnosis. Others just hit you with it; smother you with their dominance until you submit. That way is painful; having another force their energy to smother you feels like your insides are being ground to bits and pieces. That's how alphas like to punish lesser wolves who displease them."

"That night when Joseph attacked Richard and I his friends seemed to be in a trance," I noted.

Rick nodded. "Richard packs a wallop. I've never seen an alpha as skilled as he is. Even Daryl does not have the refined control he has. It's almost like he actually has a kind of psychic. Richard has always had a way with people, both werewolves and humans. I thought it was just his natural charm..."

He trailed off, I saw he was looking at Richard with a thoughtful expression.

His words made me think of the night of the party. When Richard lost control, and we shared some kind of connection.

I still remember the terrible need that I knew now had not been my own but Richard's. How had he been able to make me feel that?

Humans could not sense werewolf auras or be manipulated by another alpha. That's what Lucas told me, even humans with werewolf blood were immune.

But maybe it was a soulmate thing. Could our bond be so strong that I had a sense for Richard's aura or even be affected by it?

"Will he be alright? After tonight I mean. I know his reputation in the pack is a messed up now," I said.

"Richard did make a mess. But I wouldn't worry. That boy is smart and will build his reputation back up in no time. Though, with Derek now out for his blood he will have to work extra hard."

"Can't he just challenge Daryl before Derek?" I asked.

Rick laughed. "Sure, but he would get his ass handed to him. Daryl is a mean motherfucker in a fight, and his alpha abilities are more refined than Richard's or Derek's. They both know that. Daryl hasn't had to actually fight a wolf in a long time. His power is so great he uses his aura to force a wolf to back down before the fight can begin."

"Doesn't being a Pack King give you an extra boost in power or something?" I asked. "Lucas once mentioned how Pack Kings can gain power from their pack."

Rick smiled.

"Your last boy-toy kept you well-informed. When you are a Pack King, you are connected to everyone in your pack; their strength is your strength. So yeah, when you become a Pack King you get power, but it depends on how many wolves you have in your pack and their loyalty to you. The more loyal a wolf is to their Pack King the stronger the bond is, and the more power is shared between them. Now, if a wolf is deciding to switch sides or thinks another alpha should be Pack King, then the bond weakens and less power is shared between the two, making it easier for the challenging alpha to win."

I could see why that would make having the pack loyal even more important. I never imagined that the connection between a Pack King and his people was so powerful. It made me realize why Kent was so concerned about Lucas and I. I knew he was worried what the others in the pack would think but now I understand it was more than a matter of loyalty.

"That's why Frank was so concerned about this ruining Richard's image with the pack! He wasn't just worried about popularity he was worried how much power Richard would lose!"

Of course, just like with Kent. Frank was afraid how my relationship with his son might hurt his sons rule as Pack King. Ironically, it was more Richard's fault than mine for any damage done to his reputation with the pack.

"Bingo. Pack politics are complicated. It is always wise to make allies before you take over so your rule is easy. But the more wolves in your pack who are loyal to you, the more power you get as a result. A Pack King may be the top dog, but even he needs his pack, as much as his pack needs him."

I rubbed my head. "Man, I am seriously going to have to take lessons on all of this. This is a lot to take in, werewolf politics can be a real devil's game," I said.

"Don't worry. If you ever need help, you have me and the Farkas family to help teach you," he said.

Daryl called for the pack's attention. It was time for the transformation to begin.

I had seen Lucas and his friends transform before, but never on the night of a full moon. I had never been allowed to be there when his pack gathered for a run.

All the werewolves gathered closely to one another. Some had disrobed and gave their clothes to the humans to look after while they went off hunting.

The rest of the human pack members stood together and watched the transformation happen. There weren't many human. Not all of them had showed up tonight. Including me, there were fifteen, including the ones who had been too busy to show up tonight, it was thirty.

The children had their eyes covered by their mothers so they wouldn't see the nudity. Nakedness wasn't much of a big deal with werewolves but for us humans with our delicate sensibilities it was awkward.

The wolves all stared up at the moon; it reflected in their eyes.

They all looked at if as if the Moon was speaking to them, whispering something sweet and wonderful.

The air was silent, no one spoke.

Suddenly a rather disturbing sound could be heard. Like rope being pulled too tight-quickly followed by groans.

Then one by one they began to change. The ones who were pure bloods were graceful and smooth. The fur flowed over their skin like water and their transformation was quick and almost soundless.

Some went all the way into their wolf forms while others went to their hybrid man-wolf form. I knew those were alphas, only they could assume the hybrid form.

Betas can only assume a wolf form. Omegas need the power of the moon to do such a thing. Otherwise they only get minor modifications to their bodies.

I remembered the omegas from Lucas's pack. I had seen some of them change. Their transformed state was humanoid with a harrier body, pointed ears, fangs, claws and altered facial features that made them almost unrecognizable.

They may not be able to make a full shift without lunar assistance, nor could they assume the hybrid form. But an omega still had the physical capabilities any other werewolf had.

I remember there was a woman in Lucas's pack, a petite omega who flew into a rage after a fight she had with her boyfriend and decimated his truck with her bare hands.

The transformation for the turned was different. It took them a couple seconds longer then the born werewolves to transform.

Their transformation was noisier. You could hear them groaning as their muscles and bones reformed and altered to adjust to the change.

Once all the werewolves had transformed the night was soon filled with the howls of the Wolf Fang Falls Pack. A few trotted over to us humans. Wives giggled as their husbands licked them, I saw one human child be lifted by his human mother onto his werewolf father's back and ride him around like a pony.

Richard came over to me in his wolf form, the fur on his back was black, but his underbelly, lower jaw and front paws were white.

It was if he crawled on a floor of wet paint.

He circled around me, rubbing up against me, marking me with his scent. I reached out and pet his ears; he let out a low whine of pleasure as I scratched behind his left ear.

Liz trotted next to me and her coat was white as snow. I saw their parents; Frank had black fur and Janice had a pretty silver coat which was lighter around her face.

Susan padded over to her daughter and Son-in-law. I saw her fur was the same white as Liz's fur. She rubbed her head against Janice's face and Janice nuzzled her lovingly.

Even in his wolf form Frank look sternly at us, (though he had a special glare saved just for me), he barked and Richard and Liz went to join their parents, though Richard did look back at me as he ran off.

Susan nipped at Franks ears and gave him a stern look. He glared at her and turned around and ran out into the woods with the rest of his family following him.

Liz told me Susan and Frank butted heads a lot. She was open minded and warm while Frank was stern and stubborn.

But she still loved him for being a good husband to her daughter and a good father to the twins.

Frank thought she was too soft, but he respected her for her wisdom and role in the pack. Even werewolf families can be dysfunctional.

A woman walked up to me with a little boy by her side, it was the same woman who put her son on top of one of the wolves. She had grey eyes and blonde hair. Her son had dark hair, but his eyes were the same color as his mothers.

"Hello Jeremy. My name is Jackie. Richard asked me to look after you while he is gone. I work with your mother at the hospital," she explained.

"Aren't you Trevor's mom?" I asked.

She nodded. "I am. My husband is Trevor's stepfather. I met him when Trevor and I moved here ten years go. He was a deputy, and we started dating and eventually we got married."

"Was he already a werewolf then?" I asked.

"No, he was not. He knew about the werewolves though. He got badly shot by some drug dealers during a raid, and Rick saved his life by turning him."

"Wait, Rick? I thought the Pack King was the only one who was allowed to turn someone into a werewolf?" I asked.

"One of the first rules Daryl made when he took control was to have it that any human pack member that is in danger of dying may be turned by any werewolf. They had to tell me of course, it took some getting used to the idea that werewolves exist."

"My dad is a werewolf, isn't that cool?" the little boy chirped.

"Yes, it is," I said giving him a smile.

"Many years later Trevor developed leukemia and Barry and Rick requested permission for him to be turned," Jackie said.

"And when I grow up, I am going to be a werewolf too!" her son exclaimed happily.

Jackie smiled at him. "When you're much older, Leo. It is hard enough raising a human child and a werewolf teen."

"Was it difficult for Barry and Trevor to become werewolves?" I asked.

"It always is, some more than others. A turned wolf has to be under constant supervision. The new emotions and instincts can be a bit overwhelming. Trevor still has little tantrums now and then and Barry sometimes breaks what ever he is holding if he gets agitated," she said.

We walked over and got some food. Some of the other humans had begun to pack up the tables and what food was left.

"How long will they be out for?" I asked.

"They will run around for a few hours. They'll come back and sleep and by morning they will be human again. Are you spending the night?" she asked.

"Yeah. Luckily, we don't have school tomorrow," I smiled.

Tomorrow was Monday, but we didn't have school because they were getting ready for the upcoming formal.

"So, how does it feel to be married?" she asked.

"Don't even get me started. I still can't believe this happened. How am I supposed to go about my day when I know I am married?" I asked.

"I know how you feel, when I found out, I had a hard time believing this was all real myself," she sympathized.

I wanted to say it wasn't the werewolf thing that bothered me, but the fact I was married to one. Though I am sure having a son and a husband who are were's was difficult.

"Will you become a werewolf," Leo asked me.

"I don't plan on it. I'm fine with being human," I said.

"I'm not," Leo said crossing his arms. "I'm going to become a werewolf then I am going to become the Pack King!"

"Oh really?" I chuckled.

Jackie rolled her eyes. "It's all he ever talks about."

I bent down to speak to Leo.

"Being a Pack King is hard work. You think you're up to it?"

He nodded. "Richard says if I want to be Pack King I will have to beat him first. Everyone knows he will rule the pack next."

"Not everyone thinks that," I muttered.

"They're stupid! Everyone knows Richard is the coolest werewolf ever! And the strongest. No one can beat him!"

"He treats Richard like a second brother," Jackie grinned.

"Richard says when I become a werewolf he'll train me," Leo said looking proud.

"That's great! You'll be Pack King in no time!" I said. "If you could change anything about the pack what would you change?"

"Free pizza for everyone on Saturday. Because everyone should eat pizza on Saturdays. That when people have fun!"

"He actually wrote a letter to Daryl explaining the importance of free pizza on Saturday's," Jackie giggled, "Daryl keeps it on his fridge."

I smiled. I had a healthy respect for Daryl, and more than a healthy dose of fear. But the idea that he kept a letter from a child on his fridge made me think better of him.

"Daryl is a good Pack King," I stated.

Jackie nodded. "He is. He cares about everyone in the pack. Human or otherwise. He is everything their tribe believes in. He is fair and honest."

I remembered the look in Daryl's eyes when he spoke to me at my house. I did not doubt he was a good man. But I wonder if Jackie knew how far Daryl was willing to go to protect the pack. Because I knew if I had been a threat he would not have hesitated to silence me: Permanently.

But that was the point of being the leader. To make the tough calls and protect your people from any threat. I couldn't imagine having to deal with such a burden. To know many lives depend on your every decision and that one wrong move could end badly for everyone involved.

I talked with the other humans of the pack. Some were doctors or lawyers, or were married to a wolf. They all congratulated me and I just smiled and said thanks. When in reality all I wanted to do was scream.

I was married now. Till death do us part and all that. My life has changed so much. Wolf Fang Falls was supposed to be a new beginning away from werewolves and their bullshit.

But since I have gotten here, an alpha werewolf fell in love with me, I have made powerful enemies due to circumstances beyond my control, I almost got killed by a bunch of rough Hunters, and now, accidentally got hitched because Richard had to skim some ancient texts.

What the fuck.

A little over an hour later the werewolves started to return. Richard was one of them. The second I saw him my heart soared. He had not been gone long, yet it felt like an eternity.

A sandy yellow wolf and a wolf with ash-colored fur went over to Jackie and Leo. Barry and Trevor circled their human kin. Rubbing their cheeks against Jackie and Leo, marking them with their scent.

Leo pushed at Trevor's side.

Trevor purposely fell down and Leo jumped on him and began to tickle him.

Barry and Jackie watched warmly as their sons played. She ran her fingers over the top of his sandy colored head.

Richard walked over to me and transformed into his hybrid form, his limbs smoothly transformed and he stood upright. Since it was the full moon, he could not resume his human form.

The only way he could talk to me was in his man-wolf form. When he spoke his voice was rougher, more hoarse sounding.

"So, one hell of a night, huh?" he asked.

"Tell me about it," I moped.

"I am sorry," he apologized yet again.

I sighed. "I know Richard. But this is really going to complicate things for both of us."

"I know. God, I am such an idiot. You must hate me."

"I don't hate you Richard. I am irritated yes, but I don't hate you. We're going to have to have a serious talk though. Since I am now an honorary member of the pack and your husband, we have to discuss my place here and what my responsibilities are. I don't want another surprise law popping up," I informed him.

"I understand."

I tried to keep my eyes on his face, but I couldn't help letting them drift down for a split second. When the werewolves take on their hybrid form, it's not just their limbs and body that become more human as well.

Richard saw me look and grinned, which with a muzzle, looked like a snarl.

"Like what you see?" he smirked.

I felt my cheeks get warm, and he chuckled.

"You know, this is our wedding night. I am sure I can find us someplace in the woods so we can-"

"Finish that sentence and I will neuter you," I stated sternly.

A little while later I got my sleeping bag ready. More of the werewolves showed up and the other humans got ready for bed. I saw Jackie and Leo on the ground sleeping, resting in a sleeping bag.
Trevor and Barry curled protectively around them.

I got in my own sleeping bag. It was a nice night, the moon hung in the sky.

Liz lay down next to me, giving me a little wink. Frank and Janice lay down with one another next to us, (though Frank lay as far from me as he could).

A few other werewolves sat close to us and our little group. I recognized Susan, Daryl and his wife and son. They all circled around us, joining the pile.

I saw Rick laying with a female and a small pup. I assumed they were his ex and daughter several feet away, he nodded to me and laid his head down.

Richard remained in his hybrid form and spooned me. He draped his arm around me, he was very warm.

I stared into the fire; it was just embers now.

I felt an odd sense of....belonging. Something I hadn't felt with Lucas's pack. I knew they only tolerated me because of Lucas. Don't get me wrong; there were nice people there, and I did make some friends. But I was human, they were werewolves, and it was a barrier no one but Lucas would cross.

I closed my eyes and let the warm feeling of Richard's body soak into me.

As I fell asleep, I realized not only was I in the center of a pile made of wolves who were more than wolves. I was surrounded by my new family.

Though I was still getting to know them, the Farkas clan welcomed me in with open (and in some cases reluctant) arms.

I felt a sense of belonging, something I had not felt in a long time.

Perhaps coming to Wolf Fang Falls really was a good idea.

26

Richard

I awoke to the divine scent that was Jeremy Moonvine.

I was human now, I could feel it.

It always surprised me that I never awoke when I slipped back into my human form. You'd think the feeling of my body changing back would stir me.

Then again I was a heavy sleeper.

What's more I was surprised Jeremy had not awoken when I shifted back. I was still holding onto him. It was the early hours of the morning, the sun was starting to rise, casting a yellow orange color on the clouds.

People were already starting to pack up to head back home. I decided to let Jeremy sleep and go help everyone pack.

I kissed him on top of his head and he mumbled sleepily but did not wake.

I got up and walked over to the bag mom had packed our cloths and grabbed some shorts and a shirt.

Dad was talking to Daryl and to Howard Vernon Troyer.

He was a lawyer and dad was talking to him and Daryl about last night and about figuring out the legal ramifications of my blunder

Howard told dad to have us stop by his office later so we could go over everything.

Trevor and his dad were packing things while his mom held a sleeping Leo.

"Morning Richard," Barry said, "congratulations."

"Thanks," I said with a sigh. "Can I give you a hand?" I asked.

"Sure."

I helped them pack up their stuff and carried a few bags and walked with them out of the meadow and into the woods where they parked.

"So what are you going to do about Derek?" Trevor asked me.

"Keep an eye on him. If you hear anything let me know," I said.

"Will do. Any idea how your going to improve your image to the pack?" he asked.

"Avoid making myself look like an ass for one. All I go to do is start acting more responsible and prove to everyone I am worthy of being Pack King."

Jackie put Leo in the back seat and buckled him in. Barry started the car while Trevor and I put the bag in the trunk.

"I got your back Richard and so do the others. But you know things are going to change at school now right?"

I sighed. "I know."

Now that people knew my secret and my own blunder there was going to be a division in the ranks of the kids at school.

Several of my friends had already jumped ship to Derek, and I was sure more would follow.

But maybe this was a good thing. Times like this was a good way to see where loyalties lay. How many would stick with me? How many would join Derek's cause?

I never put much thought into the rapport I shared with the people around me. There had never been a reason too.

It had been naive of me to think I could count on everyone I hung out with to be my true friend. How many just wanted to be close to me because I was an alpha and potential Pack King?

"I admit I had my doubts and I still don't fully understand this soulmate stuff. But you can always count on me."

"Thanks man," I said.

We shook hands and bumped shoulders.

"Listen, I'm thinking after last night we need to have a little party. Something to help us all relax. Plus it will be a good way to show everyone Jeremy is cool to have in the pack."

"Sounds like a good idea. What did you have in mind?" I asked.

"We go out to the Wolf Den tonight and you bring Jeremy. We all have some drinks and chill. I'll invite a bunch of the others over. I know not everyone is willing to go to Derek's side. Some will want to stay neutral, but if we play our cards right, we could get some more on our side. I know Jeremy is cool, but you need to show the others he is a good match for you. The main concern many in the pack have is that he will make you soft that he won't be as strong as a mate for you as Mary was."

"Make the calls and I'll talk to Jeremy about it."

He nodded. "Alright, see you tonight." He patted me on the shoulder, "Think of it as your belated-bachelor party."

He got in the back of the car and they drove off.

I walked back to the meadow, passing several of my pack. Some nodded to me politely, others gave me a stern look and shook their heads.

Jeremy was still sleeping by the time I got back. I knelt down next to him and gently shook him. "Wake up Jer," I said softly.

He cracked open a beautiful violet eye.

"We're leaving."

He yawned and sat up. He stretched his arms, and I took the

moment to look at the still vacant look in his eyes. He looked so cute after he woke up.

I leaned forward and kissed his cheek. "Morning," I said.

"Did we get married last night?" he asked in a tired voice.

"Yes," I said rubbing the back of my head.

He stared at me with a vacant expression. "I married an idiot," he groaned and fell back on his pillow.

*****

Jeremy

So, quick recap:

Thanks to a huge blunder on Richard's part, a simple ritual turned out to be a marriage ceremony, so now we are married.

Now the Farkas clan and I sat in their lawyer's office to discuss what being married soulmates entailed.

After we returned to the Gates and got cleaned up, we headed over to the lawyers office. Frank wanted us to go there as soon as possible to go over the legal ramifications of our marriage.

The werewolves have their own legal system but sometimes they have to overlap their rules with human laws.

The lawyer was an African American man in his early fifties by the name of Howard Vernon Troyer. He had been a lawyer for over twenty years and was turned after a decade of loyal services to the pack.

He worked both human and werewolf clients and was the Farkas' personal lawyer.

He was a bit cubby, his hair was cut short with bits of white creeping in at the roots and he had freckles around his eyes. He was looking at a yellowed parchment Susan had brought about the ceremony and the oaths that bound the two soulmates.

The parchment was so old it should have been in a museum.

"Well, from what I am reading, as Richard's husband, Jeremy is entitled to the same rights and privileges of any other married couple. Should anything happen to Richard-God forbid-then Jeremy becomes the sole owner of any assets that are in Richard's name," Howard explained.

"So, if Richard dies then that means Jeremy gets Richard's inheritance?" Frank asked.

"Yes, that is correct. Unless you decide to alter the terms and conditions of your will. Otherwise what you leave to Richard you also leave to Jeremy," Howard replied.

Frank didn't look like he liked the sound of that. Then again, he hadn't been very happy at all since he found out about Richard and I.

"Is there any loophole or way we can get this marriage annulled?" he asked.

"Sadly no, this is very airtight. No wonder the ancients only allowed soulmates to do this ceremony. Only someone truly in love would agree to something like this. It is very similar to regular marriages however, there are a few differences. Like-." He frowned as he read the parchment. "The rule about the sexual geas."

"The what?" Richard and I asked.

"According to this, neither one of you are allowed to engage in any form of sexual activity outside your marriage without consent of your spouse," he explained.

"That's an odd rule. If soulmates love one another so much why would they ask permission to have sex with someone else?" Liz asked.

"Even soul mates can have a taste for exotic pleasures. There may be times the female in the relationship might prove to be infertile and so would allow her mate to breed with another female so his line could continue," Susan said. "But back in those days they didn't have artificial insemination."

She looked at the both of us, giving us a very pointed look. I had a feeling Susan wanted very much to live long enough to see at least one great-grandchild before she passed.

"So, if Richard and I decided to see other people we could give each other permission to go on dates and stuff?" I asked curiously.

"I don't want to date other people," Richard said sharply.

"Well, what if I do?" I asked with a stab of irritation.

"Tough shit, I don't give you permission," he hissed.

I felt another, stronger stab of irritation this time. "Why the hell not?" I asked.

"Because you are mine!" he growled.

The irritation grew into something stronger: Anger. After his screw up I didn't think Richard had any right to tell me what to do.

"Look, I got tricked into doing this Richard. I have the right to see someone else if I want," I grumbled.

Personally there was no one I did want to see. After last night I don't think I could date anyone even if I tried.

But I didn't like the possessive tone Richard was taking. It reminded me way too much of Lucas; right before we split up and the more I tried to put some distance between us the more aggressive and territorial he got.

Alpha or no alpha, just because we are married now does not make me his property.

"Is there anyone in particular you want to see?" he asked. I could tell from the look in his eye if I did name someone they would meet an untimely end.

"No, but I am thinking ahead, you know; down the line, Richard," I said harshly.

"What don't you get! There is no down the line for us! We're together forever!" he said raising his voice.

"Well whose fault is that?" I asked.

"Well if you hadn't come to town, then we wouldn't have met!"

"Oh so it's my fault?" I asked giving him a cold look. "Maybe if you had read the fucking book, we wouldn't be in this mess!"

"Looks like the honeymoon is over before it even began," Liz sighed.

"I can't believe you even would consider going out with someone else after what we shared last night!" Richard went on ignoring Liz.

"Don't make me out to be the asshole I was just asking a damn question!" I yelled.

"You two can discuss that later, for now let us focus on the rest of the meeting," Daryl said raising his voice.

Richard and I quieted down. I stared down at my lap still fuming.

"But at least not all hope is lost for grandchildren," Frank said looking hopeful.

"What else is there?" Daryl asked Howard.

Howard looked over the parchment a few more times. "Nothing, just the usual stuff." He took off his reading glasses and set them on the table. "So, I already got the forms ready."

"What forms?" I asked.

"Legal forms. For you and Richard to sign; Since you and Richard are not yet old enough to get married according to the human judicial system, these are simply to allow one of you to inherit the property of the other in case one of you dies."

"But I don't have property, I am seventeen. I don't have a lot of money or own land or anything for Richard to own," I said.

"Werewolf law dictates you are not only married but you are each other's inheritors. When you both turn eighteen and decide to marry the human way, we can make new documents to sign," Howard replied.

He went to his file cabinet and pulled out two sheets of paper. "Daryl, you need to sign a form as well. Richard's family normally can't be witnesses to the signing as per the law, but you can as Pack King."

"Very well," Daryl said.

I looked over the document real quick. I frowned when I noticed mentions of words like 'mate' and 'tribe' and 'pack'.

"Isn't it a risk for someone to see these? I mean they would look odd if a human reads them?" I asked.

"These documents do not go to the human system. Werewolves have their own judicial branch and they will be sent to them," Howard explained politely.

That made me wonder just how connected to the human world the werewolves were. And where would these documents be sent?

Or rather to *whom*.

Richard went and signed his paper as soon as Howard gave it to him, slamming the pen on the table when he was done.

I looked at the paper, reading every line. I could feel Richard's eyes on me. No doubt waiting to see if I signed it or not. He already signed his paper so I might as well sign mine.

It didn't really matter if I signed it. From what I read from the paper these documents were just for legal purposes.

I signed it, though not as quickly as Richard did and to show him what proper etiquette was I gently placed the pen on the desk and politely handed the document to Howard.

After Daryl signed his paper saying he witnessed Richard and I sign our paperwork and neither of us was under pressure or duress and that he had witnessed our union we left, thanking Howard for his time.

"Welcome to the pack Jeremy," Howard said shaking my hand. "I understand things are a bit hectic for you. But if you ever need legal help, please give me a call."

"Thank you," I said to him.

Richard drove me home. The ride was quiet and a little awkward. Neither of us knew what to say.

And after our little tiff back at Howard's office neither of us wanted to talk to the other.

Mom wasn't home; she was working the morning shift today. God, how was I going to face her and act like everything was okay?

I wanted to tell her so badly, I wanted her advice. Knowing mom she would hunt down Richard and shoot him. I am not in the mood to become a widower just yet.

Richard followed me inside the house. I sat down on the couch and he sat next to me.

"So....we're married now," he started.

"Yep," I said.

"You know I didn't mean for this to happen, right?" he asked.

"I know," I sighed.

"Do you...really want to see other people?" he asked quietly.

I looked at him. I could see in his eyes he was waiting for me to say yes. He had that look a person gets when they are expecting to get some devastating news.

"I wasn't trying to hurt you when I asked Howard about us seeing other people Richard. After last night I feel different. I do believe now without a doubt you do love me. And I admit I do love you."

His eyes brightened.

"But this is all going too fast Richard. This isn't normal. I was comfortable with the way things were going between us. When Lucas and I were together, I let myself get swept away by my feelings for him. I let my love for him rule me and I paid the price for it. I don't want to have that happen again."

"Jeremy...look at me."

There was such a pleading note in his voice. I looked at him and saw he was looking at me with such sincerity and love.

"I know I fucked up badly Jeremy. I fucked up real badly. But I have to admit. A part of me is glad this happened." He took my hand and began to rub his cheek against it. "I know that is selfish of me to say that, but I can't help it. I promise I will make amends for this, I promise I will fix everything and I promise you will be happy."

He took my hand and kissed every single finger. Every time I felt his lips touch my skin I felt warmth seep into my skin and travel straight to my heart.

"I need you Jeremy. I need you like I need air. I was afraid when I first met you. This pale beautiful human just pops into my life and makes me feel things I never felt for another guy. I was confused and angry, I resented you for making me feel this way. But now I feel blessed to have you in my life. I love you Jeremy Moonvine, with all my heart and soul."

Before he could react, I jumped onto his lap, gripped his face tight in my hands and kissed him. At first he was surprised, but it didn't take him long to melt into my embrace.

We have kissed a few times. But this time was different. This was not about feral instinct, or the joy of surviving a near death experience. Yet it was all that and more. This is how a kiss should be.

Ever since last night, ever since we had the ceremony, something had been building inside me. My attraction to Richard was much stronger now. Because I now know beyond a shadow of a doubt, he loved me. I felt it, felt his love coursing through me like another blood flow; like when I peered into his soul and he into mine something got left behind.

You don't do shit like that with someone and not have a powerful bond form.

I hadn't really meant it when I asked about the open marriage thing; the idea of being with anyone but him now, just seemed impossible. It was not until I voiced my question that I realized the only one I wanted to be with was Richard.

It just seemed....right.

A deep growl escaped Richard's mouth, his whole chest vibrated, and I felt a thrill of delight run through me.

He gripped my ass tight and stood up. I wrapped my legs around his waist and he took me to my room. He kicked the door open and used his foot to slam it shut.

He tossed me on my bed and the look he gave me was positively feral; it was joyful, prideful, primal, lustful, and possessive. It made my heart beat harder in my chest and made me feel all tingly.

I could still feel his lips on mine; soft, plump and so kissable. I imagined what those beautiful lips would feel like on other parts of my body.

He does have really nice lips.

He took off his shirt, showing off his wonderfully muscled chest. I have seen him naked and covered in blood, I have seen him naked as both a man and a man-wolf and no matter the situation, I couldn't help but think how perfect he was.

He is an alpha, he is a man. He is my alpha and my man. He is mine just as I am his. A part of me was saying this was going too fast that I wasn't thinking right. But I didn't care.

My heart needed mending; I was tired of being alone. I needed this, and so did Richard.

He took off his shoes and removed his socks. His toes wiggled free, he had big feet; a size fourteen if I had to guess. I had a strange desire to rub his feet, hell I just wanted to touch him period. I moved to the side and patted the spot I made for him.

He smiled and stalked forward. His smile was....well...wolfish, he jumped on the bed, stretching his body, looking like a model for Abercrombie and Fitch.

I got up and moved to the bottom of the bed, he watched me with a curious look. I smiled at him and moved his feet so they were in my lap.

He grinned when he realized what I was going to do and purposely wiggled his toes. I rubbed his feet, and he closed his eyes letting out a deep sigh, his whole body relaxed as I began to massage his soles.

This was what I missed; intimacy, affection, bonding. I miss sex a lot too, but we were working on that. Right now I wanted to shower Richard with the same amount of care he showered on me.

In the past, I had always tried so hard to resist him and his damn charm. God knows there were plenty of times when he tried to get into my pants. And there were plenty of times I wanted to give in and let him have his way with me.

But using every ounce of willpower I had, I would stop before it got too heavy or serious. But now after last night, I couldn't resist. I wanted him. I wanted him so badly.

Plus we were married now, so what the hell, right?

"God, you have wonderful hands," he purred.

"You have no idea," I said suggestively.

He gave me a heavy look. "But I will find out."

He moved and suddenly and I found myself pinned beneath him once again his hands and mouth were everywhere. I ran my hands over his back, feeling all those wonderful muscles underneath that perfect tan flesh.

"You have no idea how long I have wanted to do this," he whispered. He kissed the middle of my throat. "How many times I fantasized, dreamed, jerked off to this. Do you know what it is like during gym when you get all sweaty? All that adrenaline pumping through you and seeing all that sweat glisten off your skin; God, I wanted to just throw you on the floor and fuck you raw!"

I noticed his eyes had had turned a darker yellow and his canines had elongated.

"I wanted to claim you, mark you. Make you mine. Do you know what it is like to want something so badly it physically hurts?"

He rubbed his crotch against mine and I could feel he was fully hard. I remembered seeing him naked and aroused when he rescued me from the Hunters. But he seemed even bigger now. Then again, I had a concussion the last time I saw him naked. Maybe he looked smaller because I had a head trauma.

He sure as hell wasn't small right now.

"I have been beating my dick every day. I wanted you so fucking bad. But finally, you...are...all...mine. My little pale angel."

I chuckled. "You really know how to make a guy feel special."

"Oh, believe me; by the time I get done with you, you are going to be feeling all kinds of things."

He slid off the bed and unbuttoned his jeans and unzipped his fly. He slowly pulled down his pants and kicked them off. He hooked his thumbs into the waistband of his boxers and slowly pulled them down.

He stood before me naked as the day as he was born. The breath seemed to leave my body as I stared at him and all his perfection.

He looked like a Greek statue come to life. His body was smooth, defined by thick, powerful muscles. He wasn't like those guys who got so big their bodies were popping with veins and looked misshapen.

I wondered how much of it he had to work on and how much was just natural. Werewolves had a different metabolism then humans did. They could still get fat but it was easier for them to stay in shape and burn calories.

Nature can be so unfair sometimes.

I sat up, motioning him to come closer. For a second I saw hesitation in his eyes. But only for a second.

He was only a foot away from me now. I examined his body more closely. He didn't have any hair on his chest. But his lower legs and inner thighs had a nice amount of fuzz.

I reached out and placed my hands on his hip. The second I touched him his whole body gave a small jump, and I heard him gasp.

I looked up at his face and saw he was nibbling on his lip. I smiled and began to gently run the tips of my fingers up his skin, causing him to shiver and goosebumps began to grow on his flesh.

I ran the palms of my hands down his legs. Over his thighs and dangerously close to his groin. I continued down, feeling every bit of tight muscle and soft hairy flesh I could before I ran my hands back up his legs.

I was like a sculptor feeling the statue he had just finished creating. I was not feeling for *imperfections*, but rather I felt everything that was *perfect* about Richard.

When my hands reached his stomach and began to trace the lines of his abs, I stood up; trailing my nose and lips from his belly all the way to his chest.

I looked up into his eyes and once more saw that same doubt I had witnessed earlier. I remembered I was the first and only guy Richard ever desired.

I know he had been with women before he started dating Mary. We had discussed that when we talked about out bond and his feelings for me.

Had I been a woman I am sure he would be more confident and assertive. Whenever we would make out, he was always the instigator, the leader. The one who had me breathless.

Making out was one thing. But this was something else; maybe because of our new bond, maybe because this was something far more intimate. But whatever the reason, Richard was unsure what to do.

This time it would seem I would be leading this particular *dance*.

I admit. I felt a particular sense of excitement. I have the upper hand now. I was the one in control. Richard was going to be dancing to *my tune*.

I began to slowly walk around him, trailing my hands over his chest. When I stood behind him I placed my hands on his sternum.

I pressed myself against his back, hugging him tight. I pressed my cheek against the warmth of his skin, the was a strong musk coming off him like that of a dog. Werewolves had a strong smell like that after they transformed.

I moved my hands up so my thumbs grazed his nipples. When I heard him take a sharp breath, I began to kiss down the center of his back, stopping just stopping at the point where his back met his ass-And damn, what an ass it was!

I stood, trailing my tongue up his spine. He was breathing heavily now.

"Christ Jeremy!" he growled.

"You taste so good," I murmured against his skin.

They were the same word he said to me when he kissed me. And they were so very true. The taste of him on my tongue made the insides of my cheeks tingle.

Moving my hands under his arms and up to his shoulders. "This is how you werewolves do it right?"

I began to move back to stand in front of him, letting my hands fall down to graze over those fine ass cheeks.

"When you scent mark you like to use as much physical contact as you can to leave your stink on an object. To show ownership or affection."

Stopping in front of him, I brought my hands up to his hand and began to run my fingers through his hair.

"I'm starting to understand why you always...need to touch me. Because I love your smell. Your taste. You've marked me pretty good-placing my hands around his waist I slowly began to move us so his back was facing the bed-but I think it's time I marked you."

He licked his lips. I could feel his most intimate part between us. I was pleased by his reaction to my ministrations. "Sounds fair to me."

"Lay back on the bed," I instructed him.

He sat on the bed, resting his head on his hands, his feet rested on the floor. I took a few steps back. He followed my movements with a curious expression.

I began to undress, taking off all my clothes. I stood there naked, running my hands over my body, loving how he was looking at me now. Loving how hungrily his eyes roamed over my body.

This was the first time he had seen me naked. And if his glowing amber eyes were any indication: he liked what he saw.

My heart was beating hard in my chest.

Not in fear or in lust. No, I felt a strange sense of excitement. Since our relationship began Richard has always been the one in charge. The one to arouse my feelings and turn me into a hot mess.

But this time I was in charge, this time I had the power, and I was going to enjoy every moment of this.

I walked over to the bed, I climbed onto it. One of us was trembling, or maybe it was the both of us. I wasn't sure which. All I knew was when I slid my body up his, he moved his hand so they rested on my lower back.

He was so warm; if I didn't know he was a werewolf, I would say he had a fever. But werewolf temperatures run a little hotter than humans. Especially when they are in a very emotional state.

He leaned up and kissed me. I kissed him back as our tongues battled for dominance.

I pulled back so I could kiss down his jaw, moving down to the part between his shoulder and neck. I kissed the spot gently, then bit down softly on it.

"Yes!" he hissed.

"You like that?" I asked.

I began to bit down harder this time.

"Stop!" he warned, trying to push me away.

I pulled back and looked at him worriedly. "Did I hurt you?"

He shook his head and kissed my nose. "No, but you need to be more careful. Bite me any harder and you'll break my skin."

"Oh shit!"

"Yeah."

I had almost made a terrible mistake. Werewolves don't turn you with a bite; but with their blood. One drop, doesn't matter if it's from an alpha or an omega and you'll find yourself howling at the moon.

He suddenly latched onto the same part of my neck where I had been kissing him. I cried out as I felt sharp teeth dig into my tender skin. It hurt a little, but I kind of liked it too. He began to suck on that spot hard, I knew the bastard was going to leave a hickey on me.

"Good thing I don't have that problem," he said.

He gripped my ass cheeks. He pulled back his left hand and gave me a sharp smack that caused me to let out a sharp cry.

"God, I love how your ass jiggles when I slap it. It's so soft, smooth and creamy."

He brought his left hand up my back and to my head. His thumb gently touched the bruise Joseph had left when he kicked me.

Richard kissed it softly, like he always did. I knew he hated it because it always reminded him of how close he came to losing me.

Rachel had been helping me use makeup to hide it from view. If my hair hadn't been cut so short it would have been easier to hide.

We continued to lazily explore one another. Touching and teasing. Searching for the secret spots that with enough attention would yield the most perfect reaction.

Richard was less cautious now. He was gaining more and more confidence.

But we hit a small bump when my hand started to fondle his genitals and he gripped my left shoulder so hard there was nothing pleasurable about it.

I cried out at the sudden sharp pain that broke through the haze of joy and pleasure.

Richard moved back from me, I touched my shoulder and winced. I was sure it was going to bruise.

He quickly began to apologize, panic rose in his voice. "Shit, I am so sorry Jeremy I forgot your human!"

I figured something like this would happen. I wasn't just his first male lover. I was his first human lover as well. Werewolves were much more sturdy than humans. They were far from bullet proof but they could withstand far more physical trauma than any normal person.

Lucas had more experience with humans, but even he sometimes left a painful reminder of how accidents can happen between a werewolf and a mortal.

"We should stop," he said, "this is going to far too fast and we should-"

I lurched forward and captured his lips in a silencing kiss. I didn't want this to end. I knew he didn't either. We were both to close to the edge, and I was not going to let one little accident stop us now.

"It's okay," I whispered. "I'm so close Richard. I need you to finish me off."

He growled in response.

He moved us so I was sitting on his lap. Our lengths were sliding against one another. The fluid that leaked from the tips provided the lubrication needed to make things wet enough that it was enjoyable.

He grabbed the back of my neck and pull, forcing me to lean back and causing my dick to sliding against his.

He latched onto my left nipple and I moaned as I felt sharp teeth against my skin and a wet tongue tickling my nub.

I knew it would lead to this, with Richard asserting his dominance in some way. Werewolves are by nature territorial and aggressive; alphas even more so; it was their instinct to be dominant more so than the others.

The bedroom is no different. for them.

He thrust his hips forward, causing his manhood to slide forward against my own. He began to rub it up and down, sliding himself along my length.

He leaned in and began to plant kisses, licks and little nips along my neck and shoulder. I could feel his canines bite into my skin but not hard enough to draw blood.

I always wondered why the myths say a werewolf bite turns you into a werewolf. A werewolf of any breed or rank could bite a human as much as they pleased and it wouldn't make them a werewolf.

The one thing I liked about Richard is he was more careful with his bites; gentler. Lucas had drawn blood a few times when he did it. I liked it rough but not that rough. Lucas would apologize and say he lost control.

I would be pissed and deny him any more sex. But that bastard could use his words to melt butter, and before long we would be going at it again.

Sometimes he was able to keep control, other times he couldn't.

Did Richard have better control? Was it because of our connection that gave him the extra discipline he needed to keep from really giving me some love bites?

Don't know and don't care.

"Fuck, I want to be in you so badly!" he growled.

"One day Richard, one day," I breathed with anticipation.

"One day, I will be making you beg for it. Then I will make you scream for it," he panted.

What a day that will be I thought to myself.

He let go of my nipple-which felt overly sensitive. He pulled his hand back and once more brought it down on my cheek. A jolt of delicious-sharp pain surge through me like an arrow.

"You like it, don't you? I can smell it! Your heart spikes when I slap that fine ass of yours!"

"Yes, I love it!" I growled.

His eyes were full-on wolf now. His nails had lengthened into small claws. His muscles were harder and there were more veins running along his neck and arms. A small amount of hair began to grow on his chest and belly.

I could tell he was close. I didn't know how I did but I knew it wouldn't be much longer now.

It was just like the night of the party at Hunter's Meadow. Only it wasn't a terrible need or longing I felt. It was pure peace and calm. A sense of bliss that I never felt with Lucas.

He may have loved me, but we were never equals.

I wrapped my arms around his neck and kissed him, he let out a snarl of approval. I had to be careful because of his canines; one of my early lessons in kissing a werewolf was learning that wolf teeth can be really sharp.

We were both sweaty; it ran down his chest, his hair clung to his forehead and he licked every bead he could find off me.

I dug my nails into the back of his shoulders. We clung to each other desperately, our hips gyrating against one another with such friction that the whole bed shook.

"Ri-Richard!" I gasped.

The heat was starting to pool low in my belly. I could feel my balls start to tighten.

"Almost there! Almost there!" he cried.

I reached between us and gripped our shafts together. The added pressure was all it took to cause the heat between us to erupt in warmth and liquid.

He threw his head back and a long deep inhuman howl escaped his mouth. I came at the same moment Richard did, my bones vibrating from the sound of his howl.

Our stomachs were coated in thick white ropes and my hand was drenched.

We sat there, him holding me tight, and I-exhausted and blissed out beyond what I thought possible-feeling so tranquil.

His canines returned to normal and so did his nails. He opened his eyes, and they returned to their regular honey brown color. He was breathing hard, like he just ran a mile. He smiled sweetly at me.

"That was fucking awesome!" he gasped, looking extremely delighted.

"Amazing," I gasped.

He smiled. Pleased by my praise. "Did I do good?" he ran his hand over my shoulder. I was sure once the endorphins went away it would hurt more.

"I've never been with another guy so I wasn't sure if I was doing anything right."

I smiled. "Like I said. Amazing."

He looked down between us at the mess we made. He looked like he had accomplished a great triumph, in a way I suppose he had.

"We should clean up," he said.

I moaned in response.

He laughed and kissed my swollen lips. "I know. But if we're going to cuddle, we need to...dry up."

He picked me up, and I wrapped my legs around his waist. He carried me to the shower and sat my on my shaking legs. We took our time washing. Sharing some more kisses as we washed away our essence.

When we got out and dried off, we went back into my room. The air reeked of sex and I sprayed air freshener while Richard changed the sheets, replacing the dirty ones with clean ones.

He climbed on top of the bed, his long tan body glowed with post-orgasmic bliss.

I felt the urge hit my fingers full force, and I grabbed my phone from my pants and laid next to him.

"What are you doing?" he asked; though he already knew the answer.

"Marking the occasion," I responded.

I aimed the phone, making sure to capture as much of our bodies in the frame as I could. I took the pic and checked to see if it came out good.

The image showed me with Richard behind me, his arm and leg lazily draped over me, showing off the curve of his ass perfectly; he smiled at the camera, some of his hair rested on the side of my face.

I looked at the picture, admiring how good we looked together. My slender body fit perfectly against Richards larger form.

"Looks perfect to me," he said kissing my neck. "Send it to me. I'll make it the background on my phone."

I chuckled and sat the phone on my bedside table. "How about we just keep this between the two of us."

"Yeah, knowing our luck it would get leaked to the whole school." He began to run his hand over my side. I could feel goosebumps form where his fingers trailed over my flesh. "And I am the only one who gets to see you like this."

I turned my head to kiss his cheek. "Ditto."

He held me close, his hand now gently traced patterns on my stomach.

I let out a sigh of pure contentment. I felt absolutely at peace. I knew we still had plenty of issues to deal with. But for now we were just two guys in love.

I closed my eyes and for the first time in a long time, I slept happily. Eagerly awaiting when I would awaken and find Richard's face beside mine.

27

Richard

After a nice two hour long nap we both go up and got dressed.

I came up behind him and wrapped my arms around his waist. "You smell like me," I whispered against the mark on his neck.

"We smell like each other," he replied patting the side of my face."

"Perfect," I purred.

"Come on lets go get something to eat," he said.

The second he mentioned food my stomach let out a growl. I had enjoyed a couple rabbits last night but didn't have time for breakfast; and after our little activity I was feeling famished. We walked downstairs and into the kitchen. Jeremy held my hand the entire time, and I felt like I could skip with joy.

Last night may have been an accident, but as far as I am concerned it was a good accident. The connection between us was stronger than ever and he now knew beyond a shadow of a doubt I cared for him.

I offered to make him something to eat (being the alpha and the dominant one it was only right) but he made me sit while he worked.

I watched as he moved about. Grabbing bread and other ingredients to make us some chips and sandwiches.

I frowned when I saw him rub his shoulder, I had forgotten what happened earlier.

"Does it hurt?" I asked.

"What?"

I motioned to his shoulder, and he shrugged. "It's a little tender but it will be fine."

"Here, let me make the food," I said.

I went to get up to finish for him but he gave me a stern look. "I got this! Sit!"

"Okay!" I sat back down.

He sat my plate on front of me. I grabbed my sandwich and with four bites it was gone. I looked over at Jeremy who was watching me with a look of shock and disgust. He had barely touched his own sandwich.

"Sorry," I apologized, "I was hungry."

"Obviously," he cracked a smile.

We ate in silence for a moment. I watched him as he ate, slowly eating my chips.

He noticed I was staring at him and he blushed. "What?"

I shrugged. "Can't a guy look at his husband?"

"You stare at me all the time," he replied.

"Well...it's your own fault for being so beautiful."

He smiled, his hand shot out and snatched my chip from my hand. "Hey!"

He laughed at the indignation in my tone.

"Thanks."

He popped the chip in his mouth and chewed it. "So how did you like your first time with a guy?" he asked wiggling his eyebrows

"It was...different. But very nice," I answered.

"I could tell you were nervous," he said.

"I was not!"

I actually was. We had kissed and made out before. But as much as I enjoyed what we did I was happy to let him take the lead because I have never done anything close as to what we just did with another guy.

If he had been a girl than things would have been different. Though I admit I did enjoy letting him lead the show.

"I just need some more practice is all," I said leering at him.

He rolled his eyes. "Sex fiend."

"Wait until you see me during the winter."

"Why what happens during the winter?" Jeremy asked.

"You don't know?"

"Know what?"

"Winter time, its mating season for werewolves," I said.

Of all the things about our kind Lucas *didn't* tell him, it had to be that!

"Mating season, what like animals?" he asked. "That's a thing for you guys?"

I ran my hand through my hair. Of all the awkward conversations to have it had to be *this!*

"Alright...you know how female wolves-real wolves, go into heat in late winter?"

He nodded.

"Well, for werewolves a similar even occurs. It happens when we reach sexual maturity. Between mid-to late winter both men and women of my race enter a heat. Our instinct to procreate goes into overdrive and we are overcome with a need to breed. If we mate during mating season a she-wolf will birth a litter. In our pack, no one is allowed to conceive without the Pack King's approval. Otherwise, the pack would grow too big."

"Wow, it must be difficult for you all during that time," he said.

"It is. The older werewolves can handle it better. But for werewolves of our age, it is horrible. We become obsessed with sex, well, more obsessed I should say. I remember when I had my first heat. For the first few years you have to be chained up in special holding cells. The need to mate is so powerful that if a young werewolf was allowed to roam, we would find the closest thing to fuck. Human, werewolf or wolf," I explained.

He got an odd look on his face like he misheard me. "Wait....wolf?" A look of understanding washed over his face. "You mean....you can mate with....normal wolves?"

"I don't!" I quickly said. "No one in this pack does! Even we have a concept of bestiality. But when you are a young werewolf going through your heat, it doesn't matter where the sex is coming from....as long as you get it."

He shuddered. "I hate to ask, but like many people, I have a sick sense of curiosity...is it possible for a werewolf and a regular wolf to produce offspring?"

"It is, but.....it is forbidden. It's one of the laws of all the tribes in fact. 'Thou shall not lay with the wolf-kin'."

I shuddered. I have heard stories about werewolves who escaped from confinement. But I can't fault them. I would do the same thing if I escaped.

Like I said it didn't matter where you got the sex from as long as you got it.

"Dare I ask why?"

"Well, the offspring are werewolves but-I flinched-they are wild. Even by werewolf standards. Think of them as reverse-werewolves. Or wolves who take human form. We call such creatures Amorak. You ever hear of the Beast of Bray Road?"

He nodded.

"That was an Amorak. It was a rogue one though; it had no pack. But once it started to attract media attention, it was quickly killed. But it wasn't the only one. Plenty of other Amoraks have existed throughout history."

"So, do you kill them on sight?" he asked.

"Some packs do, others may decide to keep them and try to help them as best they can. Like I said, they are more wolf than human. Very primitive, they mostly stay in their wolf forms."

"Are they dangerous?"

"In many ways, yes. Like I said, it is impossible for them to live among humans. They draw too much attention and have no restraint. Many humans have been killed by Amoraks because they thought were harmless hobos."

"What about these places where they keep you during the heat? Are you still going there?" he asked.

"Yes. It's not as bad as when I was twelve, though. During mating season all the young men and women of the pack are rounded up and taken to separate facilities. The elder members, usually the parents, watch over their children. The men look after the boys and the women after the girls. During this time it is forbidden for a member of the opposite gender to visit the compound holding the other sex."

"Why?"

"To prevent an older wolf from sub-coming to the pheromones of dozens of fertile young werewolves," I answered.

"I thought you said the older werewolves have better control during this time?" he asked

"Better control yes, yes. But even a full-grown werewolf can't be around one of the opposite sex when they are in heat for a long period of time before he or she gives in to their instincts. After a while, it gets to you and the need to breed becomes too powerful. So, the older men and the older women look after the young werewolves they share the same gender with until the heat it over. It is their job to make sure none of us get loose."

"Has anyone ever broken out?" he asked.

"Not in a long time. Like I said, we are restrained and guarded around the clock. We are put in cells with a bed, some clothes, and are fed regularly. We never share a cell with anyone else because in our rage we might fight and kill one another." I took a deep breath. "It's the one thing I hate about being a werewolf. When you are in heat, your body turns against you. All you can think about is sex. Your cock is constantly hard and the only relief you have is your hand."

"Yeesh. How long does it last?"

"Thankfully, only a week."

He was quiet for a moment. "Man. I thought being a werewolf was easy."

"You're not weirded out about it are you?"

"Richard. You're a werewolf, it is already weird. This is just one more thing. But what are we going to do when mating season rolls around? Now that you and I are bound, how will that affect things?"

"I only want to have sex with you, that won't change. When a wolf finds their soulmate they won't have sex with anyone else," I said.

"But you had sex with Mary," he pointed out.

His tone wasn't judgmental or jealous, which I was grateful for. I had a few lovers before Marry and she got angry if I ever talked to any of the girls I ever slept with.

"I was only able to get it up with her when I was thinking about you. Now that I have come to terms with us, it won't be a problem, as you just found out," I grinned.

Jeremy grabbed our now empty plates and took them over to the sink.

"If we wanted to could we...be together when your next heat hits?"

As much as I wanted to shout *yes!* My reply was a stern-

"No!"

He looked at me, surprised at the vehemence in my tone.

"Remember when I hurt you earlier?" I asked.

"Richard it's fine really-"

I held up my hand, stopping him. "There have been times when a werewolf escaped confinement and killed a human they raped."

The blood drained from his face.

"Like I said, when you are in heat you don't care where you get the sex from. Or if it is consensual or not. It gets better with age. But...you know how strong we are. Imagine if I squeezed your shoulder so hard I severed you arm from your body. And even than I wouldn't stop."

Fear began to waft from his body. I instantly cursed myself for my choice of words.

"I am not that bad," I said waving my hands, "I am just giving you a very...very poor example. If we did decide to have sex when I hit my heat, I am sure I could stay aware enough to stay in control. But once we started to fool around, I don't think I could trust myself."

He walked over to me, he bent down and touched my hand.

"Hey, we got plenty of time to talk about it. If we do have sex, it doesn't have to be when you're in heat. Besides, you said it gets better with age."

I let out a deep sigh. "You'd think I would enjoy talking to you about werewolf sex. But it's so damn embarrassing."

"With a touch of terrifying and a dash of fucked up," he said.

We both laughed.

"You know, we should go on a date," I told him.

"A date?" he asked. "You realize people date than get married right?"

I shrugged. "So we skipped a few steps."

He nodded his head, I could see the idea pleased him.

"Sure. God knows I could use some downtime."

"Okay. How about tonight?" I asked.

He smiled. "Okay. Where do you want to go?"

"Trevor thinks it would be good for us to go out tonight. He's going to invite some people to see if we can get them back on my side," I told him. "We have this club called the Wolf's Den."

"Original much," he said rolling his eyes.

"As a member of the pack it would be smart for you to socialize with the pack as much as possible. If we can show the others, we are stable it might help with my image."

"So our first official date is a political move?" he asked.

"There will be lots of alcohol," I commented.

"Alright, sounds fun," he grinned.

"Don't worry about tonight. Just be yourself and everything will be fine," I told him.

"Is there any protocol I should be aware of?" he asked. "A way I am supposed to act and behave?"

"If one of us rubs their cheek against yours that is okay. But if they bite your neck or touch any of your private areas, then let me know. Also don't show your neck unless you wish to show respect or submission."

"Just like in Luca's pack," he commented.

"We may come from different tribes but our rules for decorum is the same," I said.

"Is there anything else?"

"If anyone gives you shit let me know," I said.

"I can handle myself," he said sternly.

I chuckled. "I know. But you're still human. If someone threatens your or insults you what are you going to do?" I asked, "challenge them? Fight them?"

"Right because I am a puny human," he said bitterly.

"Hey now, don't be like that. It's just how things are. If you were a werewolf, I wouldn't be so worried about you getting into a fight with one of us. But the fact is you wouldn't stand a chance against an omega. Even a Hunter needs weapons just to be able to fight even one of us on equal footing."

I placed my hand under his chin and gently made him look at me.

"You're my mate, an insult to you is an insult to me. I know you are stronger than you look. But you're still just a human. If someone decides to challenge you they have to fight me by proxy. It's the rules."

"I thought we were going to have fun and make friends?" he asked dryly.

"We are. And hopefully everything will go smoothly tonight. But if we want respect, then we need to show we are not to be taken lightly. We won't be respected if we are seen as weak."

"I may be human, but I am not weak," he said firmly.

"I know. That's one of the things I love about you," I said, kissing him on the lips.

*****

As I drove home, my mind kept on replaying what happened. The sex I had with Jeremy was so intense, not even Mary got me off like that.

I hadn't seen Mary last night after the ceremony. I know she had to be devastated, any hope she had of us getting back together are now crushed.

Thinking about Mary made me think about Derek. We were going to have a fight, I knew it. I couldn't let him take any more supporters from me. I was still pissed all those so-called friends of mine ditched me because I was with Jeremy. But I was also grateful for the ones that stayed.

Real friends are the ones who stick around when things get tough. But it is also good that it happened. Now I know who I can really trust.

I thought back to my conversation with Jeremy. As much as I would love to go through a heat with him I am not going to risk it. I needed more time to learn control with him, we had both been lucky I hadn't hurt him worse.

Control was key, and sex is about not holding back. About letting loose and going all at it. If he were a werewolf than I would be more than happy and willing to have *real* sex with him.

Perhaps next year we could try. I could finally kiss that godsforsaken pit goodbye and not have to be chained up and left to suffer alone.

Going from a whole week howling for sex, to a whole week of nothing but sex. An improvement for sure.

Times like that made me envy the yellow tribe.

Especially Uncle Eldred. He told me one time how the yellow tribe actually has a special holiday. During mating season, members from different packs of their tribe are chosen to breed. It was their way of mixing bloodlines and such.

It was one of the reasons why the yellow tribe was the largest and had the most pureblood werewolves of all the tribes.

I was in a pretty good mood when I got home. Sure, I was going to have to do damage control with the pack and deal with Derek. But Jeremy and I were married, and after what happened earlier at his house, I had high hopes for our relationship.

But, as I entered the house I caught a familiar scent.

"Richard, come in here!" I heard dad call.

I groaned. I had been hoping I could get a shower before I ran into anyone. I walked into the living room and found dad sitting down with Jason, Mary's dad. I was glad to see he was alone; I didn't want to see that prick Derek right now.

"Jason," I said giving him a respectful nod.

"Richard, I-"

He stopped, he sniffed the air and his face twisted into a mask of disgust. Dad was glaring at me as if to say *How dare you come home reeking like sex!* Well jeez, if I had known we were going to be entertaining a guest, I would have showered over at Jeremy's.

"I see you wasted no time in consummating your relationship with the Moonvine boy," Jason said.

"Jeremy and I enjoyed one another's company, but he is not ready for that step yet. We may be married, but it is only due to my own stupidity and not natural cause and effect," I said.

"Glad to see you are taking responsibility for your actions," Jason acknowledged.

"Richard, Jason has come to try to bridge the gap that now grows between our two families," dad said.

"I am glad to hear that. I am sorry for hurting Mary. I did try to resist this, but she deserves someone who loves her, instead of someone who pretends to."

Jason sighed. "I believe you, Richard. I can smell the truth on you. Hell, I sensed the energy you and the human made last night. Please have a seat, we have much to talk about."

I sat next to dad. I noticed he started breathing through his mouth, no doubt trying to avoid smelling the sex on me.

"Mary is willing to forgive and forget all this under one condition," Jason started.

"What?" I asked.

"You take her to the fall formal," he said.

"A very reasonable request," dad added.

I had been hoping to take Jeremy to that. I planned on coming out that night to the whole school by taking him to the dance and kissing him in front of everyone.

It was very romantic and a good way to earn brownie points with him.

But if this can help smooth things over with Mary and her family, then I would do it. But I was going to have to talk about this with Jeremy.

I wasn't going to take my ex to the Fall Formal and there would be more dances for us to go to.

I was sure he would understand, unlike me, Jeremy was very level-headed and could control his emotions.

"I will do it. But it will just be as friends. I would like for there to be peace between Mary and I. I do care for her; just not how I used to care."

Jason nodded. "I understand that. But I fear Derek is another matter altogether."

"He said when he becomes Pack King he is going to banish my family from the pack."

Jason's face hardened and Dad looked sharply at me. "He said this? When?"

"Last night."

Dad looked at Jason. "I did not know about this, Frank. I will have words with Derek about this, believe me. Our families have been good friends for too long for it to end in such a way. Derek is very upset. He cares deeply for his sister and seeing her in such pain turned your friendly rivalry into something more serious."

"Once again, my fault. I take the blame for that as well."

"I know you do. But Derek is young and stubborn as all young men are. I will see if I can talk some sense into him. But I can't stop him from trying to become Pack King. Grudge or no grudge."

"I wouldn't ask you to do that. If Derek wants to challenge me in the ring or in a game of politics, I will answer that challenge. I just wish for there to be peace between our families again."

"Well said. This whole situation is unfortunate, to say the least."

Jason stood and shook hands with us both. "Thank you, both. I will go tell Mary the good news."

He left, leaving dad and I alone. I had a feeling there was going to be another conversation. I was right.

"Well, glad to see you are trying to fix this mess you made," he began.

"Well, I wasn't going to ignore the problems I made," I retorted.

"Watch your tone, boy!" he snapped. "Bad enough you come home reeking of that human! I won't have you talking back to me!"

"And I am not going to have you constantly remind me of how bad I screwed up!" I snapped back.

"How dare you speak to me like that! I am you father!"

"I'm not a pup anymore dad, so stop treating me like one!"

"If you didn't act like a pup, then I wouldn't have to treat you like one! Why couldn't Liz have been born a boy, at least she isn't such a disappointment!"

My stomach filled with a burning combination of hate and shame.

"Fine! To hell with you, too!"

I spun around and headed for the door. "Richard, get back here!" dad yelled.

I ignored him. I passed mom, she tried to stop me but I kept on going. I slammed the door behind me and went to my car. I pulled out of the driveway, burning tire and headed for the only place I could go.

Jeremy's.

28

Jeremy

Okay, so werewolves go into heat. Freaky, but I have to confess...there is a lot of potential there.

What Richard and I did earlier today was incredible and amazing. So when we actually do have sex I can't even imagine what it will be like.

Though after Richard's story about werewolf sexual-deviancy, I felt a new level of caution at the idea. My shoulder was starting to feel sore, a reminder of what he told me about werewolves who lose control.

Lucas and I had the same talk when we first started sleeping together. But unlike Richard he had more experience with humans so he had a better sense of restraint.

We may be married and soulmates but there was still a lot of things the both of us need to go over. A lot of conversations about our personal lives and little things like sex and having a family that needed to be talked about.

Truth be told, I was really looking forward to tonight.

Just Richard and I having a nice, normal meeting with his friends. Nothing werewolf-y about that whatsoever.

Mom was still paranoid about me going out, but if I told her I would be with Richard and his friends, it would make her feel better.

I wasn't sure if I should tell her if I was dating Richard or not. She would tease me about because I would do the same thing to her. Not that she didn't already suspect something was going on between me and Richard.

She loved him, he had charmed her, and I had a feeling she would love it for the two of us to hook up.

I was going over what to wear. I decided to wear the clothes he got for me to wear to Liz's party. If he plays his cards right, he might just get to see me in that red underwear.

Just then the doorbell began to ring. I went downstairs and opened the door to find Richard standing there.

"Hey, you're kind of-" I stopped. He was angry; I could tell from the look in his eyes and the way he stood. "Richard what's wrong?" I asked.

"Can I come in?" he asked.

"Of course."

I moved to the side, and he walked in. He went into the living room and sat down. I sat next to him and put my arm around his shoulders. "Is everything alright?"

"I got into a fight with my father," he said.

"What happened?"

He told me everything; about the deal he made with Jason, and the words he had with his dad.

"He called me a disappointment," Richard said, his voice thick with sorrow.

"He is just angry right now. But at least you are trying to make amends with Mary and her family," I soothed.

"So, you're okay with this?" he asked.

"I think it is a wonderful idea. Who knows, maybe Mary will finally realize that you don't love her anymore."

"But what about you? Who will you go with?" he asked.

I shrugged. "I won't go. I don't think she would like seeing me there."

"But, it's the Fall Formal," he reminded me.

"I have been to plenty of Formals. It will be fine."

I really was okay with it. After everything Richard and I have been through, I was not worried at all. And if this could help make things right between their two families, I was all for it. The last thing I wanted was to cause a war.

I have seen what happens when werewolves have a beef with one another, and trust me, it is not pretty.

Granted, that was Lucas's pack, and I wasn't sure if the rules were the same. The white tribe seems more civilized than the red tribe who were all about fighting and proving who was top dog.

God, what am I going to do when Lucas shows up? He is the Pack King of his pack now, and has a wife and a kid on the way, but there is a lot of bad blood and unfinished business between us.

I just know when he finds out that Richard, and I are married he is going to raise a stink. Not that he has any right to make a big deal, but I just know when he comes to Wolf Fang Falls, he will cause drama.

Hopefully, we can fix this issue with Mary and her family before he shows up, the less drama the better.

"What are you thinking about?" Richard asked me. "You look like you are miles away."

Knowing better than try to lie to a werewolf, I decided to be truthful with him. "I am thinking about Lucas and what will happen when he arrives," I said.

"   You're worried?"

"Of course, my ex is going to come with his pack and celebrate some big werewolf holiday. And there are a lot of issues between him and I."

"Fucker starts shit, I will pound the fuck out of him!" he growled.

"I doubt he will cause shit for the pack. But I am just warning you, there will be drama."

"I thought husbands are supposed to deal with each other's drama?"

I smiled. "Still going to need some time to get used to that idea. Me, married."

"Tell me about it. Though I won't lie, a part of me is pleased about it," he smiled.

"Why?" I asked.

He gave me a look, a loving and warm look that made me feel all kinds of tingly. "Because, now you are mine, and I am yours."

"You're not mine Richard; you are your own person," I said.

"No. I was yours the moment I laid eyes on you. And now, I finally have you all to myself."

I frowned at him. "Love isn't about ownership, Richard. I know you werewolves are big into that, but don't think I am going to just act like a domesticated little house-husband."

He smiled. "Why would I want you to be domesticated? I like you like this; full of passion and fire. That's what I love about you. You may look like a pretty flower, but you have thorns. I love that about you."

"How is it you can go from irritating, to sweet, to irritating again?" I asked him.

"It a Moon given talent," he said with a smile.

Just then his phone began to ring. He pulled it out of his pocket and looked at the number. "It's my house number. Probably mom calling. I will be right back."

He left and walked out to talk. Judging from the fact there was no yelling or cursing, it must have been his mom. I hated the fact that Richard was fighting with his dad. I wish he would lay off Richard and stop being such a hard ass.

Richard came back and sat next to me. "Is everything okay?" I asked.

"Yeah. Mom was just checking on me. Liz is going to stop by and drop off some clothes for me for tonight," he said.

"That's neat, we can just hang out for the rest of the day."

He got this look in his eyes and I knew he was about to do something mischievous. He leaned forward and pinned me against the arm of the couch.

"What are you doing?" I asked him.

I had a flashback to the night he did the same thing when he came over so we could work on our report.

God how things had changed since then.

He continued to smile. His left hand reached into my shorts and he began to fondle me. A soft moan escaped my lips as his warm hand wrapped around me.

"Doing my duties as your husband," he replied, kissing my neck.

He moved down my body and pulled off my shorts. He was about to swallow me when I stopped him.

"Easy there, don't just shove it in, you have to be gentle," I gently scolded him.

"Okay."

He opened his mouth wide, and I felt nervous when I saw all his perfect ivories. "Try and pucker your lips, let's try to avoid all those teeth," I instructed.

He puckered his lips. I hoped he didn't wolf out while he was down there.

"And don't be afraid to use your tongue, okay." I added.

He frowned at me and I got the message.

"Okay, shutting up now," I smiled.

He went back to work, and I kept my mouth shut. I felt his tongue lick the top of my head and felt his mouth wrap around me. I closed my eyes and laid back and let him do his *husband-y duties*.

I could definitely get used to this marriage thing.

29

Mary

I tore through my closet, trying to figure out the right dress to wear. Dad came home and told me the good news; Richard agreed to take me to the dance.

This was my chance.

For an hour now I have been trying to figure out what to wear. Normally I don't put this much effort into these little formals, I mean, it's not like I had to put a lot of effort into looking good.

I have a collection of tiara's to prove that.

But this was different; this was my last chance to get Richard back. I don't care if he is married now. We will cross that bridge when we come to it.

I was going to have to buy some new makeup and definitely get bottled Moon Flower perfume. No werewolf man can resist an alpha woman wearing Moon Flower perfume.

I was so busy I didn't notice Derek walk in.

"Mary?"

"What is it?" I asked as I examined my old dresses. The ones I knew Richard liked I kept on the bed, the rest I tossed to the floor.

Maybe I should just by a new dress? Something new. Something that was a mixture of all the dresses Richard liked.

I grabbed a pen and notebook and began to write down all the things I knew Richard loved about the way I looked, what he liked about all the dresses I ever wore.

Most women are too dumb to ask their men what it is exactly they like about what they were. I always made sure I knew what Richard liked so I could alter my wardrobe to his tastes.

"What are you doing?" he asked looking around the disaster that used to be my room.

I rolled my eyes at him. "What does it look like, Derek? I am getting ready for the dance."

"But that is not for another week."

"No shit, I wish I had more time to prepare. I take it you heard the good news?" I asked.

"I don't know why you are getting so worked up. Excluding the fact they are married, you felt the energy they released."

I dropped the pen and notebook. Because if I didn't I would have destroyed them both. I clenched my fists. I used every ounce of willpower to block that memory out.

"What Richard and I had was just as special. I just need to get him away from that little twink and remind him of how good we are. That is where I went wrong; I didn't give him enough attention, and he strayed. Mom always says a good woman always smothers their man with love."

"Mary, you were around him every day," Derek stated.

"Why are you being so negative?!" I snapped at him.

"Because I don't want to see you get hurt!" he growled.

"I am not a little pup Derek, I can handle myself!" I exclaimed.

He grabbed my shoulders and made me look him in the eye. "You are obsessing over this Mary. It is clouding your judgment. It doesn't matter how much you pretty yourself up. Richard loves the human now.

You need to accept that and move on; for the sake of your own sanity."

Anger began to rise in my chest. "How can you say that? Don't you want me to be happy?!"

"Of course I do, but I know that trying to win Richard back isn't going to work! He's married to the human now, you know our laws!"

"We'll figure something out, love always finds a way!" I insisted.

"But he doesn't love you!"

I pushed him away. "You just want to be Pack King; that is what this is all about!" I yelled.

"No it isn't, I am just trying to look out for you!" he snapped.

"Liar! You think you can use me as an excuse to wage some stupid alpha male war with Richard!"

He growled, and I felt his power beating at me. I let my own power out to push against his. I wasn't going to let him intimidate me. He may be older than me, but I was no omega!

"This is more than about me! If you would stop obsessing over Farkas, you would see that!"

"Whatever, just leave me alone, Derek!" I yelled.

He let out an angry huff and slammed my door shut as he stormed out. I ignored his childishness and continued to plan. Stupid Derek, figures he wouldn't understand.

He has never been in love, not like Richard and I were. He doesn't know what it is like to have some stranger show up and steal the one you love, right from under your nose.

But I'll show that little bastard! He had no idea who he has messed with!

Once I get Richard back, I am going to make Jeremy's life a living hell!

I grabbed the pen and notebook from the floor and began to take notes again. I was going to have to call in a lot of favors. I know my girlfriends and mom and dad will help out.

I just have to be perfect in every way. I can't lose Richard! He is my reason for being! This is just a test. All great loves are tested somehow.

I'll win Richard back and everything will go back to the way it used to be.

30

Richard

"You know, I have called lots of guys cocksuckers. But now that I have tried it myself, I have to say it is not so bad," I commented.

We were on the couch. I had just finished giving my first blowjob and despite it being my first time I think it went rather well.

Jeremy was resting his head on my shoulder. I could feel how relaxed he was; smell the afterglow of his pleasure and his peace. My wolf was thrilled; this is what we had wanted so badly.

"You sure you haven't done it before? I thought you were a little too good," he teased.

I chuckled. "What can I say, I am the gods gift to man."

He punched me gently on the shoulder. "So, everything will be smooth sailing right? You will take Mary to the dance and fix things with her family. Then we will have that celebration and deal with   Lucas, and then we'll be able to live the rest of our days in peace?" he asked.

I kissed the top of his head. "Yep, then we can live happily forever after. I will fix things with the pack, then one day become Pack King, and you will want for nothing."

He looked me dead in the eye. "I don't need luxury or status to be happy, Richard. I don't care if you are Pack King or not. None of that matters to me."

"Then what do you want? What can I give you to make you happy?" I asked.

"Richard, I don't need a gifts and presents to be happy. I just need you. This right here? What we are doing now is exactly what I want. Us being together. It's all I will ever need."

"Seriously?" I asked.

"Of course."

"Sorry, I guess I am just so used to giving presents to impress someone, you know."

"Well, I wouldn't mind something every once in a while," he smiled.

"Sheesh, make up your mind," I laughed, kissing his neck.

He chuckled, and I held onto him, feeling much better and much more confident about the future.

Just than I heard a car pull in the driveway.

"Your moms here," I said.

He sat up and pulled his pants up. "Thank God you have super-hearing."

By the time Diane walked into the house Jeremy and I were watching TV. We had just enough time to sort ourselves out and make ourselves presentable.

"Hey mom," Jeremy called out.

Diane walked into the living room. "Hi sweetie-oh, hi Richard."

"Hello Diane," I smiled at her.

"How was work?" Jeremy asked.

She let out a huff of air. "I swear, it seems like the full moon brings out the crazies-Jeremy and I shared a look-either makes people psychotic or stupid."

"If you want something to eat before bed I made you a snack in the kitchen," Jeremy told her.

She smiled at him. "I raised you so well."

"Hey mom, Richard wanted to take me out to hang with his friends tonight. Is that okay?" Jeremy asked her.

Diane was quiet, I could tell she was thinking it over. I stood up and walked over to her.

"Don't worry Diane, I won't let him out of my sight. In fact I might not be letting him go period."

She gave me a funny look. "Oh?"

I stood straight and looked her in the eye. "I really care about your son. I know we haven't known each other for long and it seems odd but I think you should know I am dating your son."

I heard Jeremy make a gasping sound.

Diane stood a little straighter, the weariness in her eyes melted away to be replaced by something sterner.

"Oh?"

I suddenly found myself feeling intimidated. But I pushed down my sudden sense of trepidation. I had to do right by Jeremy; especially after last nights blunder. And this would be the first step. I know Jeremy and his mom were very close, and I wanted Diane to like me. Not that it wouldn't be easy to charm her. I am very charismatic after all.

"I know you must be scared. I mean he has almost died twice."

"Richard!" Jeremy snapped.

Diane raised her hand to silence him. "Go on," she said to me.

"But I give you my word I will look after him. He is very precious to me and I want you to sleep soundly knowing your son is the most well protected guy in this whole world."

Diane looked past me to her son. Then to me.

"Well Richard. I really appreciate your candor. I admit, I have had suspicions about your feelings for my son."

She smiled. and I felt some of my nerves vanish.

"But you are right. It will help me sleep better knowing you are looking after him. I can tell you truly care for my son."

She looked at Jeremy. "Of course you can go. Just don't drink. You have school tomorrow."

She looked at me and opened her arms, inviting me in for a hug.

I bent down to accept her invitation and as she wrapped her arms around to pat me on the back, she whispered sinisterly into my ear.

"My kid has already been hurt once. If you do anything to cause him pain, I don't care what your family name is. I will stab you with a rusty knife. Remember, I am a nurse. I can make you hurt in ways you will never recover from."

I froze.

She let me go and patted me on the cheek. "Take care of him okay?"

She walked away, heading for the kitchen.

I turned and walked back to the couch and sat down next to Jeremy. I sat down and placed my arm around his shoulders.

I looked at him to see he was grinning. "She threatened you with physical harm didn't she?"

"Didn't your mother take the Hippocratic Oath?" I asked.

"A mothers oath trumps all," he replied with a smile.

31

Jeremy

Richard, Liz and I were on our way to the club outside of town. We were driving to Glenwood which was little over thirty minutes from Wolf Fang Falls.

Liz dropped off Richard's clothes when she showed up at my house to pick us up. She was excited about tonight. "Wait till you see how werewolves party Jer-Jer," she said to me from the back seat.

"I've seen how your lot party. I hope you brought plenty of towels for the blood," I said.

Liz cracked up with laughter. "I can promise you we party a little more tamely than the red tribe. We're not so *dramatic* as them."

Dramatic? That was one word to describe them I guess.

"See you finally decided to wear the clothes I got you," Richard said as he observed me.

"Well it is our first date, so I figured I should dress nice."

"Can I assume you are wearing the red briefs?" he asked with a grin.

I smiled and pulled my jeans down just enough to show him the red lining of the briefs. He got this hungry look in his eyes and I felt a thrill of victory.

It's always nice to know you can get a reaction out of people like that.

It seemed like the walls I had been carefully setting up between us were quickly falling down. We're married and have now engaged in sexual acts. Not exactly how I wanted things to go, but damn if it wasn't good!

"Play your cards right and you might see the whole thing," I told him.

He licked his lips slowly, I watched as his tongue move over those lips and the memory of our earlier activity made me shudder.

Richard wore black jeans, black leather boots with a metal ring on the side, a sandy colored t-shirt with a black inky design of a skull with wings and a leather jacket.

He looked absolutely mouthwatering.

"Gods you two smell like you're in heat," Liz gagged covering her nose.

"Good thing we showered before you showed up," Richard said flashing me a toothy grin.

I blushed at the memory of the shower. I had gone first expecting us to take turns, but then Richard had surprised me by joining me and I spent more time staring at his naked wet body then washing myself.

Not very many werewolves live in Glenwood, most preferred to live in the safety of the Gates. But they had to have some members of the pack live there to keep an eye out for trouble. More or less border patrol Richard had said.

The pack had one of the largest territories in North America, the entire county was under their jurisdiction.

The club was called the Wolf Den. It was actually an old warehouse that had been gutted and redesigned to be a club. There was a bit of a line but the bouncer let us in. I had to show him my leather wrist cuff Richard got me before he let me in.

"So, was he a werewolf?" I asked, referring to the bouncer.

"Yeah, the pack owns this club. We get in for free, and any humans that are with us get in for free as well," Richard explained.

I thought that was kind of unfair for us normal humans but if it meant free drinks for me, then I'm game.

"Being in a pack can really rock even if you are a human," I said.

"And we get a discount on drinks," he said with a grin. "Don't worry about an ID. As long as you are with me you can drink as much as you want."

"Don't werewolves follow the underage drinking rule?" I asked.

"Please, you know it takes a lot to get us drunk," he replied with a smile. "You can drink too as long as I am there to vouch for you. Human members are allowed alcohol if their fifteen and have a wolf present."

"Aren't you all afraid of this place being busted for underage drinking?" I asked. Werewolves didn't seem to fear breaking any laws but their own.

"We have some people in the police department up here. As long as we make sure no humans get hurt or injured, it's all good."

"I thought the white tribe was about law and order and all that?" I asked.

He smiled. "We do. Our own laws that is. The white tribe has more rules and regulations than all the other tribes. We believe in order. We believe in peace. But we know that human rules and our rules are two very different things but we still try to respect those rules."

"And how is letting minors get shit-faced respecting human laws?" I asked.

"Do you see any other minors in here besides you? Besides, you humans are always breaking the laws you make anyway." he shrugged

Hard to argue with that logic. I had my first beer when I was thirteen and got grounded more than once when mom found out I had been drinking.

The inside of the club was enormous, the wall behind the bar was lined with more alcohol than I have ever seen. Strobe lights flashed from the ceiling and fog machines dispersed fog.

Richard and I moved through the crowd, and I recognized many faces in the crowd from the pack meeting-slash- impromptu wedding ceremony.

Some nodded politely, but others didn't even look in our direction. But a few did offer to buy us drinks, and we took them up on their offer. Glad to see some people were happy about us being married.

We met up with Richard's friends Keven, Trevor, Cora, Vivian, Scott and Henry who were having a good time. We joined up with them and played pool for a while.

I didn't do too badly, but of course my skills were no match for theirs. Damn enhanced reflexes and all that. I didn't bet money knowing damn well they could school me.

Instead I watched as they played their games, cheering for Richard and rubbing his back when he missed a hole. Richard had a very competitive nature even by werewolf standards and didn't take loss very well.

At times I found it enduring and other times I found it irritating. But he did look cute when he pouted.

Over time more and more people came to chill with us.

Trevor had done his best to get as many of the Commune Kids to come over to the Wolf's Den tonight. There was Bob a tall guy with a humble disposition and light brown hair and a freckled face and arms like tree trunks. He was an omega, but he was not like the omega's from Lucas's pack. Richard had not been kidding when he said the Wolf Fang Fall's pack treated their omega's differently than the Cambridge pack.

The omega's there had been timid and bitter things, bullied and picked on by other werewolves unless they had a strong wolf to help protect them.

But Bob was not like them, it was obvious no one gave a shit about his rank. They treated him like he was any beta wolf.

Then there was Scott with curly black hair and hazel eyes and a smirk that never left his face. I knew right away he was a prankster, my theory proved true when he jumped onto Richard's back and gave him a sloppy wet kiss on his cheek.

He jumped off him and Richard took a friendly swipe at him but Scott just cackled like a hyena and evaded his blows.

They were his inner circle of friends. Trevor, Keven, Henry, Bob, Cora, Vivian, Scott, Liz. They were his best friends and strongest supporters.

They were the people who did not want to be friends with him just because he was an alpha or because he came from a wealthy family. But because they recognized a good leader when they saw one.

Richard was the kind of guy people naturally gravitated towards.

He was handsome, charming, and larger than life. You felt special just by being near him as if he had an aura of happiness that you wanted to surround yourself with.

And they welcomed me into their fold with surprising ease. Lucas's friends were nice to me, but there was always this sense that me being a human was something that kept them from truly bonding with me.

They treated me like I was Lucas's little brother whom he got stuck babysitting. But Richard's friends didn't care if I was human or not. They accepted me for who and what I was.

After everything that happened the last few weeks tonight was a welcome relief.

Then Trevor decided to buy the newlyweds, (Richard and I), some drinks. Not just any drinks. Moon Lust; a special drink that was made by using several ingredients and Moon Flower nectar. It was the most expensive drink the club had to offer, but it was well worth it. Richard said it was like sacramental wine for werewolves. The Moon Flower gives it a bit of a kick for the werewolves.

Trevor went to the bar and got us all cups. He carried them over on a tray and we all grabbed one. We all raised our drinks and Trevor made a toast.

"To Mr. and Mr. Farkas! Richard you are my best friend and I never thought you would marry another dude. But you're still my brother from another mother and now I can call you a fag and you can't hit me for it! Here's to you and Jeremy, hope you guys have a happy marriage!"

"Cheers!" we all shouted.

We drank from our drinks. Moon Lust was definitely sweet. It had a fruity taste with a sweet after taste like wine.

Richard put his cup down and pulled Trevor in a friendly headlock. "Call me a fag and I will beat your ass!"

"Careful, don't want Jeremy to get jealous!" Trevor cackled.

We all laughed. It was nice to see not all of his friends were going to ditch him because of this marriage thing. But I think it had more to do with the fact Richard married another guy.

But I put those thoughts aside. Tonight I was going to have a good time with everyone.

"Hope you're ready to go on a trip Jer," Keven said clapping me on the back.

"What do you mean?" I asked.

"Richard didn't tell you?"

"Tell me what?" I asked looking around at everyone.

Everyone was looking at Richard who had a disturbingly familiar expression on his face.

"Shit I forgot!"

"Damn it Richard!" Liz said slapping him upside the head.

"Tell me what?" I repeated feeling a little panicked.

"This Moon Lust isn't made from the same Moon Flowers like at Hunter's Meadow. The extract from this type gets us buzzed but humans develop hallucinations," Cora said looking at me nervously.

"Oh...well shit," I said.

*****

For the record, Moon Lust is the shit!

Before long, the lights were looking like a kaleidoscope on the ceiling; they looked like one giant rainbow shining light on us all. But I realized that the light was actually dozens of beams of lights that shined from the wolves. It all twined together like a ball of yarn, only to branch out and connect to other wolves.

My skin seemed to become more sensitive and I could feel the sweat breaking out of my skin. And Richard and his friends seemed to turn into anthropomorphic wolves.

Though I did notice not everyone looked like this. I spotted many in the crowd who still looked human. I spotted one girl in the corner making out with a guy with a wolf head.

It was awesome!

"Hey? Is it just me or are their wolf-head people running around?" I asked.

"Looks like someone is tripping," Scott sniggered.

"Way to go Richard you got your husband high," Liz chastised.

"Trevor got the drinks, not me!" he growled at her.

"Oh it's okay," I giggled and fell onto Richard's chest. "This is actually nice."

"Sorry Jer, I forgot what Moon Lust does to humans," he said kissing the top of my head.

I nuzzled his chest. "It's okay, let's go dance!"

I dragged Richard onto the dance floor. They were playing some awesome heavy metal music and the energy in the air seemed tangible. Or that could have been my drug-induced mind talking.

I placed Richard's hands on my hips and we began to dance.

I stared into his honey brown eyes. They were like a bottle of whiskey, warm and intoxicating. I leaned in to give him a kiss but pulled back just as his lips were about to touch mine, teasing him. He smiled and pulled me closer to his body, his hand on my hips were gentle yet firm.

I pulled my head back; baring my throat to him.

He began to sniff my neck, letting out a pleased growl and began to kiss and nip and my throat. I looked up at all the pretty colors on the ceiling. It looked like a multicolored rainbow was dancing in the air.

But there was something else as well, a beautiful white wolf dancing in the sky. Her hair was white as snow and she had a beautiful mane of fur that moved as if an invisible wind was blowing. She had dark eyes that sparkled like a star-filled nighttime sky.

She watched us all with kind and caring eyes; smiling at our joy, chuckling when we made fools of ourselves and she shook her head when we got too rowdy.

She looked down at me as if she sensed my gaze on her beautiful form; she smiled and gave me a wink.

Man, I have got to try this Moon Lust more often.

Richard and I were all over one another. He knew how to dance and so did I. I caught many people watching us, some looked scandalized, others delighted. I smiled, a part of me enjoying the audience; enjoyed showing them Richard was mine that I was his.

His friends joined us and we danced together on the dance floor, soon it seemed like everyone began to dance as well, drawn into the beat of the music. Some girls showed up to dance with us. The guys danced with them, some more intimately then others, though the ones with girlfriends kept things platonic.

Richard kept close to me. A few times some random guy got close and tried to get a little touchy feely with me, not that I wasn't flattered, but I was a married man now.

My husband on the other hand, did not take too kindly to strangers groping me. He would get up in their face and snarl at them and they would scamper off.

Richard's friends really warmed up to me; we talked and told jokes and laughed. I was glad we were able to get along. They had their reservations about me; they thought I was like some delicate little flower who was afraid of having a good time.

But I showed them I can play with the big dogs.

It's been such a long time since I've had so much fun. After everything that has happened to me I can finally just let it all go and be a carefree teen again.

Richard and I danced, staring into one another's eyes, ignoring the world around us. His hands slid over my ass and my hands ran down his chest. I leaned forward and kissed him.

I leaned my head back and gave him access to my neck again. Werewolves were big on kissing or nibbling on necks. Richard took my silent invitation and began to assault my throat with sensual kisses.

I looked up and saw the lights on the ceiling were bending and twisting. I raised my hands. I wanted to feel those lights on my hands; to run them through my fingers like water.

I could actually feel them on my fingers. They hummed like an electric fence. I couldn't tell if they hurt or felt good. As I played with them they seemed to pulse like blood veins.

"Dude, Richard, turn it down, man!" a voice I recognized as Keven yelled over the roar of the music.

Richard let out a low growl.

"I don't give a fuck if people are looking at us!"

"Dude, your aura is fucking with us again!"

"What?"

Richard let go of me and I looked to see what he was seeing. Many of the wolves were getting a lot friskier with their partners. I saw one she-wolf pinning a guy against the wall, she was getting too aggressive with him and he was struggling to escape from her clutches.

Over by one of the tables a werewolf had a woman laid out on the table. They were fully clothed, but the way they were going at it you would think they were about ready to have sex.

Cora who was meek by nature was getting a body shot, Vivian was trailing her tongue up her stomach. Some of the other werewolves were cheering them on, I noticed their eyes looked wolfish. There was a loud bang by the bar. Two wolves were growling at one another. A woman hid behind one of the wolves, looking afraid. I couldn't really hear what was being said but I read their lips and apparently the woman was one of the wolves' girl and the other wolf was trying to get fresh with her.

Everyone was getting a little frisky. Not just the werewolves but there were plenty of humans who were doing some serious PDA.

One of the bartenders was leaning over the bar to kiss a customer passionately. A woman had allowed a couple of men to dance with her, they pressed themselves against her while their hands roamed hungrily all over her.

I lowered my hands and leaned into Richard's ear. "Are you doing this?" I asked.

"I didn't think.....that's.....but I thought I was shielding," he said, confusion written on his face.

Things were starting to settle down now. The guys were beginning to behave themselves. The couple on the table realized how hot and heavy they got and the guy helped the girl on her feet and they looked a little red in the face. The wolves by the bar shook hands and avoided a fight.

Cora seemed to snap put of her daze and was red in the face while everyone else cheered for Vivian who threw her arms up triumphantly.

But the humans were also calming down as well.

"Damn man, we need to keep you two apart when you are around other wolves," Keven said with a chuckle.

Richard still looked confused. Like he didn't understand what happened.

"I think we should be going soon," he said sounding a little distressed.

"One more dance, please?" I begged him.

32

It was past midnight when Richard drove me home. I promised mom I wouldn't be out too late.

Liz caught a ride from one of the others to give me and Richard some alone time. As Richard drove, I leaned over and kissed his neck.

"Jeez Jer, you want to cause a wreck?" Richard asked his voice husky.

"What? You look so fucking hot, I can't help it," I said.

My hand went from his leg to his crotch and I began to rub him. I could feel him starting to harden and a deep husky growl escaped his lips.

"Jer, please," he begged.

"Oh, the big bad wolf is begging. I love that," I said nibbling on his ear.

"Jer, you're drunk," he said.

"I know, it's awesome." I laughed.

I tried to unbutton his pants, but he gently moved my hand away.

"No Jer."

"But Richard, I'm horny. I want to go down on you."

Alright, I confess. When I get drunk, I get a bit....sloppy. It wasn't something I was proud of. I mean, lots of people act stupid when they are drunk. Plus it's nice to let loose and be out of control every once in a while, God knows I need to after everything that has happened.

He sighed. "Goddamn. Jer, if you were sober I would love to take you up on your offer. But I won't, it would be wrong to do anything sexual while you are like this."

I kissed his cheek. "Oh Richard, I love you so much it makes me sick.......no, really, I feel sick, pull over!"

Richard quickly pulled over, and I hopped out. I bent down over the side of the road and unleashed the contents of my stomach onto the grass.

Richard was by my side, his hand rubbing soothingly along my back.

"I knew this was going to happen. All the alcohol you had plus the Moon Lust really fucked you up," he said.

I wiped my mouth. "Are you nuts? That shit is good. Even if it is a little bit trippy."

I felt another wave of nausea come on and threw up again.

"Your mom is going to kill me," Richard muttered.

"My mom adores you for saving me, remember?" I said.

Another wave of gut-clenching sickness hit me and I puked again.

"So what was that at the club?" I asked.

"You mean everyone getting freaky?" he asked.

I nodded. "I thought alphas couldn't influence humans."

"We can't. Humans can't even sense our aura. But I swear they were effected by my power as well."

"This has happened before I take it?" I asked.

"There have been times when I cause a few incidents with people in my pack. When I was young if I got angry people around me would get angry. If I was happy other people were happy. I never really spent much time around humans if I could help it, and I have been training to control my power for years. I didn't start losing control until..." he trailed off.

"Until what?" I asked.

"Until I met you," he said with a smile.

"Is that a good thing or a bad thing?" I asked.

"It's just something I have to work on. There was an incident weeks ago-lets just say I lost control and my friends got caught up in my power."

"It's almost like mind control or hypnotism," I commented, remembering the looks in the guys eyes the night Joseph attacked Richard.

No one at the club said anything to Richard about what happened though many seemed to be disturbed by what happened.

A lot of the other werewolves were more respectful to Richard. Those who refused to talk to us or looked at us with disapproving expressions were a lot nicer and some even showed their necks to Richard and me.

Apparently they thought he purposely messed with the werewolves at the bar as a reminder of how strong he was.

We didn't correct them. The whole point of tonight was to fix his reputation. If we couldn't do it with a few drinks and a good time, then I wasn't afraid to lie.

Besides, if they knew Richard lost control of his power it could hurt his standing in the pack even more.

Lucas didn't have this kind of power. I had seen him force werewolves to transform, but never effect so many werewolves so subtly that he could hypnotize them.

"Even Daryl can't do what I do. I had to go through serious training when I was growing up. I didn't want to be a freak who mind fucked his pack by accident. I want my people to respect me because I was a good werewolf. Not because I could force them too," he said

"I think you'll be a good Pack King one day. You're already a good friend and you care about your pack."

"I've been screwing up a lot lately," he said, his shoulders slumped a little.

"Good leaders are made from trial and error. They are not just born."

"You think so?" he asked.

I shrugged. "No one is perfect. We all make mistakes. As long as you try to do better that is all that counts."

I suddenly got this feeling like we were being watched. It was an icy chill that ran down my back and it wasn't nausea. It was fear.

I looked up, and I saw it: A wolf. It stood in the field looking at me. No, not looking, glaring hatefully. I shouldn't have been able to see it in the darkness that covered the field. But its fur was blacker than the darkness that surrounded it as impossible as that sounded.

I could see it perfectly. I saw how huge it was; about the size of a large grizzly bear, bigger than even a normal werewolf. Its eyes were pure white, like the eyes of a corpse. But there was not death in them, just hate; pure hate that made me sick to my stomach, and it wasn't because of the alcohol.

It was because all that hate was directed at me. The wolf opened its jaws and revealed it's deadly sharp teeth.

"Richard, who is that?" I asked.

"Who is who?" he asked sounding confused.

Didn't he feel this sensation as well? Didn't those superior werewolf senses alert him that we were not alone?

"That werewolf. No way is it a regular one," I said.

"What werewolf?" he repeated.

I stared at him like he was crazy. "The one in the field right in front of us."

He looked around. "I don't see another werewolf."

He had to see it. Werewolves had better night visions than humans. And if I could see that *monster* than Richard should see it as well.

I looked at him, he was frowning as he gazed out into the field. I raised my hand and pointed my finger. "But it's right-"

The wolf was gone.

I looked around for it. But I could not see it. There was no place it could hide. The field was vast but barren of trees or boulders.

"I think we need to get you home," Richard said.

"Yeah, I think we should," I agreed.

We got back into the car and drove home. I tried to forget about the black wolf I saw. I was certain it was the exact same wolf I had dreamed about.

It must be the Moon Lust in me. First, I am seeing colors and dancing white wolves and evil looking hellhounds.

Mom was asleep on the couch by the time we got back and Richard draped a blanket over her. He took me to my room and got me a glass of water which I drank gratefully.

"You are going to have one hell of a hangover tomorrow," he commented with a grin.

"Don't underestimate my endurance, Richard," I smiled.

33

"Ohhhhhhh, fuck," I groaned. It was lunch and my friends sat with me.

"You look like shit, man," Gabe said.

"I feel like it," I mumbled.

"Wow Jeremy, you must have had one hell of a night," Heather said.

I smiled, if you're going to party with werewolves you better be ready to party hard. I had dark shadows under my eyes; partly because I was up later than I should have been, and partly because I had a hard time sleeping.

I kept on dreaming about that wolf; the one I hallucinated I saw in the woods last night.

In my dreams I was in a dark forest, surrounded by dead trees, their twisted and gnarled limbs seemed to reach out and try to grab me. It was not the first time I had dreamed of that horrible place.

The wolf would appear, slowly stalking toward me, his teeth bared and fur bristled. Then I would wake up in a cold sweat, my head aching and sweat running down my head. I was never trying Moon Lust again.

"So, what is up with the Commune kids? Things seem tense in their little group now," Rachel asked looking at the tables where Richard and his friends usually sat.

The Commune kids were all sitting together now. Mary sat across from Richard and was looking a little happy. But there was still some obvious tension in the group. Most of them seemed to sit further from Richard and closer to Mary and less seemed to be sitting with Richard.

I shrugged. "Who knows," I lied.

Richard looked over at me with a slight frown on his face. He was worried about me. I tried to tell him I was fine, but he knew I was lying. Those nightmares I had about that black wolf really messed with me.

But I didn't want him to worry, so I just shrugged it off.

Richard said something to his friends, and they all got up. They grabbed their lunch and moved from the table they usually sat at and headed straight for us.

"Uh, guys," Gabe said nervously.

Richard and his friends walked over to us, and Elizabeth was with them, of course. Lots of other people noticed the strange migration; lots of heads were turning to see where they were going as well.

The group stopped in front of us. "Hey Jer, can we sit with you?"

I looked at the others. This was their table long before it was mine.

"Sure," Rachel answered.

"Fine with me," Heath agreed.

"Of course," Heather said.

"I don't-" Gabe was about to say.

"Perfect," Richard said sitting down, with his friends following.

There was an awkward pause as the Commune kids sat down. I looked at Richard and he just smiled as if this wasn't a bad idea.

"So, nice day we are having," Rachel said, breaking the silence.

"Yes, lovely. Though I dare say Jeremy can't appreciate the lovely sunshine outside," Liz said with a teasing smile.

"Had a little too much to drink last night, huh, Jeremy?" Trevor asked with a grin. I glared at him because he was partly to blame. After all, he and the others were cheering me on as I drank all those bottles of beer.

"You were partying with the Commune kids?" Heather asked.

I was very much aware of my friends' eyes on me. They didn't know I had gone out with Richard and his friends last night.

I wasn't ashamed of my friends. I was really glad I had them in my life. When Lucas and got together, I slowly distanced myself from my human friends and spent more time with Lucas and his group.

I was determined not to let the same thing happen again. But I also wanted to keep the part of my life that now included Richard and werewolves separate from my mundane life. I learned the hard way that the two could never mix.

"Oh, didn't I mention that?" I asked.

"No, you didn't," Gabe said, not sounding too pleased.

Gabe of course, was going to be the angriest about this, and I couldn't blame him. Richard and his friends had tormented him for a time. Now here they were, at his table, acting like none of their bullying had ever happened.

I would be pissed too.

"Hey, are you guys doing anything tonight?" Richard asked my friends.

"Why?" Rachel asked.

"I was thinking that we should hang out or something," Richard said. "How would you like to come to my place?"

My friends looked like they had been slapped in the face.

I stared at Richard in shock. There was no way in a million years his dad would let a bunch of human teens into his-

*****

Richard

"Awesome home!" Heath exclaimed.

"Thanks," I said closing the door behind him.

We all took off our shoes and set them aside. Jeremy leaned in close

to me and whispered in my ear.

"How the hell did you get your dad to agree to this?" he asked.

"I didn't, Liz did. All she had to do is bat her eyes and beg, and he crumbled like a sandcastle to water," I said.

He looked over at Liz and she winked at him. "Not that I don't approve, but why are you doing this?" he asked.

"Because they are your friends and I want to get to know them better," I explained.

"Your friends don't seem too enthusiastic about it," he said.

"The only reason they agreed was because the guys had a lot of fun with you last night. You showed them that humans are not so lame."

"Geez, werewolves are just so nice," he muttered.

We all went into my room. Liz got us all drinks and chips and in an instant the TV was turned on and they began playing Modern Warfare.

Liz and I worked together in getting everyone to interact.

Despite the time they had spent with Jeremy they found it awkward to be around humans, especially ones who didn't know our secret.

"Give them time, they will open up once they get to know them," Liz said.

I looked over at Scott. I could tell he was especially interested in Heather. Scott didn't have a girlfriend, but I doubt Heath would be pleased to know Scott was taking an interest in his woman.

I could smell it and sense it in his aura. As long as he didn't try anything that might cause a problem, I would leave him alone.

Scott was the kind of person who liked to mess with people to see what their reaction was.

He was a trickster and even though it had gotten him in trouble a dozen times he still could not resist the temptation of pissing someone off.

But Scott was a loyal friend, and we had something in common. You fuck with our loved ones and we fuck with you right back.

But whereas I will beat the shit out of you Scott is more devious. He is very calculating. He will wait when his prey is least expecting it, studying them learning all he can about them. Then once he has learned the best way to do it, he will get revenge. He can be a pain in the ass, but he is patient and his fury is cold and merciless.

I noticed Jeremy's one friend Gabe did seem to be a little upset. I knew he was still pissed at me for being a dick to him. I couldn't help it. I mean, he was so scrawny and easy to intimidate.

I know for a human it sounds like a terrible thing to say but werewolves are predators. We prey on the weak. Plus, it was fun chasing after him after school.

He runs fast for a human.

But he was Jeremy's friend, and it was time for me to man up for what I did. I need to stop being a jerk and grow up. My stupidity caused a lot of problems, and it is time I changed.

"Hey Gabe, can I talk to you for a minute?" I asked him.

"What for?" he asked, suspicion in his eyes.

"I think I have some left over pizza, and I am going to need help carrying the plates and drinks in," I lied.

"Alright," he said.

He followed me out of the room and into the kitchen. I turned and faced him. "Alright, I lied. I wanted to talk to you alone and apologize to you."

"What for?" he asked, his voice thick with suspicion.

"For being an ass to you for all these years."

"Why are you apologizing now?" he asked, his eyes hard.

"Because. I did something that pissed off a lot of my friends and it made me realize I need to change," I explained.

"What is going on between you and Jeremy?" he asked.

"What do you mean?" I asked in turn.

Jeremy's friends didn't know we were together. None of the humans at school knew. Jeremy wasn't ready to reveal our relationship yet, and I respected that.

"Don't give me that bullshit. I know something weird is going on between you two. For years, you and the rest of your friends treated the rest of us like we didn't even exist. Now Jeremy shows up and you are trying to be all nicey-nice."

Damn, he really is perceptive.

"You act all nice with Jeremy and give him that wrist cuff, and why is Mary always glaring at him like he-"

He stopped. His eyes went really wide, and seeing how his glasses already made him look a little bug-eyed, they really looked overly large now.

"Oh my God! You and Jeremy are together!"

"Shhh! Shut the hell up!" I growled.

"Oh my God! All those times you called me and all your other victims gay and fags, and you're one yourself! You're such a fucking hypocrite!" he exclaimed.

"Look! It's true, Jeremy and I are together. I ditched Mary for him."

"And she didn't try to slit his throat?" he asked sounding truly shocked.

"What do you mean?" I asked indignantly.

"Oh please, she is crazy, everyone knows that," he said.

"No she isn't," I said offended he would describe her as crazy.

"Remember two years ago when that foreign exchange student Kimiko was found naked in the woods and refused to say what happened?"

"Hey, she said Mary's ass looked fat in her new jeans."

"Or that one girl who had to drop out of school because she had a breakdown due to all the mental abuse Mary heaped on her because people told her she looked better than Mary did in the same pair of shoes they wore."

"Women are sensitive."

"Or that time when our ninth grade teacher had her cat killed and left on her doorstep after she gave Mary detention."

Well, he had me there. Mary was known to have a bit of...temper. I never put too much thought into it because I felt she had been in the right or didn't care enough to look too deep into the matter. One of my many faults.

"Okay, so she has some issues. But I made a peace offering with Mary; I will take her to the Fall Formal to appease her," I said.

"And you really think that will please her?" he asked with a disbelieving look.

"I have dated her for the past four years, so yeah, I think I know what makes her tick," I said.

"Why Jeremy? I find it hard to believe the school's biggest asshole would turn gay overnight. Rachel has great gaydar, and she didn't even get a signal off you."

"Look, it's complicated. I didn't mean to fall in love with him, it just happened, okay. I know that sounds stupid, but it's true. I love Jeremy. It caused some shit to go down with my friends. I want to come out to the school about us but he doesn't want to make things more difficult for me."

"You are really lucky, you know that?" he asked.

"I know. Jeremy has had a good effect on me. He is making me realize I have to change to become a better person. I won't ask to be your friend, after what I did, I wouldn't want to be my friend either. But I want to get along with you, for his sake."

He was quiet for a moment. "I need to talk to Jeremy about this. It's a bit much. But let me tell you something. I don't care who you are or how tough you are. Jeremy is a good guy, too good for you, and if you hurt him, I will find a way to get back at you," he said.

I smiled. "Damn, I didn't think you had it in you to be tough."

"I may not be tough, but I am smart; that's much more dangerous."

I was three times his size and I could tell from his scent he was serious. Anyone willing to fight for their friends was okay in my book.

I extended my hand to him, he looked at it and recognizing the sign shook my hand. Staring me in the eyes as he did so.

Normally it is never advised to look into the eyes of a werewolf, same reason why you don't look into the eyes of an aggressive dog. It can be taken as a challenge.

But instead of anger or indifference I felt respect for Gabe. I had tormented him for so long, he should be terrified. Yet here he was laying down the law and looking at me, man to man.

We walked back into my room and everyone asked where the food was. I told them I was mistaken and there was no pizza. I made it up by ordering five pizzas which were delivered to the house and quickly devoured.

I was feeling good about myself. Who knows, if this night goes well maybe Jeremy will be ready for us to come out to everyone and we won't have to hide it anymore.

I respect his desire to keep it secret. But I won't to be able to hold his hand and kiss him where ever and when ever I want.

And if anyone doesn't like it to bad.

34

Eventually we all decided to go out together and hang out in the woods.

Things were going so well, and the night was still young, and everyone thought it was a good idea. I brought a couple of six-packs and we drove out into the woods. We drove to our usual hangout; a nice isolated spot where we could not be found, and where we liked to do all the things, our parents told us not to do.

We started a little fire and turned the radio on to listen to music. We were all having a good time. Kesha started to play, and Rachel, Heather, Cora and Vivian began to dance together while the rest of us cheered them on.

Jeremy didn't drink; he was still reeling from his hangover. I was happy because he was happy; he was pleased our friends were getting along. They were talking more and just interacting in ways that never happened before.

The Commune Kids never mingled with the normal kids unless they had to. The humans thought it was a division caused by money and status. Never knowing it was due to a difference in species.

I never thought much about humans. They were just there, you know? Like your friend's pet you don't mind, but don't care for either.

Why should we pay them any mind? We were stronger, faster, we healed quicker. Why should we spend time with people who were our inferior?

The white tribe prided itself for living amongst humans; for trying the hardest to bridge that gap between the species. But now I wonder if we ever actually put any effort into it after all. I mean, how can you pride yourself about integrating with people when you lived behind Gates and walls?

Did we ever try to truly connect with them? We had human members and had human spouses, sure. But we almost never invited a human family outside the pack to our homes for dinner, we never asked the human teens to come to our homes to hang.

Watching us all tonight I wondered why we had been so foolish. Did it really matter how different our peoples were? Look at how much fun we were all having.

But living among humans could be tiring and worrisome. The werewolves had to stay hidden from the world. It gets tedious trying to pretend your something you're not.

That was why the Gates were built. So we could have a place where we didn't have to pretend to be human. Where we could just be ourselves and not have to worry about being discovered.

But the old me would never have had these thoughts. The old me didn't fall in love with a human.

"Hey Jer, can I talk to you?" Gabe asked.

Jeremy got up. "Sure."

"Let's go into the woods."

Gabe and Jeremy walked off into the woods. I had a funny feeling I knew what they were going to talk about, and judging from the knowing look Jeremy gave me, he also knew what it was about.

I already warned him that Gabe knew. Jeremy had been nervous, but I assured him Gabe simply wanted to understand.

Heather walked over to Heath. She was almost drunk, a bit tipsy, but almost there. I didn't have to smell it on her to know; you could tell from the way she moved.

"Hey babe, I need to go to the bathroom, come with," she said.

"The hell do you need me for?" he asked.

While Heather was dancing Heath, and I had been talking about football. Heath was on the football team at school, he was a quarterback. His build made him perfect for offense.

"Duh, we're in the woods. What if I get attacked by a bear? What if another psycho like the one who attacked Richard and Jeremy pops up?"

My friends and I shared a knowing smile.

Heath rolled his eyes and waved his hand at her. "You'll be fine. Just don't wander to far from here."

She frowned at him, clearly upset. I could tell from her scent she didn't need to go to the bathroom, rather she wanted some *alone* time with Heath.

"Whatever," she snapped. She stomped off into the darkness. A few minutes after they left, Scott got up.

"Be back, need to take a piss," he said.

I quickly got up and followed him, grabbing his arm. "Scott."

He stopped and turned to look at me. "Yes?" he asked, trying to look innocent.

"Don't go and do something stupid," I warned.

"I swear on the Moon, I need to take a leak," he said.

I let go of his arm. "Go on."

He may have sworn on the Moon but I know Scott, and he was up to no good. But I knew he wasn't going to hurt anyone either.

I walked back to Heath who was now talking to Trevor and Keven. Rachel was talking to Liz and the girls; they were talking about Gabe. Their anniversary was coming up, and Rachel was thinking about maybe changing her hair to impress him.

"Man, these guys aren't so bad," Trevor remarked.

"Yeah, Richard. We should hang with them more often," Keven nodded.

"Yeah, you guys ain't bad yourselves. Always thought you were kind of stuck up but you're cool," Heath said bumping fists with the three of us.

I grabbed some beer bottles and handed them to the guys. "Here is to the beginning of new friendships."

We clinked our bottles and drank from them.

35

Scott

I didn't lie when I said I had to piss; I really did. But as soon as I finished, I quickly went looking for Heather. I knew exactly why she wanted to go out into the woods; Heather's scent betrayed her true intentions. Heath either didn't know or didn't care. His mistake.

I have had my eye in her for some time. I always thought she was hot, and I heard lots of stories of what a freak she was in the bed. But we were from two different worlds so I never tried to get with her.

But last year things changed.

We met at a party last year at a party. Normally I don't go to human parties but I was bored and no one else wanted to hang so I had to go lone wolf.

I met up with Heather, it was before she even started dating Heath. We were both single and looking for a good time and hooked up.

We didn't date, just kept things casual. We exchanged numbers and would call one another whenever we needed to bang.

I never told anyone. I knew if my friends found out they would hound me fore sleeping with a human. Because when our elders gave us the whole 'sex talk' thing they told us how dangerous being with a human could be since they were so delicate.

Then she started dating Heath, and we stopped hooking up after that. I haven't spoken to her in a while. She never called me and I never called her.

I didn't hold it against her nor did I blame Heath. Heather and I knew what to expect from one another and that all we were looking for was a little fun.

Heath was a pretty cool guy. I have to admit, when Richard told us we should hang with Jeremy and his friends, I had my doubts.

I mean, humans can't hang with werewolves; they aren't like us. But I remembered how wild Jeremy partied at the Wolf's Den and figured we should give it a shot. And they all proved to be pretty cool people.

I heard Heather in the distance. I heard her muttering angrily about Heath. I found her leaning against a tree, she didn't hear me coming.

"Fancy meeting you here," I said.

She jumped and glared at me. "You asshole! You scared the shit out of me!"

"Sorry," I laughed.

"The hell are you doing out here?" she asked.

"Took a leak. Decided to make sure you were okay. You know, in case of bear or psychos."

"Fuck off!" she spat.

"Come on now, I am just messing with you," I chuckled

She crossed her arms over her chest. "Yeah well I am not in the mood."

I leaned against the tree. "Are you upset because of Heath?"

She sighed. "Yes. Things are...complicated when it comes to our love life."

"What, he not paying you any attention?" I asked.

She looked at me, she bit her lip than stood straight. "Heath is a great guy. But he's Asexual."

"A sexual what?"

She rolled her eyes and flicked my forehead. "Asexual! It means he doesn't have the same urge to have sex like you or me. It's like-she made a frustrating motion with her hands-it's like when a guy is really into sports but his girl has no interest in it whatsoever!"

"So, he can't get it up?"

She let out a breath of air. "Yes he can get it up! He is more about romance. The only time we have sex is if I instigate it and even than it is not often."

"Like tonight?"

She nodded. "I am sure everyone back there knew I wanted to fool around in the woods...everyone but *him.*"

I knew it must be difficult for her to be in such a relationship. She was a very sexual person and being with someone who had no sexual interest in her must be very frustrating.

"Have you tried talking to him about it?"

She threw her arms up in the air. "Of course I have! I have tried everything to get him hot for me. But it hardly ever works. Don't get me wrong he treats me good but sometimes I wish he would-"

"Let loose and fuck your brains out?" I asked.

She slapped both my shoulders. "Exactly!"

"Well. How about I help you out with that?"

She placed her hands on her hips. "Are you soliciting me for sex?"

"Remember our agreement when we first hooked up." I reached into my pocket and pulled out a condom. "No attachments, no romance-"

"No regrets." She looked at the condom packet than to me. She took it out of my hand and smiled. "Let's see if you still got it."

36

Jeremy

Gabe and I walked a little way from the group, far enough I would say we couldn't be overheard but werewolves have a godly sense of hearing.

I was sure if they wanted to any of the werewolves could listen to us if they wanted.

Richard already told me Gabe figured out we were together. I wasn't surprised. Gabe was very perceptive. He could always see the little details people would normally miss. He was planning on working as a crime scene investigator after he graduated.

When we were far enough away, Gabe turned to face me. "Jeremy, I know about you and Richard," he said.

"Yeah, Richard told me you figured it out," I said.

"Why him? I told you what a dick he was," Gabe said. I flinched at the small note of betrayal in his voice.

I couldn't blame him; Richard had tormented him. I had my own experiences with bullies growing up and if one of my friends started to date one of them, I would be angry as well.

"Believe me, I didn't intend for it either, and he had to work for it. I made it perfectly clear to him if we were going to be together he had to change his ways."

"I was wondering why he wasn't being as big of an ass as usual," Gabe said.

"Trust me, he can still be an ass," I commented.

And I'm married to him.

"Then why be with him?"

I needed a moment to think. Richard did have a lot of things going against him. He could be overly confidant, cocky, cruel. But he was trying to change; the fact that he was trying to make peace between our two groups of friends proved that.

Then there was the fact he was unconditionally in love with me and had already saved my life. When he would look at me, I would feel so loved, so safe.

"Because he loves me and I love him and I want this to work out," I replied.

"Well, I can't say I am too thrilled the guy who used to give me atomic wedgies is dating one of my friends. Just be careful okay."

"So, are we cool?" I asked.

"Of course we are," Gabe said. "I think you are a good influence on him, I mean if he is willing to do all this, he must care about you a lot."

"He does, and I really care about him. There are times when I feel so secure in our relationship, and other times I have some serious doubts."

"Don't worry about it, now let's get back. The night is still young."

We bumped fists and made our way back to the camp. I noticed Heather were gone as was Scott. Heath was talking with the other guys while the girls talked.

I sat down next to Richard and he smiled at me. "I take it your talk with him went well?"

"It did. Thank you for doing this, Richard. I really do appreciate you trying to open up to my friends as well."

"I have made a lot of mistakes lately, Jeremy. I want to make up for it all; you make me want to be a better person. Before, I only saw humans as a lesser species. Something not worth my time, and Mary thought the same. She never encouraged me to think differently, she encouraged me to think I really was better than humans, better than lots of other people as well. She encouraged my bad side, but you encourage my good side."

"If you want to become a better person, it should be because you want to, not because you want to make me happy," I said.

"But that's the thing Jeremy; I never wanted to be a better person because I already thought I was better. No one ever tried to show me differently, and there was no one I cared about enough to try to change for. Isn't true love supposed to be like that?"

To that I had no answer; having only been in love twice now, I was far from an expert on the subject.

Sometime after Gabe and I got back, Scott and Heather returned together laughing. They had smudges of dirt on their clothes and Heather had some twigs in her hair.

"What were you guys doing? Wrestling in the woods?" I asked.

The two of them shared a knowing look and laughed. Richard was scowling angrily at Scott who simply shrugged in response.

Heather walked over to Heath who hadn't even noticed she had come back with Scott. I had a sudden feeling our friends may have been mingling more than I cared to think about.

37

Lucas

I stood and watched the fight.

One of many in the pack and more in our tribe .We fight for many reasons; honor, loyalty, revenge, status, love. But this was a fight for fun.

We all stood in a circle, watching. Jessica, my wife and mate stood next to me, holding my hand. Her belly was round; our child was due in two months and we were both ready to meet him or her.

We had wanted the baby's gender to be a surprise. We both didn't care, we were just happy to have a child.

I was the Pack King now; having bested my father weeks ago in combat. I finally achieved the position I so wanted. I have had two challenges since then, it is not uncommon for a new Pack King to be challenged after his rule begins. I made sure to make a good example out of my challengers.

I didn't kill them, but after seeing what I did to them, no one would be challenging me for a long time. I had to discourage any wolf from thinking he could challenge me.

Becoming a Pack King was the most energizing thing I have ever felt; almost as good as basking in the light of the Moon, better than being high on Moonflowers.

All the pack's energies were added to mine, their allegiance and loyalty cemented the bond of a Pack King and his pack, and those bonds allowed me to tap into their collective power.

I will always remember the night I defeated dad and took his place. Standing over him victorious, the rush of power flowing through me.

It was arousing, it was enticing, and it was maddening. Had Jessica not been so far in her pregnancy, I would have taken her then and there. Instead, I had to take my needs out on a willing female who was more than happy to offer herself to her new leader.

Jessica didn't mind, in fact she had encouraged me to mate with another female. Hell she had even chosen her for me so I could have someone to vent my needs on until she was read resume her duties as my mate.

Jessica was not bothered by it. In our tribe it is common for alphas or werewolves of high status to have a few lovers.

I had a beautiful wife, a child on the way and I was finally Pack King, I should be happy. But it was not perfect; Jeremy was not here.

I had no idea where he was. Needless to say, our last meeting was not pleasant. Then he just vanished, no one knew where to. Even his mother had not told anyone where they were moving too, so no one knew where they were.

Many in the pack were worried he would betray us in revenge but I knew Jeremy better than that. He would not turn on us out of petty vengeance.

If I knew where he was now, I would do everything in my power to bring him back where he belongs. Why couldn't he see that I loved him? I really did. This thing with Jessica had to happen. Our marriage was prearranged when we were just kids. It happened a lot in our tribe.

Plus she was a strong alpha; her father was the Pack King of her pack and could give Jeremy and I kids. I tried to tell him it was okay; it was common for alphas to have both a spouse and a lover.

But he refused, even when I offered to transform him, to allow him to become one of us. Sure my father was pressuring me to do it in fear that the strain on our relationship would cause him to do something foolish, but I would have offered him the blood either way.

But even with the offer of becoming a werewolf and perfect life, he still turned me down. A part of me was kind of glad he did leave. If he hadn't, dad would have forced him to become a werewolf. It was the only way to keep him from turning on us.

But he disappeared before that could happen, and I did not want him to have to be forced to be one of us. But if the choice came to be between him being one of us or being dead, I would see him as one of us, even if he hated me for it.

I had always been drawn to him even when we were in school together. There was something about him that drew you in; his perfect pale skin, his raven black hair, those eyes which were neither blue, nor violet. Lots of people liked to make fun of him, saying he looked like a little girl, that he was a sissy.

But he was not a sissy, and he broke many noses to prove that. I remember watching him get into school fights; watched as he fought with such ferocity, how he would stare defiantly into the eyes of bullies three times his size, refusing to back down.

God, I miss him. I miss his voice, his eyes, I miss holding him. I miss arguing with him, I miss our secret meetings in the woods where we would watch the stars together.

I would do anything to get him back. Anything. If I knew where he was now, I would go to him and bring him back, even if he didn't want me to.

"Lucas."

I turned to face my father. He had fully recovered from our fight. He was proud of me for winning; the bastard didn't go soft on me. He made me work for it. Now he was an adviser as former Pack Kings become when they lose their title. If their challenger didn't kill them that is.

"Yes, dad?"

"We must speak. Jessica dear, might you give us a moment?" he asked her.

"Sure thing, I need to get away from all this blood. It's making the baby excited," she said with a smile as she rubbed her belly.

She walked off and a few of the females followed her. They wanted to keep an eye on her and to coo about the baby. Jessica was a good woman, we did care for one another but we were not in love. We did our duty to our packs as was expected of us. But she sure was pissed when she found out my affections lie with Jeremy. I was never able to tell if it was the fact he was a human, a male, or both that really angered her.

"What is it dad?" I asked him.

"As you know the Nox de Lupus is coming up and the Wolf Fang Falls pack of the white tribe is hosting this year," he said.

"Yes, I know." I nodded.

"There is something you need to know. Jeremy is in Wolf Fang Falls," he said.

My full attention was on him now. I got a little closer to him, my body tense. "What?"

"I was able to track him down. A while ago a Hunter attacked one of their wolves and Jeremy saved him. The wolf is Richard Farkas and his family has been prominent members of their pack for many generations. I happened to read about it in the paper and when I realized Jeremy was there I called Daryl, the Pack Master and told him."

"You did what?! Why didn't you tell me?" I demanded.

"Because I knew if I did you would rush into their territory and try to claim him."

"Damn right, what if they kill him?" I demanded.

The White Tribe was one of the most peaceful tribes, but even they would not allow a human to live if they knew of our secret.

"The white tribe are not so quick to shed blood. I spoke with Daryl again recently, and he informed me Jeremy is alive and well and has become a member of their pack."

"You don't mean-"

"No, he is still human. Apparently his experience with us helped him figure out their existence, and as a reward for saving Richard's life he was allowed to join their pack."

"Why are you telling me this now?"

"Because that boy clouds your judgment. If it was not for the Nox de Lupus looming upon us, I would have never told you. But seeing there is now a large chance you will run into him there I felt it best to tell you now."

"I am the Pack King now; you do not decide what is best for me!" I growled.

"You may be Pack King but you are still my son. The Nox de Lupus is our most sacred festival. If you were to cause a scene on this most holy day, it would damage your image in the pack, the tribe and in the eyes of the other tribes as well. I know you still want him back, were he not part of another pack the situation would be different."

"What else is there? I know you are not telling me something," I said.

"Well, Daryl seemed a little off when we spoke about Jeremy. I got the feeling there was something he was not telling me. But the fact alone that Jeremy is one of their pack; even a human one, changes the rules. We can't abduct him as that could be seen as an act of war to the Wolf Fang Falls pack."

I knew enough about the Wolf Fang Falls pack that they were the largest wolf pack in the state. And we had been friendly with them for years.

I wasn't going to ruin generations of peace, even for Jeremy. "Damn it! I should have turned him when I had the chance!" I glowered.

"Might I offer some advice?" dad asked.

"What?"

"Woo him."

"What?"

"If you want the boy so bad, woo him. I seem to remember he had a weak spot for you. Get him alone and use that charm of yours to convince him to switch packs."

"Would they allow that?"

"I don't see why not. It is not uncommon for a member of a pack to switch to another tribe. And it's not like he is valuable to them."

"Why are you helping me now?" I asked suspiciously.

Dad was not very enthusiastic about us before, so why the change of heart now?

"Because now you are married and have a child on the way, because now you are the Pack King. Your future is secured. But I know if I didn't tell you and you learned on your own he was there, you would have done anything and everything to get him back. I do not want you to cause a scene in front of the other tribes because of your obsession with that boy."

"I am not obsessed with him, I love him!"

"Call it what you will," he said waving his hand dismissively, "But do not ruin your image by doing something foolish over the boy. Do not try to force him to come with you, use your charm to get him to come back to you."

"You never approved of us. I still don't understand why you are telling me to woo him back. I seem to recall you were rather pleased when he vanished," I said.

"Because at the time we were trying to get you and Jessica married and Jeremy was causing too many problems. Were it not for him, you would have married her right away instead of putting it off. Had I known you were really serious in having a relationship with him instead of having a small fling, I would have never allowed you two to be together."

"But now?"

"Like I said. Now you and Jessica are married and expecting. My bloodline will continue and her pack and ours are united. You are Pack King and everything is now as it should be. Now I am okay with you having your little human lover. I don't want you making an ass out of yourself on the Nox de Lupus over a human boy. That is why I am telling you this now."

After Jessica and I married her father, Albert stepped down as Pack King of his pack and handed control over to my dad. Albert was old and enjoying his retirement.

He had been very vocal about Jeremy being killed to protect our secret; and he was more than happy when he disappeared.

"You should have told me sooner," I complained.

"Like I said, I was afraid if I told you, you would have run right into the Wolf Fang pack's territory just to see him and caused an incident. But I trust that now you will handle this situation appropriately."

"And you won't stop me should I decide to bring him back? Should I make him my lover or turn him?" I asked.

"You are the Pack King now and I will support you in anything. I have no grievance with the boy, so long as he doesn't try to cause problems between you and Jessica. I only ask that if you do convince him to return, you not anger the Wolf Fang Falls pack. Even if he did save one of their wolves, they would not make him a member without reason."

"Daryl gave no reason for letting him join?" I asked.

"No, I tried to inquire as to why but Daryl would not go into further details."

"Why do you think he would let him become a member of the pack?" I asked.

"He must be useful to them in some ways. All the tribes have a few humans on the payroll. It is advantageous to have someone who is immune to silver, wolfsbane and turning into a murderous beast on a full moon. But usually it is a human who is useful in some way. A lawyer, a doctor, a cop. Someone who can be of help, and there is nothing I can think of that Jeremy could provide. He is still just a teen and has no connections to anyone powerful."

"You don't think they turned him, do you?" I asked.

"No, that would mean someone in the pack truly values him or he did something to truly warrant the blood as a reward. But I am sure we will find out when we get there. Just please, keep yourself in check. You are a new Pack King and if you don't control your emotions, it could damage your reputation in the pack."

"Don't worry, I will. Thank you for telling me this."

We returned to watch the fight, and I was feeling very good. Jeremy was in Wolf Fang Falls, and we would be going there soon for the Nox de Lupus.

Surly this was an act of providence. Destiny, fate, it all adds up. I have a wife, I have a child coming, and I am Pack King. Now all I need is Jeremy.

It won't be easy because he can be so damn stubborn. But when I show him the benefits of being the Pack King's lover he will see. He will want for nothing; he will have nothing but the best. I will have to speak to Daryl about this first. Jeremy is one of his pack now, but I am sure he won't mind.

Jessica will be a problem though she doesn't care if I have lovers. In our tribe an alpha can have as many as he wants. But the fact it is Jeremy might open up some old wounds for her, she knows my love for him is stronger than what I have for her.

But I am her husband and her Pack King; she will do as I say. And if I say she will accept Jeremy, then she will.

I can convince him to come. Jeremy won't be able to resist me when I put the charm on. I can show him I can take care of him and provide for him. Then after that, once I get him settled into his new life, I can try to convince him to change, to become my wolf.

Oh yes, thank you Byrrus for this blessing.

38

Jeremy

"You and Richard!" Rachel squealed.

"Oh my God!" Heather exclaimed.

My friends were at my house right now. It was the night of the Fall Formal and the climate had lowered a few degrees in the last few weeks.

In the time leading to this night I had received several requests from girls at school to go to the dance but I gently let them down.

Now everyone at school knew of my orientation and I was officially known as Jeremy Moonvine the only gay kid at school.

The biggest problem I had now was people assumed I was some kind of fashion guru and I had guys and girls asking me for clothing advice.

Everyone else seemed to want to avoid me now. I would catch people staring at me, or whispering to one another as I walked through the halls to class.

I had a feeling some of the more narrow minded students would be more verbal of their distaste of my sexuality. But I was known to be *tight* with Richard's group so no one dared mess with me.

Rachel, Gabe, Heath and Heather were visiting before they went to the formal; they were trying to convince me to join them. But I told them why. Gabe hadn't spilled the beans, and I was grateful for that. I told them about Richard and I and the situation with Mary.

I wasn't going to go even though Richard and Elizabeth had done their best to convince me to. But I didn't want this to be ruined for Mary. I knew if I was there Richard would constantly be looking for me, making sure I was alright. He needed to give Mary his undivided attention.

This was her last night with Richard and I didn't want it to go bad for her. I wasn't trying to be friends with her; God knows she isn't my favorite person. But I do feel responsible for what happened to her and I want peace between us as well.

"Oh my God, it all makes sense now!" Rachel exclaimed. "I can't believe Richard Farkas is gay! My gaydar is broken!"

"And you're okay with your boyfriend taking his ex to a dance?" Heath asked.

"I feel bad for her. I know what it is like to have someone steal your man. I owe her this," I said with a shrug.

"Oh please, you don't owe her shit," Heather said. "Richard dumped her."

"Because of me," I pointed out.

"Oh come on Jeremy, please come. I feel bad that you will miss the dance," Rachel said.

"It's okay guys, there will be other dances," I said. "Just do me a favor and don't tell anyone okay? Richard and I are planning on coming out to the school soon."

"Can I ask a question?" Heather asked.

I took a deep breath, knowing her it would be something sex-related.

"Shoot."

"Is he hung?" she asked.

Called it.

"Babe, I really don't want to hear how big Richard's dick is," Heath said.

"True that," Gabe said shaking his head.

I grinned and decided to indulge Heather's curiosity. I whispered into her ear his length and using my finger and thumb I gave her an idea of how big he could get.

She looked at me, her eyes wide and her mouth open in shock. "Oh my God! Have you and Richard had sex?" she asked.

Rachel turned a shade red and began to fan herself with her hand and let out a small giggle.

"No, but we did-"

"Stop!" Gabe yelled covering his ears.

"Oh, come on. We have to hear you two talk about how hot women are all the time, give us this one thing!" Heather said scowling at the guys.

"I bet he is a romantic; he likes to fill the room with roses and scented candles," Rachel said.

"Please, I bet he likes it rough and dirty," Heather said.

"I think it is a little disturbing how much thought you two put into this whole thing," I said.

"Are you sure you don't want to come with us?" Heath asked changing the subject.

"Yeah, besides it would be awkward and I don't want to be the lonely guy on the wall with no date," I said.

I saw them out and watched as they drove away. I walked back in the house and I caught mom trying to sneak out. Tonight was her night off, but she was going on a date with Rick.

"Going somewhere, mom?" I asked.

She froze on the spot. "Damn!"

She wore a pair of black high heel shoes, matching black cotton pants, a button jacket and a pair of gold earrings.

"So, curfew is at ten, and no drinking, and if he invites you to his place, just say no. You are too young to be having sex young lady," I admonished.

She smiled and cuffed me upside the head. "Do I look alright? I don't look old or like a slut do I?"

"Mom, you look great, Rick will be crazy to think you are anything but amazing," I answered her honestly.

She smiled, pleased with my answer. I was glad she was going out with Rick. She had never gone out on many dates before. I think part of the reason why she never had a lasting relationship was because she still loved my father.

After everything I put her through, I was happy she was able to find some happiness from the mess that was my love life.

Mom left, and I walked into the living room and turned on the TV. I was kind of glad I had this night to myself though I was sure Richard would stop by later after the dance.

He had developed a habit of sneaking into my room in the middle of the night. We had not done anything sexual since our little tryst but we did make out a bit.

Things were sure to get more interesting around here soon. The Nox de Lupus was right around the corner, and werewolves from the other tribes would be arriving to celebrate their holy day.

The celebration would be held in Hunter's Meadow. Many of the visiting werewolves would be staying in the Gates as honored guests, or in nearby hotels.

From what I have learned, not a single member of the black tribe would be allowed in the Gates. Of all the tribes, the white and black tribes hated one another the most.

Liz told me once that thirty years ago the black tribe did come to stay in the Gates for the Nox de Lupus. Not even an hour after they arrived they were all kicked out.

Poor Rick is going to have his hands full. The black tribe likes to make things difficult for the tribe they're visiting. He says if there aren't any mysterious disappearances in the human community, he will be extremely surprised. The black tribe has a habit of leaving bodies in their wake.

On the plus side, I was looking forward to meeting Richard's uncle and his family from the yellow tribe. He said Eldred was Frank's younger brother who switched to the yellow tribe years ago. He now has three wives and several kids. Eldred is said to be the exact opposite of Frank; funny, warm, easy going. I was really looking forward to meeting him.

Then of course, there is Lucas. I will run into him, how can I not?

Maybe it is time I did see him again, bury all that water under the bridge and all that. It is time I moved on with my life, it is time I stop wishing for the old days.

I can't believe this is my life now; married to a rich and powerful werewolf after having my heart broken by another werewolf.

Dear Abby would have a field day with me.

Just then my cell began to vibrate, letting me know I was getting a text. I pulled it out of my pocket and looked at the screen. It was Richard's number.

Wishing you were here

I got another text. This time it was a picture. It showed Richard wearing a nice tuxedo. He was looking into a mirror, giving me a wink as he took his selfie.

I smiled and got up to go to my room. I plugged my phone into my computer and opened the tab for my pictures.

I went through my folders until I found the newest one I had made. *Wolf Fang Falls.* Inside was all the pictures I had taken since I arrived in this town.

Pictures of Gabe, Heather, Heath, Rachel. My new friends who had welcomed me with open and accepting arms. On pic showed Gabe and Rachel studying together, she was resting her head on his shoulder while he pointed to something in the book they were reading.

Another pic of Heath and Heather. They were walking through the hallway at school, he was giving her a piggy-back ride and they were both laughing at the camera. Pictures from the night we all went dancing at Hunter's Meadow. One pic showed Heather and Rachel leaning on one of the stone boulders holding their drinks in their hands. Another showed Gabe dancing like a spaz while the others laughed. Another showing Heath and I drinking from our cups at the same time to see who could finish first. The angle was a little crooked, Heather had taken the pic and had been cheering Heath on.

Of course there were pictures of Richard and the Commune Kids as well. Richard laying on my bed, he was on his side facing me, he lips parted in a silent snore. The next pic was the same except he had an eyelid cracked open with a small smile on his face. Another of me, I was laughing, Richard above me taking the pic, his hand right next to my head as he used his other to take the picture.

Dozens of pictures of Liz posing in dresses from her limitless walk-in-closet. Pictures of her in the garden with her mother. One hilarious picture of Richard sitting at the dining room table reading the books his grandmother gave him while Susan and Frank stood behind him, the both of them watching him sternly.

Pictures from the Wolf's Den of Bob, Henry, Scott, Cora, Vivian and Trevor. Dancing, playing pool, having a good time.

In this moment I realized I was truly a part of this pack. I wasn't just Richard's boyfriend....err husband. No, the werewolves actually accepted me as one of them. I felt more connected with them then I ever did with Lucas's pack.

The last picture-and obviously my favorite-was the one I took the day after Richard and I were married. When we were naked on my bed, his body pressed close against my own and our eyes shined with happiness.

I added Richard's photo he sent into the folder. I was about to exit when I saw the folder that held all the photos of Lucas and myself.

Had it really been more than a month since I last looked at this folder? Since I struggled to delete it and wipe away the memories of my time with Lucas.

Whatever it was that had stopped me before was gone now. I sent the whole folder to the recycle bin and wiped it from my computer.

And I didn't feel sad, I actually felt glad to do it.

My old life was over. My new life has just begun. And I know I will fill the memory space of my computer with pictures of Richard and my new friends; human or otherwise.

39

Richard

Derek and I sat down, glaring at one another. Keven, Trevor, and Scott sat with me. Jack, Charlie, and Dylan sat with Derek, glaring right back at us.

I once counted Dylan, Charlie, and Jack as my friends but after the ceremony they jumped ship to Derek's wagon. A lot of my supposed friends didn't even waste any time when they learned I was with a human guy.

At least now I knew who my real friends were.

The girls were upstairs getting ready, I could hear them talking. I knew they were all waiting on Mary, helping her get dressed.

"So, how is your husband, Farkas?" Derek asked.

"Good, wishing he could come. But he graciously declined so it wouldn't cause a problem for anyone tonight," I said.

"How nice of him," Derek said with a sneer.

Just then the girls began to move; I could hear them coming down the stairs. We all got up and immediately went to greet them at the foot of the stairs.

Her parents were already waiting to greet them; her mother held a camera in her hands and her father gave me a nod.

The girls came walking down, talking excitedly, all of them looking amazing in their dresses. But Mary stood out as always.

She wore a white gown that clung to her frame perfectly, showing off all her amazing curves and her generous hourglass figure. A thick white ribbon was wrapped around her waist and rested against her hip. A pair of white opera gloves and matching pearl slippers completed her look.

Her hair was tied in a tight bun and a single moon flower was above her right ear. Around her neck was a piece of jewelry in the shape of the triple moon. The quarter moons on the sides were simple gold, but the full moon in the center was pure sapphire.

That necklace must have be worth a fortune.

The smell of Moonflower was thick in the air; she-wolves like to wear it as a perfume to special events. Werewolves love the smell of a Moonflower.

She was stunning, truly magnificent; an artist would love to draw a painting of her. But it did not make me wish I was going with her instead.

A part of me felt sad for her, obviously a lot of trouble went into this, not that she had to put a lot of effort in looking good. But when she actually put some added effort into it she was amazing.

She smiled when she saw me, and in an instant she was by my side, her arm wrapped around mine, as if nothing had changed.

Her mom took a bunch of pictures of all of us, telling Mary and me how good we looked together. I could tell Mary wasn't the only one who was hoping we would become a couple again.

"You look beautiful, Mary," I said truthfully.

She beamed, looking happier than she had in a while. After the pictures were taken, we got into our cars and headed off to the school for the dance.

It was just Mary and I in the car. I turned the radio on finding a Taylor Swift song for her to listen to. Not my thing but this was Mary's night.

"Tonight is going to be perfect," she said happily.

I said nothing, letting her do all the talking.

"Sorry if Derek is being an ass, I told him to be nice but you know Derek, his understanding of nice is so messed up," she said.

"It's fine, he has a good reason to be angry," I said.

"Well not anymore, we are together again and that is all that matters," she said.

I didn't bother to correct her that this was a onetime thing. No sense in getting something started that wouldn't end well.

*****

The dance was in the school gym. The school had hired a DJ for the music. Balloons and curtains had been set up and tables had been brought in covered with nice tablecloths that were holding food and drinks.

Lots of eyes were on Mary, she loved the attention; she beamed with pleasure as envious looks from the girls and lustful looks from the boys were directed at her.

I spotted Jeremy's friends at one of the tables. I had hoped to see Jeremy with them, which was stupid, as he told me he wasn't going to be here.

But that didn't stop the small bit of hope in my heart from making me think that he would change his mind and show up with Rachel, Gabe, Heath and Heather.

I looked over at Liz. She wore a black satin dress with a floral design, her hair tied up in a ponytail. She had thick black eyeliner and matching lipstick and she put on extra black eye shadow and white powdered skin.

Bob was her date; he still looked as stunned and amazed as he did when Liz asked him to the dance. Liz was never one to wait for someone to ask her on a date or to a dance.

She didn't have a crush on him, she just needed a partner to the dance and Bob was one of the few people to have never gone to a dance or on a date with her.

"Dance with me Richard," Mary said pulling me onto the dance floor.

I obediently followed her, and we began to dance, the others gave us a wide berth. I could hear them talking amidst the roar of the music, the humans took notice we were together again, already theorizing why we split and why we got back together.

We ignored them and continued to dance. Mary seemed happier then she had in a while, I just hoped she realized this would be the last night we would dance together.

40

Jeremy

I closed the door and made sure it was locked. I pocketed the keys and began to take my walk. I got bored, nothing was on TV and there was still some daylight out, so I figured I could take a quick stroll.

Now that Joshua and his Hunter friends were dead I didn't have to worry about someone kidnapping me again.

I was wearing a red jacket and a pair of boots; the jacket had been a present from Liz. She liked to call it her 'Wedding present' to me.

I hadn't gone for a walk in a while. Most of my time was spent either doing homework or with Richard.

I wondered if he was having fun at the dance. I know he wasn't too thrilled about doing this but I hope he can at least have some fun while he's there.

Richard and I have become so close. It has only been seven and a half weeks since I moved here and the first day I met him he was just some handsome guy that went to my school. Now he is my soul mate and my husband.

I have spent a lot time with his grandmother learning as much as I can about the white tribe. Learning what responsibilities I would have if he did become Pack King.

A Pack King's wife, (or in this case, husband), has a lot of pull in the pack, but their main job is to cater to the needs of their husband or wife. They take care of their home and help ease the tension a Pack King gains from running his pack.

A Pack King's mate also looks after the pack; making sure they are all safe and healthy. That made me think of another subject Richard and I had barely talked about: Me becoming a werewolf.

The question lurked in the back of my mind. Did I want to become a werewolf?

Sure there are some advantages, but was it necessary for me to transform? I like being a human just fine.

Werewolf this, werewolf that; it seems like my every thought these days have to do with werewolves. Better than vampires I guess.

I could stay human; it wasn't like there was a law I had to become a werewolf. (I triple-checked just to make sure) There were lots of couples in the pack that were like that. One human and one werewolf and they got along fine.

I pushed it all aside and continued on my walk. Instead, I thought about my friends and wondered how they were all doing. I hope they are enjoying the dance.

*****

Heather

"Oh God, harder!" I moaned.

Scott thrust his hips harder and deeper into me, I moaned and a small growl escaped his lips. We snuck off into the girl's locker room. He had me pinned against a wall, with my legs wrapped around his waist, his pants and underwear were at his ankles, my skirt was hiked up and my panties were to the side.

Heath was off with his friends somewhere, of course he did not know about us. A few nights after our little get together in the woods I was walking home, pissed that Heath had to cancel our date to hang out with his friends.

Scott had pulled up next to me in his car and offered me a lift. We talked as he drove and feeling the need to get back at Heath and wanting another round with Scott, he drove off into the woods and we had sex in his back seat.

The next night after that, he appeared at my house, having climbed the tree next to my room. I let him in and we had sex on my bed.

I know it was wrong for me to be doing this to Heath. He had always been a good boyfriend but lately we have been drifting apart. He has been spending less and less time with me and I feel like our relationship is about to die.

I have tried to keep it going, but I am reaching the point where I am tired of trying.

I had been sitting at the table, feeling angry that Heath was talking to his friends about some dumb football game and was too busy to dance with me.

Scott sat down next to me and we started talking and I may have hinted that we should have a private dance. We made sure to lock the door before we came in and here we were.

Scott was so....I don't know how to explain it. I guess you could say lively. It was like he could read me in a way Heath couldn't. Plus he was so attentive and caring; he was quickly filling that hole Heath was leaving void.

No pun intended.

And the sex, my God! Heath was good but Scott was amazing! We could have sex and he would be ready to go again and again and again!

Plus he was one of the Commune Kids, lots of girls at school would love a chance to sleep with one of them. Not very many could say they did, but those that had all said the same thing.

Guys from the Gates are a great lay.

"Oh God I am close!" he panted.

"Me too! Me too!" I cried.

My walls clamped down on him and he gave one final thrust and filled his condom. We stood there catching our breaths. Then he set me back on my feet and pulled out. He took off his condom, tied it in a knot, tossed it in a toilet and flushed.

"Thanks, I needed that," I said.

"No problem. I didn't bring a date tonight, so I was kind of bored," he said pulling his pants back up.

I went to the mirror and checked my appearance. Scott walked up next to me, leaning against one of the sinks.

"So, what are you doing this weekend?" he asked.

"Well I was supposed to go out with Heath but I am not sure if he will blow me off again," I said with a groan.

"Why don't you just dump him?" Scott asked

"I can't just dump him," I said.

"Why not? It's not like you guys have a very stable relationship," he pointed out.

"Scott, do you want to be my boyfriend?" I asked.

He smiled. "Well yeah, I think you are smart and beautiful. Why not?"

"You're sweet, but we can't," I said.

"Why not?" he asked.

"Because I am with Heath."

"The guy who has been ignoring you and whom you are cheating on?" he asked raising a brow.

"Heath and I are going through a phase right now. It happens to lots of couples, we have to find our spark again, is all," I said.

"Why try to find a spark with someone when you have chemistry with someone else?" he asked sounding confused.

I turned to face him. "Scott, let's be reasonable, just because we had some good sex doesn't mean we are hooking up. I am with Heath and this is just a fling," I said.

"Just a fling? Come on Heather, I know you like what we have. I don't mean just the sex, I mean what we have," Scott said.

"Scott, please don't do this. I like you; you are nice and funny, but don't try to make this more than what it is. Heath has always treated me well, and this is just something to tide me over," I explained.

He looked at me with a hurt expression. Then his face turned hard. "Fine. Whatever." He turned around and began to walk out.

"Scott, wait," I called.

He ignored me and walked out of the locker room. I sighed and put my hand to my face. I admit, Scott's idea of us hooking up was tempting. I wouldn't mind going out with him. But this is just a phase. I needed a way to vent my frustration with Heath.

Still didn't stop me from feeling guilty though.

God, I feel so frustrated with Heath, I feel like I should just end it, but on the other hand I don't want to hurt him. He does treat me good.

Scott and I may have agreed to a 'no strings attached' kind of deal. But obviously the deal was off. It was in that moment I realized I was crushing on two guys. That was not supposed to happen!

I looked at myself in the mirror.

"Girl, get your shit together."

41

Richard

Mary and I were taking a quick break, having danced to five songs straight. I got us some punch, and she quickly drank it.

"Thank you Richard, I am so warm," she said.

"No problem," I said.

As she drank from her cup her eyes seized me up. I could tell she was trying to gauge my mood. "Are you having a good time?" she asked.

"Yes, I am. How about you?" I asked her, taking another sip from my cup.

I was telling the truth, I was having fun. It would have been better if Jeremy was here, but it was nice to act like it was the old days before all this shit happened.

I was actually starting to have hope that maybe, just *maybe* Mary and I could be friends. That everything could work out for us all. That one day we could look back on all this and laugh.

"Oh great, thank you so much for this, Richard." She moved closer to me and kissed me on the cheek. Then her mouth moved to my ear. "In fact, why don't I really show you how thankful I am?"

Her hand touched my groin and began to rub it.

I quickly grabbed her hand gently and moved it away. "Mary, no," I said gently.

"Why? You want to go somewhere private?" she asked with a sultry smile that once would have turned me on.

"No, you know why Mary," I said.

The beauty melted away, showing the ugly anger beneath that beautiful face. "Come on, Richard. Forget the human and come back to me where you belong."

Just then the song ended and a new slow song began to play.

"Oh let's dance again!" she exclaimed.

She quickly got up and dragged me onto the dance floor. We passed Derek and his date, Derek shot me a dark look.

Derek had graduated last year but was here as a date for one of Mary's friends Tiffany. We passed Liz and Bob who were slowly swaying to the music.

It was nice to see Bob having a good time. He didn't have the same good looks the rest of us had, but he wasn't ugly. He had a very boyish face and was considered plane by many so he wasn't as popular with the ladies the rest of our circle.

But Liz never cared much for looks. Bob was a nice guy, and that was what mattered to her. I spotted Scott who was leaning against a wall. I noticed he seemed to be glaring at Heath and Heather as they danced. I knew he and Heather were fucking around. I didn't say anything to Jeremy about it because it was between Scott and Heather. But I did warn Scott to be careful.

I knew he was getting attached to her, a dangerous thing for him to do. But I gave him my warning and left it at that.

Mary and I continued to dance and she gently laid her head on my shoulder. "Oh Richard, it's like nothing ever happened. Like it is just us again, isn't it perfect?" she asked.

I realized from the tone of her voice Mary was not going to stop trying to make this into something it wasn't. She was setting herself up for disappointment and I didn't want to anger her, I didn't want to lead her on either.

"Mary, we need to talk," I said.

"It's okay, there is no need for words, I forgive you Richard. Let us put this all behind us and move on," she said. "Things can go back as they were, with us together again."

"Mary, you know it can't. Besides the fact, I am now married and Jeremy is my soul mate. Please don't think this means we are back together," I said.

She looked at me, her eyes full of hurt. "But Richard....I...I...I did all this for you. I spent hours on designing this dress to be made; I poured thousands of dollars into it!"

"Mary, I still love you. Just not like I used to," I said gently.

"But why?" she asked, hurt crept into her voice.

"Mary....I don't want to do this. Let's just end this night on a high note," I suggested hopefully.

She let go of me and took a step back. "Why, Richard? Why....*him!*" she snarled.

"Mary-"

"What does that bastard have that I don't?!" she yelled.

People stopped dancing and looked at us.

"No one has loved you like me! I was supposed to marry you, not him! How are you supposed to raise a family with him, Richard!? Last I checked, men don't have a womb!"

Her energy poured off of her in waves, she was becoming dangerously close to shifting, and in front of the humans no less. If she so much as even risked exposure, Daryl would not hesitate to have her punished.

The humans were muttering now. Already the flames of gossip spread.

"What is she talking about?"

"You don't think Farkas dumped her for a guy do you?"

"Why is she so angry?"

"Mary, please compose yourself!" I hissed.

"I love you, Richard! Why can't you get that? What do I have to do to make you love me again?!" she yelled as her voice began to break.

"I don't love you anymore, I love Jeremy!" I exclaimed.

"Jeremy?"

"As in Jeremy Moonvine?"

"Holy shit!"

"That would explain why he has been hanging out with him."

"Farkas is *gay*?"

"Shut the fuck up!" I roared at everyone.

They all took three steps back as I glared at them. Then I smelt the scent of salty tears and looked at Mary. She was crying now, her mascara was already running down her face.

"How could you say that, Richard? After everything we have been through? What happened to our dreams? Marriage? Family?"

"Mary, please. I am sorry, but things have changed, you know that. I still care about you and want you to be happy."

"Then love me! I can't be happy unless you love me!" she yelled.

"I....I can't," I said with a sigh.

A sob escaped her lips, and she fell to her knees. Derek and their friends quickly appeared and got her up and carried her away. Derek glared at me and quickly hurried off.

Liz appeared next to me, gently placing her hand on my shoulder. "Alright people, show is over," she said waving her hand to the gawkers.

She quickly guided me out of the gym and into the hall. Scott, Bob, and Trevor followed.

"Dude, what happened? You guys were doing great," Bob asked.

"She kept going on how we were back together and things were going to go back to normal. I couldn't let her think it was true," I said.

"Mary is deluding herself. She was there when the ritual happened. She is letting her emotions get the better of her," Trevor said.

"Maybe I should go talk to her," I said.

"Are you insane?! Derek would beat the snot out of you and I doubt seeing you will make her feel better," Liz said.

"And now the whole school knows about you and Jeremy," Trevor noted.

"I couldn't care less about the school; I am more concerned about Mary. Maybe I should have kept my mouth shut," I said rubbing my face, feeling bone tired.

"No, Mary saw the ceremony and felt your aura mix with his. She is deluding herself with the notion you two can still be together. Feeding that delusion would only make it worse," Liz said.

"She does seem a little on the crazy side. I mean, I feel for her and all, but she seems to be going over the edge. I mean, she almost shifted in front of the whole school, can you imagine what Daryl would have done if she did?" Bob asked

We all shuddered. Daryl was not cruel, but you risk the pack in any way and you will find out quickly just how creative he can be with his punishments.

You can't be the Pack King by being soft. You had to be firm, protective and when the time came wrathful.

"So what now?" Trevor asked.

"Fuck if I know, I doubt Mary will be in any mood to finish tonight though," I said.

42

Mary

Derek, Rebecca, Tiffany, Zoe and Victoria stood with me outside the school. I was still crying, I couldn't believe this happened. I was so sure I had him again, it was all so perfect.

"Don't worry Mary, it will all be okay," Zoe said.

"Yeah, we'll just fix your makeup and you'll go back in like nothing happened," Victoria said soothingly.

"How can I go back in there now? Everyone knows now, everyone is talking. I can hear them all," I cried.

"Well, maybe if you hadn't lost your cool, then they would not know," Derek said.

"Shut up, Derek! You do not know what I am going through right now, so just shut up! I spent weeks planning for tonight and it was all for nothing!" I screamed.

"Mary, he is married now, you sensed the energy they released. You had to have known this wouldn't work," he said.

"Come on Derek, lay off," Rebecca said hugging me.

"This is all that fucking human's fault! If he never came here, then none of this would have happened!" I growled.

Jeremy fucking Moonvine! That stupid, skinny, weak, pathetic little bastard! All of this is because of him! If it wasn't for him, then Richard and I could be together! If it wasn't for him then.....of course.

I took a deep calming breath and smiled. "Guys, could you give me a moment please?" I asked.

"Are you okay?" Victoria asked in a worried tone.

I nodded. "I just need a moment alone. I will be fine okay? I just need to catch my breath, fix my make-up, and then I will be back in."

"Okay girl, don't worry, everything will be fine," Rebecca assured me.

I smiled. She was right; it would all be alright, just as soon as I took care of one minor detail. Then everything will be as it should.

Derek lingered. He gave me a quick hug and a kiss on the cheek. "I am sorry if I upset you, Mary. I just hate how you keep letting yourself get hurt by Farkas. You are a beautiful and wonderful woman and deserve nothing but the best."

Derek has always been my rock.

I know I don't treat him as well as I should. He is always looking out for me, protecting his little sister as best he could. But he never gave up on me.

I hugged him back. "It's okay, Derek. But don't worry, I think things will be better from now on," I said.

He gave me one last kiss on the head and went back inside. I turned around and kicked off my slippers and ran into the woods, I ripped off the necklace and tore off my clothes. I transformed into my wolf form and ran through the woods; my once-beautiful dress tore to pieces.

I didn't care though; I was on a mission now. A mission to get the love of my life back and the only way I could do that was to kill the one person who was in my way: Jeremy.

*****

Jeremy

I shut and locked the door behind me. I took of my jacket and shoes and put them in the closet. I hummed to myself as I made my way to the kitchen. My little walk had caused me to work up quite the appetite.

It was starting to sprinkle outside when I got home. It was eight-thirty now, the party at the school was supposed to end at ten. I hope everyone was having a good time.

Just then the phone rang, and I went to answered it.

"Hello?"

"Hey sweetie, is everything okay?" mom asked.

"Yes, everything is fine. How is your date going?" I asked.

"Oh, it is going great. It's been so long since I had this much fun and Rick is such a gentleman. I should be home around ten but if I am a little late, don't worry."

"Take your time, enjoy yourself. I can handle myself," I said.

"Alright sweetie. Take care," she said.

She ended the call, and I went back to making my sandwich, then the phone rang again.

"Hello?"

"Jeremy?"

"Richard?"

"Hey, listen, something has come up," he said.

I rolled my eyes. Of course something has come up. And I have a sneaking suspicion Richard is at the center of it all. "What did you do this time?" I asked.

"Hey, it wasn't me, it was Mary," he said.

"What happened?"

He told me what happened; how Mary had a serious meltdown and in her anger told the whole school Richard and I were together.

"Oh God," I muttered.

"Yeah. So don't be surprised to be the center of attraction at school," he said.

"Is Mary alright?" I asked.

"I think, but I haven't seen her since she left. I am thinking about just blowing this whole thing off. Hell, it's already over before the dance even ended," he said glumly.

"Find out if she is still there and try and talk to her. Maybe if you just sit her down and have a nice heart-to-heart you can work something out. What could it hurt to try?"

"Yeah, you're right. Enough of this beating round the bush shit. I need to just talk with her like grown adults and hash everything out!"

"Call me back and let me know, okay?"

"I will. Sorry about this. I know you weren't ready to come out to the school about us yet," he said.

"Well, if I have learned anything since I moved here, it's that my personal life doesn't stay personal for long," I said with a sigh.

"I will call you later, love you," he said.

"Love you too," I said.

I set the phone down and finished my sandwich. I went into the living room and turned on the TV.

But then I heard a loud bang from upstairs and I put my plate on the table. I quickly made my way to the closet and pulled out an aluminum bat.

I quietly made my way upstairs. I didn't hear anything, but that didn't mean nothing was there. It sounded like it came from my room so I walked there. Bat raised and ready, I turned my light on and looked around. I saw no one, but my window was open and the cold air was blowing through it.

Odd, I know I shut it.

I went over to close it but I noticed scratch marks under it. Like someone dug their very sharp knives. But these kind of looked like claw marks.....ohhh fuck!

I felt something large fall behind me, then I felt an inhumanly strong hand grab my shoulder and before I knew it I was airborne. I slammed into the wall. I fell to the ground. I think I almost blacked out, but I managed to stay awake.

I looked up, I had to blink a couple times because all I could see was white spots. When my vision cleared I saw it was Mary.

She had been clinging to my ceiling above my door, waiting for me to come in.

Most guys would be happy to find a beautiful naked woman in their room, but ignoring the fact I was gay, Mary didn't look much like Mary.

Gone was the stunning beauty that turned heads and left a wake of admirers in her wake. She had dark stains around her eyes from her mascara mixing with her tears, her teeth were sharp and pointy and her nails were claw-like. Her eyes burned with such hate, it warped her beauty into something twisted.

"You! You ruined my life!" she screamed, pointing a clawed finger at me.

She began to advance on me, snarling like a deadly beast, which of course she was. I got up as quickly as I could, luckily nothing was broken but I was sure I was going to be sore later.

If I survived that is.

The bat was too far away for me to grab, she would get me before I could touch it. And even if I did get my hands on it there was no way in hell I could hope to stop her with it.

"Mary, don't do this," I said.

"Oh, I am so going to do this. After I kill you, I can have Richard again!" she growled, an evil smile on her face.

"Mary, think about this, you know the law forbids a wolf to hurt another wolves' soulmate-"

"You are not his soulmate!" she roared, her voice so shrill it hurt my ears. "I love him more than anyone! He is mine, not yours!"

She lunged forward and grabbed me by my shirt and lifted me up in the air.

"But I am not just going to kill you; I am going to make you pay for all the pain and humiliation you heaped on me! So I want you to run! I want you to run like the little rabbit you are!"

She dropped me and I backed as far from her as I could.

"I will give you five minutes. Best run little rabbit!" she taunted.

I stumbled as I ran out of the room. I still felt dizzy from being thrown into the wall, but I couldn't afford to be slow.

I ran down the stairs, I slammed into the door, I forgot I had locked the door when I twisted the doorknob desperately. Once I finally got the damn thing open, I ran outside.

The street was quiet as I ran out. A few of the other houses had their lights on, but I didn't dare go to my neighbors for help. Unless any of them have any silver bullets they can't help me and I will not put anyone else in danger.

I looked up at my bedroom window and saw Marry watching me with a cold expression. I saw her mouth moving as she counted down.

I ran into the woods. I quickly pulled out my cell and dialed Richard's number. "Jer, hey-"

"Richard she's after me!" I yelled.

"Who?"

"Mary! She just attacked me!"

"Where are you?"

"In the woods, she is going to hunt me down!"

"Run to the school! I'll find you!"

"Richard, please hurry!" I begged.

"I'm on my way don't worry!" he yelled

I heard the sound of a wolf howl behind me. I was out of time.

I might just make it. If I could get to Richard in time he could save me from Mary.

But I had to go as fast as I could, I could not risk slowing down. Werewolves were faster than humans or wolves. I did not bother trying to guess if she could catch me before I made it to safety.

I had to believe I could make it, I could not accept the notion she would catch me.

I was not going to die.

Not today!

43

Richard

I tried to find Mary to talk to her, her friends angrily told me she was outside. I tried to find her, so I followed her scent, and when I found her slippers I knew something was wrong.

I followed her scent into the woods and found her necklace on the ground, the warning bells were really going off in my head now. A bad feeling settled in the pit of my stomach.

When I found her torn dress, my phone rang, and I got the call from Jeremy, telling me that Mary was after him. I quickly began to follow Mary's scent, as I ran I dialed Rick.

Being the sheriff and being the enforcer of the pack, everyone had him on speed dial in case of an emergency. "Hello?" he answered.

"Rick, Mary is going after Jeremy!" I yelled.

"What?" he asked sharply. I quickly told him the situation. "I'm on my way!"

He ended the call, and I ran faster. I remembered he was on a date with Jeremy's mother and hoped this didn't expose her to our world.

My wolf clawed at my mind, our mate was in danger! It was angry, so was I. There was no reason for Mary to do this, no excuse whatsoever!

I let my wolf out, I felt my body begin to change as I ran, my clothes tore as my body grew and expanded. In my man-wolf form I ran even faster.

My instincts were going wild because all I could think of was protecting him.

The wind blew, and I stopped running, a sweet and familiar scent washed over me. It was Jeremy's scent.

I followed the scent, pushing my body to run as fast as I could.

I would protect my mate, and strike down any who would harm him!

It was at that moment I smelled something that filled me with horror.

Blood.

*****

Jeremy

I hadn't had time to put on a coat or my shoes, my socks were wet and my feet were bitterly cold. As I ran for the school my phone began to ring.

It was Rick, I had given him my number weeks ago. I had forgotten I even had it and cursed myself for the blunder.

"Rick!"

"Jeremy! Where are you?" he asked.

"I am running to the school, Mary is trying to kill me," I panted.

"Damn girl, I was afraid she would snap. Wouldn't be the first time she has done something like this. Listen to me very carefully, do not stop running. Richard is trying to find you; it will be easy since you are his soulmate. I am on my way and I have called some of the pack to head your way as well."

"What about my mom?" I asked.

"I arranged for her to get an emergency call to the hospital. She is on her way there right now."

"Okay, I-"

Something slammed into me and sent me tumbling to the ground. I yelled in agony as a burning pain ran over my back. The phone dropped from my hand and I looked up to see Mary bring her foot down on the phone crushing it. Her left hand had blood on her claws.

"No one is going to help you!" she growled.

"Mary stop, Rick knows. If you kill me, they will kill you," I said as I stood up. I was trying to ignore the stinging pain from the claw marks on my back. It wouldn't turn me; if the old legends about a scratch or bite turning a human into a werewolf were true, the world would be filled with them right now.

Though right now I wished I was a werewolf, then I would have a chance at defending myself.

"No they won't. Richard will protect me, he always has," she said full of confidence. She truly was deluded.

She began to transform into her hybrid form. I knew it was pointless to run from her, werewolves were fast in human form, faster than humans, but in wolf form they were even faster.

I don't know what was more terrifying, watching her change or the manic look in her eyes. She truly believed Richard would protect her for this, she didn't think it possible he would punish her for this transgression. She truly thought killing me would bring her and Richard back together.

She was beyond all reason now, there was no talking to her. She stalked forward, her muzzle pulled back in a snarl.

"I am going to enjoy this so much. You will never hurt me again!"

"Mary, please don't do this!" I begged as I began to back away from her, trying to ignore the pain in my back.

I was bleeding quit a bit, I could feel my back become wet from blood.

She slowly began to follow me, knowing full well she had me right where she wanted me. Knowing in one leap she would end me.

Her fingers kept twitching as if itching to tear into something. I already knew what that was.

"You brought this on yourself!" she spat, spittle flew from her muzzle.

"If you kill me, you will kill Richard! I read what happens when a wolf loses his soulmate!" I cried.

"YOU ARE NOT HIS FUCKING SOULMATE! I AM!" she roared.

She lunged for me and I closed my eyes.

My mind flashed with images.

My mom, Lucas, my grandparents, my friends home and the ones I had made here. But most of all I thought of Richard.

Perhaps this was inevitable. Maybe my fate was sealed the moment I met Lucas, or maybe when I first made Richard. How many times had I avoided death?

Seems like my luck had finally run out.

Then there was another growl, deeper, but just as terrible. Then I heard a collision. I could feel the impact of two large bodies slamming into one another

Then there was the sounds of angry dog-like snarls and barks. I opened my eyes and saw a familiar black and white man-wolf in torn clothing fighting Mary.

"Richard!" I yelled.

He must have hit her just when she was about to tear into me. It had been close, way too close. But he was here now, and judging from the way he was fighting her, any affection he had for her was long gone.

44

Richard

It was when the smell of his blood hit my nose that I lost control.

Fear, panic, rage and instinct took over.

I ran as fast as I could because I could sense her; her power was like a roaring fire. She was out of control.

I could hear them talking, I could hear the seething hate in her voice as she moved in for the kill. My mate was begging for his life and I felt her sick pleasure over it.

It only fueled my rage.

I rammed into her before she could pounce on my mate. Had I been even a few seconds late Jeremy would be dead.

Mary and I rolled around on the ground, clawing and biting one another. She kicked me in the gut and sent me flying back. I landed on my feet in front of my mate.

"Stay away from him!" I roared at her..

I sent my power at her, letting her know I was serious, but her own will was as ironclad as mine. She would not yield.

"No! He took everything from me, but I will get it back!" she screamed, her voice was so deep and filled with madness it sounded demonic.

She tried circling around to get to Jeremy, she was more focused on him then me.

I could hear Jeremy behind me. Hear his heart beat frantically in his chest. The smell of his fear and blood burned my nose. Causing the seething rage boiling in me to intensify.

I had to be patient, Mary was after Jeremy, if I went after her he would be defenseless. Mary may not be as *me* but she was fast.

It would be easy for her to jump over me, or even sidestep me to get to him. She was getting impatient. She continued to move around us, looking for an opening.

"Richard...I love you!" Jeremy said from behind me.

I smiled. I stared right at Mary and spoke the words she wanted to hear. But I made sure she knew who I meant.

"I love you too Jeremy."

Mary let out a scream of rage. Her power blew out in waves.

She rushed at me and I slapped her aside. Before she could get back up, I pounced on her. I clamped my jaws around her throat and bite down as hard as I could.

She tried to fight me off, but I was too strong. I felt her windpipe crush and she let out a strangled gasp. But she was not dead yet, a snapped neck did not easily kill us.

I bit into her harder, blood exploded into my mouth as my fangs tore into her flesh. I jerked my head back, ripping her head off her body and tossed it to the side.

I dropped her body, it fell to the ground with a wet ground with a wet *splat*. It continued to spasm, then it began to turn back into its human form.

A sense of savage victory filled me. I walked over to the head and stared down at it, it was looking up at me, with an almost hurt expression.

Then it began to transform back into its human form. A single tear slid down its cheek. As I stared down at that familiar face a new emotion filled me: Regret.

I went to my mate; he was huddled on the ground. I whined and inspected his back; there were four long scratches running down the length of it. My mate was shivering; he was not properly clothed for this weather and the loss of blood only caused him to grow colder.

I picked him up in my arms, my little mate. So small and delicate. I had almost lost him again. I held him close, keeping him warm. He looked up at me, looking so happy to see me.

"Richard....you always save me," he said, his voice shaky. His lips were starting to turn blue.

More wolves came, but they were pack. I snarled at them as they approached, I didn't want them near my mate. But one of them stepped forward.

"His instincts have taken over. Let me handle this." I felt his power wash over me, soothing, calming. "Richard, focus, it is me, Rick. Please concentrate. Remember who you are. We only want to help."

Rick...yes, Rick was my elder, my protector. My packs protector.

The rage inside me began to die down, man and beast became separate and the full impact of what happened hit me.

Mary was dead.....I killed her.

I threw my head back and howled, my voice filled with pain and loss.

*****

Jeremy

It was past midnight and Richard held my hand as he cried.

They had to give me stitches for the claw marks; I would have a scar though. It was Mary's last parting gift. Something to always remember her.

I felt bad, more for Richard than her. A part of him did still love her, killing her had changed something in him. He had known her since they were kids, even if he no longer wanted her as a mate there was still a bond there.

But when a werewolves' soulmate is in danger, they don't think rationally; it becomes a matter of instinct. And instinct could be such a violent thing.

Rick and I already went over the cover story. I decided to go to the dance and was on my way when I stumbled upon Mary, who in her anger about the fight with Richard, had fled. We bumped into one another and both happened upon a bear.

I lived despite the marks on my back, but poor Mary wasn't so fortunate.

Mom of course had been notified. She cried so hard but Rick took her outside to calm her down.

I seriously think she is considering homeschooling me.

Richard wasn't supposed to be here but being a Farkas does have its advantages.

"Sorry, I am so so so sorry, please forgive me," Richard said for what must have been the millionth time that night.

He wasn't talking to me; I don't even know who he was apologizing to. Mary? Himself?

Any hope of peace between the two families was infinitely zero now. Even if it was to protect me, I highly doubt her family will ever forgive Richard for this. They are trying to keep it quiet now but I doubt it will be long before the whole pack learns what happened.

Rick assured me Richard would not be punished. As my mate and husband it was well within his rights to protect me, even if it was from another one of his pack.

Had Mary killed me, the pack would have hunted her down and killed her in retaliation. Killing one's soulmate was the ultimate taboo.

They had given me pain killers and I did feel a bit drowsy. But I couldn't sleep knowing Richard was in such pain.

Mary couldn't understand that even though she didn't have his whole heart she still carried a small piece of it. And even a piece of a heart can mean so much.

But she took it with her to her grave. I still remember the look on her severed head, staring up at Richard with shock and heart-wrenching pain. Her lips half open as if to say *how could you?*

I couldn't help but hate her as much as I pitied her. If it wasn't for her obsession with Richard this wouldn't have happened. Why couldn't she see it was over between them? Now Richard was going to have to live with this his whole life.

If only I knew how to erase his pain if only I could make it all go away.

"Richard. I know it hurts, but I promise it will get better," I said tiredly.

"But I killed her...I killed Mary, how am I going to face her parents? Or Derek, or the rest of her family? I loved her once, and I killed her like she was nothing!" he cried.

"She was trying to kill me, Richard."

"Because of me! Because once again, I fucked up! Because I had to go ruin tonight! I had to ruin everything again! Everyone is right, I don't deserve to be a Pack King, I would just destroy the pack!"

"Richard listen, Mary made her own choice. She knew we were married; she was there for the ceremony. You even told her you loved me but she wouldn't let you go. It wasn't love that made her do this. It was obsession."

"Jeremy, if you were smart you would stay away from me, you would never speak to me again, I just ruin everything," he said.

It hurt me to see him like this. So broken and full of pain. I would go another round with Mary if it meant I could take it away.

"Richard. I love you. You saved my life twice now. I know you are hurting, but I will be here with you. I promise. It will all be okay," I said soothingly.

He kissed my hand and nuzzled it.

"Richard, please sleep with me. I don't want to sleep alone."

He got up and helped move me to the side, we had to be careful because of the stitches. It hurt a bit to move, even with the pain killers.

He got in the bed with me and he positioned my head on his chest. He gently wrapped his arm around my shoulders and kissed my head.

I lay there with him and did what I could to give him some comfort.

As we laid together, I realized that I loved him. Truly and utterly loved him.

Yeah, I said the words before. But just because you say something doesn't mean you actually mean it.

When I ran through the woods, I feared never seeing him again, I feared what my death would do to him, I imagined his pain-stricken face when they told tell him I was dead. And listening to him cry, all I wanted to do was wrap my arms around him and keep him safe and happy.

Any doubt, any sliver of disbelief I had was now gone.

After the Soul Oath Ritual and my last near death experience the truth was laid bare to me

I loved Richard and after all this I would no longer deny it or reject it. Maybe if I had done that sooner none of this would have happened. Maybe if accepted what we had, then Mary could have had more time to adjust.

Of course that was just bullshit my conscious was coming up with.

Mary was deranged. Losing Richard had caused something in her to snap. I still remember the crazed look in her eyes. She would have killed me with no hesitation or remorse, the consequences be damned because she truly thought with me dead she could have Richard again.

That wasn't love. That was obsession.

Richard would come to understand that. He just needed time. And though things would be difficult for a little while I knew they would get better because we had each other.

I was able to close one chapter of my life and though it had been filled with trials and tribulations with more to come, I am glad I can continue on with my life with him.

My love.

My mate.

My Richard.

www.ingramcontent.com/pod-product-compliance
Lightning Source LLC
Chambersburg PA
CBHW071244250626
47163CB00002B/326